THE DISGRACED MARTYR TRILOGY

BOOK II

THE
GENERAL'S BRIDE

THE GENERAL'S BRIDE

M. F. SULLIVAN

The General's Bride
© 2019 M. F. Sullivan
ISBN: 978-1-7326691-0-9

Text: M. F. Sullivan
Editing: Michelle Hope
Cover Design: Nuno Moreira
Typesetting: Jennifer Cant

www.paintedblindpublishing.com
publicity@paintedblindpublishing.com

FIRST EDITION

At that he seized the bowl and tossed it off
And the heady wine pleased him immensely. "More"—
He demanded a second bowl—"a hearty helping!
And tell me your name, now, quickly,
So I can hand my guest a gift to warm his heart.
Our soil yields the Cyclops powerful, full-bodied wine
And the rains from Zeus build its strength. But this,
This is nectar, ambrosia—this flows from heaven!"

So he declared. I poured him another fiery bowl—
Three bowls I brimmed and three he drank to the last drop,
The fool, and then, when the wine was swirling round his brain,
I approached my host with a cordial, winning word:
"So, you ask me the name I'm known by, Cyclops?
I will tell you. But you must give me a guest-gift
As you've promised. Nobody—that's my name. Nobody—
So my mother and father call me, all my friends."

—Homer's *Odyssey*, Book IX,
Lines 396–411

I

Perchance to Dream

The Hierophant was everywhere. Every door she opened. Every place she ran. Even in this Void: a place she'd never meant to visit! A place she'd never known to exist until an incalculable time before. Dominia found it impossible to discern hallucination from thought from objective experience, and wondered if they differed in this place. Was this some dream? Her wife, fair Cassandra, seemed distant memory, dream, terror—sleep's chimera from many days prior, when confronted by this much more pressing tahgmahr before her.

In a half-formed study suspended upon nothing, she had found her Father. That man who had stolen her right eye from its socket as she'd fled in search of the mystic who might restore life to her wife. Dear Cassandra, who so suffered at the hands of the world. At his hands.

Hearing the voice and seeing the shape of her Father proved more powerful than either sense alone, and her thoughts skittered between the stimuli: him; his wineglass; the magnificent strings of Berlioz piping into the vast space from an artifact record player at his elbow; a profusion of memories that scattered across her eye like so many mis-shuffled playing cards. Dominia focused on the oriental rug that slithered even once her body settled into its surroundings. The Hierophant uttered a sympathetic (and condescending) tut as she swayed with obvious vertigo.

"'Be not afeard.'" He set his glass beside the gramophone while rising to his feet. "'The isle is full of noises, sounds, and sweet airs, that give delight and hurt not.'"

Caliban's speech, drawn from the finest of Shakespeare's plays, proved better anchor for consciousness than Valentinian's advice of remembering the ground, tossing stones, or shuffling cards. Everything snapped into simple clarity. Lucid as the real world.

"The real world." She almost laughed at the concept until she realized she was responding aloud to her own thoughts and managed to ask while edging across the threshold, "Are you real?"

He smiled, and filled a second glass of burgundy fluid from the keroid decanter. "As real as you; more real than my wine. Yet"—he approached to hand her the glass; his eyes crinkled as she accepted it—"unreal though it may be, it has quite the effect in this strange place."

Now she saw him close, and he appeared younger than she'd ever known him to be. The tension of flesh against bones, a certain sleekness of body brought on by hyper-advanced age's loss in muscle mass, had been reversed. All that had faded from his features after so prolonged— possibly eternal—a lifespan had returned with new glow, and fit the Hierophant with increased resemblance to Cicero. The clearest visible difference was the Pontifex lacked his son's Mephistophelian goatee.

Cicero! The General had not thought on the Holy Family's unhinged priest since taking his eye; an event which felt simultaneously moments and months before. No doubt he had no knowledge of this place; otherwise, she would have known about it, partial to bragging as he was. Cicero's discovery of such a thing would only disturb their Father's peace. El Sacerdote was a gnat, and particularly loathsome when something could be gained in the way of knowledge or power. Dominia, also, hungered for knowledge, but showed patience in learning and less cruelty in its use. In her own opinion, at least. Thus, it made some sense she was welcome in an imaginary study of her Father's where even the Eternal Son was not invited, but not by much; after all, as she insisted, "You tried to kill me. Or let Cicero try, at any rate."

"And you took his eye!" Said with a twinkle in both his dark ones. "My dear. You have waited quite a long time to teach your brother that lesson, haven't you?"

"Call me 'inspired.'" Her free hand lifted to her eye patch. "Lest we forget, this started with you pulling out my eye."

"It actually started with poor Casandra's death. Speaking of—why don't you come out, darling?" The Hierophant looked at a bookshelf against the farthest implied wall. "We are alone. No one will hurt you here."

Cold sweat prickled across Dominia's palms well before that vile thief of Cassandra's form stepped from where she—it—listened. Panic overwhelmed the General. She turned her eyes away, to the fireplace, in a look her Father followed. The creature twitched through her periphery in an effort at walking that seemed that of an alien recreating a description heard secondhand, perhaps through translation. Something within the body walked, but the body did not. As cramps of nausea clutched the General's ribs, the martyr permitted her Father to take her free hand. She allowed him kiss and pat it in that doting manner he demonstrated when he felt like supplicating his children into something, rather than ordering or threatening them. She tolerated the sound of his voice as he said, "You should know better than to think I would let true harm come to you. That I do not want to return Cassandra to you."

She almost laughed; but there again for a wink of the mind was the first appearance of the thing, outside the fire she'd shared with Lazarus and the formerly fictional Saint Valentinian. "I was told it wouldn't be able to come into the light."

"Not normal light, no. This light—my light—is much superior. All God's creatures may enter it without harm: I am like the black sun, in that respect. Please"—he released her hand to gesture toward the armchair seated across from his—"won't you sit down?"

With effort, Dominia set eye upon the vulgar recreation of Cassandra. Visible in her Father's blue firelight and standing statue still, the likeness almost passed: but Cassandra's hair was not the ink of this creature's, nor were her eyes dun and half lidded. Lifeless. Still, as the Hierophant did not wait for her to fulfill his invitation before settling into his crimson armchair, she felt obliged. In that vacuous space, any sensation was as comforting as the doppelgänger was disconcerting. She lowered herself into the empty seat and winced when that copy jerked to her side, where it knelt at her arm in perversion of Cassandra's occasional custom.

"She has a gift for you," said the Hierophant. The General grit her teeth as it brandished a crown of lush sapphire flowers once held behind its back.

"Dominia," the thing recited, trying the name and a smile. Both actions were ill-suited and ill-advised. The creature showed its beautiful teeth in a cold, mechanical way that did not alter its eyes or brows one whit. It held the crown in expectation, waiting; but when, after a time, it asked, "Don't you love me," Dominia slapped the so-called gift out of the pirated hands. The thing emitted a cry in hollow replica of her dead wife's voice that only made the General down a mouthful of wine. While it scrambled to collect the ruined crown and crouch by the side of the Hierophant, her Father clucked like the old hen he was.

"You're hurting the poor girl's feelings!"

"What does it want from me?" She stared the uncanny thing down and it shrank against the Hierophant's chair, mouth pressed to the upholstery. Its jaw warped under the pressure as though its bones were rubber while the Holy Father regarded Dominia with bland innocence.

"What does *she* want from you? Only that you should love her! If only Cassandra had so pure a motive in life."

That stung her back into her wineglass. After the burning liquid sprang her taste buds into work and tightened her jaw, she said, "That thing's not Cassandra."

"She is. She is Cassandra, and more than Cassandra."

"It's a monster. Some kind of—formless, abstract thing." What was the word Lazarus had used? "A *tulpa*."

The Hierophant rolled his eyes. "I would not put much stock into what Valentinian tells you." She did not correct him as he carried on: "The word you have just used is of Tibetan origin and means, quite simply, 'thoughtform.' Look around you! Everything here is a thoughtform. The wine you drink, your chair, each book upon my shelves, the fire that lights the room! Even our bodies here are sorts of thoughtforms, suspended upon our own unconscious understanding of ourselves."

At his words, she studied the books. The titles remained legible despite how, on a second, harder glance, the individual letters forming these words made little sense. What registered to her mind as the spine of the *Odyssey* yielded, upon closer inspection, a word spelled "TÆ CΦDVUKΘP." As her mind tangled in cognitive dissonance to marvel at such mechanics, the Hierophant carried on. "The origin of this Cassandra, within the cauldron of your memories, makes her no less real than the woman you once called your darling wife; if anything, this memory-borne bride could prove more real than your last, if you would let her."

"Now you're just lying. This thing isn't Cassandra. Cassandra doesn't move like that, doesn't even look that way. It's wrong."

"She is wrong because you have not yet invested energy into making her right. She is like an infant, newborn. Why, she would not even know how to say the name of her adored Dominia, had I not spent this whole night teaching her."

"Dominia," repeated the thing in a sullen voice that made the General's skin crawl.

"I wish you hadn't. I wish you'd kept that thing in the darkness, where it belongs."

"How cruel you are! How forgetful of all those years of love." While the terrible thing wept Cassandra's tears, the General pushed herself from her chair and paced around the bookshelves. On second pass, the nonsense titles were different in either lettering or meaning. "Forgetful of your love of Cassandra as you are forgetful of your love of me."

"I never loved you. You stole me."

"I saved you from certain death. I gave you a destiny." His pale-blond eyebrows lifted as she spared him a withering glance. "And you did love me at times, against your better judgment. You love me even now, or you would not be here. Would you?"

Dominia did not speak. When she was a teenager and he had taught her how to draw, Berlioz had played in the background then, too. It was a natural cross-discipline for a fighter in martyr culture; thanks to Saint Valentinian, patron saint of death as well as artists, any form of visual art was by and large considered the domain of soldiers, executioners, and other individuals of violent inclination. These classes to foster a creative hobby in a girl whose only interest was fighting represented a rare few times where, yes, wrapped in the moment, she looked up and realized she'd been forgetting to hate him. It made her eye sting to remember. She covered it and the patch with one hand. "I wish I'd stayed with Valentinian and Lazarus."

The Hierophant drained his glass and set it aside. "Confront the root of your dark feelings toward this poor, sweet child of a woman. Why do you hate her?"

"Please don't."

"Is it because she is a Cassandra you may safely hate? Into whom you can pour all your resentments, all those old feelings of having been used and manipulated? When she came to you at the beach, it was, for you, a pure moment, but the purity was cheapened by her intent. Perhaps this dark-haired Cassandra pulled from your thoughts is that base intent of hers brought into shape. That is why you hate her so."

"It's a thing attracted by my energy, my emotions. It has nothing to do with Cassandra. Cassandra is dead."

"And yet, she yet lives."

"No, damn you! She's dead!"

"Dominia." The thing lifted reddened eyes from its tear-wet fingers. "Why, Dominia?"

"Oh, shut up."

It resumed weeping. The Hierophant stroked its hair as though petting a cat. "Perhaps your resentment toward our poor Cassandra is meant for yourself. Perhaps you do not feel deserving of a second chance with her, after the way things happened."

On furious instinct, she took a step toward him. The arctic heart of the fire flared against its tangerine edge, and her shadow fluttered like the wings of a gargantuan black moth. "What happened to Cassandra was your fault. Cicero's fault. This Family drove her insane. She never forgot we're just a bunch of cannibal monsters."

Symphonie Fantastique, in its final ten minutes, took its sudden somber turn, and the Hierophant let his lips curl in his calmest smile. "Another truth turned Cassandra toward your unlocked gun, but I suppose it's true she might have killed herself any old way. Surely it was convenience. Not some symbol."

The gun at her hip, whether dream or no, seared her thigh through her trousers as her Father rose. His long shadow quite dwarfed hers. As she stood her ground before the towering man, she insisted, "Her final choice didn't have to do with me. The gun was something she knew. It was handy."

"It was also the gun of the woman who killed the father of Cassandra's child. The gun of the woman who killed her the first time by martyring her, thus sealing the fate of her baby."

Dominia began to storm away, but the Hierophant snatched her arm with such viselike grip she had to remind herself she could not be hurt in this place. As he drew her back to him, he continued, "The Cassandra you loved is different from the Cassandra you knew. The one you knew—the one you refused to see—never moved beyond her human life. This is why martyring adults is so dangerous. It only brings heartbreak. But, my girl: this Cassandra is new. She has become as a little child"—there he went with that fucking book—"and from the purity of her meek and humble heart grows the love for which you've pined. The kind of love you never had with the old Cassandra, despite what you told yourself."

"You're lying! Cassandra loved me. She came to me for her own reasons; but in the end, she loved me."

"Then why did she kill herself that way?"

Over and over, five times in one second, Dominia walked into their room at the exact point in time Cassandra pulled the trigger. Over and over, her wife's eyes met hers with shock to find the Governess had woken up early. Over and over, it was too late to do anything but watch.

"It took some planning, princess. It was not a split-second decision."

Oh! The impossibly soft feeling of her wife's lips as the Governess had comforted her the morning before, when she had been so unexpectedly devastated during the Walpurgisnacht Party. That powder-soft femininity and mint and warmth. Finally, Cassandra had calmed and dozed off on the sitting-room couch. Dominia had thought they could sleep in safety. She had not wished to move her wife. She had fallen asleep beside her, still in her clothes, gun not put away.

"I am sorry to say this, but she was deeply unhappy."

The cold panic on waking from a tahgmahr—no, a real day terror, a replay of her escape from her Nogales cell—to find herself alone. Her racing heart. The memory looped: calling her wife's name, clambering up, seeing the gun was gone and knowing her second of intuition had been justified, running through the halls, checking every room in their vast estate until reaching their bedroom, and there was the door, the door, so close, so close—but never close enough.

The Hierophant touched Dominia's cheek, and she came back to herself to realize she wept. Her Father wiped away her tears and held her as, forgetting herself, she collapsed into sobs. As if the past month had never happened—as if the past lifetime was erased and she was a girl again—she allowed herself to be rocked against his chest, to cry there and say, "I just wish she would have talked to me."

"There are some pains too deep to express. She did not hide it because her heart was stone. She hid it because, though she may have loved her late soldier, she also loved you, her living soldier, much as she could. And she knew the pain of her lasting grief would hurt you, in turn."

The first true thing he'd said in some time inspired a sharp breath by which she steadied her nerves. This gaslighting was insane: he was a pendulum. She pushed away from him to clear her throat. "You're right. She loved me more than you would know. Pain or no, she loved me."

"So will you cling to the intangible memory of love? Or will you come to your senses and see it waits before you even now?"

Behind him, the standing thing had shambled forth a few steps. One hand kept its balance against the General's empty seat. Still ill at the mere sight, she insisted of her Father, "That thing is a lie. A false creation proceeding from my hopes, my memories, my feelings. It's a predator. Fake."

"She can be real. And she is far less a lie than those Lazarus and his friend tell you."

Though her ears burned with fury, and denial boiled on the tip of her tongue, Dominia still nursed doubt enough to withhold comment. Her Father insisted, "Those nonsense stories of resurrection, of the stream of consciousness you knew as 'Cassandra' finding bodily resurrection in this world—they are lies."

"The only liar here is you."

"My poor, sweet angel! So trusting of your friends you will not listen to your own Father's words. I tell you, they lie. Lazarus will not help you."

"There's someone," she began, stopping because he said, "They will lead you to Cairo, and you will be disappointed."

Her stomach tightened. She stepped away, toward a fire that emitted no warmth. "How do you know about Cairo?"

"Do you think Lazarus and Valentinian are the only ones who have been through all this bad business before?" The Hierophant returned to his seat while smoothing the fabric of his suit. "'I do not know everything, but I am aware of much,' as a great devil once said; and I am aware Cassandra will not be resurrected in the way you hope. But *I* can give you Cassandra."

"You can give me a lie."

"A lie becomes the truth if told enough. Cassandra's love for you was, in the first place, a lie that became the truth. Why would it be different were it to happen again, this way?"

Somehow, the question staggered her more than any he'd posited. The simpering doppelgänger gazed through tear-matted eyelashes, lower lip trembling, as the stalwart General nonetheless insisted, "She's not real."

At her Father's smile, the General bore her teeth to realize she'd slipped by calling the thing "she." As if it were a person! It even responded. Brightened around the eyes. Dominia shuddered and folded her arms, more eerily afloat than ever in her life. Every word she spoke seemed more futile than the last. Horribly, sooner or later, she would have to acknowledge this thing in a way not dismissive.

But then—praise God, or damn Him—they were interrupted by a knock. The General held her breath.

II

The Magician and the General

"*Entrez*," called the Hierophant, his tone reminiscent of teatime conversation. (Though it did always seem such with him, didn't it?) When the broad oak door through which she'd entered swung wide, Dominia exhaled. Relief mingled with anxiety in the way it had when, in too deep at a party as a too-young girl turning toward substances and trying to pretend she wasn't a Holy Family member, she had urgently called for a driver. Instead, her Father had knocked at the party's door. Though she was all of fourteen and much, much too high, and he'd found it all ill-advised, he had arrived to save her—and embarrass her. Now, salvation and embarrassment arose to find the doorway filled not by her Father but the lithe frame of Valentinian, who leaned with his elbow propped against the jamb.

"Leave her alone." The General studied her Father's reaction to the saint's impudent tone and found His Holiness illegible as ever. "We've got a long way to go. She doesn't need you distracting her."

"I'm connecting with my daughter the only way I can! Every time I see her in real life, she runs away." A merry twinkle lit the Hierophant's eyes as he picked up his decanter. "May I pour you a drink?"

"No, thanks." Valentinian strolled over the threshold, hands in his pockets and eyes sliding around the room until he noticed Dominia's empty glass. With his scoff of annoyance, bold eyebrows lifted high and his hands flew once more into sight. "Don't tell me you drank his wine. Fairyland rules! Do they mean nothing to you?"

She was assailed by a thousand myths, fables, and legends about stupid people eating stupid things and facing stupid consequences. Oh, no. "I don't have to stay here forever now, do I?"

"What? No—I don't mean *that* level of fairyland rules. I just mean, don't eat or drink things you're given here unless we clear it. For one thing, when you're drinking his wine, you're reinforcing his reality and his power in this place even more than I could. This is new to you. You've got an impressionable mind at this phase; he could convince you of anything, no matter how levelheaded you usually are. And when you're drinking his wine, you're...connecting with him. Accepting him into you. You're drinking his thoughts, after all."

Dominia wasn't sure of the concrete harm, aside from the abstract sense of violation, but she wasn't sure she wanted to learn. It was bad enough knowing his blood flowed through her veins. His influence was inseparable from her present self, even if that self felt so removed from the woman who had been, among other things, architect and tool of genocide. As she edged toward the door, Valentinian extended his hand, and she took it without second thought. A childish impulse, she considered after. Perhaps he was right about how impressionable she was in this place, this early in her exposure. Perhaps it was his perception of that same trait that made him say, with a nod toward the melancholic replica of Cassandra, "You didn't touch it, did you?"

"Only to slap its 'gift' out of its hands," she admitted. The mage nodded.

"Good. The surest way to strengthen a thoughtform is by touch."

Though he began to lead her away, Valentinian stopped short when Dominia refused to move. "What would happen," she asked in the absent way of forced innocence, "if it did manifest in reality?"

"We'd lose," he said with a cold glance at the Hierophant. "If it manifested, Cassandra would have no hope of coming back—you would be willing to settle." Her lip twitched in an untenable defense that went unspoken; he continued in a gentler tone, "But that won't happen. This is the time we win."

"I love your optimism," said the Hierophant, black eyes curled with nasty levity. "Every time."

"Cute." The magician half laughed in his own nasty way, showing his teeth, then let the mirth drop when his expression was visible only to Dominia. "If it weren't for this place, somebody would have murdered him long ago. And I'm not talking about me; there'd be a line."

Too true. No wonder no bullet hit him, and why his speed was in excess of even martyr dexterity. Now she understood how it was he and Lazarus and Tobias had flickered in and out of existence like hallucinations. Much as this place accounted for the legend of Lazarus—that those martyrs who partook of his blood would never again need to eat human flesh and would, in exchange, never burn in the sun—so, too, did it explain her Father. Many traits, however, remained unaccounted for, and Dominia could not wrap her head around the mechanics of reality's oscillations. The idea of someone like Valentinian or the Hierophant moving between high amplitudes, rather than dwelling within them...

"I hope you will visit me again, Dominia." Her Father smiled such that perhaps he had his own form of telepathy here. Mere paranoia. "We still have much to discuss. Thank you for picking her up, Valentinian."

"Yeah, yeah." The magician was now successful in his efforts to shepherd her through the threshold; she took but a quick glance at the duplicate as the door shut, and her friend told the Hierophant, "See you tomorrow."

Valentinian did not look back, but Dominia was hung up on the Hierophant's phrasing. Like divorced parents, exchanging a daughter.

"You knew I'd go to him?"

The magician released her hand. "I had to sleep sometime, and Lazarus has been up for days... He's more bothered than I am—that you go to see the Hierophant while we're here—but, hell, I visit him all the time, too."

"You do?"

"Look around. Who else is there to talk to? I mean, sure, there are—people, some places, depending where you look. But nobody on my level. I don't have a choice. If I want to have a conversation with somebody without constantly explaining myself, my options are limited. No offense. Anyway, there's no real damage capable of being done here—not to one another's bodies—so I swing by to play cards. He's got a chess set. You have no idea how sick I am of chess."

"I can't imagine." With every step, the richness of the dark anti-landscape paled into what passed for dawn, and it was not long before those electromagnetic bands of color began to once more twist into relief. "You must be lonely. How long have you spent here, stuck as a dog on Earth with only Lazarus and thoughtforms in this place to keep you company?"

"Only about two thousand reality years," he said with cheer before adding to a flabbergasted Dominia, "this cycle."

"Two *thousand* years?"

"Yeah, well, time moves differently here. It's flown by like four hundred years to me, as much time as I spend hanging out between dimensions. See? Only a bit older than you. If you're talking the real total, though, I'm not even sure I know. How many times have I watched the world go around? How many times has the game been played in this particular fashion, with these pieces, with this set? I can't rightly say, but I can tell you this—we will win this time. Because he may be aware of much: but I know everything."

For whatever reason, Dominia believed that. She was willing to believe it, at any rate. Whether it was truth, she wasn't sure, but she was desperate to think that the magician who was also a dog had answers. That was why she was glad when he stopped and turned to speak seriously to her. The black sun, on the verge of creating the peaked horizon by breaking it, paused with them.

"He's a deceiver, Dominia. He's easy to like, and the things he does are superficially good, and it's a fact he wants you to know the truth. But he wants you to know the truth in a way that perverts it, and makes it good as a lie."

From the corner of her eye, Dominia noticed two things with a distinct chill of terror: the path of torches disappeared behind them, one at a time, two back from the one beneath which they stood; and the doppelgänger, having stalked them, was now still as one of those torches. It stood in the darkness, from which it observed in eerie silence through owlish eyes that had grown. As if the thing had learned how to hold its expression to emulate its forebear but naively exaggerated certain features to make itself more attractive. The effect failed spectacularly, into total uncanny horror. Valentinian gazed also at the silent creature, whose violet dress and long black hair—not Cassandra's at all, bearing so slim resemblance it enraged the eye—hung motionless. Dominia realized only when the magus spoke that the thing drew no breath.

"No matter how well you tell a lie," said the magician, "it can never be the truth."

"I know." Miserable, she turned from that ugly thing founded on beautiful memory.

Valentinian clapped the General upon the shoulder, then resumed his brisk pace to their camp. The sun, to their right, resumed rising. "You know better than anybody, kid. The man can spin the truth the way athletes spin their balls."

"Then why are you letting me see him?"

"Complicated answer; save my pride by boiling it down to, 'I can't stop you.'" At her silence, he noted her expression of skepticism and touched his chest. "Look, kiddo, I'm not the miracle person. I mean—I am in the end, but somebody else is in charge of making big, profound, Earth-moving miracles manifest in reality."

"Is that Lazarus?" asked Dominia. Valentinian did not answer.

"What I'm trying to say is, short of producing a miracle of some kind, I can't stop you from going to him during the night. That's just the way it is. Fish gotta swim; birds gotta fly; your Father's gotta be a huge pain in my ass. Excuse me for a second."

He ignored her to pat around the pockets of his waistcoat. As if he needed to find things, rather than manifest them like a walking Higgs boson! After a few pats, he withdrew a pack of cigarettes that couldn't have fit into his waistcoat without disrupting its silhouette. Yet, as he stuck one in his mouth and put the rest away, no sign of a box-shaped outline remained visible against the man's ribs. He didn't bother to hide that he lit it with an electrical spark cresting between his fingers, rather than his lighter.

"Smoking's bad, kids," said the fictional martyr while lifting his head. The puff of smoke he exhaled formed a bisected circle of non-entry. "But Lazarus has his stones, and I'm not exactly going to get imaginary cancer in my astral body. Not that somebody couldn't if they believed they could." He regarded the cigarette before resuming it with a shrug. "Anyway, it sticks in your dad's craw he can't reason me into quitting, so you'll have to pardon my smoke."

"How do you know each other, exactly?"

"He's the asshole who's got me stuck as a dog, among other things. I mean, *really* 'other' things. Basil is just one of many. This one incarnation many centuries ago, I somehow got hooked into an aquarium of sea monkeys." The magician shuddered. "That family's cat had it in for us. Stuff like that's why I spend so much time here until you show up."

"But how is it you *know* each other?" The General tried to study his face, but it was difficult with the both of them moving and the black sun warping all it revealed. This space seemed different from where they'd been yesterday; distant mountains were replaced by the elevated planes of mesas, and a vast gorge now split the distant world, east (if she correctly read the fields) of where far-off Lazarus smote the night's flames. There was resemblance between the men, between Lazarus and Valentinian, as though they were of the same stock; but it was not so strong a resemblance as, say, between the Hierophant and Cicero. If anything, such resemblance elevated to a kind of twinship on seeing her Father with so young and spry a form. Valentinian and Lazarus shared features: shapes echoed in noses and eyes and the magician's high-cut cheekbones, the likes of which were hidden in Lazarus by agéd beard and tangled old-man eyebrows. Yet, overall differences of stock and build—the broad old mystic looked as if he had a background of pit fighting and had nothing of the lean, middle-aged magician's wiry frame—indicated they were not so closely related as the Hierophant and his Eternal Son. "Who are you?"

With a coy smile, the man answered, "I'm nobody."

Dominia tried to shake off what seemed not so much a lie as a reference to the *Odyssey*: as though he teased her with knowledge of the books she had studied. Her face burning to wonder if this was how it felt to be schizophrenic, the General cleared her throat.

"Why won't you tell me anything?"

His look grew somewhat stern. "Because if I tell you the truth about anything, you won't believe me. You'll decide I'm lying, you'll go into the future with unnecessary predispositions, or you'll try to test me."

"More than I'm testing your patience?" she asked, brow arched.

The magician, who had been gesturing with his cigarette, coughed himself into a laughing smirk. "All right, wise guy. Let's hurry up. The old man looks impatient."

So he did: Lazarus stood in the distance, hands on his hips. As they approached, Dominia made out the tapping of his foot—and the clouds of dust puffing around his foot, as if some dirt, some real ground, had developed overnight.

"Well," the old man barked when they were within range, "did she touch it?"

"Not tonight," answered the magician. The mystic nodded as the General tried to avoid distraction from her initial question—one she cemented in the depths of her mind so as to never forget: Who was Valentinian?

"Then we still have a chance, though it's going to follow us." The thing at which she had deliberately not looked was now quite a distance away, perhaps as distant from them as Lazarus was when first she'd noticed his figure; yet, because she knew Cassandra's features so well, she saw every false freckle upon the doppelgänger's sallow cheek. With a sigh of disgust for the thing, the mystic reached into his pocket for his rocks. "Let's move this train along, folks." The day's first pebble pinged along the growing gorge. "Still thirty-three more real days to pass, and a lot of ground to cover."

"But, wait." The men ignored her, walking on, which blistered her entire being. "Hey! If you know me so well, you know I hate being ignored."

"We've never tried ignoring you before," admitted Valentinian.

"Military ego," explained the mystic without looking back. That military ego flared in real indignation while she made no move to march. They kept walking; like a pair of bubbles splitting off, the greater compass shared by the men parted from that of the General and left her with not only a poorer sense of confidence but the nauseating discovery her compass pointed back in the direction of her Father's study. In time, she would find his study always manifested north of her location: in those irritating seconds of scorn at the hands of her so-called comrades, however, the glowing tori that swept in his direction provided a suggestion, rather than an objective marker of magnetic (or other) poles.

"Have I ever refused to go on before?"

With a sigh of irritation, Valentinian paused to do her the decency of looking at her. "Once or twice. Under similar conditions."

"What conditions are those?"

"Our refusal to tell you anything. But if I tell you anything now, like I keep saying—"

"Dominia." Lazarus, who had also stopped, drew her hostile attention and watched it melt away, for the old man had a kind of infinite patience about his face and being. It was difficult here to maintain indignation before him; or perhaps being in this place clarified the pointlessness of indignation. "This same free will that lets you stand in place and stop all three of us is the same free will that makes you such a valuable treasure. You like to think on a decision before you make it, and make it with care. I understand it's frustrating to know so little. We've already told you almost everything; we'll keep telling you. But all you have to know is that you are going to save the world, and kill your Father."

"Like you said when we got here. But save *what* world?"

"All of them," said Valentinian.

"Humans *and* martyrs," she pressed. The men exchanged a reluctant glance.

Through some spurious form of telepathy (or Valentinian's puppy-dog eyes, which recalled Basil), the men decided Lazarus would be their spokesperson. "Do you remember, Dominia, when I explained to you Earth is a prison, and martyrs, its prisoners?"

A most painful kind of beauty—something like what Miki Soto, Red Market prostitute and Dominia's only real friend, would have called *mono no aware*—arose in Dominia's throat at the memory of the sermon. "Yes," she said. The old man approached her to rest a warm hand upon a shoulder she would have otherwise forgotten.

"It does not always have to be like this. Martyrs are people, too. But they are not people meant for Earth."

"Acetia?" The planet from which her Father claimed to herald, and which would not develop life for millions, possibly billions, of years. In its present state, circling the distant star of Procyon A near sacred Sirius, it remained in noxious and primeval condition. Deadly. "I never believed in it before."

"It's possible, in a sense. But only without your Father." Valentinian glanced in silence at Lazarus, then turned away to light another foul cigarette while the mystic said, "Humans and martyrs can never live together, it's true. But that doesn't mean one or the other has to die. It just means martyrs have to change. They have to be willing to leave."

"Sort of like an intergalactic Australia," suggested the exhaling magician, "before it was turned into a prison camp in half the state, and a nuclear waste and garbage dump in the other half. You know, way back when it was just a prison colony, after the Aboriginal people were horribly subjugated but before the place became prohibitively hot and most who could afford it skipped town."

"Hot Siberia, with superpowers." The irritation in Lazarus's mutter was not just for the human race but all sapient life. "Anyway, it's true. What I'm suggesting for the martyr race is scary, but you have the irresponsible pleasure of not having to worry about it."

Her mind now open (possibly for the first time in her life) to the concept that her Father was an alien martyr from the future who had somehow copied Cicero's features, Dominia asked, "Why is that?"

"Because you are our military ego," said the old man with a wry smile. "By the time the war is over, you'll already be at home with Cassandra."

Whether or not he told the truth, Dominia had to give it to him: Lazarus knew how to get her marching again.

III

Attention Deficit

The General had endured many a long march. Indeed, she'd led more than she'd endured! Though her Father's army had always been technologically well equipped, there were those locations, those battles, those infiltrations that required substantial walk and some hastily constructed encampments. Mexico was still covered in her boot prints. But, for her thousand battles and thousand-plus marches, she had known in her life no march quite like this. Not one so long. The conventional secret to marching was placing focus on anything but what was happening and what would continue to happen—as if, in not acknowledging the road, one would suddenly find oneself at the destination.

In this case, imagining was dangerous. Her coping mechanism for marches was gone, but she'd lost far more than that. Imagination was how she dealt with trauma, and, at times, how she dealt with killing—though she needed that coping mechanism less now than she had as a young woman learning the arts of hunting or war. And, in modern nights, her usual figure of distraction was a memory whose name she feared to think lest it feed the thing behind her. She dared not think of anything now. Not for a prolonged stretch, and nothing of her dead wife.

So, as the gorge broadened with the march upon their untiring legs, she instead thought how the unflagging nature of her dream-legs was a torture of its own. With the black sun still in the yet-dark sky, time froze, and though there was now more to look upon than "nothing," there was still not much. Perilous thoughts marched to the beat of her feet: her unanswered questions, her dread for the length of the trip, Cass—

No. Back to her feet. Remember the ground and the pinging of pebbles. But what about her Father? How did these people know her Father? Many questions filtered through her head, the doctrine of martyrs clashing with what she'd heard from Miki of Red Market legends. The only way the General would gain clarity was by hoping somebody told the truth.

"Is it true"—she hurried to Lazarus's side while he spared a glance her way—"my Father is an alien? Are you an alien, too?"

"Do you believe everything you hear? Do we look like extraterrestrials?"

"Neither does my Father."

"I wonder why," Lazarus dryly asked of laughing Valentinian.

The magician spread his hands. "We're all aliens, in a way."

That night, when they would camp near the opposite end of that gorge and settle in for the night, the torches would once more appear, and the doppelgänger would be gone, and Dominia would find herself drawn down this nighttime path to the study. This occasion, the mobile room sat on the gorge's opposite side. She would remark on the earlier, extraterrestrial conversation to her Father while refusing his wine politely as possible. In response to this refusal, he would say, "No offense taken, my dear: I understand your hesitance. Who knows what was said to you! But take a seat, at least."

Likely as bad as drinking his wine; but, her sitting made him comfortable to say, "You asked me of Lazarus, and Valentinian—yes, I knew them when I arrived on Earth. As to whether I stole the protein from Lazarus, as you say your Red Market friend suggests"—wry smile—"how could I have done that when I brought it from my world?"

That day, Lazarus will have said, "Cicero and I were genetic engineers together in the earliest world I recall. Him, me, and his brother, Elijah." The name of the Lamb, her ram-horned, gentler Family member, somehow alarmed Dominia to hear. "The same night I was martyred, the Hierophant swooped in to martyr the brothers with his inferior blood."

"I was originally involved, too," was Valentinian's addition, which had earned glances from both Lazarus and the General.

"Yeah," the mystic had allowed, "but I don't remember it."

"Why not?"

Dominia would ask this question twice; only the Hierophant, that night, would give her something resembling a straight answer.

"Valentinian was never born into this crest of the universe because of a wish gone bad."

There was no maintaining a straight face. "A wish? Now you're being childish."

"Don't tell me you don't believe in wishes! I've fouled up somewhere in raising you, haven't I?"

"Valentinian has no body," Lazarus explained before that moment, in those careful words, "because your Father trapped him."

"How?"

"The same way he turned me into a dog." The alleged saint, having tarried to grind a cigarette beneath his shoe, hastened to catch up. "By magic, basically."

Because of that, Dominia would later think to ask her Father, "Are you a magician in the way Valentinian is?"

"Every man is a magician in this place. What Valentinian does is not so impressive."

"But, if he were back in reality, would he still be a magician? More than you are, I mean."

The Hierophant studied her, hands folded upon his knee, the specter of Cassandra leaning its head against the arm of his chair. It had been that way since Dominia's arrival, plaintive eyes plastered upon the widow's steeled expression with all the emptiness of a statue's hollow gaze. "If every man is a magician in this place," the Pontifex decided, "then every man is also a magician when on Earth. It is a question of his means in producing magic, and how powerful he is—that is, how much energy he uses to produce how drastic of a change. A drastic miracle—or wish, if you'd rather—is something that would normally require a complex, energy-costly series of transmogrifications, but which the magician elicits with a tap of the finger." He lifted his glass to his lips. "Turning water into wine. Rudimentary business here.

"'Magic' in reality is another word for 'influence.' One uses magic to influence events, whether personally, locally, or at an even larger scale; magic often consciously utilizes science, but science never seems capable of acknowledging its magical potential. The magical man is such because of his connection to this place, among other things. Our bodies here are like the dark star of Sirius B—the occult twin of its bright-shining brother, who keeps close watch on Acetia and its procyonid sun. Once the individual reaches a level of self-awareness high enough to detect that black star and utilize its secret light, anything is possible."

"Like what?"

"Anything at all."

"Anything" was such a staggering notion she dared not think on it, for the only thing she wanted was something(one) too easily corrupted. Something(one) she could not give herself, could not manifest from nothingness. Not that same Cassandra who killed herself, who she knew and loved. Not in the reality she knew. She had accepted that fact well enough for the doppelgänger to seem less an opportunity to move forward and more a bleak reminder of all the ways the General had gone wrong. But the tiniest sliver of her heart—the tiniest spark—wondered at the replica, abominable deception though it was. She longed in sporadic moments, fraught with shame, to lay her hand upon the softness of Cassandra's cheek and feel it emulated, however false the emulation. In such fleeing moments of—yes, wishing—the creature's eyes glittered, and Dominia spurned those hopes that fed its vapid existence.

The Hierophant asked in a mild tone, "Did you inquire about their ability to resurrect Cassandra?"

"Valentinian assures me you're a liar, which my personal experience confirms."

"I never lie, certainly not in so crass a fashion. Neither one has the power to resurrect her."

"They know who does."

"You are on a fool's errand. The men lead you astray from what your intuition warns: something is not right. You do not even know half the truth."

"Why don't you enlighten me?"

Across the room from her smirking Father, the fire spent shivering light upon a glossy floor that had appeared overday as a base for the study. These tiles, alternating shades of wood, were arranged in the pattern of a chessboard and did, in fairness, render the space visually warm. This did not negate the disturbing effect of such a drastic change being engendered with no effort. After the General had sufficient time to ponder this, her Father spoke up.

"Any truth I say is bound to be dismissed by them as lie; therefore, I dare not share the way of things with you just yet, lest my honesty implant some sense of falsehood in your mind. But Cairo will see you leaving empty-handed, without your lover. All after is violence. They are keeping you upon a certain track and draining you of your free will."

There was that first time she'd met Lazarus, before the service, after Miki and the wounded (ex-)Hunter hacker, Kahlil, had dropped her off and left for Cairo. So long ago to her mind—or perhaps '*nous*' was a better word in this place of no-mind, no-time, no-thing. "Lazarus said my free will gives me power."

"It gives *him* power, too, if he goads you into making choices in service to his cause, rather than yours." His pale brows lifted toward slicked hair. "You deny your senses and lean on faith—hope!—when a solution is before you. You deny their ill intent when they've kept you here so long! Have they even told you how to leave?"

That expertly aimed question startled the General. They had not; but she insisted, "No, because we're going to Cairo."

"And going to Cairo is your choice?" At the purse of her lips, he smiled. "I have watched the footage from your DIOX-I, Dominia. I wish you had not taken it out." She grimaced to relive, in brief, the horrible surgery wherein Cicero had installed it. Would she could take it out a second time! "While I still saw your comings and goings, however, I noticed the same thing you noticed upon waking aboard that train to Kabul. The same thing I notice now: your missing diamond. Your missing wife."

Dominia's hand lay upon her breast with bitter longing for the absent stone. It had already been many terrestrial days since Miki shipped the compressed body of the General's wife to Cairo on orders of her goddess, the Lady. At the unspoken title, jasmine and lavender flowed through the study as if on a breeze not felt. The Hierophant turned his nose toward the scent as his daughter said, "We need to go to Cairo for Cassandra, yes. Your point?"

"You would need not do that at all, were it not for the actions of that prostitute who somehow befriended you. Indeed, were it not for Miki's actions, you would have the components necessary for the alleged resurrection. If nothing else, you would have the ability to seriously consider my proposals. I know you won't, as things stand now."

She hated when he told her what she was and wasn't going to do, and knew he thrived on that hatred. There was never any telling if what he said was what he honestly felt or another hollow manipulation. She forced herself to remain silent.

"You might yet leave that false diamond, all those unfulfillable promises, far behind. You are here with me—with me, and more precious a Cassandra than you might ever hope to know." His hand lay against the doppelgänger's shoulder, and it leaned toward Dominia, hands clasped between familiar, pale knees that peeked beneath its short violet dress and made the General think of how much higher up they went, those legs—of when they became thighs, and where those thighs terminated. As she returned struggling attention to her Father, he asked, "Have they described to you how space here represents space, time, and, to a certain extent, probability in the 'real' world?"

As the General nodded, he went on. "If you continue to follow them, you will find yourself in Cairo when they generously share the means of awakening. You will have made a choice about the future of our relationship, the future of this world—and you will have sealed your fate, much to my regret."

The weight of significance borne by his look pressed down upon her chest. He continued. "But you are here with me. In my study. And I could tell you how to awaken this instant, if you like. Wake up at home, Dominia, and it shall be as if nothing ever happened. Your Family will be back; I'll restore your governance of the United Front and help you bring your wife back to true life. I'll help you exercise your valuable free will. Whatsoever you desire, I'll see the world manifests it one way or another. Or perhaps you would rather continue on your own. Regardless, I would be happy to inform you of the means to leave this place. I hate to think of you stranded here, should something happen to them, or should you run afoul of one another."

"You expect me to trust you after all you've done to me?"

"Can you trust them any more than you can trust me?" was what the Hiereophant asked as Valentinian knocked on the door to collect her the second time. Both inhabitants of the study paused while its owner invited him in, and the mage entered with an uneasy but satisfied look toward the still-crouched doppelgänger. His gaze soon shifted to the new floor with a snort.

"Nice work."

"Do you like it?" asked the Hierophant in his gayest manner, terrifying, boyish mischief in his face. "I thought the place deserved some sprucing up, and Cassandra, sweet thing, reminded me of your love of chess."

"A deep love," agreed the magician dryly, offering Dominia a hand. She accepted it without thinking, preoccupied by her efforts to avoid mental recollection of the conversation just had; at any rate, she suspected it didn't matter whether she touched the magician. Between the boundaryless nature of the space and Valentinian's magical talents, there was no means of hiding information. Not from him, at any rate. "Come on, Dominia. Time's up."

As ever, her Father was gagging to leave her with questions. He insisted on adding as she was tugged toward the doorway, "Valentinian would have you believe this world is more real than reality, and with good reason: he is, in reality, a dog."

Yes, in fact, he was. Basil, the border collie. It was difficult to look at Valentinian and see a border collie; but she had often looked at the border collie and seen Saint Valentinian. That incanine, inhuman determination in his eyes as he put a stop to the rocketing train. Those moments of wry mirth and silent validation: when he saved Miki from traitorous René Ichigawa, blinded spy of her Father; shooting poor Kahlil, who had never been so much a member of the terrorist society as a kid with an easily manipulated ideology (and/or penchant for ladies of the evening). Not unlike Dominia, only less successful, and with a technological emphasis rather than the General's physical one. Indeed, it might have been said Dominia was more like the violent and sometimes base members of the infamous anti-martyr coalition than Kahlil: yet, he had been shot, and naturally reacted with more violence. Understandable—as it was understandable that she reacted with violence by cracking him over the skull. But it haunted her with guilt, that mindless crack. When would the violence end? It was all too bloody: from the moment humans were born in a screaming mess, it was a parade of violence, loss, betrayal, fear, death, Cassandra, Cassandra—anything but Cassandra.

Dominia hurried herself over the threshold that second night, her Father's words stuck in her like venomous darts. She and the magician spoke little until they reached Lazarus, who confirmed she had not touched the thing, and again said, "Then we still have a chance." Off they set again, to a day the same as before less the gorge, and less a degree of trust.

It was not their fault she mistrusted them. It was her Father's fault, whether he had spoken the truth. No scrap of information could be garnered from him unless he meant for it to be used against someone else, or (best case) to his gentler benefit. Thus, she couldn't give his words much credit. At the same time, there was marginal truth to all he'd said, and more he had yet to reveal.

Knowledge was a tempting thing. Knowledge had been Cassandra's undoing. Though she strove to forget, Dominia was plagued by the six months of increasingly erratic behavior that crescendoed in the death of her wife. This had all begun during the winter of 1996, during Lavinia's sixty-sixth Feast Night—a commemoration of the night she awakened at the physical age of twenty-four, rather than the anniversary of her birth, as it was explained to inquiring children. The Governess and her wife had flown into Europa to visit for the first time in ages.

Dominia had thought it all a perfectly lovely time while it happened. Though she was not a party person, even she admitted the fete was grand. Her sister turned ninety that night, all years counted. Therefore, the gala had been a most important and busy occasion, populated by barons, the European governors, journalists, judges and barristers, military men and women. All of them were there with their adorable, spit-shined children, half of whom looked miserable and terrified as one might expect, and half of whom—blossoming sociopaths handpicked for their "charm"—circled a punch bowl kept cold by a few cheerful frozen eyeballs. This latter group required frequent interception by servants, lest their grubby fingers muddle dirt into the pomegranate and blood of the punch. Cassandra studied the former class of frightened squibs with a half-suppressed sigh, and leaned her artfully decorated head against her wife's besuited shoulder.

Dominia laughed. "You spent an hour on your makeup and hair. Are you going to mess it all up?"

Cassandra's eyes, lashes tinted with glittering powder and lids more colorful than any parrot, lifted toward Dominia and warmed the Governess's soul. "I like the way it looks after you've been kissing me."

Oh! Her heart. She kissed her mouth, that chin, the corners of those lips. The taste of makeup sat on her tongue even still, the powder-soft clay recalling a far-off childhood, a mother applying makeup at a mirror, a time of peaceful stasis and safety existing in a separate dimension from all of this. Endless. Dominia would so often be inclined to leave after touching that soft mouth—Cassandra's safe, reassuring lips—just one time. That night, at Lavinia's party, she came near to such an abrupt exit. If only she had! If only she had...but she hadn't. The Hierophant had found them. When Dominia lifted her head, there he was with his warmest smile, having emerged from the profusion of people.

"The most beautiful couple this family has ever produced." Their Father bent to kiss both their cheeks, Cassandra more accepting and smiling to see him than Dominia, who stiffly presented her cheekbone like a succumbing cat. As she stared out into the crowd, she located Lavinia, who greeted people in the company of the somber Lamb with her blonde hair in elaborate ringlets and white ribbons. Her dress for the night was a furling, white-and-azure assortment of petticoats; the Princess looked more like a woman from the Southern United Front in ancient BL times than European royalty. Not that it wasn't charming, and not Lavinia didn't obviously love every second of the silly dress.

"Livy looks like she's having a nice time," said Dominia. The pleased Hierophant placed a hand upon Cassandra's shoulder while he watched the scene.

"I certainly hope so! We've put hours of preparation into this party. You wouldn't believe what trouble we went to, acquiring the center-piece of this gala!"

The banquet table was decorated with quite a statement-making centerpiece, though why it was such trouble to acquire, Dominia was not sure. A delicate arm had been arranged to hold a quail-egg diamond and a slew of other stones, the slender wrist emerging like one of many exotic flowers that spilled around the offering to the guest of honor. Amid all the floral sprays, sumptuous fruit avalanches, and gaudy cakes, the delicate "centerpiece" was easy to miss. "Was it so hard to get here in Elsinore, of all places? The butchers across North America are fewer and farther between, but they always have plenty of whatever cut I want. I'd think your shops overflow, Father."

"The perfect pair of arms is impossible to find among humans. How we had to search!" Shaking his head, the Hierophant added, "But, nothing is too good for my girls. And see that smile?" Lavinia noticed her sisters and, beaming, sprang through the crowd.

"Her Father's smile, no matter whose she was to start." The Hierophant said this with a broad smile of his own before releasing Cassandra.

Perhaps it was only in memory she recognized, while turning her head, the way her wife's face fell. She certainly didn't notice it then, because Lavinia was upon Dominia for a hug, and all was forgotten by the Governess amid the girl's babbling insistence they come and see the mare Lavinia had been allowed to ride into the ballroom—hadn't she a *lovely* mane! Dominia agreed, but the three-hundred-something-year-old curmudgeon in her felt a noose's tension every time the shod equine brought its metal-lined hooves down upon the lovely marble floor. The floor, the floor!

The floor.

Dominia remembered she was remembering when she remembered the floor, because then she remembered the magician urging her to remember the floor, and then she remembered her body and found herself standing at a concrete fountain amid short weeds. Before her, Valentinian punctuated something with the phrase, "You know what I mean?"

Her mouth open, she glanced, helpless, at Lazarus. She looked, too, at the black sun blazing overhead, and sensed the day had ticked away much of its time. "I'm sorry—" She laughed at herself and then, unable to help the terror contorting the edges of her lips, looked between them. "How did we get here?"

"Oh my God." Valentinian slapped himself on the forehead. "Were you seriously not listening?"

"I don't know what's going on. How far have we walked? Please." She grasped Lazarus's arm, and he, usual inscrutable expression softening, held her hand. "I'm so sorry. I got lost in thought."

"Explains why it's closer," said Valentinian, rubbing the bridge of his nose, then stopping her from turning around with a quick, "No! Trust me. It'll be worse if you see how close it is."

"That's not going to help." With sudden patience, Lazarus looked deep into Dominia's good eye. "What's the last thing you remember?"

"I remember Valentinian arriving. The Hierophant...he's all I remember. Then I started thinking and I got caught up and I remembered the floor, finally."

Fingers working over his temples, the magician perched upon the chipped edge of the fountain, which emitted, from the mouths of alternating cherubs and fish, eight streams of glittering water. "We've walked half a day already. We just spent an hour explaining the operations of Fortune to you."

"I'm so sorry." All she managed was a fluster of apologies, embarrassed to have missed a cosmic lecture for which most mortals might have killed. "I didn't even realize we were walking. It was like I fell asleep."

"You're already asleep here." Lazarus released her; she seemed steadier, despite her alarm. "The problem is the same as the benefit: you're dreaming. Your attention got caught up in another dream. Reality is malleable for the observer in a place like this. Speaking of, *magician.*"

The mystic extended his hand expectantly, and the sighing magus slapped the open palm. As his hand bounced up, a clay sphere manifested between them: a cup with a circular lid that Lazarus unscrewed with care. As he filled it from the nearest fish, Dominia looked around and, tinted by the alarming notion she dreamed, began to see the landscape in an even more menacing light.

Perhaps it was the effect of that landscape's new feature. Solitary amid a desert of nothing, the sole source of water, the only sign of life they'd seen in this disorienting place with that thing so close, the fountain was no comfort to look upon. It was a man-made fountain; they had seen no people. No one she knew had created the landscape. Who, or what, had made the fountain? She dared not think on it in so unanchored a place as this.

"If I'm dreaming"—her heart pounded in her ears as she sat to take Valentinian's hands—"can't you tell me how to wake up?"

"Kiddo," began the magician, but she gripped his hands so tightly he winced.

"Please, Valentinian. Tell me, just so I know."

"If you know, you might try it."

"What would be wrong with that? Couldn't I come back?" Her eye leapt between the men, Lazarus no longer looking at her but studying the cup. "That's the way it works, isn't it?"

"Yes, but you need training to come back and forth reliably, and to find your way around. At least, you have to come in and out a few times on your own to experiment a little, gauge distances. You could awaken in the middle of some trap, or at a bad time and place. And it's not possible to get back here when you're panicking, or when it's night—not without some creativity."

"Who said anything about me being panicked? Me, being panicked—can you imagine! Do you know who I am?"

"Buddy," said the magician, "your hands are shaking."

Gritting her teeth, Dominia released her grip and shot from her seat. "Fine. Yes, I'm afraid! Nobody tells me a thing, and when they do, it's conveniently while I'm getting wrapped up in memories of—the past." A sheen of tears glossed the General's eye; she covered it while bowing her head. "I'm afraid because I have no idea where I am. I have no control or knowledge of the situation. I've lost my life and my Family, and I mean more than one family. I've been in accidents. I watched my wife *kill* herself." The sentence, which she had never said out loud in quite so many words, solidified the event in a way that curled her lips back from her teeth like wilting flower petals. She sobbed, and because Valentinian stood to put his hand upon her shoulder, she stepped away. "I've been a prisoner of war! My own Father...my Father. I'm more afraid of him than I am of anything in the world. But I've never—*never* been afraid like this. That was all on Earth. This—I still don't understand what this place *is*. What *is* it? Where *are* we?"

"New people always insist a thing has to have a name before they understand it. Call it what you want." Lazarus screwed the lid upon the cup. "It's not hell, but it's not exactly heaven, either. Valentinian called it 'Nirvana,' but it's more like the Bardos. Catholics and martyrs call it 'purgatory,' science calls it something else. I like to think of it as similar to the Wyrd."

"Like the Norse fates," asked Dominia, hyperconscious of her eye patch while Valentinian nodded and resumed his forgotten lecture.

"In short—to redescribe to you what I've been describing—this place is a web of probability in addition to space and time. We are experiencing consciousness from a wave form instead of a particle form, and when we perceive everything else to also be information interpreted as waves, reality is malleable."

"I don't see waves, or anything except for our electromagnetic fields. I see a landscape."

"People who have made it this far while retaining a sense of self and bodily tie to reality tend to experience static images, especially at first. The more time you spend here, the more you're able to abstract it all. Hell, sometimes when I stop concentrating, all of existence is just a geometrical lattice. Like a kaleidoscope, in dimensions even I can't explain! But when people experience their final death and have no more ties to physical reality, that's their first time here if they don't have some kind of esoteric dream experience or a few drops of Lazarus's blood. With no context, all bets are off. It could look like anything. A parade of demons, a series of bodily transformations, a vast plane of nothingness. Worse, they might be trapped in the lower frequencies; VLFs and ELFs are like a prison for the crystalized soul that can change no further, can draw no closer to liberation. People who think they hear ghosts on the radio aren't always wrong. Over time, though, less crystalized people wandering here learn they can do things. Then, they can move on, or look at the data in another way. Some people can abstract all the data of reality down to the experience of a sound. When Elijah manipulates the probability of events to grant prayers—low-grade wishes, but sometimes pretty powerful ones—he's manipulating this place while remaining present in the physical interpretation."

"Will we find the Lamb here, too?" She wouldn't be able to handle both her fathers coming to guilt her night after night. Luckily, Lazarus shook his head and answered for the long-winded magician.

"Cicero keeps too close a lock on the Lamb for him to acquire my blood and physically ascend, which means the position of Elijah's shade in this place is most often tied to his position in reality. Just like the Hierophant keeps Cicero grounded because he'd lose control of El Sacerdote within five minutes of this discovery, he also keeps the Lamb from utilizing this place to its fullest extent."

Understandable. The Lamb was never far from Cicero, out of a blend of love and something ancients called "Stockholm syndrome." Martyrs called this "family ties." But it was also true the Lamb kept as much of an eye on Cicero as Cicero did on the near-omnipotent Lamb. It was entirely possible the Lamb sacrificed the extent of his powers for two thousand years simply to keep his brother from catching a whiff of this place; no doubt, the Hierophant approved. The mystic, with his own strong opinions on the matter, went on. "Better to keep him trapped in the material world, where he can be corrupted into minor tweaks to reality, than let him come here, where he can make significant changes that might solve the problems his brother caused." Lazarus slipped the clay canteen into his robe, just over his heart, and turned away. "If it were up to me, I would have given the Lamb my blood a long time ago."

"What's stopping you from showing up in his closet?"

"The horns, for one. Electromagnetic effects are warped near him so if you can find him here at all, you can't drop in on him as closely as you can with somebody else—not if he doesn't want you to. Also, I hate to admit, but I'm not as talented as Houdini over there when it comes to rearranging how I perceive this place's information. That means—for me, anyway—it's hard to find *any* person's precise location, here or in reality. It doesn't help that Cicero and the Lamb are a traveling carnival of sacrilege, going from martyr church to martyr church and taking his false blood along with them. With each day here being about a week in reality, it's extremely hard to pinpoint and intersect the physical location of a far-off moving person through any means other than chance or elaborate design. The magician, though, or the Lamb, or somebody less set in their ways than I am—they can find their way to specific people or places based on energy patterns like the electromagnetic field of our collective presence. But...even then, it can be hard to sort one person from another."

Lazarus waved at the colorful bands, which, accommodating as they did the combined space of the trio, faded enough into the edge of Dominia's visible perception that she had grown accustomed to it. "People give off similar patterns of emotional, physical, or even psychological expression. A magician like Valentinian learns how to read the spark of individuality hidden there. But, for example, the Lamb's physical brain is a receiver for all prayers of the world, whether human or martyr, and he knows their identities even if they don't. He's half in this world and half out of it all the time, so unlike those whose thought-bodies are absent because they're on Earth, his phantom is always around here somewhere. If his physical body was free of those metal horns, he'd be pretty easy to find on this plane, bodily presence or no. Normally, his spirit is a conglomeration of pleas. That's one of the reasons your Father has become such a big fan of artificial enhancements. Helping the Lamb deaden the sounds of prayers and disguise his presence here.

"And, frankly"—Lazarus resumed tossing the stones, and Dominia wondered just how many pebbles he had—"the consequences to my capture are far too vast to risk. Elijah is a gentle person in a bad position, but there's nothing I can do about his situation with things the way they are. Your Father uses all kinds of fail-safes to keep interference on this plane from getting anywhere near him, his castle, and his business."

"How is *he* coming and going? Why does he only come at night? How does his study move with him?"

"Please, will you drop this," the magician begged. Dominia was in no mood to relent.

"I've agreed to go with you to Cairo. It's in my best interest to go to Cairo; I want Cassandra back." She winced at the rattling exhalation of the thing behind her. The General redoubled her will to go without looking over her shoulder. "That means getting the diamond back from Miki, which means I have to stay here. But it would give me—psychological comfort to know the way out of here, even if I never use it."

"It won't."

"It will," she insisted, with such force that Lazarus stopped, heaved a sigh of disgust, and once more faced her.

"You want to know how to leave this place? You have two easy options. First is, get to where you want to be and let the black sun take you back—just stare into it for long enough and it will be a door for you. You want to try it? Go back now? Huh?" He waved his hand toward the sky, and she, taken aback, sputtered some useless noise while his hand lowered. "That's what I thought."

As he turned away, she thought of her Father's study, and how it—and he—appeared only at night. "What if the sun isn't out," she asked in meeker tone.

Lazarus spoke without looking back. "What's the easiest way to awaken from a dream? Kill yourself."

The General's mouth opened and shut in silent horror. Valentinian, realizing she still stood frozen, paused to shrug.

"Or let someone else kill you," the magician added. "Either way... better to wait for the daytime, right?"

Fair point.

IV

Two Souls, Alas

Death could not be the only means of awakening. That night, as she gazed into the blue heart of the fire, the Hierophant studied her face with a half-suppressed smile.

"You look tired."

"Only four more nights." The words felt miserable aloud. "Pretty easy for you, showing up where and when you please. Otherwise, you're safe at home."

"It's as though you never should have left."

While she tried not to snort, she focused on the spot where awaited the new-sprung, green-felted pool table. Arguing with him was pointless. He was too adept, and too annoying. Better to keep focused on topics in line with his one use: as an echo chamber for frustrations she otherwise locked within herself. If nothing else, her Father gave half answers, as opposed to the nonanswers of Valentinian and Lazarus.

"This place is so creepy. Why is it so dark? Where's the moon?"

"It is all around us, in a way. All things are, in this place." The Hierophant's gaze fixed upon his fireplace. He crossed to stoke it with the poker above its mantle. "Yet, all things are not."

For some reason, the thought of the absent moon evoked Miki's thousand-named goddess. Ishtar, Amaterasu, who knew what else. Those words were taboo, along with all Her other names, among self-respecting martyrs. "Couldn't there be a moon in this sky, if somebody thought of it? At least, over your study?"

"Anything might be made here. You might recreate every star in the sky." His tone was too approving for her comfort.

"You'd like that, wouldn't you? What would those thoughtforms do?"

"Only light up the night, and make it a more palatable time to travel. You might arrive at Cairo faster; perhaps your friends would thank you."

"Don't treat me like I'm stupid." As he batted innocent eyes, she turned toward the thing wearing Cassandra's face. Tonight it sat using her wife's hands to numbly manipulate a book through which it gazed as though pretending to read. Fear to foment it turned Dominia away, back to the nauseating dark. "I'm not sure of the harm, but I'm sure there would be some. I know they wouldn't be happy with me."

"Perhaps. But if they are unhappy, the root of their unhappiness will lie in displeasure at knowing you've nurtured your powers. You, Dominia, have a grand capacity for so-called magic. It is a capacity of which you have been kept ignorant. I admit I've had a hand in this, but with the secret out, I feel responsible for helping hone your abilities. These forces can cause harm when allowed to go untempered. Powerful as you are, the world might be at stake."

While rubbing her forehead, she laughed without joy. "Funny you should say that. I've been tasked, according to them, with ending the war, and seeing the martyr race off to Acetia."

"They said that?" asked her Father in near-incredulous tone, the corner of his mouth giving a twitch.

"Sort of. Why?"

"I'm only surprised. They're not often so forthright." Without batting an eye at his daughter's questioning, the Hierophant replaced the poker and began to use his pool table as if hoping she would join. She would not. "What a terrific burden to lay upon your tired mind! Have they no idea what I've put you through over the past few weeks?"

"Nice that you're honest seventy percent of the time."

He racked up the colored balls in a series of clacks that flashed her to times in barracks and bars, earning the respect of her soldiers and impressing far more than a handful of beautiful women. Cassandra, of course, had been the last—oh, teaching her to play it properly! The deerlike bend of her body! The smell of her neck—

Dominia gripped the chair to refocus her thoughts from dangerous sorrow. What had they been speaking of? Yes—her obligations to humanity and martyrdom. "It's pretty exhausting."

"Then I'm glad I need not point out that your companions intend to bring the apocalypse for our people. They would jettison us into space without so much as a return address!" After whisking away the triangular frame, he circled the rectangular table, brows lifted high in significance. She was not sure when the cue stick had gotten into his hand, and she had watched him the whole time. "I, my girl, strive only to prevent the horrors of entropy."

At the crack of his cue, the balls thundered apart, and both a stripe and a solid wheeled into opposites corners. As the rest arranged themselves, the Hierophant adjusted his tie, loosed the buttons of his jacket, then resumed his prowl around the table.

"You think I am bad. Think of them! My efforts at culling human populations are for their own good, the good of the planet—most of all, for the good of our religion. For God, my girl!" *Crack!* A solid whirled into a side pocket. "Fair Earth cannot sustain the human race when it balloons to such extents as the past would have encouraged. At one point, it was necessary to spread one's genes through as many heirs as possible; now we must think of the Earth, for the humans do not. Why else would the Lord have put us on her face, were we not to control her population? Martyrs manage the human population, and I manage the martyr population."

"And who manages you, again?"

"The divine wisdom of the Lord. You should know that by now." *Crack!*

He was a fine one to talk of his God-given responsibility toward the environment. Much of the technology responsible for wrecking the planet had been pushed into development by him, even before his public appearance alongside Cicero and Elijah in 2045 CE, otherwise known as AL 1. He alternately reveled in destroying and rebuilding—perhaps because when something was rebuilt by him, he did so in his own image. That was what he did with people, after all. Still, she did not want to waste time arguing tangents. Another ball cracked off into a pocket's void. In the corner of her good eye, the doppelgänger sat in her Father's chair, rapt as they spoke. "I don't know." She glanced from the ugly sight. "They have a point. I think the humans were better off managing themselves."

"This guilt over your own existence is unhealthy. Martyrs are necessary. You are necessary. But what is not necessary is the end of the world. Not at this point in time."

Annoyed he mixed a valid point about her emotional state into an unrelated one about the conflict at hand, she nonetheless decided to play the Hierophant's advocate enough to extricate his opinion. "I don't know. I haven't made up my mind about any of this. They've hardly told me anything, aside from my responsibility. I mean, what happens if we stay on Earth? We'll colonize space eventually no matter what. Humans continue to perfect and spread the terraformed state of Mars, and with technology you paid to develop."

"But your friends would see every martyr wiped from Earth's surface. It is not a matter of colonizing other worlds; it is a matter of exiling an entire species before it is ready."

"Why not bring them here?"

"I admit: one reason I have encouraged population growth for the past several years is the vain hope we will find another mutation like Lazarus."

"A Lazarus you can control." At his mild smile, she pressed, "You teach his blood is the damnation of martyrs."

"It always is. I have never met a martyr who does not taste of his blood and wish to overthrow me straightaway. This is the real story of Regulus. But perhaps, if the Family had a child with blood as extraordinary as that of Lazarus who remained loyal to the cause, I might guide the initiation of my more educated children. This is fruitless, but one never does know."

"So you really have lived through all this before? Lived through this war, then gone on to colonize Acetia just to come back and start it again?"

"Yes."

"How many times?"

"Once." *Crack!*

He scratched. The white ball bounced around, twirled into the corner pocket, and took nothing with it. Dominia smirked as her Father offered the stick. "Care for a turn?"

With a glance for the too-close doppelgänger, the General made her way to the table. The Hierophant's smile as she accepted hovered between mocking and paternal even more than usual, and she strove to ignore it as she turned her attention to the game. Eight balls left—no, six. Every time she looked, the number changed: the order, the colors. She tried to focus her wandering eye and force her muscle memory to work.

As she arranged herself, her Father said, "Your abilities are far vaster in scope and possibility than merely bringing about the end of the martyr world. I told you I could give you anything you liked, but the fact is I would only be showing you how to get it, yourself."

"I know how to get what I want on my own." She pocketed two balls at once, in side and corner pockets. As she worked her way around, she refused to look at him, lest the order change again. "I don't need your help."

"You do if you're to keep yourself from being corrupted. From devouring lies. They hide so much from you! Why, they have even forbidden you to take advantage of your own, holy body! They have encouraged you to think it would be some crime against your wife to make love to her shadow—"

"Corner pocket," she interrupted, waving the cue to indicate the four ball and her target.

"—when in fact it would honor her. Bring fair Cassandra closer to reunion with you."

The announced ball propelled home with a gunshot's crack. "It wouldn't be the real Cassandra."

"What defines the real Cassandra? What is real here? You said your-self, you might well create the stars. Your body, too, is a thoughtform, as is mine. Here, you are as real as Cassandra."

"I'm always as real as Cassandra." She didn't bother calling the next and pocketed it while saying, "That thing's not Cassandra."

"By that logic, Valentinian has little to do with his canine counterpart."

"I'm not sure I follow."

"My dear girl"—he put heavy emphasis on his next words—"everything here is a thoughtform. What has a dog to do with a man? Nothing. But a dog might be imagined to have the *spirit* of a man, and be reflected as a man."

Now, it was her turn to scratch, though rather more dramatically than had her Father. Her cue ball, propelled by too much force, leapt from the table to bounce across that nice chessboard floor. While the General grimaced, the false-Cassandra-thing hurried after it with a laugh and the disgusting chide "Dominia!" from a hostage voice.

She shoved the cue stick to her Father. "What are you babbling about?"

"Only what I have tried to tell you for some nights." The doppelgänger returned the ball, smiling dumbly as it did, and her Father set it on the table. "You are being deceived, lest you should realize the truth and see what fool you've been for listening to their lies. They will not even tell you the truth about your eye, will not let you lift your patch!" She had forgotten about her missing eye in this place where she barely felt the body parts she had. Her left hand tightened. The eye had not mattered as she played pool, but, now reminded of it, the weight of the elastic band dominated her consciousness. Her depth perception, as though remembering it was supposed to falter, did. As with all strange things here, she fought to ignore it.

"So, then: What's the truth?"

"Valentinian is as much, or more, a thoughtform as your dear Cassandra here—and equally created by you."

Crack!

The General did not see if the ball had sunk; she did not care. A strangeness overcame her. She insisted, "That's stupid, of course he's not," even as his words evoked the first night Valentinian had collected her from the Hierophant. When he'd asked her, on touching her, if she had touched the doppelgänger. As she recalled all those times in which he'd laid on her a comforting hand or she'd gripped his arm for support, her Father continued speaking, continued shooting on a table whose number of balls returned to eight when the cue was passed between players.

"It makes less sense that a man should be turned into a dog. I told you Valentinian was trapped here for the sake of a wish gone awry, did I not?"

"Yes. I've also heard Valentinian is trapped here because you tricked him."

The Hierophant turned so she might see his dubious expression. "You mean to say I turned a man into a dog? My girl"—he laughed, and her face burned as, with relish, he resumed shooting—"we have talked from time to time of magic, but let's not be absurd. The amount of energy required *alone* would be cataclysmic. Nuclear. It is as vain a hope as the hope your Cassandra could rise from the dead. Yet how easily one talented in magic might accidentally imagine a dog as a man, lest they be alone with a mad old mystic!"

"Lazarus is supposed to be his father, though, or something. Originally. Right? Didn't they work with Cicero and Elijah the first time you came to them?"

"Mere fantasy. I have never seen Saint Valentinian in the waking world, not in all my many nights. Not in this world, or any other. When an imaginary being cannot reveal it is imaginary, it must concoct an elaborate backstory to earn its host's support."

"If he's imaginary, and from *my* imagination, then why have you put him into paintings all these years?"

With a pitiful look, the Hierophant leaned his hip against the table. "He has done such a number on your mind you cannot see you have it backward. Saint Valentinian is a symbol of *death* to the martyr. He is a fictional saint, a false star crafted to fill a hole in our culture's spiritual constellation. This place is a place of death, and your soul knows it. Therefore, though you may not be physically dead, to be here is to accept a visionary experience that shares many of death's qualities. It is only logical a thoughtform in the shape of Death should greet and guide you."

"No, that's wrong. He's taking me to Cairo—they both are. Lazarus wouldn't support his story—"

"Unless Lazarus, who remembers more than even I, feels Valentinian serves his ends. What could a thoughtform of death want more than a mass sacrifice in war's bloody climax? What could he crave more than the deaths of seven million helpless martyrs—for, my child, it seems we are many, but that *is* the true number of our populace, I remind you. A speck beside the bacteria colony of mankind! And what of those many servants"—de facto slaves who signed away human rights for cushy paychecks as the result of a lifetime of social brainwashing—"who depend on us for food, shelter, their entire social infrastructure? For *these* make up the majority of martyr-controlled towns and cities. Their livelihoods would dry up, and many would not be accepted back into human society after working with us for so long. What are they to do—follow us to the stars? Helpless women and men and children sent to uncertain fate in the vicissitudes of space? The premature birth of an entire species? Indeed, perhaps *then* he would have the energy to craft his physical body."

"We could go to Mars." Her eye glassed with tears of doubt while the Hierophant waved his hand in dismissal.

"Then when they have finished ruining the first marbled planet of which we were once custodians, they shall come to defile the new one, and chase us from *that*. You do not understand what humans are like, Dominia, because you have never seen them have free rein. They are *violent*. They are *savage*. They are apes, unevolved and unconscious animals hooting and shitting in the Garden of Eden." His use of profanity always shocked her into attention. "We must not just be gardeners but zookeepers. Of course they resent us. They call us depraved and evil and insist we are better off floating among the stars because they have been 'left behind' with us and their sin in a Rapture not even described in the human Bible—a Protestant invention, a device with which to question our claim to the throne of the Lord. But we are the children of God, and they are larvae beside the glory of our imago. To think you have allowed yourself lured off the righteous path by some imaginary fiend." Disgusted, her Father resumed his game. "I tried to save you from all this, you know."

Despite knowing better, she mentally succumbed to his talent for shaming ungrateful children. Despite knowing better, she tried to explain to herself why Valentinian couldn't be a thoughtform. "But he could have turned himself into a dog, if he's…" She couldn't bring herself to say the words, "a magician," because the sentence still sounded absurd. She looked, embarrassed, at the table. The eight ball sat alone.

What if she was wrong? What if, all this time, she had been quite literally letting her imagination run away with her, and because of that, she now found herself on the opposite side of—what? Rightness? Decency? Divinity? What was God in a place like this, in a world like this?

"Whose wish was it that trapped him here?"

"Yours." The Hierophant took aim, savored the moment, then mis-struck and sent the white ball askew when a knock reverberated the heavy door. Dominia lacked the schadenfreude she reserved for such things. The usual semi-relief of Valentinian's arrival was displaced by unaskable questions.

The doppelgänger shambled to get the door, and the magician stepped inside with a look of displeasure. "Ugh! It's opening doors, now." This, punctuated with a pointed look that expressed uncomfort-able knowledge of Dominia's thoughts.

"'Speak of the devil and he shall appear.'" The Hierophant trans-muted his displeasure for the unmoved eight ball into a wry glance at Dominia. Head bent to light a cigarette, the magician loped to the table and ignored her Father's sniffs of puritanical disdain. "Need you do that in here?"

"What are you talking about, 'in here'? In where? There's no ceiling, no walls. We're not inside anything, except the miasma of imagination. Goddamn." He stopped by the table with his blue eyes bright, treacherous cigarette dangling from the corner of his mouth as he rolled his dark sleeves to his elbows. "I love a good game of pool. About time you got something new! Something new and decent, I mean. May I?"

Forcing himself to smile, an effort evident in the quick-upturned, then relaxed corners of his still-shut lips, the Hierophant passed the cue to the magician. Valentinian rolled his shoulders, balanced his cigarette upon the edge of the table (Dominia felt her Father's eyes upon it), and bent forward.

"The key to a good pool shot is all in the breath." He exhaled, that exhalation guiding his stick into the cue ball into the black-eyed eight, which bounced in playful fashion against the nearest edge to spin into the opposite side pocket. "That"—he handed back the cue with a (doggish?) grin—"and the ability to ignore distractions. You ready to go, Dominia?"

She wasn't eager after that conversation, and glanced at her Father with a mind that whirred from thought to thought in a useless effort to evade questions. "Run along, my girl," said the clairvoyant Hierophant. "We can resume our conversation tomorrow night."

"Unfortunately, he's right." The magician waved. "Come on."

The General had anticipated Valentinian would try to take her hand, as usual; but this time, he went to the door, cementing his obtrusive study of her inner thoughts as obvious fact. Suppressing her irritation to the fullest extent possible (not much, in truth), she strode through the door, then winced as the thing in the study called, "Goodbye, Dominia."

"Why the fuck are you telling me goodbye?" She paused on the threshold to narrow her eye in the profane thing's cringing direction. "You're going to stalk us all day, aren't you?"

"Actually, I will be keeping her behind. We have some lessons, I think."

"That's great." Valentinian attempted to guide Dominia out by the shoulder and was left rolling his eyes when she stormed down the path of the Hierophant's torches. "People get so touchy."

"I'd be less touchy if you'd stay out of my head."

A certifiable statement of the mentally ill, considering she might be speaking to her imaginary perception of a border collie—specifically, her projection of the patron saint of death upon said border collie, assuming Valentinian even had anything to do with Basil in the first place. Could be he was just a smart dog, and she'd made a false connection. Or, if it was true Valentinian was a disembodied spirit from the first iteration of the world, had Valentinian's martyr spirit attached to the dog's material body specifically to direct the course of events? She tumbled through an infinity of paranoid thoughts and considered his mention of previous incarnations during even this cycle of reality. What else had he been in her life? A tiger at the zoo that led to Cassandra's job teaching Noctisdomin school? The job that gave her wife a reason to live as long as she did in the wake of a series of unfortunate choices leading to undesirable immortality?

It was almost *more* logical Valentinian should be a thoughtform, though short of serious mental gymnastics, it was nigh unimaginable she could have ever created him. But it might make sense if things happened again and again, and thoughtforms got more power with every interaction. In that case, it was possible Valentinian was a thoughtform created—summoned, manifested, whatever—in a repetition long ago. From that point on, he could have existed in linear fashion from the start of many other universes, each time perpetuating some bullshit claims even Lazarus couldn't remember about a life he probably didn't live as a researcher alongside the mystic, the Lamb, and Cicero. With all this talk of lies becoming real, it was impossible to tell what might have been truth: and when everyone's truth was so incomplete, she wondered if they weren't petitioning her with their versions of reality, rather than trying to deceive her.

"Which place is more real"—she decided to ask of the magician—"this place? Or reality?"

"Consensus, material reality is real by definition. As close to 'real' as you're going to get. But you have to real-ize—ha-ha—after you reach a certain point of understanding that one is untenable without the other. Both this place and reality are the same amount of real."

Dominia could have screamed for such nebulous answers piling around her, and he knew it. "It's not helpful. I'm sorry. Think back on our film analogy. Is the series of static images making up the reel of film more real than the movie projected? More appropriately, which is more real when you're reading a novel? The individual words your brain decodes into experience? Or that experience of the story, undergone by your consciousness?"

There again were the books in the study, "TÆ CΦDVUKΘP" somehow unstable in its own existence but nonetheless emblazoned gold upon the side of a lapis-blue tome. She had since seen the *Odyssey* upon his shelves twice, and neither time had the title resembled its prior arrangement; yet, each time she registered the meaning of the text as if it were spelled the expected way. The most recent appearance was in nonsense-full Greek, and still she comprehended it; but it seemed a falser representation of the word than the variant before. This, she recounted to the nodding magician.

"A good metaphor. Ultimately, the arrangement of letters underlying the words you see don't matter as much as the overall meaning. The less observed something is, the more abstract and true to itself it is, because it contains a wide swath of possibilities. Infinite. But, the more you observe something, the tighter it becomes. The more crystalized. You understand it in a comprehensible way—maybe you're even able to take it into the real world with you. But the thing is then less true to its highest self because your observation has tuned its frequency to the band necessary to render the experience of it static. The Greeks had a three-faced goddess, Hekate—one of the ways Ishtar manifests, or vice versa, if you'd like. Her name means 'far-darting one,' and the arrangement of Her body and faces mean the most men can hope is to see two at a time. We can never see all three, like a Heisenberg uncertainty principle of metaphysics and creativity. There is always some information lost in translation from abstract to concrete: yet the abstract cannot be wholly comprehended by the three-dimensional perspective, so, to the human and martyr mind, the abstract is less real, even though it contains a perhaps higher truth."

"And to your mind?"

He shrugged. "I've spent a long time here. It's all the same to me. But I pine—oh, how much!—to walk with my own body through the world."

"Have you, ever?"

"In this world, this time? No. But many times, I have, and after all this… Your Father is a liar." He punctuated his abrupt turn by tossing his finished cigarette in the direction of the black sun, which had hefted most of its body above the horizon. "I keep telling you, yet you keep listening. It's always this way. Why? What can I do to get you to listen to me like that?"

"Try telling me the truth. Who you really are and what this is, and why you want to jettison my people into space." When Valentinian offered no response, she scoffed. "You can't even admit that. Even after Lazarus told me before, you still can't bring yourself to talk about it! What is it with you?" The blister of her fury swollen sufficiently to burst, Dominia grabbed his shirt.

"Why am I here? Why all of this, why me? Why won't you tell me the truth about my eye?"

"Because if you take off your eye patch one second before I tell you to, everything we've worked for is lost."

"But why?"

"If I'm not back to myself in the world before your eye here opens—and especially if the Lady isn't restored—there's no way for me to help you, and I have to move on to the next Dominia."

"Sounds like more bullshit to me."

"It's the truth. Your Father claimed sending martyrs into space sooner rather than later would be like giving premature birth to a world; real premature birth is removing your eye patch." While she was baffled by this, he blew right on without explanation. "You know what happens when you open your eye? You wake up. You *really* wake up. You wake up so hard, in a way beyond waking, that the truth itself creates a new world. You can't open a portal to a new world if you aren't ready to move through it. Rifts like that only have the energy to sustain the movement of one body through their substance, and even *that* is dependent on there being an empty space for the body to go.

If they don't have an empty space, they'll have to make one, or risk destroying the whole system. Guess who's ready to jump through a universal rift *and* happy to make himself an empty space?" The agitated magician waved his hand in the direction of her Father's study, a path empty of doppelgängers for the first, blissful morning. She could not appreciate that absence with the magician mad at her, because she couldn't follow his babbling. "You don't understand how any of this works, do you?"

"Of course not! You won't explain it to me!"

"Because every time I have, you've fucked it up!" The normally composed magician raised his voice, and Dominia was so surprised she released him. While he straightened himself out, he continued, "You fuck it up again, and again, and again. Well over forty times, a hundred times I remember, you have fucked it up! I hate to break it to you, kid, but you fuck up a lot. Big, unfixable fuckups. And each time one happens, guess what else happens? Everything! Every-fucking-thing happens over, and over, and over again. And you know why? Because you take off your eye patch too early, or because you manifest Cassandra's *tulpa*, or because you decide to go along with your shitty dad, or because of forty-something other reasons I don't even want to remember! You fuck up *repeatedly*. Because of that, Lazarus and I have lived an eternity and you have to keep doing this again, and again. Have to keep living your miserable life again."

At the pain that crossed her face, Valentinian's tone and expression softened, but he was not deterred from saying, "You have to watch her die again."

"Why would you say something like that?"

"It's true."

She slapped away the hand that tried to comfort her. Briskly, she turned toward the study of the Hierophant. The sun did not sink with her, perhaps because Valentinian did not pursue. He merely called with a sigh, "Kiddo, come on, come back. We should go."

"What, can't you come after me?"

"There's no point if you don't want me near you."

"Why? Because a thoughtform has to be wanted?"

"Yeah, okay." The sighing magician turned from the General with a wave of that slapped hand. "Do what you want. So this is the clichéd part of your journey where we have a falling out? I can take it. I've got a thick skin, to use another cliché. But if you get lost—"

"If I get lost, you've got more to worry about than I do."

Dominia hastened her retreat to the Hierophant's study and away, as far and fast as possible, from Valentinian. The rising black sun revealed a distant, shadowy river that went unappreciated, for she was as annoyed by herself—and by the magician's refusal to follow her—as she was by his cruel points. No matter how accurate. The thought of eternally walking into their spoiled bedroom, shame in Cassandra's eyes, a second too late, the silver barrel in her mouth, *Crack! Crack! Crack!* forever—it made her too sick, and her conversation with the Hierophant left her too disoriented. She felt like she had as a girl hanging upside down for an extended length of time. When she straightened, she found a new surreality, and wondered for a strange moment which way was "up." The mere thought made her slow her steps and spare a reluctant glance in the direction of her friend, who waited to see if she would return.

Perhaps because he waited, she decided she wouldn't, and dashed on until he was far from sight.

V

Are the Stars Out Tonight?

This childish habit of running away emerged from childish pain, and Dominia grew more aware of her own inescapably embarrassing motivation every meter her legs dragged across the dark ground. Valentinian seemed trustworthy after his actions as Basil, but now she could not be sure. She could not be sure of anything they'd told her. Oh, yes, her Father was a most notorious liar among those who were not sheep gamboling about his bloody flock. But he told the truth with pleasure when it benefited him; and Valentinian had not appeared interested in or able to refute the planted ideas, assuming he knew what was discussed. Yet she harbored a certainty, deep-rooted as a United Front redwood, that both men had told as many truths as they had lies. It would be far simpler were things clear-cut into the black-and-white lines of liars and honest beings. Instead, truth was not just veiled: the notion assumed a different shape behind those veils, depending on who did the talking.

Of course, the ambiguity of truth didn't justify running away: so she felt with greater acuity each step farther from the magician. All the while, the sun rose. The torches of her Father had disappeared, and horror dropped a mocking hand upon her shoulder to remind her she wandered alone in an alien desert with no path to guide her back. No trail of bread crumbs or Lazarus's stones—nothing but her lonely set of fields, claustrophobic without the cumulative space of three people.

Maybe she should have been leaving playing cards behind. However, as she dug into the ammo pouch for the deck given her by the magician that first night beside the fire, the Hierophant's office presented itself as a distant speck. Unfortunately.

Dread tightened the General's jaw even as relief tried to loosen it, for she couldn't bear to listen to the Hierophant pontificate for an entire day. On what, Lamb only knew; however, neither could she bear to return to Valentinian. She braced for her Father's smug expression when she knocked upon the disembodied door. No answer came, and she opened it to find the study empty.

Not just empty: a still life. Remarkably static without his presence. As if she'd penetrated the hollow shedding of a cicada. Like that husk, the dimmed books upon unsteady shelves seemed brittle. Not only was it intensely eerie to observe the study by herself—was it not somehow worse reinforcement when she observed it independently of him? Did that make the location more concrete, as it drew upon her fields to form her perception of her Father's thoughtform study? They vanished as she crossed that threshold, their daytime colors flexing against the invisible walls and fading into the bookshelves. Did they render her Father's reality more, as Valentinian put it, "consensual"?

Still: with the doppelgänger also missing, and some of the comforts of home (a sense of space and the illusion of depth), she could not resist. Could not help but think if her so-called friends wanted her back so badly, well...they could come and get her.

She pretended the source of her bitterness was unaccountable as she sank into her seat and assessed the postmodern wine decanter arching like the neck of a lily. Two glasses, hers still empty from the prior night, waited to be filled. She squinted at them to see if they were smudged by prior activities, yet they were clean, as if some metaphysical maid had swept through the unoccupied study to make its contents fresh again. Somehow, this infuriated her. A mockery, this spurning of detail and causality.

Her frustration was not the exclusive fault of the thing walking in Cassandra's skin. That honor lay with the burden. The sheer, unimaginable burden that her Father hastened to clarify. To decide what to do with her own people! To decide whether they should live on Earth and make others suffer, or alleviate that suffering and threaten the life of her entire species! Old friends who now thought her an enemy of the state; ex-girlfriends who'd once read her military exploits in the paper and had sometimes sent longing Halcyon account messages at one in the afternoon; children who'd never had a say and wouldn't hurt a human being for many years. All of them, up in a rocket gunning for nowhere, deluded into believing a nubile planet awaited guiding hands.

Real or fake, wine was wine. That desperation driving conscious-ness to escape present circumstances was never particular in its means of evacuation. The glass of wine Dominia poured contained every glass of wine she'd ever poured herself, from tacky disposable cups imbibed at teenage parties to those many flasks of whiskey downed during her military career. Most of all, it was that first glass of wine with Cassandra, in that wonderful house on the coast where Dominia went to escape herself and what she'd done after her last military campaign. That beautiful house, where she had never expected to bring a woman so gentle, so beautiful and human. So un-self-conscious. Natural. Always laughing. Gazing at Dominia with such adoring eyes.

How that had changed after her child's death! Cassandra's flowerlike way of blossoming with joy hollowed through the years, no matter how she loved the children she taught. Dominia had never become conscious of that loss—not in almost a century, until she looked back in pain. Then it was all so obvious.

The Governess's drinking had been proportionate with her wife's unhappiness, though Dominia never blamed her for being depressed. Drinking wasn't a problem as far as her hyperefficient martyr liver was concerned, so Cassandra never found a decent argument against some-thing in which she herself engaged on Noctisfreis and holy nights. Alcohol poisoning for a human meant drunkenness for the so-called master species, which was good, because most martyrs found it some-where between desirable and necessary to be drunk as often as possible. But this drinking Dominia did in her Father's dream-study swiftly became a bit much even for her. The decanter never emptied, though its amount fluctuated whenever she returned from her thoughts for fear of falling too deep into any memory, any fancy, any idea. Her foot tapped in the empty room to keep her from thinking too much about anything, especially Cassandra—

Obviously, she needed music.

Wine upon the end table, she knelt to flip through the assortment of albums in the nearby bookshelf. How heavy each movement was! As if she sat in a bath of tar. The square cardboard sleeves containing large vinyl pancakes were difficult to move and more difficult still to read: far more difficult than the spines of books. Perhaps just because her limbs felt heavy.

The wine sat beside her elbow. Had she put it there? She took a sip, resumed her work, and at last read "Mozart"—muddied with some Cyrillic, but legible. Instantly, she stood before the record player to find her prize the composer's Requiem. Had it been there because she expected to find it in his collection, or had it been there because it was there? Because her Father put it there, by will or imagination? The wine sat beside the record player. She took a sip and carried it back to the chair; if it was going to follow her, she might as well consciously bring it along.

Now that she considered it, that had been her reaction to Basil, the cute dog Valentinian had been. Or the cute dog he remained, when one met him upon Earth. She lifted a hand to her patch; if only this world were more real than its counterpart. Then again, how could she be sure it wasn't? She felt this was where she came in her dreams. Perhaps she had even glimpsed these moments in her waking, and only now experienced them in linear condition. The sound of Mozart's Introitus rang more powerfully in her ears and chest than ever before, the force of the music flushing her face as much, or more, than the wine—as much as any lover. Her head tipped back and she fell deep into its flow, forgetting even her own body.

Not unlike being pierced by the sound. As if her flesh were stripped away and her consciousness, purely contacted by the psychedelic experience of the art. Her lips parted. Somehow, she sipped her wine. No wonder her Father spent so much time listening to music! No wonder human and martyr flesh so craved music when it afflicted the soul thus.

It inspired a heat, a hot and furious anti-sexuality, founded in deep-set nerves she had never before felt and which the uninitiated might never understand. Behind closed eye, the world was naught but color, the formless texture of music more real than a body. Her fingertips did not exist, yet they filled with sublime delight. *Were* sublime delight. Perhaps it was the nature of the music, written for its composer's own mortality: a grand celebration of life and a humble genuflection to the awe-inspiring power of death. She had already died once she knew of; how many times had she died eternally? How many times had Valentinian skipped from Dominia to Dominia? Who knew! She kept drinking.

All was well and fine until she reached the Benedictus. Then arose logical memories of Nogales, which had been, at the time, the worst experience of her life. The Battle for the Reclamation of Mexico had been horrific: one of the most profound wastes of martyr life in all military history. It proved a mark upon the lives of many humans, too. She never let herself forget that. Being a helpless prisoner changed her; or maybe it was her jailer, Benedict, a bright-eyed kid barely twenty-one who had been amazed to see that his charge—not only the infamous General but the only survivor of her ill-fated unit that dark night—looked all of twenty-six years old.

"I'm two hundred and forty," was her curt response from behind the wood-and-iron door. Primitive, but its reinforcement served to trap her in that stone room reeking of shit and piss and rancid meat and base, animal sorrow. Too frequent a visitor in dreams, that room.

"Oh, gosh"—the boy laughed at himself—"I'm sorry."

At the time, his laughter seemed mocking. "You're going to apologize for that?" There was no humor for her while she huddled upon her bench, forced to stay awake all day to navigate her cell lest her flesh encounter that square of sunlight her captors refused to cover. A sleepless prisoner now mocked by a child, she snapped, "Don't insult me. You killed my people. Good men and women with families whose children have already been orphaned or abandoned by one set of parents. Now you've orphaned them again, you keep me here like an animal, and you apologize for thinking I'm twenty-six? Like I give a shit how old you infants think I am."

The boy blanched. "I don't mean to apologize, it's just—I'm real sorry, ma'am."

If only something throw-able had been left in her possession. In reality, she was lucky they'd left her with shirt and pants—were she a man, they wouldn't have. "Don't call me that, and don't apologize to me." She pressed against the cell door, having strode through the patch of sunlight that the boy apparently thought impassible: so quick, he barely had time to jump. "I could rip your tongue out through this window. I don't want to hear another apology. Frankly, I don't want to hear the sound of your voice, but if you don't talk to me, I'm just stuck here listening to you breathe, and that's worse. Since you mongoloids are going to put me on trial instead of killing me right now, we've got a lot of time to fill. That's a lot of wet mouth-breathing—"

"Mouth-breathing," repeated the flabbergasted young man while the General railed on.

"—I'm forced to hear without interruption. So do me a favor and, if you insist on talking to me, talk to me about something— anything!—that isn't an apology."

With his brows knit in an expression that initially recalled worry, the boy slipped his hand through the tight-fit bars of the antique cell and startled her by touching the hand that gripped her window. "You're right. I guess it's disingenuous to apologize to you, since I didn't have a hand in the battle and I'm only here to defend the things I care about. I just got here yesterday!" The boy laughed nervously and released her hand, sliding his own dampened palm back to safety with a glance down the hall. "They're desperate for men. There's a bunch of us here and more on the way, so don't get any ideas...but you did a number on us, too."

The boy had looked back at her with a hard, significant glance, one hand lifting his feldgrau rebel's cap while the other scratched his blond hair. It occurred to her, despite his deep tan, he was from nowhere near Nogales, or even Mexico. The 64th Jurisdiction of the Front had long been a subject of conflict, and the seat of terrorist activities whose impacts stretched not quite as far as the Jurisdictions of the Canadian Winterlands—this was why the General had stayed in those generously dark and quiet states during her twenty-year sabbatical, until Operation Sole Sovereign was put into motion and the Hierophant ordered her return. During her absence, hundreds of citizen militias had popped up across the Front, and all of them champed for an opportunity to slaughter their martyr oppressors. The idea had been to abandon unsuccessful drone tactics and take Mexico City by city, the good old-fashioned Roman way; and there was no one to lead such an assault but Dominia di Mephitoli.

The problem was intelligence about human military capacity proved wrong, time and time again. While things had started well and many target locations were secured, the martyr army—more brainwashed human slaves than martyr overseers, truth be told—was harmed by its own prior efforts to deny Mexico necessary supplies. What supplies the Mexican citizens had were funneled by the South American Resistance Army troops and various other Hunter cells; the same could be said of the weapons, which were easily passed along routes built to exchange precious goods. All that was to say: martyrs had expected a primitive and scrambling group of testy animals, and were met with many waves of well-armed fighters, guerilla or otherwise, who so wore the General's army down over the four-year campaign that, by the time the strike was launched on Mexico City, defeat was inevitable. Four years they had marched around in circles, and their human troops were stymied by malnutrition. Of her sizable unit drawn from the whole during the Battle for the Reclamation of Mexico, Dominia was the only one shipped to long-since ruined Nogales—the only survivor. She was shipped up, and Benedict, down, to a location that had become a storehouse for the tiny smattering of living martyr soldiers captured alive. She deserved it. Benedict, decidedly, did not.

Dominia drained her glass and filled it again, and wondered how many times she had repeated the motion. How many times had the record skipped, waiting for her to pick its successor? How long had the doppelgänger leaned against the bookshelf far behind her Father's empty seat, pale cheek pressed to the cherry wood? It looked more physical: a more compelling rendition of her deceased wife. With that horrific thought, the thing bit its lip as though acting coy.

The General's eye narrowed. "What do you want?"

The thing continued staring, the hand not braced against the book-shelf lifting to play with the dark curls tumbling down its neck. They were lighter in color today, those curls; the neck they surrounded seemed so like Cassandra's fragrant one that Dominia felt herself kissing it. She took a burning swallow of wine.

"Don't look at me." Her faltering words strengthened. "Don't look at me, you thief."

The parody did not move, though it did smile in that horrible shark's way. So unlike Cassandra's it sent a shiver down the spine. As she rose, the General demanded, "Did you hear me? Do you understand what I'm saying?"

"Dominia," it whispered.

The wine was on the verge of backing up her throat. "Don't use her voice."

Gaze unfaltering, the abomination took a step. Did it ever blink?

"Don't you love me, Dominia?"

The question ended in a shriek as the General hurled her glass past the thing, which lifted its arms over its face and cowered against the bookshelf. Dominia approached it for the first time, to grip the front of its dress and rattle it as a wolf might a rabbit.

"You bitch," she said into the vacantly fearful face. As Dominia spoke, she reexperienced all the times Cassandra had called her the same: their most violent fights, times of fury and panic early in their marriage. Those first few troubled years, when Cassandra had pushed her and slapped her and accused Dominia of ruining her life. Of taking everything from her. All accusations from which Dominia could not possibly defend herself, because they were true. What was she to say to things like, "You killed the man who should have been my husband," or, "If it weren't for you I wouldn't have to stay alive," or, the worst: "I wish I hated you, so I'd have a reason to leave you."

How had those fights come about? Dominia had never been able to discern. She once ceased drinking in hopes it would help them get along, but when the fights didn't stop, she doubled her previous alcohol consumption. All those failed attempts to make her wife happy—to get her to move past what seemed increasingly to Dominia like a blip near the start of Cassandra's otherwise beautiful life of ninety martyred years—made the General a miserable wretch. Every time her wife wept over life not lived and death not died, the Governess felt so inadequate she often wished she might just disappear. But things had improved with time, and distance, and love, and patience, and communication: until one day, many years later, it became apparent they weren't communicating at all in the necessary ways. After all, Cassandra would rather be the confidant of a bullet than the then-Governess.

It had not been Dominia's fault. She had told herself that, and so had everyone else, but it was hard to believe. Hard to ignore the resentment now that she held this false Cassandra. This lying Cassandra. Her Father had a point when he said Cassandra had always been a liar. This was merely the amalgamation of her lies, or perhaps her lies as personified by Dominia. This thing stared through a convincing recreation of Cassandra's largest, most terrified eyes, and the General laid a heavy slap across its face.

This was not the first slap she had laid across Cassandra's face, but it was the first that felt good. She did it again, and as it cried her name, she grasped its delicate jaw as though to shatter it.

"You're not Cassandra. You'll never be Cassandra, and if you keep talking to me like you're Cassandra, I'll kill you."

"Dominia," the thing sighed, half whining, squirming in her grip and against her body. She glanced down and saw its own, naked beneath the thin fabric of its violet dress. The General might have let her fingers push new holes through its pale cheeks had she not noticed the motions of its hand, pinned between thighs she knew too well, had missed so much, were not real, were not there. Yet—

Her hand was there, too, like it was one hand. The General's kisses lay bruises on those lips as she dragged the vile thing, writhing, to the floor where she pinned it. There, it keened at and reached for and begged of her in ways Cassandra never had. Cassandra had been more inclined to make sure Dominia watched her undress. Her motions would slow to sensual drag, and cream shoulders came rolling out of her blouse like the soft hills of breasts already spilling from the chocolate lace bra. The hair would come down, followed by the panties. Then she'd recline upon the couch, the bed, the floor, and look at Dominia in nude expectation that reminded her so much of the first time, so much, oh...the General never had any choice but crawl to her side in devotion. How she had loved Cassandra! She had hated their fights, but craved their tenderness!

But: this thing. She loved abusing it and hated it more than ever now that it rolled her over with its sex-hungry body and pulled its dress over its head. There she was. Every bit of her. Tragic, beautiful memory, profaned. The thing bent its head over the General's belt, over the stolen, fumbling fingers. Dominia wondered if this was less or more a betrayal of her late wife than would have been a jaunt with Miki in the train or the pawnshop or the dentist's apartment. As she winced, then relaxed into the caress of the thing's cold tongue, she became aware of her Father's distant voice, and felt she sat again in the chair across from his now-filled one. Around the edge of his seat, there was herself, lying on the floor with the doppelgänger's head between her legs. Incredible, to be so out-of-body: yet, from time to time, she felt its mouth.

"Sexual fantasies"—he spoke as if in answer to some query and was either oblivious to the activity behind him or, more likely, felt toward it the distant interest any alien scientist might reserve for a pair of coupling subjects—"are a misapplication of the creative libido down into the sexual drive, rather than upward, toward God."

From her position sprawled upon the floor, she turned her head to watch with her good eye herself in that velvet chair. Her Father, on rising, took the skipping needle from the record, then withdrew from the sleeve collection an album she could not see. As the black sun sank and with it night cooled all remaining definitions of environment, the cobalt fire spontaneously emerged in the fireplace, and the thing between her legs redoubled its efforts for her attention; efforts that, undeniably, had effect, so Dominia panted and struggled to divine the lyrics of the ancient United Front ballad she'd heard more than a few times growing up. It went almost unrecognized in the wet heat of pleasure. The whole world was muted by the long curls of dark hair that tangled around the General's fingers while she pushed ever tighter the creature's jaw against the apex of her thighs. All the while, the Hierophant talked on. "The average man is incapable of salvation because he is so wrapped up in the material world that he cannot see that his own lust for flesh is truly a lust for a higher power. The average martyr, even, cannot be saved, and the best he can hope for is a close connection with his community in the form of the living Church."

The song was one the Holy Father had sang playfully to her so many times. Its eerie tune, its themes of eyes and stars and the moon in a superposition of existence and nonexistence, were a playful paternal melody in those nights. She even turned around and sung it to Cassandra! Now she knew the song of devotion for what it was: a teasing promise of that fateful night at the McLintock farm. As her Father poured wine, then abruptly reappeared in his seat, his voice carried on: "When we find our lover manifested in the flesh, we derive from them a surge of inspiration because the soul is liberated from the surly bonds of lust. Our fantasies are revealed as the poisonous wastes of time they have always been. Idle hands are the Devil's playthings." He lifted his glass in toast to her.

"You really are the Devil." She marveled to watch herself, eyes glassy, stomach churning at the thought of more wine but brain unable to stop the movement of her hand to the glass to her lips. Her Father smiled, onyx eyes as burning as his fireplace while darkness ended its descent.

"Labels like that seem such primitive notions in this place, don't they? 'You' and 'I,' 'Valentinian' and 'Basil,' 'Cassandra' and 'it'"—for the first time he acknowledged the scene behind him with a glance and, from the floor, Dominia met his black eyes and looked away, not embarrassed so much as furious he would interrupt this moment of what was supposed to be private shame. The Dominia of the chair was calmer: perhaps because of the wine, or the conversation, or the way her Father said—"'God' and 'the Devil.'"

She was capable of only mechanical motion while the Dominia upon the chessboard floor, exhaling, forbade exaltation of her pleasure.

The thing carried on, carried on, carried her away. The darkness around the study quivered. She chronicled its motions through one hazy eye that dissolved into a burst of color and pleasure along with the rest of her, then recollected to discover a new ceiling upon which was painted quite a fresco. An old religious story called the Assumption of Mary. A primitive, pre-Hierophant interpretation of the Truth, but a small part of the story after the addition of the Post Testament. The music had also changed. She recognized neither it, nor its lyrics, but she heard a distant keyboard and saw from her chair that her Father had moved. Now, he tended the fire.

"You have been alone so long, and refused yourself an outlet lest you offend your dead wife. All this time you've clung to the hope she'll return as once you knew her. But would she want that? If you brought her back, would you ever find peace? All these questions, poisoning your mind. What relief awaits you, if only you'd accept your pet!"

On the floor, the thing crawled the length of Dominia's body to kiss her mouth. She gritted her teeth but nonetheless found herself absorbed into its kisses while her Father carried on. "This pursuit of fantasy has been the ultimate in distractions. A lesson on the life-ruining power of inaction, of lust. Poor child, poor girl, poor daughter! I cannot stand to see you throw away your life on so fruitless a cause. My tragic angel; your hopes are being manipulated by cruel and greedy forces. You are trapped in a dream—a tahgmahr such you cannot remember the girl you were."

He was back in the seat across from her; the poker, abandoned, leaned against the marble of the fireplace. "My girl, first plagued by bad dreams, as so many young martyrs—who then one evening looked so prideful, victorious, over breakfast."

And she was that girl, sitting in that too-big, ornate wooden chair at the expansive dining room table of their Vatican home (where they stayed frequently to bribe her into good behavior, for the child was always in a better temper when upon Mephitolian soil), silver spoon grasped in her hand as was the wineglass pinched in her fingers. Had she not broken it? Had it not shattered behind the cringing *tulpa*?

Even now, it fell from her hand to break once more upon the floor: in the Vatican, her Father asked, "What's pleased my princess this fine evening?"

"I figured how to stop my night—tahgmahrs." At his curious "Oh," she nodded. "First, I realize I'm having a dream. Then, I decide to open my eyes."

"Of course, of course!" The Hierophant laughed and exchanged smiles with the other adults at the table, his beloved Cicero and adored Lamb and a few transitory favorites from the Mephitolian court. "How simple. Would all problems had such easy solutions."

Was he saying those words then, or now? While she was in the chair, or on the floor? She struggled to orient herself against the mouth of the thing until its fingers edged up her face: for a fraction of a second, it attempted to caress her cheek. Then the black band of her eye patch shifted against her ear.

Her drunken, dissociated head cleared as if by the ringing of a bell that focused her consciousness to one point. She grasped that hand and, with a grip automatic as it was steely, broke two fingers. It cried against her mouth in a voice so terrible, so unreal, that the General no longer recognized it as any way related to Cassandra. As she shoved the creature away, she glimpsed its true form, and cried out at the edge of one horrific gray mandible while midturn for the poker. By scrambling to her feet and twice nearly falling, she reached her goal and was ready to fight: it had fixed itself by the time she turned back, though the Cassandra-flesh it wore rippled as if ants crawled beneath. The General saw in it nothing of the terrible bulging eyes and profusion of teeth floating in the adrenaline-drenched recesses of her mind. Her chair was empty. She had collected herself. The only Dominia to be seen stood with her back to the fireplace, brandishing the poker against the thing, which, naked and weeping, retreated behind the Hierophant's chair.

Someone knocked upon the door. Edging to throw it open without taking eye from the scene, Dominia found herself more ashamed than ever when the man who entered was not Valentinian but Lazarus. He observed the room, then Dominia, his expression tight.

"I take it you touched it?" When she managed a reluctant nod, he sighed. "Well…there's still a chance. I'm glad you were honest."

"How could I have hidden it?" Her voice shook as she glanced down. To her surprise, her clothes were in perfect order. Belt and all.

"The truth renders us naked," the Hierophant said, reaching behind his seat to pat the shoulder of the doppelgänger. "Poor Cassandra's fingers! It will take her a whole day to recover. I hope you're happy."

"I know I am." Lazarus glanced at the poker Dominia forgot she held. As he removed it from her hand, she felt more like a sullen child than ever. "Come on. Let's get back on track."

"But it's not morning yet." No one had ever told her she couldn't leave her Father's study before the morning came. Even so, the idea of leaving it prematurely numbed her every limb. Lazarus shook his head.

"It's soon to be."

"That can't be—the sun's just set."

"The time you spend here is in what you do, not how many minutes you spend doing it. Other measurements are more important."

Eye watering, Dominia struggled to avoid seeing the doppelgänger. "I didn't screw up, did I? This isn't an unfixable fuckup?"

"Nothing's unfixable as long as we're friends. Are we still friends?"

"Of course."

Just slightly, Lazarus smiled. "Valentinian will be glad to hear that, I'm sure. He's waiting: come on."

"Actions have consequences, Dominia." She turned back to watch the Hierophant as she allowed herself led down the path of lights. "How many times will you slap my offered hands?"

"As many times as it takes for you to get the message," Lazarus responded. Over the threshold, he released Dominia and doubled his stride.

Relieved to escape that place of stasis and surreality, she hurried along with one last glance over her shoulder. "Will it follow us again?"

"Probably not today, not since you damaged it. But you'll see it tomorrow, I'm sure, good as new."

Her bones lurched at the thought of what had happened, of more days and nights wandering through this desolate place. She stopped, the back of her neck breaking out in the putrid sweat of a hangover. "Do I have to keep going back there? Why? Why can't I just stay with you all night?"

"I told you already about time. It's doing things that makes the morning come. Otherwise, we would have to wander in the dark; and whether you believe it or not, that's more dangerous than enduring a nightly visit with him."

"How could that be more dangerous?"

"You could completely forget who and what you are—or, worse, drop to lower frequencies. It's easy for any of that to happen in this place no matter what, especially for somebody unprepared or with no will of their own. But in the darkness, when you can't see your body or anything else, you can forget what you are. Become something else."

"Something like what?"

"It's one thing for a man's physical body to be swapped with a dog's. It's another thing if the soul thinks itself a dog. The same is possible for you. Get caught up in a flight of fancy, and with no body to act as a frame of reference, you could become anything: a dragon, an eagle, a tiger. It sounds great, but when you're doing it, you forget to enjoy it. You forget that it was ever any other way, and become so caught up in being that thing you could live a whole lifetime. Trust me: your Father would love that."

Worrying her tongue against her teeth, the General asked, "About what happened before—"

"You don't have to talk about it if you don't want."

"But what have I done? I got drunk and it just...things happened, but I didn't mean—"

"Gazelle don't mean to be eaten by lions. But you still fed it, and reinforced it *and* your Father's study. Valentinian talked to you about the wine."

Yes, the wine. It hadn't felt like any alcohol she'd had—like any drug. So heavy and strange to imbibe; yet, its effects had already disappeared. The mystic nodded at that.

"You're drinking his spirit. His thoughts, his ill intent...it's poisonous. The more you drink his wine, the more you'll accept his way of thinking, and the more you'll be tempted by his servant. But it only has power over you while you're engaging with it in his reality bubble." Her own luminous bands, their edges fading in with the graying morning light, were evoked at that term. The furniture and the space of the study had been formed by her Father's fields, *were* her Father's fields—and her fields, too, while she visited. All other fields, by virtue of the observer, were drawn into the system of the imaginary object. And, as with the thoughtform, it reflected the inner essence of that observer.

It was more than a visible demonstration of electromagnetic fields, this series of neon streaks encircling them. It *was* them in so many ways; ways she could not articulate; ways that so stirred her she migrated the subject back the conversation at hand, and the mystic's description of the memory bride as her Father's servant.

"Did he send that doppelgänger? It seems...close to him."

"No. You attracted it without knowing. But your Father likes to think himself compassionate toward all things, thoughtforms included; he doesn't care that it's a compassion that comes at the expense of compassion to humans, and even martyrs."

For the first time, Lazarus hit a nerve he himself had exposed. "You're a fine one to talk about compassion to martyrs. Wanting to shoot a whole species into space."

"I'm not talking tomorrow," said the old man, looking as annoyed as she felt. "And you're jumping to conclusions. I never said anything about outer space. That was *your* idea. Not mine." At her astonished expression, he barged on: "Look: when your Father is killed, there will be a schism among your people. However you slice it, his death will cause so many problems that martyrs will lose their grip on the power structure of the planet. You know that. You also know that your Father needs to die."

She lost any hope of adequate response, and chose to linger in troubled silence as he continued. "You know things can't proceed as they have. All this suffering is unnatural: you know it, the good martyrs hidden among the population know it. Those good martyrs, and the good martyr we choose as their leader, will see that it is not only in the benefit of humans to depart Earth. It is in the benefit of martyrs."

"How will we eat? What will we do for all those centuries of travel? Surely you don't want *me* for leader after him, right?" Now, it was Lazarus's turn to remain silent. Finally, her lips pressed thin, Dominia tried one more nagging question. "Please. Is Valentinian real? A martyr? Or is he just some dog, some fictional character, who only exists because I've convinced myself he does?"

After studying the General, the mystic admitted, "As long as I've known Valentinian, I have been personally unable to remember when I met him, or how I knew him. Valentinian says he was once my son, and that he regrets not salvaging my consciousness from that first world."

"I thought it was your blood that caused your memory to come back—why wouldn't it contain the memory of that first time?"

"The blood allows it, but I think he's responsible for it somehow. He won't admit it. I've sort of given up caring. He seems lonely. It's one of the reasons why he makes me suffer this eternal existence, I guess: so I don't forget him again. Apparently, his mother in that place was the woman who became, in all universes thereafter, the current manifestation of the entity known as the Lady. I *do* know her. Trisha," he said with longing. "But we never had children. Hell, we never had more than one date before she sort of fell off the map, and I was too embarrassed over a misunderstanding to track her down. Now, I see that misunderstanding wasn't a coincidence. It was designed so she and I wouldn't be together: so she could become the Lady, and Valentinian could never be born."

So that was the space her Father had made for himself. "Do you believe him about his parentage?"

Lazarus shrugged, which was becoming the physical expression of choice around those parts. "Someone has to be responsible for all this. This conflict, this eternal loop, this struggle against your Father. If he wants to take credit, I'm happy to let him."

"But if he can extract your consciousness and restore it to your new body, why can't he do that for me?"

"Do you *want* him to do it for you?" At her grimace, he nodded. "We did try that once, actually."

"How did it go?"

Following an ominous pause, he answered, "We decided it was better you don't remember your past...attempts."

She shuddered, and tried one more point: "If he's a magician, can't he turn himself into a martyr instead of staying stuck as a dog?"

The old man chuckled. "The material world is, by definition, more concrete and static than this one. It takes a higher power than that of mind alone to change something as vast as the molecules of a being's body, or to replace one being with another. Valentinian is a great magician, it's true, and he has tremendous power, but...let's say it is prohibitively difficult for a man operating the body of a dog to upgrade to bipedal, sapient primate."

"Is there a way to help him?"

"Yes." In the distance, the red-and-black figure of the magician appeared to be packing his true fire as though coaxing it into an invisible kennel. "But if you want to help him, you'll have to make a choice."

"What choice is that?"

"When we get to Cairo, there will be an opportunity for a miracle. You can have a wish granted: something restored. But you only get one wish, so you have to choose."

Beneath the anchor of his meaning, her heart began to sink. "Restore Cassandra, or help Valentinian?"

Lazarus turned toward the magician, who noticed them, and waved. "Sometimes," the mystic said, "the fastest way is not the best."

VI

Tyger Tyger

Valentinian's mood had so improved by the time they reunited that the General was forced to consider she had been the only one upset. She even felt she was the only one in a tizzy about the *tulpa* business, though it was possible they only pretended not to be upset, lest the emotional energy remotely heal it. On reaching his side at the shadow-gray apotheosis of dawn, the magician asked in the knowing tone of a bosom buddy recovering from his own night on the town, "Good morning! Did you have a fun night?"

She somehow felt the only appropriate answer was, "It was great."

"Good!" The twinkle in Valentinian's blue eyes was so different from the one in her Father's, yet so much the same. "Let's get a move on."

"We haven't lost a day, have we?"

"What did I just tell you twice over about time?" asked Lazarus. "You sort of did us a favor."

"Yeah, we basically partied all day. I won four hundred bucks. You know, theoretically. Eventually. When I have a body with a wallet again."

"Does this bum even know how to use money?"

"I've been running the stock markets since before you were born," grumbled the old man.

"That's just informed gambling," she said, and he answered, "Not if you know what's going to happen." Dominia considered this was true, and thought, with a faint pang of sadness, not just of gambling

Miki Soto but of René Ichigawa. He seemed the gambling type and surprised her with something worse. A big brick in the foundation of her trust issues with Valentinian and Lazarus, that professor. They hadn't done anything untrustworthy outside withholding information; but Lazarus had a point. It would be horrific to remember every possible (and definite past) method of death. What a paralytic notion! On top of that, knowing all the times she had failed Cassandra...all the Cassandras out there, dead forever. It ached her.

And she ached more to consider she might need to leave Cassandra dead forever, even if for the good of the world. Of the human race, and the martyr one. Oh! Who could be asked to make such a choice? Who dared even call it a choice? Only the most selfish soul would entertain it: but she must have made the choice once or twice, in her litany of unseen mistakes. The phantom weight of a familiar body pressed her arms. She dismissed it, lest it produce a second, more horrible duplicate. She focused on where she was: following the men as they trudged through a barren landscape whose hues gained saturation, for what was once black and white warmed into sepia. Or perhaps, having been there so long, her mind gave the grit at her feet an artful flaxen cast generously shared with the day-gray sky. When—at last!—some distinction emerged in the distance, Dominia cried out and dashed beyond her friends.

From a distance, this protrusion in the landscape resembled a gangly tree; but, on her approach, it resolved into a signpost whose two roots furled roughly south by southwest and north by northwest in the form of long paths laid in clay brick. The marker at this juncture, hand-carved of teal- and bright-pink-painted wood (though Dominia had seen no real trees), was marked with characters that appeared that same combination of readable and unreadable as her Father's books: here, mysteriously, the characters appeared a kind of dream-Arabic. Though she did not know the language in real life, she read the signs just fine. The left-hand one declared "CAIRO," while the one pointing right indicated "JERUSALEM."

"Not much farther," said the relieved mystic. "I'm always happy to see this sign."

The General was pretty amped, herself. "How much longer? It should only be a few more night cycles now, right?"

"About two." Valentinian crushed another cigarette filter. "Just a while to wait. Then, you can have Cassandra. If you want."

He watched as if waiting for her to broach Lazarus's warning, but she could not yet speak on it. Her face turned away, toward Jerusalem. "Earthly cities appear here?"

"No, no. This just puts you in the right direction. Like Lazarus told you before, you can leave this place by looking at the black sun for long enough; it'll take you to a specific point in Earth's space-time based on where you're standing and the sorts of things you've done. However, that takes practice, so kindly magicians such as yours truly make signs."

"Magicians such as you? I wouldn't call you 'kindly.'"

"For all I do to help you," asked the man in a mock-wounded tone while the mystic sighed in disgust to which neither of them paid attention. "To help you save the world and your wife!"

"If you're such an amazing magician, why haven't you helped me to the finish line before?"

"Ouch! There's just so many ways to go wrong. It's hard—impossible—to know what any given iteration of the universe will hold for us. Your Father remembers it as well as we do, so he's liable to tweak his strategy each time. We just have to do the best we can at piecing together past experiences, and hope we know enough to get through this time."

The weight of her patch seemed almost painful against the right side of her face. "If I'm such a threat to the Hierophant's world, and he knows the future, why did he martyr me at all?"

A jolly bass voice emanated from the blind spot that hid Jerusalem's path. "Because you, Miss Mephitoli, are too valuable a commodity to be passed by: no matter the risk."

Dominia and Valentinian turned toward the disruption Lazarus had long since noticed. The approaching figure drew his hood from his face, and there he was in all his white-toothed glory: Dr. Tobias Akachi, the dentist who fixed her teeth and removed her DIOX-I, then betrayed her by assaulting her Family during the tragic Kabul marathon. He tried to win the General to his side; worse, he showed interest in acquiring her powerful sister, Lavinia, whose memetic curse brought many marathoners to their mortal end—before the bomb detonated by the dentists' men murdered more.

Her chest tightened along with her itching fist. "What are you doing here?"

"Looking for you! Do you know how long you were missing when I came here to find you? Nearly an entire lunar cycle! Almost a month!"

"You're al-Mawta. Hunter trash—and the king of the trash heap, at that." To Lazarus, she said, "At least one cell of Hunters stole some of your blood, didn't they? Their most initiated members come here?"

The mystic, rubbing the temple of his forehead, managed, "Yeah, they come here all right. Come here and annoy me."

"Our founder was a man first tricked by the Lazerene faith, who then saw the light. He recognized the cult was but a means of pacifying humans into perpetuating the endless struggle against martyrs, rather than destroying them. One of these days"—the cheerful dentist looked to Lazarus, dark cheeks creased by the breadth of his grin—"I am going to catch you. Then all my men, and all worthy humans of the world, will come and go from this place as they please. It will be nothing to destroy the martyrs."

"You're the leader of *all* the Hunters." Dominia corrected her misperception in astonishment as Valentinian, crossing his arms, shifted his weight so both men—rather unnecessarily—stood between her and the dentist. Then again, she supposed it was for the human's good, no matter how impermanent death was in this place.

"You're wasting your time, Tobias. She's not going to Jerusalem with you. Run home to the rest of the Hunters."

"Oh, I know Miss Mephitoli will not be going to Jerusalem with me today. But I have come to extend the option, because she may change her mind in the future. It would be immoral if I did not give her a way out of what she must otherwise face!"

That a Hunter—their leader!—should lecture on morality was laughable, but what got her attention was something else. Talk of the future in any context alarmed her these nights. "Don't tell me you've also been through all this before?" she asked. That provoked a hardy laugh.

"No, no, my friend, oh, my, no. Why, compared to your single lifetime, I am practically a boy! A mere fifty-three years old. But even at my young age, I have learned much of the workings of the world, of martyrs, and of you. I know the path down which you trek"—said with the slightest ironic grin for the bricks beneath their feet—"is a shortsighted and petty one. If you think your people will ever submit to starvation floating around the void of space, you are a fool. If your Father is the only martyr to die, it will begin an unceasing war. Your friends would destroy the whole world to cure the blight of martyrdom. One does not kill the body to extract an abscessed tooth."

"The only shortsighted one is you," Valentinian insisted, but the human didn't stop for breath.

"This place exists for a reason, and it is not to shelter martyrs as your Father would see fit to use it; nor is it a means to manipulate the world, as would this heretical magician. This place exists to protect humanity from martyrs! Lazarus holds the key to salvation, but hoards it!"

Disgust rose in the General's heart. Though she'd had her share of hypocritical moments, she would never be as blatantly false in self-representation as Tobias. "For someone who professes to hold such love for humanity, you never mind when your terrorists kill humans by the hundreds. What about that marathon bombing? My family didn't get a scratch; a *pile* of human corpses filled that crater. For that matter, how often do your people pray to the Lamb for help conquering cities or destroying innocent lives in the name of your so-called mission? You have no problem appealing to the saints of the Holy Martyr Church when it serves."

There was no use in logic. Everybody in this place had an answer for everything, and the dentist was no exception. "Those individual lives must be forfeit for the sake of the whole. It is indeed a tragedy, but when Iblis stoops to genocide, what can be done? We play by his rules."

"'Iblis'—that's the Islamic term. I thought you were Christian."

"Oh, yes, of course. But our organization is full of people who understand that the cause of eliminating martyrs is the *true* holy war, and when a Christian works with a Muslim, he soon realizes that 'Allah' and 'Iblis' are simply another language's names for 'God' and 'the Devil.'" Dominia fought against the chill that crawled through her to remember her Father's words. "We are Muslims, Christians, Jews, and men of all Eastern faiths: even Buddhists join our cause, so it must be righteous, for they are peaceful and hold the destruction of all life as sin! But the faith of the leader at the top does not matter to those who join our cause. It matters only that he possess the vial of Lazarus's blood, and prove capable of seeing this place and living on. This is all very secret, you see. I only became involved with the Hunters while attending a school for those humans lucky enough to buy their way into safety by serving martyrs, working in vocations your idle people refuse to perform. A slave, yes? Only given the opportunity because Iblis refuses to enlist the help of artificial intelligence like the rest of the sentient world. Not that our artificial intelligence is anywhere near the quality it should be, given the amount of time and resources we've spent at war with your Father for the last two thousand years!

"You can imagine, Miss Mephitoli: during my so-called European internship, I saw much suffering. What terrible pains your Father inflicts upon the Earth, upon humankind! I could not stand for it. I escaped to join the Hunters. When it comes to the issue of martyrs, you see, there is no such thing as 'Muslim' or 'Christian' or 'Jew.' Not even 'Buddhist' or 'Hindu'!"

Dominia's irritation was on the verge of boiling over. "Of course not. Because they're just bodies to you. Tools to be used as you see fit."

"You act as though I am as bad as your Father. I assure you, Miss Mephitoli: I am the one who will be legislating in the wake of war. Not him. If even a Buddhist will join our cause, your life must be worth less than a tick's; martyrs are worse than subhuman. They are entropic. A species of primitive apes without the decency to develop the concept of cultural taboo."

"You and the rest of the Hunters"—Valentinian draped an arm around Dominia's tensed shoulders to steer her toward Cairo, away from the man she trembled to punch—"think that because you're a bunch of modern primitives, so you see primitivism everywhere. Hooting in your stolen *tanques* and tossing bombs like cartoon villains. Wastes of space!"

"I cannot bring myself to lie to you," Tobias called after them, still near the signpost. "I cannot promise you the life of your dead wife, as so many others have: that is something only the Lord can give, and He can only give it on the Day of Judgment. Nor can I promise you any particular power, for that, again, is a matter of God. But I can promise you two things. I can promise you exception from the doings that need done against your people, that you might keep your martyr life under fulfillment of certain conditions; and I can promise you, Dominia, that you will be doing what is right. You will be doing what is good by all humankind and by God if you come with me now, to Jerusalem. Your soul might still be saved."

"And if I continue with them?" She jerked free of Valentinian. "What'll you do?"

Akachi's eyebrows lifted and his expression remained humorous; but a new, rotten tone curdled his words. "Then you are as much an enemy of mankind as your Father, and I will see you killed."

Still as an ice sculpture, the infamous General assessed the dentist and said in her own warning tone, "You know what's disappointing about you? Everybody I meet lately has some ulterior motive. I guess I was stupid for hoping you were an altruistic person."

"Ah, Miss Mephitoli. You speak of disappointment, but I assure you: the feeling is mutual." Tightly, the dentist smiled, then turned away while pulling up his hood. "I shall see you in Cairo, my dear."

"I hate that guy." Valentinian made an obscene gesture with his forearm while Lazarus resumed tossing pebbles.

"What do you expect? Humans who get a taste of the black sun are insufferable know-it-alls. Anybody who spends all their time in this place has to be a pain in the ass."

"Yeah," said Valentinian absently. Dominia's laughter got him listening too late, and he caught on with a sullen, "Hey," while the mystic offered a sly grin.

"Even I have a sense of humor," said Lazarus. The magician rolled his eyes.

"Yeah? Where'd you leave it?"

In that moment of genuine mirth, the stirrings of the Hierophant between her and her friends lay so far away. It occurred to her she had hardly batted an eye when it was Tobias's chance to manipulate her. Chalk that up to the men's reaction to her brush with the doppelgänger. They treated her as if nothing at all had happened. She had to believe they were worth trusting—had to believe that the spirit of that good dog was her friend, and not one of the imaginary kind. Thus, alone with Valentinian while Lazarus went to early sleep that night, Dominia watched the magician tend the fire and, after a time, said, "I'm sorry."

"I should be sorry! I lost my temper. I try to be patient with you, but you've got a pretty short fuse yourself, buddy. Easy for one spark to light another." After watching her from over his shoulder, the magician returned attention to the crackling blaze. "Something you want to talk about?"

"It'll all be okay, right? I mean…won't it?" She felt like a child again, a sad girl trying to find some sign from the universe that the world was not cruel as she'd come to fear. Upon the blanket the magician had unfurled for her, Dominia pushed long strands of dream-hair back into the ponytail corralling them. "I haven't done something unfixable, have I?"

"With the doppelgänger? No, not yet. If you keep going back to it, maybe. But if you can help yourself, we'll be okay."

"What about Tobias?" For some reason, she had not anticipated meeting a Hunter here; and this specific Hunter stirred other thoughts. "Did Miki know about him?"

"No, but the Red Market does. They use their girls like spies and distribute them accordingly, whether the RM agents in question are aware or not. You thought your eye was streaming a lot of information? Hah! Every phone that's had Miki Soto's ID number in it has been a recording device since 4031."

"If you're a dog in the flesh, how do you know so much about Miki? I mean, I know you've lived many times, but—"

"That, and eternity is a long time—so long it's 'always.' From this space I've gotten much information. Even people—read the fields and atmosphere correctly, and you can find anybody. There really are a lot of people here, although"—he chuckled into the darkness—"it doesn't seem that way. But, it's better to walk seven days here with no people and no sun exposure than forty days on Earth with the profound threat of Hunters."

"What about here? Aren't they a threat here?"

"Everything is and isn't a threat here. I told you before: get killed, wake up. It's disorienting, but it's not so bad except for the lost time and the difficulty of precisely finding your way back."

Satisfied enough, Dominia closed her eye against the eerie dark. "What do we do if he follows us?"

"We'll deal with him. Look, General: I know you're used to planning. You want to have control of the situation. Don't we all! But now's not the time. Now, just go to sleep. You want to know if everything will be okay? Well, I promise. You have a hard time putting faith into other people's words, but believe me: I wouldn't have invested so much time and effort helping you if you weren't the key to a grand and terrible prison. If I didn't like you as a person and think you worth helping. There are a lot of 'yous' who haven't made it this far…who don't think to ask the questions you're asking, or put them together in the way you're putting them together. Because of that, you're the only 'you' that will make the right series of decisions."

That was all well and fine, and comforting—or would have been. But, after the events of the night prior, her nerves were on edge in the dark. Valentinian applied the same dust he had each night, and like each night, she tumbled off to deep, velvet sleep: but she continued tumbling again and again, for many times she awoke and thrashed upon the blanket only to fall back unconscious. It was as though she fought off some virus, though the only virus that plagued her was one of her thoughts. Not even the magician's sand might keep her from fear of herself, fear of her own lust, fear of Cassandra's disappointment. From thoughts of Cassandra, dead and unable to feel anything, let alone disappointment.

Good point: when (if?) she eventually returned, surely Dominia's wife would not be so broken by the General's loneliness- and pain-motivated infidelity. Not as much as her ego imagined. It was not Cassandra's disappointment she needed fear, but her own. She thought of the book in the Hierophant's study while awaiting his torches; of Odysseus, returning to Penelope after years in the arms of Circe and Calypso. Surely the wife of that man skilled in all ways of contending did not begrudge him those caresses transpiring at the whims of goddesses! But surely also, as Dominia once had heard Cicero joke to the Lamb, there were two versions of the *Odyssey*: the version Odysseus told Penelope, and the version he told fellows in the bars. Would there were but one truth! Would she were pure enough, good enough, to carry only one back to her vivified bride.

Eventually, muscles aching with tension she was unused to feeling in this space—and perhaps only felt because her sleepless mind expected as much of its restless body—Dominia sat up to assess the sleeping men. Valentinian snored into his arm and Lazarus lay like a corpse, mouth hanging open and no observable breath disrupting his chest. Even so, and even though she had slept as "long" as nights before, the path of the Hierophant had not appeared.

This should have proven relief. As if she cared to see him, or that thing! She tried to assure herself that her passing scorn was misplaced. Her Father mentioned it would take time for the doppelgänger to repair. Perhaps he and it had taken the night off? Too good to be true.

Something was wrong. No path would be forthcoming, she felt. Perhaps if the path did not come, day would never break. She considered waking Valentinian but knew without having to try he would not awaken. Like the day, he would not rise until she had gone to the Hierophant, or accomplished some other strange task. As long as she lay doing nothing, the light would not come.

Anxiety filled her with the truth. The only way to reach his study tonight was to find it, herself. After some delay in the hope Valentinian would spontaneously awaken, she placed a foot into the black Void beyond the firelight.

For days, her mind had wondered at the substance of that darkness. Was it a true void, like outer space? Some unknown, tarry matter?

Or, would she would step into the darkness and stop existing? She expected all those things to varying degrees, but as it happened, none occurred. She remained herself: she was simply now herself standing outside the circle of light, in a type of dark that cooled the muscles of her body, the overdriven thoughts of her brain. More alone at the edge of the light than she'd been with the sleeping men, she closed her eye to think of the Hierophant's study. Where might it be located? She could not see the ropes of her compass, that marvelous diffusion of not just light but perhaps all the electromagnetic spectrum, including regions then unknown, unmeasured, by man. But there had to be some way. The men had indicated several times that one could find one's way by tracing some sort of energy pattern, but the General saw nothing in the dark. What about the concept of attraction, though? Her electromagnetic field was not absent, just invisible. A compass you couldn't read was no good as a compass, but what about the magnetic component of the device? Was she not a walking magnet? The mortal coil through which a current of consciousness ran?

If she had attracted the thoughtform, could she attract the study?

She tried envisioning it, its checkerboard floor and broad, filled shelves springing out of space. The music replayed in her head. The more she ruminated on the study, however, the more ill at ease she became. Perhaps thinking of the study would create a false variation: her own perspective of his study, rather than the actual thoughtform. Maybe this false study would even house a *tulpa* of her Father. Then there would be two of them. Dear Lamb, how could she prove there weren't already? Was that something breathing in the distant dark? Pray for her, Elijah!

With utmost caution, she thought on her Father. There were times in the real world when thoughts of him made her brain crawl in specific regions, mostly around the amygdala. She needed care in turning down those slippery slopes of thought. Instead of thinking concretely about him, she evoked the feeling she experienced when she did, tried to feel as if she already sat in his study, talking to him, lungs full of sandalwood and cloves while his sickly fire licked its chops within its marble cage. There was the cold floor on her back and the taste of the wine and not the doppelgänger—not Cassandra. Instead, the clacking of pool balls, and the velvet of the crimson chair beneath her hands. Feeling small in that chair, like a child; feeling like a child again; feeling memory cut a different path: her hands flexing past that velvet, into fists, the Hierophant laughing to watch her box with Cicero in one of Mnemosyne's gap-filling flashes. Above the huffs and puffs of a girl fighting her brother like she wanted to kill him, her Father said to the Lamb, "She is my little tiger, isn't she."

That word echoed as if spoken aloud. "Tiger." The slide through her memories and the association of her consciousness terminated there. Like a mind on the cusp of sleep, it grasped that final cogent thought, and rolled into it with a different kind of momentum than the one Valentinian had described. This was not the escape velocity by which a consciousness might slip free the surly bonds of Earth. This was more like falling: ecstatic falling. With the word "tiger" came all the associations of tigers, of being a tiger, of fur and teeth and claws. Facts: the tiger was the world's most vengeful animal, could crush a skull with the swipe of a paw, went extinct due to poachers and climate problems in 2093 and was artificially renewed in 3545, 113 years before Morgan, unlucky human prototype Dominia, was born. But who was Morgan? She was not even sure of Dominia.

Her mind was predisposed to seek the energy of a thing imagined, being in search of her Father's study: with her heart so open, her ribs unfolded, and she turned inside out. The General lost sense of herself to her memories, then to her thoughts, and soon had so faint a notion of body it seemed perfectly reasonable she was a tiger, yes, a tiger, a beast of hot breaths and tremendous, heaving muscles that thundered into the darkness like an embodied storm, its shoulders, paws, jaws ready to strike with a might shaming the very lightning for their fury. To be a tiger was to be the physical condition of hunger, and that running hunger craved to be filled: sought the invisible meat it felt in the darkness. There arose the sensational hope of satiation to hear the breathing of a distant other, then the sound of that other's feet upon the formless earth. Neon body flickering like a candle, this tiger rocketed through the black air into which its dark stripes melted until its eyes found that which it sought, a broad-soled and double-tusked beast that shook its long gray snout and galloped into the dark. After, after! Her heart pounded in her ears. There was no existence but for muscles, and the movement of muscles. She had no fear of getting lost, no sense of running farther from the fire, from her friends, from the Father for whom she had wandered into the dark before forgetting. There was no sense of self for her, this tiger. Only the hunt, the prey, so close she tasted it—

"Dominia."

The familiar sound was so unexpected that, in the context in which the tiger heard it, the syllables seemed the foreign voice of the sail-eared beast it chased. Only on second repetition did it falter the cat, who paused to study the shape of the call in its ears. This sound was not the deep and breathless grunts of predator animals, nor of the prey that she lost as it vanished into the darkness. This sound gave some sense of self and context and space outside "this" and "that," outside the arrow drive of primeval hunger. Indeed, it spoke to a deeper hunger: a deeper craving. The tiger thundered after that deeper craving, while within it Dominia stirred at the sound of her own name. She felt again the word "tiger" and recalled an ancient poet whose utterance, "Tyger! Tyger! Burning bright" repeated in her head. A vibrating mantra in her Father's voice, the deceptive humanity of which shaped her back into a woman as the poem ran its course.

Perhaps it was the memory of her Father: of how, as he recited the poem while tucking her into bed, he would put such growling emphasis on the word "dare" that she would giggle despite herself. Because, to children who knew better, he was yet so playful and charming and kind that one never hated him as much as one wished. Even now, she heard his words: felt him closing up her ribs with tickling hands that restored a body she knew.

"What immortal hand or eye *dare* frame thy fearful symmetry?"

A woman, she tripped in the darkness as if she'd reached the edge of some invisible cliff. Perhaps she had; she seemed to be hurtling as such. The General fell such a length, at such exhilarating speed, she had no time to be afraid: only to marvel at the sound of wind whipping past her ears. The blackness plunged into her skull after the sound, filling it with immense pressure. Would her head explode?

The farther she descended, the slower she fell, and the more the darkness assumed newer, colder embrace. It was impossible to tell at what point "darkness" became "water," or if there had ever been a difference. Perhaps it was a matter of changed depth, viscosity, and perception. The difference was not a concern that came to Dominia's mind, nor did thoughts of drowning trouble her until she considered she ought to be drowning. Light, though, began to grow in the water before her, for at some point, "down" had become "up"; in that same quantum sphere where "darkness" tangled with "water," so, too, did these lack discernment. There was only the goal toward which she pumped her burning limbs until, with a violent splash, Dominia emerged from the water, gasping and coughing, good eye too blinded to see until well after she discerned amid her sputters for air the hush of feminine whispers. After a good wiping with her wrist, her eye opened, and the General was taken aback—though far from disappointed—to find herself surrounded by a coterie of exquisite women. Two of them nude, and one draped in wet cloth (which was somehow better)—plus two more pricked their heads from the bushes at the bank. Who knew how many more yet unseen. Odysseus, indeed!

"Excuse me, ladies." The General tried not to take too much advantage of her own femininity and looked politely at the nearby trees. "Sorry to bother you, but I have no idea where I am. Or"—she grew aware she stood in a lake no more than waist deep, the way she'd come having been, evidently, closed off—"how I got here."

"You are in the True West, although it seems that, to you, this is the East." The clothed woman rested a hand upon her shielded breast; another sought to smooth the speaker's hair until one of her sorority also helped. "You are a stranger here."

"No kidding." As Dominia's eye adjusted, it became apparent that these were not human women, for they were beyond the pale of earthly—or mortal—perfection. Some breed of nymph? Their hair, through of golden luster in the sun (the sun! The golden sun! The General only now registered it as it glowed unburning in the straw and chocolate tangles of the hair that haloed them) revealed the seafoam sheen of algae, and certain regions of flesh where most women's skin grew darker carmine or dusky brown were here illustrated in the same fragile ivies as the luscious flora surrounding their clear spring. She could not think to speak, but the creatures appeared as content to study her until their clothed leader asked, "You are a woman?"

"Of course."

"It is not often women find our pool. Women with your needs do not often come."

Marveling past the beautiful creatures, at the distant golden orb that did not burn, the martyr said, "Well, I'm here, though I don't know what needs you mean, or where 'here' is."

They so laughed that Dominia blushed. The water splashing around the limber legs of the clothed nymph rose to her hips; she waded to meet the General, who remained fixed to the spot.

"I know you now. How did I fail to recognize you? Because you did not recognize me, perhaps?" The girl's glistening lips parted in a smile. "How pleased we would have been for a woman's touch! But how pleased I will be, General, to lead you."

"Are you thoughtforms?" tried Dominia, somewhat weakly. The nymph before her paused to laugh, that gay, sweet ringing further burning her face until the giggling offender turned back to see her displeasure with a click of the tongue.

"We are older than thought. We are older than form."

With a hand as cool as the darkness from which still-delirious Dominia emerged, the nymph touched the General's face, lifted her palm, tried to draw her from the water. "Excuse me." Dominia's efforts to pull away were foiled, the ethereal woman's grip deceptively strong. She marveled as she was tugged past the unclothed nymphs and to the bank of the pond. "Where are we going? Who are you? Do I know you?"

"Not yet. My name is Gethsemane." The smiling nymph stepped up to the grass, and as the water beaded upon her skin to be dried, dot for dot, by the sun, the color of the woman's flesh resolved from celadon tinges to more human tones. That strange beauty, however, remained.

"My sisters and I are the Water Bearers. We are here to aid you."

"Me?"

"Yes, you. Lady Dominia di Mephitoli, Governess of the United Front, General of the Hierophant, Bitch of Europa, and Serpent of the Southwest." The girl embraced a slender tree, which, to Dominia's astonishment, bent its boughs as though to return the affection. When they lifted away, the nymph stood in light armor of bark, with a skirt resembling leaves. "I have awaited you an eternity: you, after all, are the one who crafts the eternity in which I wait."

VII

The True West

Dominia's people did not approve of drugs, but that had not prevented teenage experimentation. In the end, she was always partial to liquor, but she dabbled in tobacco, tiptoed into reefer, and, as a young woman during slivers of peacetime, gone through a phase of psychedelics that lost her more friends than it earned spiritual revelations. She had done enough substances to know out-of-body experiences and hallucinations of this degree were, to put it mildly, rare: the closest she had come to something like this was dimethyltryptamine, but even that tended to reduce reality to the pattern of a Persian rug and enhance her imagination rather than take her to any true faraway place and convince her she was awake while it happened.

This place made her awake and whole as she might have felt on Earth, or more. Yes, more awake than awake—if that last place had been a dark place of dreaming, this land, bursting in hues more exquisite than those she knew, was a land of hyperconsciousness. It was decidedly not Earth. Beneath the merry sun (a wholesome star whiter than Sol, with his angry sheen of city smog and summertime wildfire smoke in the UF), grass reflected an emerald she had seen nowhere on the face of her beloved planet, and the wind whistled a song through every blade. With it carried a fabulous scent, as if to indicate the walkers of this world breathed not some lesser gas like oxygen but rather sweet perfume. Yet, for all the glories of nature that assailed her as she was led from the spring to a distant road that curled along an unmade bed of hills, that most glorious was the spirit guiding her by the hand.

"Gethsemane." The General repeated the name and was rewarded with the lifting eyes of the nymph. Now she had to find something to say. She cleared her throat. "So—did somebody tell you to collect me?"

"Yes. We have long awaited your arrival. I am sorry I did not recognize you at first; most humans look the same to me."

"Oh, I'm not—"

"There are no martyrs here," Gethsemane corrected before Dominia made her mistake. "There is no one for the sun to burn; there is no need to shed another's blood. Not unless it is the will of the king."

"A king, huh?" Dominia eyed the girl's armor and felt for a moment she had fallen into the song of an ancient crew of earthly composers named for an outmoded style of dirigible. "Was he the one who told you to wait for me?"

"I wait for you because it is my duty. But, no. The king and his queen are on vacation in the East."

"I thought you said this was the East."

"Your East. We are the West, properly called the True Western Kingdom in the Time of Felicity. It is much easier to say 'West,' however, or 'Kingdom.' At any rate, no matter where you are, General, there is always an East."

"I suppose...uh"—coming out of a daze, or the spell of her dreamily chattering new companion, Dominia thought to ask—"where are you taking me?"

"To the City, to meet the magician called Valentinian."

With perked ears and sweet relief for the familiar name, Dominia said, "Valentinian! He's here?"

"If not already, he will be soon, because you are here."

"So, he knew we were coming... I'm still not sure how I got here. Is this the same place as before? The dark one, I mean, where I came from."

"In a sense. Everything that surrounded you before surrounds you. It has been rearranged."

Quite an understatement! To compare this place to the Void was an impossible task. They did not seem in any way the same, and Dominia was certain that mapping them (if mapping the Void was possible) would elicit two different geographies. "It was so dark there; it's hard to believe this is the same place. I feel as if I've been dreaming, and I've just woken up."

"You have, if it was night's darkness in which you wandered. The mind dreams in that darkness, which is filled with formless spirits."

And formed spirits. Her mind struggled to reconstruct the beast in that darkness, that snorting thing that watched her even before she'd wandered off and lost track of her body. Glimpses of gray, and long horns—no, tusks. "I saw an animal while I—dreamed. I thought I was an animal, too. Then I heard my name." Spoken by whose voice? In the manner of an interrupted dream, the memories refused to resolve into a functional image.

"Someone prayed for you, General." Gethsemane's explanation was so matter-of-fact that Dominia barked out a laugh.

"Prayed for me?" A thousand stuffy sermons swept to the forefront of her mind. "I never thought that did any good."

"If one is not connected with the spirit, it may not, except by accident; and it has no material use but to bolster the self in the waking day. But you must learn the benefits of prayer if you are to aid in the Lady's cause."

"The Lady...you serve the Lady."

"I am Her Bearer."

"Then—do you know Miki Soto?"

"Not in this place, at this time. In a different place, and in a different time, yes."

Someday, someplace, Dominia would meet a person who gave straight answers. For now, she'd given up worrying about it. Failing to keep sarcasm from her voice, she asked, "So, what are the...*benefits* of prayer?"

"You've felt the real benefit. It reinforces the souls of those who pray and those for whom they pray. One must be in the Unspoken to observe the impact of thoughts and speech upon Earth."

The Void, the Unspoken, the Bardo, Purgatory! Pick a name! "Does that place have anything approaching an agreed-upon title?"

"No," said Gethsemane, in a tone flat enough that the General once more laughed. The nymph smiled slightly at the sound. "Your holy books tell a story called 'the Tower of Babel'...that place is like the tower. It cannot be directly communicated one way for all to understand because your people speak so many different languages, and each believe only one of those languages correct. I speak of spiritual symbolism, General. Not true language. It is hard to find a neutral word that can describe something across all tongues without ire, just as it is hard to find a neutral symbol that can describe something across all faiths. But there is a man in the East—*our* East, General—who is a very wise man: the Wisest in the World. When he is in the West, he must labor to repent for crimes he committed out of arrogance. But, when he is in the East and has worked off his burden, he is called the Engineer, and he is as good to his people as any king. I have spoken to him many times before, and he once told me Earth's globally preferred term for the Void. He said learnéd men believe it is what they call 'the Ergosphere.'"

"The Ergosphere," repeated Dominia. "Isn't that—isn't that the area around a black hole?"

"A rotating black hole of the sort once a sun; yes, those are the words that people of Earth prefer to describe these places."

"We were in a *black hole*," enthused the General, mouth opened, hand releasing Gethsemane's in surprise. The girl, without any sense of wonder, looked plainly up at her.

"No, General. We are currently in it, or, at least, upon what you would call its event horizon, where all the information of eternity is stored. The black hole that waits at the end of time for all life to return home is existent in your time, has been existent since the creation of Sol, and before. It does not seem as such, because time's illusion has hidden it; if you viewed all things from the black hole's perspective, you would understand all things simply are."

Her hands upon the top of her head as though to contain its contents, Dominia marveled up and around. "But there's a *sun* in the sky," she tried. The nymph nodded.

"The sun exists, General. Therefore, the sun must be here. Long, long ago, your scientists corrected the notion that black holes are mouths made to devour reality. They are mouths that *speak* it: holding all words upon their tongues until the moment they must manifest as sound, yet containing them even once they have been spoken so as to use them again in a different way, during a future conversation."

It took some fantasy naiad to tell her a science fact that would have made her understand the Void weeks ago! "Why didn't Valentinian and Lazarus just explain that to me?"

"Such a notion is frightful to those who fear standing at the end of eternity; and while in that space where the Ergosphere has exposed the malleable field of the universe that magicians call 'aether' and scientists call 'the Higgs field,' misunderstanding this revelation can cause total destruction of the body and mind. Anything one thinks may become reality there. Even brief thoughts of total annihilation can be deadly. Therefore, one must come to understand the nature of the space when they are upon solid ground of one form or another; it keeps them from being carried away." With another look at the sun, Gethsemane extended her hand. "If you please, General. We have some ways to walk, and the day here passes as it does on Earth: regardless of how we spend its minutes."

Pretty embarrassing, to have spent so much time in the Ergosphere that basic facts of reality needed re-explained. "But if we're in a black hole now and when we're in that—Ergosphere, what is the black sun in the sky?"

"It is Earth, General, standing at the end of time, at the outer edge of the Ergosphere along whose inner edge you walk. When you look up into the black orb, you are putting your attention back on your home planet and time: 'coming down to Earth,' you could call it."

Behind the nearest hill sprawled a vast and well-manicured orchard. Seeing it, Gethsemane cut off the main path. The house was so large it seemed not a home but an inn; Dominia suspected this was so based on the two sets of sprawling stables. Amid the trees, she was back begging for help from the ill-fated McLintocks; but the parallels only increased when Gethsemane, rather than using the orchard for a shortcut and passing by the house, stopped to knock upon the front door. After a moment, a gentle-looking woman lined by middle age answered them, smiling pleasantly, her "Yes?" becoming an "Oh!" when she recognized the General. "Oh, *my*," said the lady, and Gethsemane smiled.

"Please, miss?" The Bearer seemed to be asking something implied, and the woman inside looked delighted by her unexpected guests.

"I didn't know they were *my* horses... Eric"—the woman called to a boy unseen—"would you watch the pot? I have to take care of something."

The woman, wiping her hands upon her apron, stepped outside and shut the door behind her. As Dominia tried to find something recognizable in her face and found nothing—to her relief, as she'd half expected Carol McLintock at the door—the smiling woman assessed her in return.

"*Well*," said the stranger. "Well, would you look at this!"

"I'm sorry...do I know you?" It was becoming the question of Dominia's lifetime.

"Oh, everybody knows everybody when they come to live here." With a wave of her hand, the woman led them to the smaller set of stables. "You just don't remember that, because you haven't come to stay. Though you'd ought to consider it sometime."

"She will," said the nymph. "Eventually, in a long time. She cannot, not until—"

"Oh, of course. That certainly would keep her from settling down in comfort..." Behind the doors of the structure painted merry pinks and blues like no stables Dominia had seen (but akin to the magician's signpost, she noticed), a humdrum of conversation buzzed; but, as the woman pushed open the doors, a few whispered noises hurried the others to silence, and the hinges swung wide to reveal a perfectly mute, normal collection of horses. More stocky and primitive—older models, say—than the ones to which she'd grown accustomed, and doubtless slower than the mechanical variety favored by animal-rights activists—but horses nonetheless, and fine ones, at that.

"Take whichever two you need. I'll just have Eric jot to town and pick them up from the hotel tomorrow. Have you eaten?" she asked

Dominia, then turned to Gethsemane. "Has she eaten?"

"Not since coming," the girl answered for the General, which elicited a maternal click of the woman's tongue.

"Take some fruit on your way out. And why don't I get you bread—"

Remembering Valentinian's warning about "fairyland rules," Dominia tried to politely decline by saying, "Please, don't trouble yourself," but the lady had already darted for her house, perfectly comfortable leaving two strangers alone with her horses.

"If everybody here is so friendly," said the General, "I might be tempted to stay after all."

"Everyone who visits is tempted; but no one ever does before the time is right. It would not be the same if you had another calling elsewhere."

Maybe so. Still, she remained tempted, for, yes, everyone *was* as friendly as the woman whose name Dominia realized she hadn't gotten while they rode away. As they resumed along the main road, now seated upon a pair of marble mares who knew the route, she found new license to marvel around her. Passing vast fields of colorful crops and pens of docile oxen, she found these no more extraordinary than the animals to which she was accustomed; and it was safe to say the startled bird that just went screeching from the nearby tree was a redheaded woodpecker and not some miniature dragon.

Yet the General sensed an ancient magic about the place—or perhaps projected such qualities upon it, since she had spent so long navigating the Ergosphere with a magician and a mystic. Stunning to think herself upon its other side, walking the surface of a black hole as convincing a planet as any other—yet a kinder, gentler planet than the one she knew. Upon that road, they began to pass friendly person after friendly person, and Dominia was astonished by every smile and wave and doff of a cap. Humans in her world had been so long terrorized that, passing a stranger, one tended to avoid all eye contact and hurry one's pace in case that stranger was a martyr.

There were no martyrs here, Gethsemane had said. But were there humans here? Were these people human? Was *she* human while visiting here? She could not rightly say; but she sensed it was somehow improper to describe these people as anything, let alone "human." From her experience in the Ergosphere, she had retained most poignantly the notion that it was useless to try to name or discern anything. She had asked more questions than she could remember, and their answers did no good. Even the satisfaction of achieving a model compatible with her preferred worldviews (that her Father was no closer to God or Eternity or anything than anybody else, among other aspects) did her no good, per se. It did not teach her *how* to do anything; it did not tell her *why*. She could ask forever "what" and "but" and never be satisfied, and not because she was not asking the right questions. There were no right questions to *ask*. The experience was communicated piecemeal, over—and by—time.

And how loath was the curious General to accept that notion!

Still, it was good to be where one could think on anything, and the world around would remain in physical place. Good to listen to the birds, and not the constant chatter of the men. And pleasant to do so in the company of a beautiful woman, who studied the General from time to time, riding respectfully along her left side. Yet, the blonde curls of that woman—

"Stop, General." Dominia leapt as Gethsemane stirred her from thought with a hand upon her wrist. "I do not mean to intrude upon your meditations, but I hear their ripples in the Waters and know the shade does, also."

"Oh," said Dominia, her tone bitter enough to curl her lip. "Even here?"

"Even on Earth, though in a muted and indirect way. But here, it is clear; the medium by which we move now is not mass, but potentiality, who, fleet-footed, carries information in a wink."

"And in the Ergosphere?"

"Light," answered the girl.

"So Valentinian is using light to read my thoughts. Like the red eye that reflects out in a photograph; that's somehow carrying information from my brain, into the Ergosphere?"

"All mediums of energy are also mediums of thought; it is a matter of the thoughts being communicated in different ways. When thoughts are given sluggish mass in the material world, they must communicate over time and through more obvious means. You must give your thoughts energy of their own, whether by speech or by giving them physical form. But in the Ergosphere and in the Kingdom, those who are sensitive and who know the secrets of the Water can hear much if they listen. And those who *are* the Water, as is the shade of your wife, cannot help but hear all communications, subtle or otherwise."

"So you're saying it can't help but torment me," said Dominia, disappointed to feel such an ugly way in such a beautiful place. The girl, her affect as muted as it had been since they'd met, nonetheless looked upon her with a particular gentleness. Taking the General's hand, she lifted it to her lips and kissed its knuckles.

"In a sense, this is so. But to it, it is not tormenting you. It seeks you, as you seek your wife. If you are to find her, however, you must not be so pained and regretful. I hope to make you less so."

Flustered into a thudding heart and annoyed by her fluster, the gruff General slipped her hand out of the girl's and primly took her own horse's reins. "Thanks for being honest. Can you lay off the thought-reading, please?"

"Certainly, but I will not need to read your mind to know your next set of thoughts."

"Oh?" asked Dominia, not seconds before her stomach growled. The girl laughed, and the General recognized that the sensation of vague nausea that had been growing since her arrival was not nausea but hunger. Normal hunger: for food, not for flesh. With a muffled, alien cheer, the nymph slipped her hand into the picnic basket packed against the saddle and withdrew a handkerchief full of jerky along with a chunk of dense, soft bread.

"You will be shy about eating, perhaps, but you must not be. You have to eat while you stay here, or else you will starve, just as you would starve on Earth were you a human."

"These aren't some creep's evil thoughts?" This elicited a small smile from the girl, who removed a hunk of soft cheese and a bright ruby apple from the pack.

"As much as any other foodstuff. I must also eat if I wish to stay on land, though I will not starve; I will evaporate. Food keeps us grounded here, you see?"

As if through the thickest of fogs.

"Fog," Dominia said aloud. "Water Bearers. You serve the Lady. She actually exists, huh?"

"Even after all this time, you have not believed."

"I've been skeptical. Lazarus is a known quantity—and criminal—to m...y people, but the Lady is fictional."

"To you, and, as you said, to your people. She is real to everyone else; even the people here know of the Lady, although She does not walk about this place. Her avatars do, as any other person here. But the Lady is the substance of this place."

Kind of a weird thought. "So I won't meet Her here?"

"One of Her avatars," answered the girl, gaze caught by something glinting in the distance that also drew Dominia's eye. As if punched in the solar plexus, the General gripped the reins of the horse and observed the distant disk of the glittering City.

"Incredible." This, from the woman who had seen a thousand towns and decimated half as many. But for those many glorious cities, there were none so radiant as this: circles within circles, twisting spokes like the rays of a sun lapping upon itself, or an egg dividing in the womb, or perhaps a spiral flower. The marble of its buildings glistened in the distance and seemed to breathe with life. A thin cornflower ribbon of river trailed through its center yet didn't break the pattern of buildings so much as highlight them. With a smile, Gethsemane admired her stunned face, turning away only when the General returned to herself well enough to look over.

"You should see it at night. All the candlelit and gaslit quarters look so soft...and there are a few electric quarters, but they are tucked deeper, so they cannot poison the sky. *They* see the sky, of course; but the City is built so it spirals within itself forever, and the more unsightly quarters therefore rest within its coils."

"Sounds like a terrible place to get lost."

"The best place. If you become lost in the City, it means it has a surprise for you: a gift, or a lesson, or even a friend that you never would have given to yourself."

Dominia knew only one thing she wanted, so it wasn't hard to give her something she wouldn't consider. Yet, she sensed it wasn't the usual flimflam peddled by "psychics" and snake-oil salesman; perhaps this place was more causal than the Ergosphere, but she sensed it was just as much ruled by synchronicity, or more.

Many people milled along the slope of the final hill between them and this extraordinary fractal, some pausing to wait for friends, some chatting along their way to join the line through the gate that seemed mere formality. There, a chipper guard in silver armor recognized the Bearer—and, after a moment of consideration, Dominia.

"Aha! She came. Thank goodness! The magician's been on my back about you for a week."

Oh, her friend! "He's been here for a week?"

"Well, I don't know I can rightly say *that*... He tends to come and go without the gate, so I can't keep track of him." This irked the fellow but mildly, and he adjusted his helmet with a hearty laugh. "Not that what he gets up to is any of my business, but, well, it *is* my job to keep track of folks coming in and out. Just for census purposes, mind."

Behind them, someone politely coughed, and he appeared to remember there was a line of people extending quite far along the road behind the women; he chuckled. "But look at me, yammering on! Go on, ladies. Good to see you now, Gethsemane."

"And you, Martin." With a wave, the girl urged her horse down the populated main street.

There was no place like this—not in all the world. Though she supposed it *was* the world, if Gethsemane had spoken truth. Her world, and all other worlds. Even Acetia, if it wasn't fictional—or even if it was. This much was revealed as true when she saw not the Renaissance fair she expected but a dreamlike mishmash of cultures, peoples, and *times*. That, perhaps, was the most startling thing. Some guy wearing goofy neon shorts and carrying a big black box playing ancient music passed a gentleman whose clothes resembled the pre-martyr era known to humans as "Victorian," whose style Dominia recognized because

Lavinia was obsessed. Yet she spied plenty of sport coats, T-shirts, and many woman wearing pants; there was no shortage of varieties and no telling upon whom or what one might lay eye. And all of that did not begin to touch the buildings! So many facades, of an extraordinary variety of styles that only distinguished themselves as more than generic but beautiful buildings of ultra-white stone when one drew near enough, or viewed them from straight on—as if an effect of light shaped the building's purpose. Were it not for the horses, Dominia surely would have been bumping into passersby. The nymph smiled at her inattention, and the thoughtful furrow of her brow.

"You are bothered, General?"

"Nothing here is what I expected...not even the clothes. I guess I had a certain...vision. When I saw you, and your outfit."

"The City has a way of defying that. It is an interesting place! There are many who dress like me—in simpler cloth or silk, not bark. These are native Westerners."

Born in a black hole? Her mind reeled but the girl hardly paused. "Some are born in the City, but perhaps more are born in the Country without it, as was the queen of this Era. Often, these move here after waiting their whole lives, and they are more excited than anyone to be here, more curious about everything they see. These tend to make friends with their neighbors because they want to know all about them and the times they are from. And then there are many, many in the City who are refugees; all these are the ones in strange clothing."

"Refugees?"

"They do not belong here originally, but the City has taken them in. Our world, this black hole. It is"—the girl frowned in irresistible thought—"like a storage space. I do not know..."

"Like a hard drive?"

"Yes, General, perhaps; the Engineer would tell you, even while still the Doorman. I do not think we will see him today, though that is for the best... He can be long-winded."

"I know someone like that," said Dominia, thinking of her Father. Her lips quirked in a smirk the girl echoed.

As usual, the General's stream of questions may well have carried on without end all the way to the hotel: but, near the arched entrance of the marketplace—passed beyond the bridge over that sweet, crystal stream—a shout and commotion let up from her blind spot. Jerking her horse to a stop on instant defense, Dominia reached for her gun and hoped it had not been waterlogged into uselessness. No sooner had she turned her good eye to the noise's source, however, than she recognized the sound of her name on the lips of a certain breathless *Jun'yō* first mate: and there he was, running up to meet her. The chubby sailor, Tenchi Ichigawa.

Would you get out of town.

VIII

Bumps in the Night

Throughout her long career, Dominia had encountered more than a few people she'd previously victimized. Survivors thereof, at least. Of all these, the survivor of the *Jun'yō* massacre was by far happiest. "Dominia"—he cried her name while tripping down an aesthetically modern curb and only barely found his feet upon the cobblestones— "oh, wow, Miss Mephitoli! How are you?"

He halted before her, swabbing his forehead while huffing for breath, and bowed a few enthusiastic times she returned in awkward manner from atop the horse. "I didn't know I'd see you here! Not so soon, anyway. I'm sorry about my cousin. You know what a coward he can be..."

"It's all right." Dominia tried to smile. "You can't control René, and neither can anybody else... Anyway, I never expected to see you here."

Though confusion darted through the man's pursing lips, it soon resolved. "Oh, I see! My goodness—what a thing, time!" As he laughed, Dominia turned a look of concern to Gethsemane. While Tenchi had been a rather cheerful, almost dopey fellow, he now seemed to be rather, well... "doped up." That didn't concern the nymph.

"You are from the General's future." She stroked the neck of her shifting mare while the sailor nodded. "I urge you, hold your tongue."

"Yes, ma'am! I wouldn't say anything. Only...ah, I'm so happy to see you, Dominia!"

Not her Tenchi—the Tenchi she'd known—but the Tenchi of the future. A disturbing notion. Oh, she'd gathered the eternal nature of the City from the clothes of its inhabitants, but she hadn't stopped to think that eternity included all future as well as all past. Which passing faces would be familiar in some future visit?

"You are a refugee," observed the nymph of Tenchi, drawing the General from her thoughts as her companion took up the reins of her impatient mount. While she spoke, she urged the animal forward, and Dominia's followed. "I was explaining the hotel—about to, at any rate."

"Oh, you haven't checked in yet? You'll love the hotel, Dominia. I'm the courier!"

"You work here?" she asked as the man fell into stride with her good side.

"You have to work someplace if you're going to stay." His eyes glowed with the earnest depth of his words. "Contribute to society as a helpful member! I guess on Earth they'd call this place 'communist,' huh? But it's not like that... I mean, it's true, I just got through delivering Mrs. McLintock's paycheck, and she'll just give it back to the—"

"Mrs. McLintock?" The name shocked her so to hear that Dominia practically felt her own pupil shrink. Tenchi didn't notice.

"Yes: she's a barker at one of the vegetable stands. A refugee like me...a little different, though."

The nauseating snap of Carol's neck, seconds after the quieter one of her daughter's. Dominia trembled with horror and shame, her fingers tightening around the reins. Horror and shame—yet, hope.

"Mrs. McLintock was a Lazarene?" asked Dominia of Tenchi, whose eyes sprang in the direction of the nymph's back. "Is her son here, too?"

"Well—that is, I don't—"

Gethsemane, hiding her annoyance for the babbling sailor, turned to say, "Mrs. McLintock was made a Lazarene in childhood; her son and daughter were not inducted into the philosophy, as she never entirely believed, and her husband did not trust even a martyr such as Lazarus."

That hope dissolved into nothing; Dominia sat back upon her saddle. "Forced to be here without her children? She can't want that."

"No one is forced to be here," Tenchi blurted, his voice a defensive pitch. "If she is here, it's because she wants to be."

"Yet this place is supposed to be a black hole encompassing everything?"

"All space, General, all time. All things are here—all planets, all stars. Ours is not the mere black hole of an ordinary galaxy; when one is upon its event horizon, one understands all black holes are the same black hole, for they will eventually all submit to their own dismissal. Like a slate wiped clean."

So where was the McLintock boy? She couldn't stand to go into the marketplace and ask Carol in person. Not after she had shot the child in front of the harried mother, whether Dominia had a reason or no. The General dared not contemplate what would happen then, what had happened after the boy died, no more than she could contemplate what had happened before the boy, before she, before anyone, was born. She had tried to conceptualize that state while on her journey and found it almost impossible. How could something emerge from nothing? Consciousness from unconsciousness, matter from space? How did the magician create something from nothing? The Higgs fields responsible for giving particles mass was a fine explanation, but what was that field? What, really? God? Then what had Dominia to do with the oscillations of reality? She could not think on it too much. Could not think that all things happened in patterns, that she eternally put a bullet into the head of Mrs. McLintock's son, just as Cassandra had done to herself. That was surely why, when Tenchi said, "Maybe I can introduce you, and you can see she's happy," Dominia forced a polite smile.

"I don't think that we'll have time today. Soon. But what about the innkeeper? Or—hotel clerk." It was hard to think of this place having a hotel rather than an inn, but she tried to erase the preconceived notions of language. "Who sent you to pay Mrs. McLintock?"

An important question, because sending this courier at this time to that woman was not anything close to coincidence. Perhaps it was the synchronistic nature of the City, but this smelled deliberate. Gethsemane all but confirmed this when, in response to Tenchi's exclamation that, "She's a great lady," the nymph corrected, "*the* Lady."

Was it rude to snort? She couldn't help it. "Your goddess is an inn—a hotel clerk here?"

"My goddess's avatar…or, rather, the spirit of the woman displaced when the goddess possessed her body. This old soul of the vessel does good works in the City to pay for her stay, like everyone else; she is responsible for managing the refugees."

"This was Lazarus's girlfriend?" asked the General.

"Not for many cycles, not since she first birthed the magician. But the magician has since become a self-created man with no need for a mother, so his mother is liberated to achieve her true potential as an individual."

"Sounds like she's anything but an individual. She submitted her body to an alien consciousness."

"No. She discovered the divine within."

Any further questions were silenced by the ringing of the crystal clock tower towering above the busy market. Startled, Tenchi looked at a watch he didn't have, patted his head as if in search of a hat, and said with an apologetic bow, "Is that the time? I should go, Dominia, but I'm happy to see you! Please come to stay soon."

"Okay." Off he dashed, at a pretty brisk pace for his size. "Bye for now, Tenchi."

As he disappeared around a corner, Dominia realized Gethsemane had stopped before a building whose anachronistic facade was still rather disorienting to behold. It resembled an historic San Valentino high-rise, built of that same ultrafine substance (a kind of post-white stone that glowed like marble, resembled sandstone, and felt like silk) the rest of the City had used. But, compared to the split-level roads rolling past quaint shops and spiraling in all directions to reveal more lovely white buildings, the yawning hotel resembled an invasive species. Even its gargoyles, hanging animatedly from their pedestals in the midst of acrobatic tricks, were a design feature apparently unique to this neighborhood.

Yet no matter how interesting its exterior, Tenchi was right: little compared to its insides. If a tall building without, within it was infinite, and made no effort at disguise. Upon entrance to the gilded lobby, the

General spent so long with her head craned in search of a miles-distant ceiling that she almost bumped into one of an immaculate pair of chiseled lions that, flanking the entrance, lifted their paws in greeting from the fronds of sumptuous ferns. The sprays of orchids, a perfect aqua like none she'd seen, startled her with the revelation that she *had* seen the color before: woven into a crown in the hands of the *tulpa*, and sprinkled around the pond of the Bearers. She was then drawn to examine the quartet of gold-and-marble columns disappearing into the distant heights of that infinite ceiling. Everywhere she looked, another stunning objet d'art awaited, and that included the woman at the counter: she looked from her paperwork with a brusque sigh, which blew from her lips a flaming lock of hair.

"Another new guest." She spoke more to herself than to them as she turned to consult a wall of keys stretching beyond reach, or reason. "And staying how long?"

Gethsemane folded her hands upon the edge of the pearl counter. "Only one night, and with me."

"You have a room here?" asked Dominia of the nymph, who nodded.

"I am a creature of water, but also of land, and when I come to land, I must have a place to stay here in the City... It would not be right of me to keep a house if I did not use it every day."

While Dominia's brain tried to work out the amphibious nature of her companion, the hotel clerk lifted her scarlet cap to tuck that obtrusive hair, only a few shades less red, beneath. "That's good," she said with a relieved glance at the General. "I was getting tired just looking at you. You're a perfectly fine woman, Dominia, but you wouldn't believe the paperwork required when somebody needs a new room."

"I'm sure," she said, not surprised that the woman whose name tag read "Trisha" knew her name. "I don't know you, right?"

"Do you know anyone, anymore?"

With a small smirk, the General tried, "Will I ever know you?"

"Not as you are, and not in a personal way. But maybe in a Biblical way." She winked at the blushing General and added, "If you play your cards right."

"Aha." Dominia laughed and coughed, her brain whirring for focus. "Well…what's our—uh, our room number? Gethsemane?"

"606," answered the nymph, who accepted their key from Trisha. Free, the chuckling clerk merrily tapped her fingers along what Dominia recognized as an invisible keyboard of the sort popular when she was young, when the "in" thing was to have a computer so unobtrusive you could easily forget where it was and wind up knocking it from your desk.

"Breakfast is at five in the morning and runs for four hours." While she explained the rules, Trisha sometimes raised a delicate finger to tap the almost extra-dimensionally thin screen only visible from her side of the desk. "Leave your dirty towels on the bathroom floor and, please, try to keep it down after eight in the evening. We have a lot of older guests, and a lot of unwell guests who need their rest."

"We'll be good," answered Gethsemane, which may have been the first not-serious thing Dominia had ever heard her say. The laughing porter wiggled her fingers as the nymph made her way to the elevator.

"Aren't you always." Then, noting the General hesitated to leave her desk: "Is there something else you needed?"

The name "Carol McLintock" sat on the tip of her tongue, but for whatever reason, she could not make herself say it. Not that, or anything else about Tenchi. But, Tenchi did bring to mind his work; so, forced to come up with something to say, she asked, "Do I need some sort of job?" When that elicited a blank look, she pressed, "To stay here? People need to work, right?"

"Oh!" With a glance at Gethsemane's back, then at the General, she said again, "Oh!" and laughed. "You don't *know*! Goodness, I remember those days…kept like a mushroom, as my grandfather used to say. 'In the dark and covered in horseshit.'" Trisha waved her away. "No, darling, you don't need to work. You already have a job! It's perfectly fine."

"Is that job 'ending the martyr world'?" she asked grimly. The woman smiled in a way that flattered its host more than its recipient.

"It's rather more complicated than that, dear, but yes. Will you be needing the workout room's location?"

"No," grumbled the General, who made her way over as Gethsemane hit the brass elevator call button. "I think we'll be fine."

Only once the polished doors closed to sweep them to their sixth-floor room did Dominia think on her own hesitance to so much as speak of the McLintocks. She had killed many people, and Tenchi's presence positioned that thought in the forefront of her mind even before considerations of the boy. But this child's death sat poorly with Dominia. Children had been killed by her before, indirectly. The Black Night had been about 20 percent children in the final statistical reckoning. She had decimated whole cities in Japan and Mexico until the Hunter cells they sought could be called "eliminated." But, like most cancerous cells, they only receded, mutated, and awaited a day they blossomed again. Akachi was their tumor. But, Akachi was also human.

"You know"—the elevator opened to their floor with a joyous chime—"I would like to make Tobias Akachi the last human being I ever kill."

The nymph held the door for Dominia. "That is a very nice idea."

"Do you think it's possible?"

"For you, General, anything is possible; but, please, don't be disappointed if things do not work out that way."

In a room less modern than the lobby (or even the plushly carpeted hallway down which they'd moved in silence), Dominia's attention remained tuned elsewhere. For instance: What had Carol McLintock looked like? As she wandered into the nymph's room, the General tried so hard to remember that she barely noticed the thin deerskin upholstery of the chair into which she slipped, or the dark-wooded interior which matched the "rustic" frame of the shabby-if-large bed across the room. At the time of the tragedy in the outskirts of the almost Jurisdiction-wide San Valentino, the General had been rather distracted; but she almost pieced together those aspects she'd failed to absorb. There was that tired beauty glimpsed as it fled through the house to please the Hierophant like a bird bashing against the bars of its cage. There was the edge of a plump lip, the glint of a mossy eye; but there was no whole, which, for some reason, filled the General with regret.

The nymph, having sparked a light in the glass lamp by the bed, drew her from her thoughts by resting upon the arm of her chair. "You are in most intense mourning, General."

"How do you commune with your goddess here"—her voice was hoarse as she unbuckled the Bearer's curious bark boots—"if the woman downstairs is the woman She inhabits, and She's supposed to be the substance of everything?"

"You know her." The milky curve of a perfect calf left the General shuddering while she worked free the next boot. "The Lady is found in every woman. As much in you as in me, or more."

"Okay," said the General, usually willing to agree with anything said by a cultist to end conversation, and always, for obvious reasons, willing to agree with anything said by a woman edging into her lap. There was as much self-flagellation among the religious martyrs of her barracks as mutual flagellation in any bedroom of Dominia's. It was as if, in the absence of any meaningful God, her deity had become violence, and that violence suffused everything about her. Cassandra had known that violence, though not always (and not always consensually, either); she had known it implicitly, like Benedict's skeleton enclosed in the foundation of their relationship. But her wife had found pleasure in those small acts of violence, too, and Dominia had enjoyed her share of love-laced agonies. Perhaps it was just that when she thought of Cassandra, Gethsemane slapped her face.

"Shit," said the General as the Bearer clutched her restored hair.

"Miki Soto is right: you are a man, as much as any I have met. Your troubles are a man's troubles."

"They're a person's troubles," protested Dominia while struggling to extricate herself. "But I've heard I fight like a man, too, if you want to find out."

As she attempted to twist away, she confirmed herself no stronger in this place than an extraordinarily athletic human—not that she minded, when she noticed the free hand of the nymph had unzipped her jacket and now slipped a cold set of fingers beneath her cotton shirt.

"I am not concerned if you fight like a man, General, but I am curious if you fuck like one."

Scandalized, somehow, to hear such a word from this illustrious entity's Cupid's-bow mouth, the General turned her blushing face away and found no escape when the nymph straddled her lap. "I'm married."

"And if your wife were here, I would have her, too." Oh! Those lips! How soft they were: impossibly plush, so much so that Dominia sagged hers open at the lightest touch of them upon her jaw, her cheek, her mouth. "I told you when first I saw you and mistook you for a stranger that it is not often women of your needs arrive to us."

"And when we do?"

"We drown them, as we do the men." At the horrified sputtering this elicited, the nymph loosened the buckle of Dominia's belt. "Never fear, General. We are on land now; the bathtub is not large enough to drown you in, I think."

"Why do you drown them?"

"Why?" The nymph, who had knelt between the General's splayed legs in effort to better unzip her trousers, now looked up with pure curiosity filling the eyes beneath her golden curls. "No one has ever asked us that, General. Most just assume we eat them...but I suppose we do it because they are so happy when we have all played together, they submit to being drowned because they do not wish to tarnish the moment by allowing it to recede to memory. They would rather dwell there forever and allow us to dissolve their energies back into the pool of the Lady. Perhaps you will understand why."

"But my wife—"

"Will not be upset." Gethsemane lifted that wandering right hand to touch Dominia's good cheek. "Would she wish you to be so restless? So ascetic? Lonely?"

"Lonely." What a horrible word. Oh, Lamb, what a horrible word! Pain welled in the General's breast, and in her good eye. She shut it against the nymph's touch and turned her face away. All this time, surrounded by people, she had never had time to think of herself as lonely, but she was. She had been lonely since that final, horrible moment of Cassandra's life. She had been empty. No more the smell of sidewalk chalk on wholesome hands after school nights; never again the light in her eyes while extolling her new favorite book; lost was the way she looked at Dominia, sometimes, when she thought the General slept. The way Gethsemane looked at her now, with adoring innocence and deep concern.

"The gun stays close," she said, minding the holstered weapon clipped to her belt. "And the eye patch stays on."

"I would never dream of touching them, General."

Mysterious. The idea of sex had been repellent since Cassandra's death, and now in the space of—well, a few days, from her perspective— she had succumbed twice. No doubt the doppelgänger had sensed her weakness, and that was why so much nothing had so quickly swooped in to mock her with her dead wife's face. The guilt, too, played a hand. There was no way of knowing why the creature found her so quickly that first time: but it was easier to detect the cause this time, when the thought of repellent sexuality provoked immediate thoughts of the fiend. Thoughts unavoidable no matter what her limbs, tangled with Gethsemane's, got up to in the bed of the City's hotel. Yet the nymph, lips against the General's jaw, spoke no admonishments. She did not urge the General, as before, to turn her thoughts from that semi-formed study where it seemed she remained, nauseous, drunk on false wine and shame.

"Dominia." The voice of that thing, rooted in her memory, yet emerged from that memory to float, sourceless, within the room.

"It's here," breathed the General, turning through the haze of pleasure in search of the naiad's eyes. "Gethsemane—"

"Sh." Those lips planted upon Dominia's. "This hotel is its own space. Closer, perhaps, to the Ergosphere than to the Kingdom; yet the Kingdom leads to it more easily than the Ergosphere. It is the function of the attendant to repel pests that slip into the hotel from that place, you see, General—and to keep them from leaving the hotel at full strength. Once it is wounded, it is free to leave, for the guardsmen can eject it easily."

"But this pest?"

"Dominia," whispered Cassandra's voice. The General recognized with a clench of infantile terror that it emanated from under the bed.

"Surely there's something we can do." She turned her face in the silence of terror to regard with her good eye the edge of the bed and the leather jacket left upon the chair across the room. At least she had trousers to pull up. "What will it do if we try to get down?"

Gethsemane, unconcerned by her nudity, shrugged. "It will try to devour us."

Shock, cold and white, streaked through the General's body. "Valentinian said it can't kill us," she protested, though she heard him appending the words "in the Void" at the same time the nymph appended, "There. Here, it's more desperate to couple with you than ever. This place is a space of high density, eternity: you are more physical than you were in the Ergosphere, where falsity and reality are meaningless distinctions. You are of even higher density here than you are on Earth, though you could not possibly measure or perceive this effect. There is gravity to everything. Here, terms do have meaning. Here, General, words are everything. The thing in pursuit of you wishes to take advantage of that meaning. It wishes to reach you in a place from which it can easily slip into the real world and take on physical presence. Wouldn't you, if the alternative was a life of shadows and darkness?"

As Dominia reached for her gun, still at hand, Gethsemane stayed her. "Do not forget what the attendant said, please. We mustn't trouble the other guests."

Teeth clenched, she instead tore part of the pillowcase away and sprang neatly upon the floor four feet from the bed, a simple matter to any former child afraid for their life every bedtime. As her bare feet landed upon the wooden boards, an intake of breath like a lover's gasp hissed from beneath the box spring and left shuddering Dominia to dart far from the noise. With her eye set upon it, she backed toward the armchair, and the darkness beneath the bed breathed at the pace of the thing concealed. That thing sometimes twitched: a motion that, with Valentinian's light (as was all light in that place), illustrated mere glints of its bulbous gray shape. She cracked the coatrack over her knee in a grimacing act a deal harder than anticipated, which also left her glad she took care to exercise in her nightly life. Many martyrs relied on their advanced metabolism to increase their speed and strength, like her useless brother Theodore, or (she presumed) skinny Valentinian. In a place like this, without the endurance from actual training, they'd be as physically weak as kittens. Even Dominia bruised herself in the process of trying to snap the rack and came to the final solution of shattering it over the armchair, which also shattered—and yielded a more desirable proto-torch than anything she might have crafted with the precious seconds given her. After selecting an upholstered piece of wood for the nasty spring protruding from its tip, the General edged toward the nightstand and its waiting lamp.

With a howl, the horror whirled from beneath the bed; Dominia cried out along with previously unflappable Gethsemane, who bolted upright as the odious thing received a gouge across the—face?—courtesy of the General's weapon. Infuriatingly, the thing wheeled in the direction of that precious glass lamp. Jostled from position, it shattered on the floor.

The dark room shuddered as the laughing creature slithered off to regroup in some far corner. As the General clambered upon the nightstand, the nymph whispered, "Are you all right?"

She received no answer. Dominia's toe bumped the pack of matches with which Gethsemane had lit the lamp. In silence punctuated only by the arrhythmic sound of infected lungs rattling after moist breath, the General bent, took them in her hand, and struck a match.

Mixed feelings bloomed in that second of light. Relief, namely, because had she struck that match but half a second later, it would have been upon her. However, it was hard to deny the sheer terror that poisoned her body as that blipped image revealed it mere centimeters from her: the clearest and most fang-filled vision of its hanging, tattered flesh she'd yet to receive. A visage like that made even the General scream. The thing screamed, too, and, blinded, retreated beneath the bed. Jaw set, Dominia struck a second match and, deciding her torch to be too unfeasible a proposition, set the edge of the bed ablaze. Gethsemane cried out on instinct, for she still sat upon the mattress, and moved to quell it, but she recoiled when she saw that lurching, six-eyed fiend that, with a shriek out of time and space, threw odious gray arms above its writhing mandibles to retreat from the light into the shrinking shadows of the room.

"We have to kill it," Dominia insisted again. "I think we've made plenty of noise by now."

She drew her gun, and wondered how long—and how well—it had dried since her emergence from the pond. She feared its ability to fire, but, as always, human engineering impressed the martyr General, who shot a trio of bullets into the shape. It screamed in a duet of agonized voices: that of her dead wife, and that of something else.

"It found you by your grief and shame," said Gethsemane while sliding from the bed to back against the wall. In the shadows, the thing's blood oozed with unearthly viscosity. "But it would have always found you in your guilt, anywhere. By bringing it here, we can cripple it."

"Can we?" she was forced to ask, for it began to stagger up: but it did so from its position behind the door, which, thank the Lamb, flew open. Light from the gold-carpeted hallway streamed in to reveal, in glorious silhouette, that miraculous Lady named Trisha.

"I thought I told you girls about our noise policy. And I thought, Gethsemane, that we discussed our visitor policy already."

Ruby heels clicking with every step she took after the thing that fled her light, the attendant stooped to collect a piece of shattered coatrack. After regarding its heft, she used it to impale the screeching beast.

"All visitors must enter through the front and register with the desk. Absolutely no exceptions! Can you imagine what kind of loony bin this place would be if I allowed my clients to run roughshod over me like that?"

The thing howled; the porter edged it closer to the dust-caked window, heedless of its efforts to pull itself the length of the stake. Indeed, Trisha emitted a pettish noise at that, and with a mighty shove baptized the thing in the flames of the bed. Its cries rose to alarming pitch, and the otherworldly *tulpa* thrashed in agony: while it lost control, the redhead stuck it through the dusty window as though the glass were made of plastic wrap, and the creature she expelled like a prosciutto-wrapped date upon a toothpick. She was not some toned woman of military or other physical might, yet the act was so careless Dominia was flabbergasted—more shocked, perhaps at the column of moonlight unleashed by the act, for she had not realized night was upon the city. She dashed to the window to watch her wife's profane imitation fall, screaming her name in thirty horrible voices, a final few feet before its deformed body shattered on the pavement.

Far from victorious, the General felt ill at the sight. Trisha dusted off her hands in theatrical symbol of victory and said, "There! No harm, no foul. I understand how these things can happen. This place is...special."

"I told her," Gethsemane said, pounding the blaze that started to overtake the bed. The General, still near the window, insisted, "Not soon enough."

Outside, the thing's pelvis twitched to kick its legs into a horrific mimicry of activity. These twisted limbs tried to drag its walking body east until its yet-unruined arm had to get in on the job. The forearm looked shattered, but the elbow, judging by the uncanny, crustacean pace and method of movement, remained intact.

"Shouldn't we go kill it?" asked Dominia.

With low urgency, the porter returned to the hall for a fire extinguisher she used to aid the nymph. "That's someone else's job now, dear. The guards will come and sweep it away, and that'll be that. Just try not to attract another one."

Grimly, Dominia stuck her head out the window to track the thing until it disappeared down some nondescript alleyway. Would they really find it?

"There." The blaze managed, Trisha planted hands upon her hips and pursed her lips to blow aside a lock of hair. As it moved, her expression flipped into a smile she allotted between her guests. "Aren't you glad we have such a strict noise policy?"

"Thank you for your help," Dominia finally remembered to say. The woman, a twinkle in her eye, doffed her cap.

"If I can give some friendly advice: guilt and sex never mix." As the General blushed, the porter laughed, and even Gethsemane smiled. "Neither do feelings of hopelessness and sex. Sex should be fun!"

"I'll try to keep that in mind." At Dominia's visible embarrassment, Trisha laughed.

"She's *very* shy for a military lady, isn't she."

"Very," agreed Gethsemane, who looked quite attractive draped nude upon the unsinged side of the bed. "And loyal as any. I hope you are not hurt, General, that our activities were meant to summon the thing; and I hope you are not hurt for the sake of your wife."

"Oh, now, there's no shame in fun! I'm sure Cassandra would know that." The name twisted Dominia's stomach as it came unexpectedly from the mouth of Trisha, this woman who the General had only met an hour or so before. "This is a different sort of thing, after all. Spiritual, for one."

"Our love was spiritual," said defensive Dominia. Gently, the porter laughed, glanced at her watch, then strode over to peek down the hall.

"Of course. I didn't mean to imply otherwise." Satisfied the way was empty, she leaned back into the room and, causing another, different flutter in Dominia's stomach, locked the door. "But there's spiritual love between two people; then, there's…well. Something else. Something just as deep, in the opposite direction. Honest, naked physicality"—the first few buttons of her top opened at the slight touch of her hand—"can be as deep a route to the divine as any profound, self-sacrificing love."

Dominia opened her mouth to object but found that she could not, because she had never opened her mind to the notion before. For no real reason, she remembered Cicero's stupidest catchphrase: "If one opens one's mind too wide, people will throw garbage into it." Maybe that was because Cicero couldn't distinguish garbage from jewelry. As the porter crossed the room to kiss the Bearer of that goddess both her new friends served, Dominia found her own line between trash and gems perfectly clear.

IX

The Orbit of Dominia$_0$

There was no more thinking of Cassandra that night, except in narrow corridors of thought between starbursts. Yes: beautiful, carefree fireworks. Dominia didn't know how close she felt to any divinity, but there did seem something liberating in renewed ability to surrender to someone who had nothing to do with Cassandra. Gethsemane alone had not allowed this surrender, and the General had resisted Miki's playful come-ons due to the seriousness of her quest. But, perhaps because the horror had (for now) been purged, she nearly floated above the ruined bed. The nymph dozed at the foot, curled like a cat, to make room for the porter. Body contorted around the burned spot, Trisha dreamily traced the lines of the General's palm.

"Is this place heaven?" Dominia asked, and her lucid bedfellow chuckled.

"I suppose it might be for some, but there are more heavenly places than this. It is a fine place, though."

"Where do souls fly on death, if not the event horizon of the black hole?"

"Oh, it depends. Some go in the direction of earthly Jerusalem, but as its substance in the Void—its interference pattern, if you'd like. Valentinian likes his movie theater metaphors, but I prefer holograms, because it's more accurate. That's what the Lady, the black hole at the end of time, is doing to us. Projecting us back to the beginning of time—creating time. Within the Ergosphere is the interference pattern of reality. Therefore, the interference pattern of Jerusalem is the same as physical Jerusalem, and the souls sense it. Much confusion has been caused by ignorance. Exoteric teachings of any church, taken without thought for the true profundity of the encoded metaphors, pose danger to the soul and cannot free it from the hologram. Whether they're part of the projected image, or the interference pattern, if they cannot rise above it and reenter it willingly, it's all the same. Mecca has the same problem, as does any holy city... Irreligious souls—the souls of materialists who don't believe in anything, for instance—tend to float around, waste away, if they haven't developed their own frame of reference to get themselves someplace like this. Some never even became conscious enough to experience death, and these don't even notice they've died...they generally don't have souls, though, except in some cases."

"What do you mean, they don't have souls?"

"Just that. The soul is a product of sentient consciousness mated with the ego, the sense of self, whatever you want to call it. If somebody only has an ego and never achieves this consciousness, they're in something of a pickle. One can't exactly sail the seas without *some* vessel. Even a barrel will do in a pinch. The blood of Lazarus is physiologically triggering the production of a soul through manipulation of the genome; in fact, a theory I developed before I hosted the Lady—never published, understand—was that the successful development of an individual's soul could be indicated based on the associated genetic markers triggered by the process, but you understand why it would be hard to convince the materialist scientist crowd to see the pattern if they don't believe in souls. Goodness knows I used to be one, myself!"

She could relate. Did Cassandra have a soul? The General had long since taken the nonexistence of souls for granted, but now she was bothered. "What about reincarnation?"

"I suppose that exists, but not in the way you mean it." As she spoke, she pressed her lips to the General's knuckles, then rose to re-dress. Dominia pursed her lips.

"You mean it in the sense of living the same life, over and over again."

"Until you become conscious, yes. Trying to escape that hologram, aren't we, dear."

"Doesn't that seem torturous?"

"That's what the Bible means when it talks about hell, or what the Buddhists call *saṃsāra*. Only the material world that your Father grossly claims to be his is so full of pointless death, pain, and boring restrictions on metaphysical truths. Real hell is being stuck living in his cycles forever without ever becoming conscious enough to pull yourself out." She bent to reclaim her abandoned undies, and Dominia struggled to focus on the conversation. "But even that isn't so bad... after all, you used to be one of the unconscious horde"—she slid the panties over those creamy thighs while the General sighed—"and you don't remember it, do you?"

"No, but it's frightening. So nihilistic. The idea that I'll experience it again."

"If you're actually conscious, you'll never have to." The porter crept around the room while engaging in her reverse striptease, her words a murmur. "I understand why death seems frightening—I felt much the same—but these days, I understand it better. It's not as bad as we all make it out to be; I mean, it's not as if they don't still exist, those members of the soulless dead."

"Where are they, then? If without a soul they drown—I guess, *are* the black grounds of the Ergosphere—then how could they be saved?"

"What do I look like," asked Trisha, buttoning her blouse, "the Lady?"

"But I thought—"

A sharp knock rapped upon the door. Annoyed (but, due to her career, used to being interrupted after, or even during, intimate moments), the General draped a blanket over stirring Gethsemane, then retrieved her shirt and pants. "Just a moment," Trisha called, one lascivious eye upon Dominia.

When it was appropriate, the demi-dog came trotting in upon the porter's say. "Didn't mean to interrupt your sleepover, ladies." Typical that Valentinian's first sentence to her in what felt like too long should have been a half-assed apology. "Refreshed?"

Behind the bed, Dominia zipped her leather jacket. "I could have used some time to rest."

"There's time to rest when you're dead, as my grandmother always said." Valentinian turned to Trisha with a lecherous quirk to his smile— wasn't she supposed to have been his mother? A long time ago, Dominia supposed. He was a martyr, after all; the Lamb and El Sacerdote, lest she forget, had once been brothers. A few hundred years passing by changes your mind, and breeding is never a concern; what was some extra friendliness among flesh-eating relatives, then? So most rationalized, but Dominia stubbornly maintained that, rather than some bizarre sign of superiority, incest was gross even in cases of adoption. Maybe she just felt that way because she hated her Family, or because the Hierophant was aggressively asexual and hammered the point that all sex was ultimately the same fruitless time waster among his violent people. Therefore, she had to take the opposite stance by drawing a line somewhere, and she wasn't alone, because about 40 percent of martyrs in any given poll of the populace stood right there with her.

That didn't stop Valentinian, though. For once ignoring her thoughts, he dug out his smokes and waggled a brow. "You want a cigarette, Trish?"

"Oh, no, darling." She laughed and patted his chest, sliding past him in a weird way that gave Dominia the creeps. "You know I quit smoking."

"I still have questions for you," the General called after her. The porter paused to listen. "Is it true you were Valentinian's mother?"

"Once, the first time, a long time ago. But he's a self-made man, now. I don't think we'd be passing any DNA tests on the subject."

"Sorry, babe. Lots of mutations, traveling through all those dimen- sions and all those worlds. Not to mention all those animals!"

Dominia laughed at him, but kept pressing. "What about the McLintocks? What do you have to do with them?"

With a giggling glance at her watch, stylishly positioned to face her inner wrist, the porter adjusted her hat. "You'll have to address that to Mrs. McLintock." A sassy wiggle in her hips, Trisha strolled from sight, and the magician watched her go before turning his arched brow to Dominia.

"A-plus, am I right?"

"Please." The General pinched the bridge of her nose, her eye squeezing shut. "I'm sure you've, like...transcended mortal values, or something, because you've spent so much time in either the—Ergosphere, or the bodies of animals, but...you've got to know how creepy you are."

"Ah, things are different here. The information is organized differently. Didn't Gethsemane tell you that? Hey, kiddo." He acknowledged the sleepy nymph, who lifted her head to force open heavy eyelids. "Thanks for collecting her."

"It is my honor, sire." That head lowered back and disappeared beneath the blanket. "The General is a hero."

"She sure is."

"Well, she *feels* like a fool." Arms crossed, Dominia glanced over her shoulder at the shattered panes. A breeze trickled in to sweeten the room and prove that not even a broken window was an objectively unpleasant experience here. "I'm sorry I wandered off into the dark like that. I didn't mean—"

"You didn't do anything wrong." The magus crossed to examine the frame. "The night had to pass somehow."

"You might have warned me, though." The annoyed General accepted one of the cigarettes he withdrew; after considering she might be smoking his thoughts, she let him light it, anyway. "I was worried I'd never see you again. That I'd never see *me* again."

"That'll never happen, buddy. I'm sorry you were afraid, but I'm glad you made it here."

"I'm still not *sure* what happened." When she struggled to recall the wandering, she still felt her body's muscles were those of that otherworldly predator. "I was lost in the dark, and then the dark was the water."

"I told you, General," insisted Gethsemane's soft voice beneath the blanket. "Someone was praying for you."

"Probably Miki," agreed Valentinian. "She's a pious girl. You should ask her!"

The idea of Miki Soto as some pious nun made Dominia laugh. Valentinian smiled in perfect patience.

"You'll see her soon enough...ready to go?"

"Where to?"

"Earth! Sweet relief." A tinkling sound caught Dominia's attention, and she looked in time to see what her brain first mistook for rain. Broken glass refilled the window frame as though the magician rewound time. Once the pane sat as good as new, he pushed the window open to finish his cigarette.

For a funny moment, Dominia felt the window had only been put there in the first place because of his courtesy. That the City and the man were somehow the same. Such a thing was easier to fathom in the Ergosphere, where the concept of definition was nothing but a meaningless hamper on thinking. That the Hierophant and his study should be one was less incredible than the idea that Valentinian—this goofy, lazy, chain-smoking (of tobacco and pot, it seemed) martyr saint trapped in a dog's body—was somehow inextricably tied to this strange place tucked within the event horizon of oblivion.

Yet, as he turned, and those electric eyes set upon her, they provoked a crackle in her blood. She felt obliged to tell him, "That thing followed us here, or was summoned by us, or something. I'm sorry. Hopefully the City's men will be able to control it."

"It was bound to show up eventually. Now that it's crippled, it'll need lots of time to recover, and won't be able to follow you around. Certainly not to reality."

Squinting through the smoke of her cigarette, the General asked, "Did you tell Gethsemane to do this?"

"What"—he touched his ear with one hand and flicked his cigarette out the window with the other—"who? Me? Huh? I can't hear you."

"You really are a terrible liar."

"Still can't hear you."

"You heard me," she said, trying not to laugh.

He raised his voice to ask, "Why don't you try speaking up?"

"Did you—" began the General loudly, eliciting a shush from the nymph.

"General! Noise policy!"

The magician had used this time to beat it to the hallway, of course. In a combination of irritation and wry amusement, Dominia considered her own half-burned "herbal" cigarette, then drew the covers from the nymph's curly head. With a smoky kiss upon those soft lips, the General asked, "Will you come back to Earth with us?"

"I am already there." Gethsemane patted Dominia's cheek, then rested that delicate hand upon her shoulder. "You will be so surprised when you see me, General."

"How is it possible for you to be in two places at once without leaving here?"

"Everyone on Earth is in two places at once, General, all the time. The Kingdom is Eternal. The most amazing thing is what you and all those Lazarenes do: you can choose at any moment to reside only in Eternity, then change your mind. Most can never change their mind."

With one last study of the delicate woman's beauty, Dominia placed the cigarette in the corner of Gethsemane's mouth, patted her pert little rear, then exited the room with only one pang of regret. Surprisingly, not regret for what she had done, but for leaving the nymph behind.

It was naïve, considering her age, but Dominia had never understood the mechanics of casual sex. Granted, she'd had plenty of it. Women (sometimes literally) tripped in front of the infamous General for a chance to visit her bed, and more than a few had courted, coaxed, and coddled her in hopes of becoming a member of the Holy Family. Only Cassandra had ever been worth that, but Dominia had enjoyed the attention before that fateful seaside meeting. What she had not enjoyed, however, was the procession of selfishness, hurt, and loss that came with every woman who wanted less than she did. She'd always felt the painful need to know the insides of another person as well as she knew her own, and to be known in kind—as if that knowing made her more real than her historic record. It *was* the real, tender side of her. Not the violent side of her.

But was there a real side of her? Were both real? Did she only dream her tender side was the "real" side, or did her violent impact upon so many lives make her existence as servant of death the truer Dominia?

Without the bridge of another being, she feared she was destined to drift along, unknowing, trapped within the cell of her own body.

When trapped in a real cell and given the opportunity to make a platonic connection, she'd wasted it. Her interactions with Benedict—this young man fresh-shipped far from his home, his mother, and the girlfriend he didn't know to be pregnant—must have seemed, to the human, a kind of friendship. To her, it was a slow, careful, conscious manipulation that she could plan twenty-four hours a day/night cycle, every cycle, until she blacked out or got free. She had sensed from their first meeting the depths of his innocence, that innocence that sparked in him a silent but obvious hope he might somehow redeem her with his friendship. One too many United Front movies about the goodness of people, perhaps. Fine by her; small wonder her Father paid to produce so much shlock when it brainwashed them into delusional mercy.

First, she demonstrated a need. Easy enough to pretend to be lonely. She let him hear frequent sighs and made sure he was around to watch her wander the cell. As she paused by the door, she'd gaze out its little window with the most somber expression manageable, then wander out of view. It did not take many repetitions—two or three of his shifts—before she noticed him reading, and asked him about the book.

"Just my mom's old Bible. She gave it to me when I left, and I've been trying to make it through this thing my whole life, so I thought I'd give it a shot while I was here, but...it's a pretty heavy book. Fourteen pages of 'And So-And-So begat Such-And-Such, and Such-And-Such begat What's-His-Name...' No offense." He offered a meek smile. "I know martyrs are religious."

"I'm not. Not really." For instance, she had to wrack her brain for a book from the human Old and New Testaments, rather than the more important martyr Post Testament. "But I always did like the Book of Tobit. It's short."

Then, after a second's recognition for the suitability of the text and the suggestion it would place in his mind, she lifted her eyebrows. "It's a fairy tale, about a young man who frees a woman from a demon."

There it was: that light of transference, of false hope sparking so bright from his irises their afterimages floated, ghostly, upon the cell wall. He would make his mistake when he returned to yammer excitedly about the story the next day, to talk to her all about the adventures of Tobit and his friend, the disguised archangel Raphael—and the dog, there, in the background.

She hadn't thought about that dog in years. On the way down the golden elevator, she wondered about it the same way she wondered about Valentinian. What was the point of the dog in that story? What was the real goal of the magician? By his own admission, he was a kind of thoughtform. With no earthly body, he could say, "I used to be real," until his face turned blue. That didn't mean he was real now, so far as it concerned Dominia and the world where she lived. Yet, he was real as anybody or anything here, and was clearly *known*, as by Trisha, who tapped the invisible keys of her computer and blandly tolerated the flirting of the magician leaning with his elbow propped against the desk. A man as any man, albeit several degrees smugger. Like a man with a great poker hand and a terrible poker face—or a terrible hand and a great face. Impossible to say.

"Here she is. Checking out?" Outside a hat left askew and a naughty edge to her smile for Dominia, the porter acted as if nothing had happened. The General coughed.

"Sorry about the room."

"Don't fret. You wouldn't believe the things that happen in this place. And most people don't tip me nearly that well." With a saucy calendar-girl wink, Trisha turned the screen in Dominia's direction, which had the odd effect of looking like she summoned it from space by spreading it between her hands. "Sign here"—she indicated—"and here, and here."

"What am I signing?"

"You know"—with an attractive frown, Trisha turned the screen back in her own direction and nibbled the inside of her cheek—"I can't say I know the answer to that."

"Eternity in a black hole, yet nobody has time to read fine print." The laughing magician leaned across the counter to kiss the porter's cheek. "All right, Trisha, have fun, be safe."

"I should be telling *you* that, shouldn't I?"

"Nah. Age doesn't matter in a timeless space, but if it's a contest...I still win."

To be sure, the magician had lived forever if he had lived a day. Flat-out reading her mind, he said, "Same goes for everyone. Shall we?"

"What?"

If she was annoyed when he responded, not with words, but by dropping his hands on her shoulders and turning her around, her annoyance melted into awe as she noticed what she had missed the first time: a square fountain in the center of the lobby shielded—along with rows of ferns and begonias that she'd thought to be the entirety of the centerpiece—a tranquil sitting area with black leather benches and a firepit waiting empty like the mouth of a cauldron.

"We're going home," he said.

"And what does a nice sitting area have to do with getting us home?"

"You remember when we had that conversation about projectors? And Trish talked to you about holograms, right. You understand it all better now, I think. If, in reality and the Ergosphere, we're in the movie and the film—"

"The hologram and the interference pattern"—called the porter, to his eye roll.

"—then this is arguably the '*real* real world' of images being filmed, scanned, super translated, whatever. And not just for this film, but every scrap of footage that was ever shot for any film: back in reality, we'll become editors of our one film again. Or you will, at any rate." With a grin and a pat on her back, he strolled to the sitting area and expected her to follow. "I'm just a supporting actor."

"Are you saying I'm the editor, the actor, or the projector?" He ignored her question and stood with his hands in his pockets, chin craned high and eyes angled as if in search of the ceiling. He gestured she should do the same, and she did, but failed to see. "Okay. What are we looking at?"

"The ceiling."

"I thought we were supposed to stare at the sun to get home. There's no way you can see the ceiling from here! Aren't there infinite floors in this place? Look at it up there!"

"You remember how you got here?"

"I remember walking into the sun." As she started to look down or at him, he urged her, "Just keep looking. Tell me about it."

"Well, I was—I was about to be captured by Akachi and his men. Then I saw you. Or...Basil. Out across the street, in the shade." She frowned. Her eye, struggling for purchase throughout the infinite floors, must have constructed one, for she now imagined she did see a ceiling: so far away, it appeared a pixel. "Is that—"

"Then what happened?"

Annoyed, she answered, "Well, you walked out into the sun, didn't you? That's how you get back and forth, from reality to the Ergosphere. You and Lazarus told me that." Yes, that was definitely a ceiling. And growing. Or descending?

"Consciousness is all about momentum, vibrational states and the electromagnetic spectrum. However, all things, including consciousness, are subject to the principle of inertia; that goes for creativity, too. If information is the basis of reality, you can understand how information that already exists requires certain conditions—certain levels and types of energy input into the system—in order to reach an appropriate escape velocity from unconsciousness to consciousness. You're a logical woman, General, you were all right with higher level math in sixteenth grade. Think of it in purely numeric form, with the Mandelbrot set, otherwise known as the first fractal."

"That creepy, black beetle fractal?" It discomforted her just to think on it.

"Reminds you of your old man, right?" While they both laughed, he said, "Because it's an appropriate mathematical symbol for how you escape his world. Stop me if you've heard this one before—the Mandelbrot set is generated by iteration, or the repetition of a process, in this case, quadratic polynomials." The numbers of the floor at the lowest level of her vision, printed across the columns by the stairs (who could take the stairs in such a place!) changed from a real number into the example form $z_{n+1} = z^2 + C$. "In the Mandelbrot set, $z_0 = C$, so if $C = 1$, so does the first iteration of z. You are our cheeky variable of

z, and Lazarus is our constant of C. You started off as z_0—*Dominia$_0$*, if you'd prefer—and applying the function of reality to you yielded *Dominia$_1$*...which we iterated again."

The floor numbers flashed from $z_1 = z_0^2 + C$ to $z_2 = z_1^2 + C$ to $z_3 = z_2^2 + C$, and trailed beyond at a pace outmatching her capacity to observe. They were passing those floors by: this whole time, they'd moved. He had stopped her from looking down because she would have seen how far they already were above the floor. Over her astonished gasp, he continued, "The list of generated numbers is called 'the orbit' of z_0 under iteration of $z^2 + C$. You can use this function for a mind-blowing amount of models, including reality itself, you now understand. There are two primary results with iteration: in the case of a positive constant in the example I just gave, the orbit tends to infinity by growing larger each iteration. But with a constant of zero—no constant, no blood of Lazarus, no hope, no soul—the orbit remains fixed for all iterations. Snore! You Father just keeps winning, and winning, and winning."

"You're as responsible for controlling probability as the Lamb, aren't you? You've been altering the odds in Lazarus's favor and keeping him on the right side every time."

"And keeping that sweet, sweet blood of his available to you and all the others in need of a way out of the loop." Yes, they flew: the floors whipped past, a thudding wind that accompanied the shifting of colors as layer on colorful layer whirled by, peeled away, dissolved into the next. "That mutated blood activates the CRY gene; in humans and normal martyrs, it isn't fully functional. Fruit flies and birds, among other beings, use that gene to perceive magnetic fields and so much more. Activated in a human or a martyr by Lazarus's blood, we see the same but struggle to put names to them as other beings don't. Yet, we are able to use the blood of Lazarus, through the lens of the gene, as other beings don't. When high-frequency wavelengths—like those of blue and ultraviolet light—interact with the mutated CRY in our eyes, our molecules are excited to such extent that it becomes possible to travel through those frequencies of light and beyond the Plancks of reality. Light travels through the optic nerve, into the brain and down into the nerves of the solar plexus, which is where we perceive the source of our fields. They indicate far more than direction, by the by. They measure the electromagnetic spectrum and connect you with devices and people sensitive to it. The Ergosphere itself is not radio-active, but individuals who have returned from it briefly are, because they have traveled at frequencies unrecorded by Earth's populace; their bodies, and their realities, have been reconstructed by what a great man once termed "Hawking radiation," the electromagnetic field around black holes that is responsible for their diminishing mass. It's pulling information back out to be constructed elsewhere, realized by the Higgs field: a result of the constant activities of souls in and around the black hole, backward across time."

"And when this black hole's mass is completely diminished?"

"An almost infinite amount of time from now? Don't worry...it's all the same black hole, anyway. If I'm being honest, the black hole itself is just a door to the highest reality there is...but this nesting doll of meta-phors has to stop somewhere for your three-dimensional brain, right?"

As Valentinian spoke, that distant ceiling grew ever larger, ever closer, and at such speed that her bones felt on the verge of bursting. They moved so fast, a hundred floors passed them in a second. What a speed at which to fly! It was almost more like... "Wait," she cried, "are we *falling*?"

She took his lack of response as confirmation. "The blood of Lazarus creates a spiritual yearning in those who take it, because it has created a soul with or without their knowing. It takes a soul to experience the Ergosphere; most people never consciously experience it, even with the blood of Lazarus, because they never learn to mount that soul. But when the body knows it's but an organ of the soul, well...your organs have to come along, too, right?"

Clutching his arm, Dominia screamed, and tried to indicate that the ceiling—decorated with a mosaic depicting the swirling rays of a sun—prepared to crush them. As if to indicate these highest floors were somehow larger than the ones below, the work of tile stretched the length of a North American football field and was intent on grow-ing. Grinning, the magician pointed to something black upon the face of that ceiling: a sunspot, the pixel's width the whole mosaic had been at first glimpse. While this black dot grew, the magician said, "You can go anywhere, and even humans will be unaffected by their own body's radioactivity... They should take a shower before visiting with friends and neighbors, though. And it's not instant teleportation when it's a chemical reaction within the body, but it's better than nothing. It could be engineered to give the answers to actual teleportation, though, if men look."

To Dominia's relief, the mole resolved into an open skylight and the night beyond. She relaxed her grip on her friend's arm, and asked, "I can do this from anywhere? Go back and forth, up and down, the electromagnetic spectrum?"

"It's safer to come to the Ergosphere from the earthly day, but you can leave it at any time. And the trip from the Ergosphere back to the planet is, from our perspective, faster than this one. From Earth's perspective, it doesn't matter."

Close though they were to home, and Cassandra's diamond, and what she hoped would be the end of her journey, Dominia was nonetheless seized by a wave of sorrow. "Will I be able to see you with my own eye? Is there really a way?"

"Of course, buddy. You'll see Basil."

"But, I mean—as you are now. A person I can talk to. Sometimes." They shared a grin and she turned her face toward the skylight that had grown so close and so large it pushed away the golden tiles of the sun. The cosmos beyond swirled so clear that the General was chilled by the sight. She had never seen such stars: swirling columns of gas beckoned them close, and sweeps of color tantalized with iridescent glimpses of neighboring galaxies. She still had too many questions. "Are you real?"

"Is anybody?"

"Are you really Death?"

"Your Father says I am. Pretty flattering."

Turning to see him with her good eye, she pressed, "Are you God?"

"Who, me?" With a cheeky grin, the magician turned a sparkling eye her way. "I'm just some dog."

She didn't manage to catch that Planck wherein he transitioned into the mangy-but-adorable shepherd dog. As he spoke, the skylight leapt for them—closed that last gap, itself—and on its other side, the General found herself adrift in outer space with Basil. It was all so abrupt she gasped. Tried to, anyway: her airless mouth, mere information being recompiled into her physical body with a new location associated—thanks, she supposed, to Hawking radiation, the Higgs field and Valentinian-only-knew-what mechanics, produced no sound in the vacuum of space. It was Basil's softly wagging tail that galvanized her resulting fright into exhilaration. She sensed no harm could come to her in this transition period, and suspected that she flew through time as much as space. In particular, the planet Mercury formed seconds before she was hurled past it. Miles and millennia passed in microseconds, and the tail of a timely comet revealed, like a curtain drawn away, the distant face of blue-green Earth swirling in a more beautiful—and more astonishing—vision of home than any she'd seen.

Legs paddling through the void, the dog twitched its ears with a look of such pure animal delight that she almost forgot—that quickly—he had ever been a man. But she would stubbornly hold on to everything learned from this place. She would take every scrap of knowledge and make it another component in the weapon she forged of herself. A weapon meant to destroy not just Tobias Akachi but her arrogant Father as well.

If it was possible to go any faster, the pull of Earth's gravity did it. On instinct, Dominia lifted her hands above her head, but, in turning her face away, was astonished by the source of her journey. Still floating at the edge of space, she rolled upon her back and looked the way they'd come. In the distance burned the naked face of the sun, which propelled them, its little sunbeams, the eight minutes and twenty seconds it took to get to Earth.

Her throat tightened. She imagined Cassandra's radiant face and looked away, urging her eye not to leak half-real tears lest they freeze to her face, or boil when they regained physical form on contact with the atmosphere. Incredibly, against all logic or rule of physics, they slowed. Dominia had undergone a palpable shift in dimensions experienced only by her sensory relationship to her own body, which grew solid enough to establish a clear difference between a thought-body and a real one. Vertigo twisted her renewed stomach as she turned back to Earth and saw they plummeted for the continent of Africa at increasing—but material, and therefore somehow comforting—speed.

Who could waste time being terrified by a sight so marvelous? Free to bark, Basil did, and Dominia grinned against the whipping air. Home! Home! Oh, her beautiful planet. She had never been to Cairo, but every part of Earth was home to her now, and as she fell to its good grounds, she let that tear escape.

The speed with which the skylight leapt to meet them was as quick as the bustling city of Cairo—more dense with highways, bullet trains, and sky-scrapers than its ancient founders ever envisioned—distinguished itself from the landscape. Like most cities, Cairo stretched to such an extent that even its mighty pyramids, dwarfed by mega high-rises, resembled children's toys. Astonishing to think that, from the black hole at the beginning of reality, they could hone in on an exact point in space-time: yet, she saw the indigo diamond of the Lady's temple well before they hit it, apparently not quite solid as she'd anticipated. The General and the dog whizzed with harmless grace through several closed floors before they landed, as if always there, upon the crimson carpet of Miki Soto's bedroom.

X

There's No Place Like Home

The notion that this was Miki's bedroom took a bit of doing to puzzle together. Her ears, once filled with the high-pressure "welcome home" scream of sweet oxygen, clamored with feminine voices, a shouting man, a barking dog, and a woman saying, "What the fuck? What the—Dominia? Holy—"

Her eyes resolved hints of bronze tapestries, which distinguished the crimson walls of an octagonal room. Its door was impossible to find amid the ornately dressed women whose sabers and halberds were drawn from veils so translucent it was amazing they concealed anything. All the while, a voice she recognized as Miki's called, "Stand down! Stand down, would you people just relax? She was probably the point of this thing, right? Right? I don't know, *you* guys are supposed to know this. You're the priestesses or something, right?"

On the round bed that was the room's centerpiece, Miki's glowing face hovered between curtains of gauzy silver and emitted a high-pitched squeal. As the baffled women began to (almost) relax, Basil was so overcome with delight that he chased his tail. Glad to be on Earth, herself, the General laughed. "I never thought I'd be so relieved to see you," she said. "Or so confused."

"Not as confused as you're about to be." Lazarus, of all people, sat up behind Miki's painted face to reveal a trimmed beard and a hairstyle that had been moderately managed. "Glad you made it back."

As if reaching his own escape velocity, the dog plunged past the armed women to leap upon the bed and dash in small circles around giggling Miki. "Basil! Basil! There's my Basil! Who's a good boy?"

"Definitely not the dog running all over the bed." The naked old man grumbled his way up and stooped to collect his pants while a grimacing Dominia shielded her eye. As he covered himself, he said something in Arabic, and the women stood down. Miki crossed her arms over her loosely closed gold kimono with an indelicate snort.

"Real nice. I thought you were supposed to listen to women! To *me*! Not some dude."

"Some dude who knows more about all this than you," Lazarus said. "No offense, Miki, but just because you're the next Lady doesn't mean you know anything now. For all you know, this is Dominia's doppelgänger."

The General rubbed her forehead. "Don't say that word," she pled, almost too exhausted to consciously integrate the piece of information Lazarus had slipped in. (And too distracted by her missing hair—heartbreak!) Miki, the next Lady? Miki *Soto*, serving as the avatar of some trans-dimensional goddess best interpreted, maybe, as a pool of water upon the event horizon of a black hole, or even the substance of the black hole and therefore the basis of both reality and eternity? Soto Miki-chan, cramming her mouth full of falafel, shaking her short-shorts, and swearing like Tenchi Ichigawa never could, the next head of the Red Market and its global cult of pagan women for two thousand years?

It was easier to focus on the *tulpa*.

"It can't come here, right?" she asked Lazarus, who strode over, she presumed, to shake her hand. "I mean, to Earth."

"Not without your help, it can't. The physical body is like a portal to those things."

Then, he did reach for her—but kept reaching past her hand, up into her mouth, where, like a grandfather yanking a baby tooth, he popped her recently implanted right canine out of her mouth.

"Elijah," she screamed; the old man investigated the thing while Miki shouted similarly.

"No"—he showed her the speaker before he crushed it between his martyr fingers—"Lazarus. You want me to do the other one, too?"

Oh, how she'd hoped he was crazy when she'd met him in the basement of that record shop where he told her Akachi listened through her teeth! Removed from earthly concerns as she'd been, she had all but forgotten about those things, and was now forced to pull the remaining device with a terrible series of eye-watering cracks. Much worse than the one Lazarus had pulled; she should have had him do it. As, gasping, she tore it free, Miki's horrified face emitted the word, "*Sugoi...*"

"Uh-oh." Lazarus frowned, investigating the tooth. "This one doesn't have—"

Dominia's shriek of fury quickly crumbled his facade into laughter. "I'm kidding. Good God, I'm kidding! Don't look at me like that... Everybody's so serious around here." After demonstrating to Dominia's tear-filled eye that this tooth was a location-tracking device, Lazarus crushed the thing, and said, "How about we get you some new ones?"

"Before or after somebody tells me what I walked into?"

"Just, like, a ritual," said Miki, as if that explained everything. "You know."

"That explains the plum incense, but not..." She couldn't bring herself to vocalize—or even form the thought—and instead waved vaguely in Lazarus's direction. The Lady-to-be grinned.

"*Well*, it's like, like a sacred marriage? Lazarus is symbolic of the energy that's supposed to be entering me, and—"

"Okay," said the General, "I've heard plenty." While trying to erase the last few seconds of her memory, she forced a bloody smile for Lazarus. "New teeth, you said?"

"Better: your *real* teeth." Having slung the neat white robe of a spiritualist over his shoulders and adjusted its high collar, he marched for one of the tapestries. Miki whined.

"I was just about to tell you all to buzz off so I can talk to my"—her voice lilted into singsong—"best-friend-in-the-world, because-she-has-been-gone-too-long."

A smile quirked the General's swelling upper lip, but, from the cluster of rearranged guards, a low voice spoke in a cadence familiar even if the tone was not.

"Neither the General, nor the magician, may see the Lady while unclean."

Heads turned, Miki looked annoyed, and Dominia tried not to reveal her abject embarrassment at the thought of meeting Gethsemane's physical persona with a swollen, bleeding mouth. It was impossible to hide the shock, however, or perhaps the delight of finding her to be so *different* in this place. The fair nymph with lips so pale they were almost sapphire and hair as blonde as Lavinia's curls had been replaced by a slender ebony Amazon, who, though dressed as the other priestesses in the room, seemed to Dominia's eye a thousand times more flattered by the sky-colored bodice and those many flowing veils. Ignoring or missing Dominia in the act of picking her jaw off the floor, Miki snuggled the tail-wagging mutt with an expression of motherly defense.

"Basil is a clean dog!"

"I don't know about that," muttered Dominia, watching an animal that accepted belly rubs in so convincing a way that she might have doubted Valentinian's existence had the memory of his arm not remained so real in her hand. From the door, Lazarus snorted right along with her.

"Even if I could begin to tell you how wrong you are, Gethsemane is right. He's mildly radioactive at the moment." Miki's hand jerked away and her lip curled with a little "ew" while the mystic shrugged. "Doesn't matter since you're going to be resistant in about an hour and immortal soon anyway, but rituals exist for a reason."

"He is correct." Gethsemane slipped past her peers and took Dominia's hand with her gloved one. "The General is much the same. She has returned from eternity, and its energies have followed her as well as Basil. Even Lazarus required purification before entering this holy room. They should not be allowed to touch the new Lady until they have been cleaned."

The woman nearest Miki hefted the border collie, struggling to hold the wiggling dog and evade its cheek-seeking kisses. As Dominia took a protective step forward, so, too, did another pair of women, but Gethsemane calmly tightened her grip.

"There is no need for conflict, General. Please: Nein takes him for a bath, as I take you."

Just like that, she was much less concerned about Basil. Dominia grinned crookedly. "Should we be talking about this in front of everybody?"

This elicited a slap from the Bearer, the pain on her bloody mouth an unimaginable fire in her long-missed body. "Please, General," said Gethsemane above the giggles of the other women and the ringing of the martyr's cheek, "this is a holy room."

Just slightly, the woman cracked a smile, and Dominia repressed her own smirk as she allowed herself led out. "What about Kahlil?" she called before exiting. Miki rolled her eyes.

"Oh, he's around." Her tone told Dominia more about the inter-actions of her friends over the past weeks than they would tell her, themselves. "Probably in the gardens."

The General would have to ask him what he thought about all this when she got the chance. Or not—she didn't want to rub it in, after all. But she couldn't imagine Kahlil was thrilled by the thought of Miki, at whom he looked with obvious and ill-fated stars, engaging in ritual sex or sacrificing her body to some goddess. Dominia wasn't sure about that, herself. But there wasn't anything he could do about it; it was Miki's body, and though he may have been able to talk her down to Earth if given time alone, the future avatar had surely spent every waking moment attended to since their arrival in Cairo, and no doubt didn't want to be talked down at all.

In the hallways, Dominia was stunned again—not by Gethsemane's beauty in the brighter light but by the light itself, doubled by the rosy marble of lapis-accented columns that served as canvases for many murals: from what the General glimpsed, of life, the afterlife, and the worship of the Lady, but it was hard to make out details as she was being hurried to the baths. There was a lot of emphasis on the numbers seven, eight, and nine, if she was counting right—and colors. Many colors. Specifically, arrays of colors she recognized as a rudimentary depiction of the electromagnetic field that had bent from her ribs. Still bent from her ribs, her mind, though she couldn't see it with her eyes. Seeing this depiction, this rainbow of stripes (like wings, she thought as she was whisked past a large image of an ascended soul) only heightened the beauty of what she had seen, but which could not be grasped by memory, because there were no words to describe the colors there, nor cones in physical eyes sufficient to translate them to sight. Perhaps in the fabulous mantis shrimps, with their bullet claws and magical eyes: she had always loved those creatures. Always wondered what it was like to be one, and now she knew. She wanted to reminisce, but even memory, when bound to her mind, failed to reproduce in true strokes the tori of her spectrum. Somehow, rudimentary though the exquisite images were in comparison, looking upon the murals of the temple brought those memories to clear, almost tangible life. Had she known how quickly everything would unfold, she might have urged Gethsemane to wait, and let her take time to examine the beauty of scenes that would not exist much longer upon the planet.

Instead, she studied the profile of the woman who guided her—who had technically guided her from the first moment she'd emerged in the event horizon. "I knew you for Gethsemane the second I saw you, somehow."

"I am amazed you recognized me, General... I have dreamed of the woman I am bound to in that other place, and she is not like me."

No, not at all. Just as beautiful, but a completely different kind of beauty. If the nymph's beauty bore whispered resemblance to the name "Cassandra," the beauty of her aligned human was the elegant compound word of a foreign language. What language that might be was impossible to discern, and somehow pleasing to keep a mystery. Without the attachment of heritage, she still seemed a pure, dreamy beauty, as all things in the Ergosphere and event horizon seemed the purest versions of themselves. Gethsemane's earthly form was so perfect to Dominia's eye that the priestess was a walking rift by which one glimpsed that other world where boundaries dissolved.

Yet, that rift reminded her she was not in that other world. Technically she was, the magician or the mystic might lecture her. But that was just it—she couldn't hear the magician lecture her in this world. Ergo, it was different. Only a few moments after she had fallen to Earth alongside a dog who in that other place was a man, the memories of her experience in the Ergosphere possessed that obscured quality particular to memories of dreams, rather than of real events. She bore a certain guilt for what she had done there, but those mistakes felt understandable now in her actual, causally bound body, hair cropped disappointingly short against her head and clothes notably more ragged than they had been in that other environment. Not to mention starkly different. As happened in dreams, she had forgotten the ruin of her leather coat; René's tattered jacket and shirt had also been abandoned. But even this crisp white button-down Miki had bought her in Kabul was soaked with Hunter blood—not dried, she noted. As if she had just been at the battle with the Hunters and her Family. And, boy, did she ever feel like it! Her body ached for rest.

Wasn't it pleasing, though, to be exhausted again? Connected to her senses, she was once more in control of her thought process and reassured nothing "magical" could happen without extraordinary circumstances—and by the Lamb, she appreciated it.

The General cleared her throat as they entered the baths, and those (mostly) controlled thought processes wandered to a different place. The steam-thickened room was dense with the cloying aroma of honey—and lavender, that scent that followed Miki Soto everywhere she went. All of it—the scent, the steam, the air she breathed—formed to the General some kind of protection from the beautiful woman who shut the door to seal them alone in the wide pool room. One of several in the complex, Dominia assumed.

"Have you never been to the Ergosphere?"

The woman shook her head at the General's question while arranging all number of towels and weird froufrou oils whose mere bottles aggravated the martyr's sinuses. "No, General. Bearers are not meant to travel to the Ergosphere unless urgent circumstances require. The Lady's attendants there are too pure, too powerful; if we discover firsthand our true selves, all the human in us will be subsumed by them and the beauty of the Kingdom. We will forget why we ever came to

Earth, and our aligned spirits must start again many years later with a new body. Just being in the Ergosphere may cause this, but the first time I enter the event horizon, I will never again leave. I will not desire to. Not all are made to come and go as you, General. But I dream of it often, and have sometimes seen it in waking, as one sees through an open window."

"What do you do here that's so important? Not to be rude, I just mean—I understand why you'd want to stay in the Kingdom. I guess I'd ruin things if I did it, since I'm—annoyingly—integral to this... function"—she remembered Valentinian's formula, perhaps the clearest detail from her entire journey, and promised herself she wouldn't forget it—"but what's stopping you?"

"Our duty is to carry our Lady. Most cannot even touch Her. But we Bearers have adapted to suit Her, or, rather, have been adapted by our contact with our higher selves. Therefore, I have no concern for your physical state."

Here Dominia and Basil had been accused of radioactivity: if the Lady was a black hole contained in the body of a woman, She must have been a walking atom bomb. "Why doesn't She walk around Herself, if people can't touch her? Genetic mutations that make you and other women radiation-resistant are fantastic, but wouldn't it be easier if—"

"Because the day that She is forced to walk, General, the world will end. The same is said of Her voice. If She used Her mouth to speak, we would remember we have no ears."

As the woman turned to undress Dominia, the martyr lifted a staying hand. "It's for the best you don't remember what happened between us. That place was like a weird dream. I'm a married woman, and here..."

Cassandra waited. The thought rose in her with a giddy flash, the bird of her heart fluttering once to prove itself not completely dead. Yes, sweet Cassandra, or what was left of her: that diamond of ashes, stolen by Miki. Soon, she would be reunited with the precious gem. And maybe—oh, fairest of words—maybe she would hold her wife in her arms that night!

She dared not dream such a thing. The thought made her more sorrowful than happy, and she stowed it away at Gethsemane's soft smile. "Yes, General: and here, were my kisses to stray from this mouth"—the priestess brushed the martyr's lips and provoked a shudder—"I would be a martyr within a few days without self-control. But I must treat you; what we said is true. This is a holy place, and all within are to be purified. Especially for the Lady's wedding to Her new host."

"Well"—wary Dominia watched the priestess unbutton her shirt, much as the nymph had unzipped her jacket only a few hours before—"I guess it's been a while since I actually relaxed."

Not that this bath proved actually relaxing. Stripped of her clothes and the eye patch, which, in this world, was not some key or metaphysical symbol whose removal had strange consequences not yet comprehensible, Dominia was dunked into the pool. The human soon joined her, then began to scrub her as brutally as a human grandmother scrubbing a child. There was, sadly for Dominia, nothing sexy about the experience: but, just as well. The Ergosphere may have felt a dream, but in its last moments it had become a refreshing, pleasing one. As a result, the General felt quite shagged and a bit baked, an effect impossible to receive from dream alone. To keep her mind off the feeling of her skin being buffed in water so hot it dehydrated her, Dominia asked about the temple.

"I'd think a worldly General would know more of it...but, the theaters of your Father's wars have not yet extended to Africa, so you've had no cause to visit. He is wise to avoid the continent and make peace with the people upon it, trading through the waypoint of Malta as he does; he knows the land will do his people less good than someplace far to the north, and knows our own northernmost countries would be quick to punish any slight by crushing Malta before moving into Mephitoli. I think he only refrains from taking the land and improving its climate for his people because he has other priorities: if he could but have his Jerusalem along with that pesky (true) branch of the Catholic Church that fled his acquisition of the Vatican, he'd sweep from there across the Middle States. A systematic conquest of the African nations would be his next move...perhaps you will see the continent then."

"I will never be his general again."

"Then whose general are you, General?"

She did not know how to answer that question, and pressed on, "But this temple. I've heard of the pyramids, but—"

"Why would your Father let your people know of the Lady's temple? Cairo has always been a heart of religious tradition. This place was built by the now-fading Lady when first She took the throne two thousand years ago. It was this Lady who centralized our faith and founded the Red Market as we know it; before, Her worshipers only loosely connected with one another, and the only ones who followed Her bodily avatar were those who had met the Bearers, or who were the Bearers. Even now, our services are practiced in secret, and are more often than not private visitations between the priestesses and those who pursue our brand of divine connection."

Sacred prostitution had once sounded to her like a goofy excuse for paying to fuck, but she had to admit that after her visitation in the Kingdom, she wasn't sure anymore. At least, the General was open-minded enough about it now to seriously compare it to her child-hood faith. "Sort of like the early years of the Holy Martyr Church... it began underground, the way the Lazarenes are now. Cicero and the Lamb preached the faith and had this...cabal of groupies, I guess, musicians and artists and famous actors. Martyrs came out because one of them was prosecuted for murder and the Hierophant went public to defend him under an assumed name, though he was living in Russia at the time, spreading the faith there while pretending to be a Catholic missionary, so he wasn't in danger like all the martyrs living in North America. He loves to tell stories from those nights, when martyrs could kill with abandon because that was what people expected of them." She remembered her audience and tried to change to a lighter memory. "Sometimes he'd pretend to be Slavic, sometimes flat-out Russian, but then he'd imply he was Italian, or he'd talk about being raised in France...nobody could figure out where he was from or even who he was."

"Many books have been written, General, speculating on the nature of his identity."

"Have they?" She laughed to think there was something she didn't know—another type of book censored from her, outside of holy books. Ill-fated scholarly works striving to debunk her Father and his Church! "How funny...I guess we all take it for granted that he's from his alien planet, or in some way divine." To say such a thing now seemed shockingly rotten in her mouth: Was this a growing sense of sacrilege? "I don't know if I should talk to a human about our period of persecution, because it was natural, and we deserved it, but during that time, those groupies fled across Europa and the United Front—States, then. They carried on the Mass in secret...martyrdom used to be passed through the faith, not parenting. That changed when the HMC took possession of the Vatican, and the souls of superficial people who thought it was all variations of the same thing."

"That is why the Lady and the Lazarenes are both so important. They save as many as they can, not just in body, but in soul."

When the (disappointing) ritual bath was deemed finished, Dominia was hauled out of the pool, dried, and anointed with heady frankincense oil. To her surprise, however, she was redressed in a broad-shouldered man's kimono of forest-green cotton. "Isn't this Cairo?"

"Her Majesty-to-be is Japanese. It is the bride who designs the wedding."

She supposed that was true, but it was funny to think of Miki as a bride, let alone the stereotypical harried version arranging an over-the-top ball. Miki was a tomboy, which led Dominia down another byway of consideration. Did the Red Market women know that the geisha selected as their next Lady hadn't always been a lady externally? Perhaps that was what had factored into their selection. But, more than likely, it didn't matter, and nobody cared. It was far from Dominia's place to ask, and guilt stirred in her for even wondering, though there was no rational reason for that guilt. Curiosity was natural when it came to the particulars of this occult business. If what she assumed to be an...incarnate, multidimensional pool needed a body, and wanted to make that body into a woman, and it had all the powers of a goddess, well, who was anyone to limit the original biological sex of the host?

Other pieces began to fall together, like Miki's insistence on getting Dominia to Cairo despite the prostitute's total lack of firsthand knowledge about the location of Lazarus. Her motivation for doing anything at all, come to think of it, was clearly rooted in this. Would her body be altered by the possession? Furthermore, what would Kahlil think? The General was sure he had never known about Miki's past, and sure he was crushed by the idea of losing her to a religion in which he didn't believe.

As it happened, Dominia saw him on the way back to Miki's room, but not in the gardens. Kahlil came sulking around a corner, arms crossed over his poorly fit kimono, *taqiyah* slightly askew upon his head, and was utterly unprepared to run into the woman who had once allowed him to be shot by the antique gun now concealed in the convenient sleeve pocket of her kimono—safety on. Though, she could have sworn the safety was on when Basil shot him; but that was a different conversation.

Regardless, given that—and the concussion with which she'd left him after his foiled attempt to claim that gun—Kahlil resembled a cat upon the sudden appearance of a dog. "Dominia!" His voice leapt to the high tone of a man trying make terror resemble pleasant surprise. "You're back?"

"I just got back," she said, nodding as Gethsemane offered to take her clothes to be washed. As the priestess vanished around the same corner from which Kahlil appeared, Dominia jerked a thumb after her. "She's a nymph in the place where I was."

"All...right." The man studied her face in search of some visible evidence of insanity. Instead, he noticed, "You lost your teeth."

"They were bugged," she said, which did not make her sound much less insane, and provoked a short laugh from the human.

"Bugged? What? By that dentist? No way."

"Way. Turns out he runs the Hunters. Didn't you know?" Kahlil had gotten his back up about mentioning his line of work in front of Akachi, but that could have been a charade. Nonetheless, irritation tightened the human's face at the mere mention.

"Please. I've been pestered with this for weeks already. Before my concussion, I didn't know anything worth knowing; I'm a low-level tech guy. I've told you this before. Tobias told me who he was while he was treating my head wound and tried to get me on his side before we went to Cairo, tried to say he'd 'forgive' me for helping you—but I had the feeling he was selling me a load, and when we heard about the bombing on the radio after Miki got sick of her music a few hours later, turned out we were right."

Dominia hadn't even thought about that, the car's connection to the music store: that would have kept Miki from overhearing any radio broadcast hijacked by Lavinia's virus in the early part of the marathon. What a fascinating lucky break: the boy went on. "Anyway, I don't think anybody but the highest higher-ups really know who's in charge of the Hunters. If they let people know who was in charge, human governments would have him. And, I mean—a dentist? If the peons knew, they wouldn't listen to anything he had to say."

"How do you think he got into power?" He had fed her some story about being set to be a slave to her people and joining the Hunters but had left out the part about his ascent to the throne.

Shrugging, Kahlil said, "I guess he impressed the right people at the right time. Or killed them. I don't know—you know more about violence than I do."

Wincing at the bitterness of his words, Dominia folded her arms in semiconscious mirroring of his body language. "How's your head? I'm sorry about before, I...I'm sorry."

"It's fine," he said, clearly aggrieved by the memory. "They've got a bunch of doctors here. They checked me out while trying to interrogate me about the Hunters way more intensely than you just were."

"Can't say I blame them."

"I can! They've been harassing me. Watching me. The only way I can feel like I'm not being watched is by going on walks, because they can't keep track of me without obviously tailing me all over this crazy temple. I've been here forty days"—the number startled Dominia to hear, though she abstractly knew it—"but it took them two or three to make it clear I'm prisoner."

"Come on, I'm sure they've treated you well." She felt the weakness of her argument even before she lamely pressed on. "Clothing you, feeding you, I'm sure you have plenty of opportunities to be with beautiful women..."

"Oh, I've slept with, like, twelve of them since I've been here." While Dominia laughed, Kahlil grinned in a way that was clearly despite himself. "I don't care about that." His smile faded into an expression of absent darkness. "You heard about Miki, right?"

"I was just thinking about that."

"She's making a huge mistake. These cultists—I guess I shouldn't be throwing stones, since I'm part of the Hunters, and they can attract some real crazies, but I'm not one of those nuts. All I've ever tried to do is be a good Muslim, and a good human. That was why I joined them. Because I thought it was the human thing to do, defending ourselves against you. I sacrificed a law-abiding, secure life for what I thought was right. But Miki...she's sacrificing her existence. She's talking crazy. You know what she told me the other day?"

The boy's eyes had assumed a soft tint. "'I know you think you love me, Kahlil, but after the ceremony, there won't be a 'me' to love.'" His face strained with a combination of horror and incredulity, his posture relaxed enough for him to spread his arms in demonstration of these feelings. "Would you tell me what that's supposed to mean, Dominia? Look—can I ask you something...personal?"

With a shifty look, Kahlil folded his arms and focused his gaze somewhere around the belt of Dominia's robe. "You don't have to tell me if you don't want to talk about it, but when your...wife"—it was admittedly bold for the man to even acknowledge her wife, considering the homophobic culture of the Hunters, which only widened her mind's openness to his concern—"died, did you...I guess—do you think you'll ever get over it? Losing her? Allah, I'm so stupid to ask... You won't. You're on a journey to resurrect her, right?" They both laughed together, hollowly; the boy removed his glasses to rub the bridge of his nose, to hide the red of his closing eyes. "But how do you go on? How do you even wake up in the morning?"

"I don't," she teased. "I wake up in the evening."

In one tearful note that jerked his shoulders, Kahlil laughed behind his hand, and sympathetic Dominia considered touching him before she thought better of it. "I wake up because I have to," she said. "Because it's what Cassandra would want for me."

"I don't think Miki ever wanted anything for me... Hell, she never wanted *me*."

A horrible feeling, that. "You can't let yourself think something like that. She's a prostitute, but she's also a person, and it seems like she spent a lot of time with you. She talks fondly about you to me, anyway. You don't know what she's thought, what she's wanted, while visiting you. I'll bet she was just as happy to be with you as you were with her. But it's not about you, what she's doing. It's about herself—what she believes, what she wants." The General faltered, and realized she spoke to herself. Kahlil's eyes had opened, and he watched her now from behind replaced glasses. Quietly, she told him, "You can't let her decision to do this to herself ruin your whole life."

"Probably too late." The young man chuckled. Down the broad hall, the Lady-to-be rounded a corner with a trio of Bearers. On seeing Dominia, she gave a cry of delight. With a snort toward the sound, Kahlil turned back to the General and lowered his voice.

"I feel culpable in this, you know. She's been brainwashed. She's going to let these psycho women keep her captive and brainwash her more and more—take her whole life away, even cause her death. Are you going to let that happen? Am I?"

"Ultimately"—the martyr adjusted her tone and expression to reflect excitement on Miki's high-speed approach—"it's her religion, her body, her decision... Hey, Miki!"

"Hey, girl, hey," squealed the future Lady, blasting past Kahlil to throw her arms around the General's neck. "Damn, you look fine in that kimono! What's up, Kahlil?" She turned, still clinging to Dominia, to nod at the man.

"Just welcoming Dominia. I'll let you two catch up. Be careful on your stay, General...who knows what these people will convince you to do." With a disdainful glance for the Bearers, three older women who openly watched the Hunter's tech guy as if at any second he might assault Miki, Kahlil ducked away from them and went down the hall from which Dominia had come.

"He's just bitter"—Miki whispered to Dominia—"because he feels like I spurned him... He doesn't understand. The problem with long-term clients. They always want to save you."

Yeah: that was all Kahlil wanted. Just to save Miki, and to have that salvation rewarded by her love. Those shards of herself that the General found in him and his hopeless love inspired natural pity. What was infinitely more desirable about a woman whose love was somehow tainted? Why was that woman always worth so much more than all the honest women in the world, those gained at lesser cost? The General would never understand it, not in all the time she lived.

Maybe it was because a complicated woman knew she was complicated, and had to take better care of herself than a woman who was sane, straight-laced, and harbored no tragic secrets. Had to put on a more alluring front or pay greater attention in areas of self-care: Miki's makeup-whitened face looked pure as the plumage of the snowy herons and cranes that patterned her shimmering kimono. Even as she yammered at the frenetic pace of a chatty person denied adequate conversation for more than a month, the effect was doll-like. "Dude," this doll exclaimed, "I've been *dying* here without you! I was driving away from that antique music store—who uses records, anyway, I mean, what?—and Kahlil was up in the front seat and he looked and me and was just, like, 'Are you crying,' and I was like, 'What? No way, stupid, I don't cry,' but of course it turned out I was and I cried for, like, twenty minutes, so that Kahlil had to drive for a while, and—"

"Why were you crying?" asked Dominia, to the prostitute's exasperation.

"Because I was afraid I would never see you again! Idiot." Falling back upon her own two legs, Miki began to fan herself with the long sleeve of her glorious robe while her two huge eyes rolled toward the ceiling. "If you make me cry again, I'm going to have my servants whip you."

"We don't do that," said one of the Bearers.

"We're not servants," said the second.

The third qualified, "Not yours, not yet."

"Quit spoiling my power fantasy," shrieked Miki, hands balled into invisible fists while the General laughed. "If you're going to follow me around like a bunch of baby ducks, just play along!"

"I missed you, too," said Dominia to the little woman, who regained her grin as if it had never gone. "But I'm happy to see you now, and I'm glad I'm back in time for your—wedding." Only barely missed that beat.

"Oh, I knew you'd make it! The Lady said the wedding was scheduled based on your arrival, not the other way around. Anyway, you want to walk in the gardens with me? I'm not going to be allowed to walk on unconsecrated ground anymore after the marriage. The next time it happens will be in two thousand years, when the next avatar accepts my body—unless the world ends, in which case, I'll walk much sooner!"

"You knew what you signed up for with this gig, right?" Dominia thought specifically of Trisha the hotel porter, with a background of Kahlil's (frankly, valid) concerns about Miki's retention of self-identity.

With another wave of that vast *furisode* sleeve, the devotee of the Lady said, "Sure, I knew! I mean, this past forty days, I've had everything I've ever wanted! Forty days of servants, getting my face stuffed..." She was, as it happened, looking "softer" since last they'd met, and Dominia smiled; Miki grimaced. "Dude, we have to get you new teeth today." That smile vanished. "Sorry, just...needs another few minutes of healing, looks like. Anyway...I've been allowed to basically do whatever I want, other than be alone. Honestly...I'm tired of it. But it won't be my problem much longer, right? This way!"

It was amazing to Dominia how brave the woman was. Perhaps unaware of her fate, or perhaps imbued with divine valor, Miki led the way to the gardens while going on like a magpie about all the things she'd done and seen in Cairo over the past few weeks. Everyone here felt a reverence to some abstract goddess—the substance of darkness, itself—but Dominia felt a reverence for Miki, who had come far from the place she started in life and now rested at the cusp of a long dream's fulfillment. That reverence only doubled as the girl chattered on: "And I've just become—*super* religious over the past few weeks, like...praying every night"—memory stirred in Dominia even before Miki continued—"for you, too! Especially for you. You're why I started praying again at all. I haven't since I was a kid."

The prostitute's self-conscious laughter for her emerging spirituality was ended by the General's embrace. "I heard you," she said, to Miki's wide-eyed surprise. "You saved me while I was there. Thank you."

"Oh...oh..." Visibly unsure how to respond to this kind of emotion from Dominia, Miki stiffened up, breathed with a hiccup, then began to sharply pull away. "Well...well, don't get all—all soppy about it, stupid! And don't hug me so tightly...you'll—smear my face..."

Miki's tears were bound to do that on their own. Springing from the martyr with the haste of hidden emotions, the avatar-to-be pushed up her long sleeves and pointed forward. "Let's go!"

Beneath the rising moon, Dominia took her first breath of fresh air—air from her home and her world—in far too long. The temple was thick with the humid scent of women, beautiful in its tapestry of perfume, sex, and powders, but the martyr's senses, hyper-tuned to smell flesh on account of her natural hunger for it, were as relieved by the gentle aromas of innocent nature as her eye was relieved by the low light of the torchlit garden. She hadn't seen landscaping like this since her last trip to Europa: something at Kronborg or Versailles, maybe. Yet, she might go so far as to say Cairo's garden was more beautiful than either of those. The effect of rolling hills and a kind of mystical forest had been achieved within an enclosed palace court-yard. A thousand plants flourished, exotic flowers and vines artificially engineered to resemble the impossible plants of the Kingdom within the event horizon. Not even these matched that beauty, but they came close with cotton-candy-pink flowers springing in clots among orchids resembling the crystalline petals with which the Memory Bride wove her crown.

But the extraordinary element was not the flowers. Dominia was most enamored by the arrangement of its walking paths, which reminded the General of the contemplative labyrinth advertised for the patients of the Kyoto hospital. Far from a maze designed to confuse, this arrangement of open paths nonetheless tangled into what

Dominia perceived would be, if viewed from above, a decorative knot of Celtic origin. The chords of the knot were distinguished from one another by low-set hedges, much like the hospital labyrinth, and were crossed with similar ease should the fancy to move to another path come to the mind. Yet even this beautiful design was not the most striking feature, for as they drew close, her eye resolved the four paths that led into the knot were guarded by statues: images of goddesses, whose marble gowns pooled about their feet with such liquidity that mere material garments dared not approach their grace.

At first glance, they were but marvelous artifacts of ancient time, these lovely statues: on the left, a maiden bent to wash clothes in an invisible stream, her hair in one thick braid that tumbled down the cloak upon her back, her head eternally lifted in alert at the approach of fleshly visitors; on the right, a madwoman, who gripped some hallucinated adversary by the throat while a trio of ravens in flight tore her age-thinned locks; but ah, the center! That helmeted Valkyrie who gripped a halberd with one taloned hand while the other, low by the armor of her hip, beckoned to the path at her right: a detail almost missed by Dominia against the background of the raven's wings unfurling from the deity's back.

"Who is that?" asked Dominia, her hush giving way to synchronicity's chill when her friend answered, "Oh, Her? That's the Morrigan."

She had never heard that word before, because it was, like all other epithets of the Lady, illegal for martyrs to speak.

Miki then went on, so excited to chat that she missed both Dominia's visible fright, and its increase as the martyr's eye neared the statue. The face beneath the partially opened helmet plainly resembled her own; the General felt exposed as must have Valentinian when first he saw, through whatever animal's beady eyes, that the Hierophant rendered his likeness in paintings. Desperate to pretend this was a coincidence and to keep Miki from noticing, she tried to devote her attention to the conversation at hand.

The garden was arranged in honor of Trisha's predecessor, way back when the now-departing Lady claimed the throne in 1974. Or when She began the process of claiming Her throne, anyway. "The transference takes a few years," Miki said. "I've thought about it lately, and it's been happening slowly, a bit at a time, my whole life. It's just now, I'm approaching the epicenter, and things are happening so fast..."

With a sad hiccup, she laughed, and Dominia took her hand. The human smiled, looking genuinely bashful for what the martyr suspected to be the first time in her life. "I don't have anything to say that could comfort you." The General felt queasy about it, herself. "But I'll be by your side for as long as I'm allowed."

"Thank you... Anyway, it's said on the eve of her coronation, this Lady saw into the future until the end of time, and demanded the creation of this, the finest garden ever seen on Earth, because of your Father." As Dominia laughed, the human protested, "It's true! It was impossible to keep him from knowing where they were located, She saw; but She also knows him as well as you do. He could never bring himself to destroy a thing as beautiful as this garden. It's said he's even invited to walk in it, if he comes alone. The legend is the invitation pacifies him into leaving Africa in peace; he's never taken us up on the walk through it, either. Good thing, because this is where"— she dropped her voice because of the trailing Bearers—"we keep the encrypted hard drives with the Red Market data on it. Hidden in these statues." While the General tried not to laugh at the ease with which her friend spilled state secrets, the human went on at normal volume. "Let's all pray he never comes."

"Not in this life," Dominia said as they passed the hooked claw of that warrior Morrigan.

Within the maze, the only difference in the paths was the order in which one encountered the statues. At each juncture rose another piece featuring one of many figures she did not recognize. Miki took joy in their naming: Venus, Minerva, Juno, these, the General recognized from their prevalence in the artifacts, plays, paintings, and myths that her Father prized. As the skeleton of the Western world ever decayed to a more hollow state, these goddesses had been so overwhelmed by their male counterparts they must have felt, to the Hierophant, "safe." Robbed of any liberating meaning. The same could be said of the Virgin Mary and Mary Magdalene, who stood and knelt on the left and right-hand side of a juncture near the center of the maze. But many other names had escaped even Dominia's well-read knowledge due to her Father's curated electronic library, which censored many books from her digital accounts over the course of her three-hundred-year life. Ishtar, she had known only because it was a dirty word, one let slip into the public presumably to keep them from wanting to know more. But there were more permutations than the General could have anticipated. Inanna, Isis, Izanami, Astarte, Nuit, and more than even Miki could identify when you got into the plethora of faces given Her by the Hindu or Buddhist societies. Not even all the Greeks had been in Dominia's education. She had not known of Hekate except in Valentinian's passing reference and references in different folios of *Macbeth*, nor long meditated on pale Persephone, whose appearance (moon-whitened marble hair tumbling over one winsome, bare shoulder, with aching doe eyes turned sadly toward the viewer) recalled, to her pain, fair Cassandra.

In her enthusiasm, as ever, Miki did not notice Dominia's moments of introspection. "Hekate is the Greek Lady of crossroads, in three parts, like the Morrigan. Or three-faced, at any rate. Crossroads are also sacred to Izanami"—she waved as they passed the divided goddess, whose proud and elegant appearance held the leash of a ghoulish duplicate crouched in the middle of birthing a heinous monster—"but I prefer her stepdaughter!"

With an imitation of a trumpet's fanfare, Miki raised her arms as they rounded the corner and found themselves before a statue most beautiful, indeed: a woman whose Rapunzelian hair, trailing down her back, was nearly long as the kimono that pooled so far down the pedestal it trailed behind, as if the goddess had been exploring and made it back to her place just in time to be viewed. "Amaterasu," said Miki, who, even in her own beautiful *furisode*, did not hesitate to kneel and kiss the statue's hem. "The sun goddess. *My* sun goddess."

Who seemed to shower her languid smile upon Dominia. The General noticed this when she looked up from her study of the incredible detail of the goddess's delicate hand, clutching as it did the marble-bamboo handle of her parasol, and found that beatific expression waiting for her. The goddess's gaze focused on the white orb cradled in the statue's other hand. This, for some reason, summoned in the General the uncanny notion that she prepared to drop the sun into Dominia's hands. Despite the silliness of it, the martyr moved from the way as Miki said, "Her story was what brought me here. Why I started to wake up all those years ago… I saw her." She searched Dominia's face for skepticism and was emboldened by its absence. "She woke me up and told me I could be whoever I wanted to be. That she would help me, and I would help her."

When Dominia looked away from her second, safer scrutiny of the statue, Miki intensely studied not the goddess but the martyr; the human looked away, but the General pondered the look's true meaning as her friend carried on. "Amaterasu's best story is about how she was driven by her shitty brother to hide away in a cave, so all the other gods had to lure her out by throwing a party. The goddess of dawn and dancing threw off her clothes and put on such a goofy show that all the gods were in a hilarious uproar, and Amaterasu had to peek out of her cave to see what the hubbub was about. Lo and behold, they'd set a copper mirror outside, and she was dazzled by her own reflection! She saw herself, see? The sun."

"And then?"

Lamely, Miki shrugged. "Then they yank her out and cut off her brother's nose or something. It's a fairy tale, you know how it ends."

"Happily ever after," Lazarus answered. His voice so startled Miki that, with a cry, she sprang in the direction of her meandering Bearers only to trip over the hem of her kimono; the man was forced to skip over a hedge to join their path and catch her. He had emerged from the Norse Fates, but who knew where he had started? Dominia sensed she hadn't seen a quarter of the statues here. A peacock, likewise startled by the sudden noises, shrieked past as Lazarus set Miki upright, then adjusted the saffron fabric of his own kimono. "Good thing the Lady doesn't have to walk," he joked.

"You surprised me, you dope! You can't surprise people in a messed-up world like this one."

"Then we better get around to fixing it, because I hate walking on eggshells."

"Why did I get put in a man's kimono, again?" Dominia asked of Miki, noting as she had the fabric and texture of Kahlil's and having the difference brought to mind by Lazarus's appearance. With a sniff, Miki said, "Because you're a man."

As Dominia rolled her eyes, the girl insisted, "Well? There are two types of people allowed at the wedding and the coronation: Red Market women, and men they've slept with. And you're not a Red Market woman, so you must be a man!"

While Miki laughed at her, the General pinched her butt with a discrete hand and elicited a squawk so similar to the startled peacock that, in the distance, the bird answered. As if she had done nothing, Dominia asked, "Where's Basil?"

"Inside, waiting for you with the Lady." While Dominia's pulse skipped, Lazarus said, "I'm here to bring you to Her."

"Is this it," she murmured, afraid to hope. "Do we get to—Cassandra—"

"You can have her back," assured Lazarus, "but I'd like to talk to you first, if you don't mind."

Anything at all, just to see that diamond again. "I'll see you later, okay, Miki?"

"You'll sleep in my room," said the girl with a cheeky grin. "There won't be any escape from me, don't worry!"

On their return along the path, Lazarus fell into slight lead, and was silent until out of earshot of the Bearers. When sure they were alone, he said, "You know what's weird: there are often lots of differences between iterations, like how things are done or said or formatted. But no matter how many times I've lived this life, this garden is always the same. All the statues in the same place, all the chords intersecting into knots at the same points. How is that possible? Even throwing dice, they'll fall differently every time if it's a nonfatal roll. The chords of this garden are not fatal in their format, yet every time they appear in the same manner, the same order. The same statues."

"Maybe their order means something," observed Dominia, follow-ing, from the corner of her eye, the earnest face and clasped hands of kneeling Mary Magdalene before she passed from view. "Like a sentence for the initiated."

"Could be. Probably is. I guess I never think to ask them about it."

"Sort of surprises me that you don't know."

"Why should I know the Red Market's specific esoteric symbol set? I already know what they're driving at. You're the one who needs the symbols. All you people who haven't lived what I've lived and seen what I've seen."

"I suppose that's true."

As they emerged from the labyrinth, Lazarus took a breath and turned, frowning, to Dominia. "There are many other things that do not change. Fatal things. History-altering events. Vital moments in games and war: these do not change once a track is picked, so this is the only chance I get to speak to you before certain events occur. I urge you, Dominia. Please don't forget about Valentinian."

The joyful promise of Cassandra's diamond still fresh in her mind, the General had indeed forgotten the way the men had, in that dream-space, urged her to choose the magician over her wife. Mirth fell from her face, and from behind her deflating spirit, she assessed Lazarus with an eye not just wary but weary.

"Cassandra is the whole reason I looked for you in the first place."

"I know." The old man's tone was as miserable as she felt. "I know. I wish I could help you the way you were told that I could. But you know how these legends go. They turn into lies very easily, through nothing but simple misunderstanding. I can't give you anything. The Lady can. But She can only give you one thing, and only one thing is the right thing."

Bitterly, Dominia asked the question she had asked at least once in that Void, but in her head a thousand times. "If the magician is so powerful, why can't he do it? You can talk to me all you want about closed systems, and my Father denied him a body, and whatever: if it's possible for the Lady to do it, why isn't it possible for some magician?"

"Because the Lady can hardly do it, Herself. You said it: once the world is set into motion and a cycle has started, it's a closed system. Like a human being born into the human race, made up of hundreds of atoms replacing themselves over time and brought to the body from places far away: that seems like something new is being created, but it's just an emergence of life within existing units of matter in the system. You can't add to the total number of these units, which means interferences with the physical body are mostly entropic in form. It takes willful intercession from another force, antibiotics or a surgeon or whatever, to add some needed element back into the game, and it is neither good nor possible that such operations should be frequently engaged; even that isn't adding something that doesn't exist. But in the material sense of what can actually happen, something has to be traded for healing. For the human body, that might be money, or vitality, or time. On this world, the transference of the Lady from one body to another is a lateral transference of energy; during this transfer, other energies can be traded up or down, if you'd like to think of it in basic three-dimensional terms.

"The distortion during the moments where the Lady's true appearance is exposed makes it possible to bend the rules of entropy the way they're bent in the Ergosphere, because the Higgs field is being exposed in the same way: and the more people who are around to observe the distortion, the more powerful it is, and the more drastic the vertical transformation that can be made. Miracles are easier to observe when they happen in private, but they are much, much more powerful when they are accomplished in the presence of multiple people at once—infinitely more powerful when such an event occurs before a temple of fervent worshipers. What you trade up doesn't have to match what you're trading down, in that instance. If you have enough additional energy from a mass of witnesses, you could trade lead for gold, a diamond for a woman, or a dog for a man. But you can't have multiple miracles at once. Not this way."

As he spoke, they had reentered the temple and made their way through its halls, but the General had not even realized it. A sickness claimed her. Lazarus watched from the corner of his eye and turned at a juncture that revealed a pair of crimson doors decorated by that infamous lotus, here emblazoned gold. "It is true Valentinian is potentially powerful enough to restore your wife from death. To find her spirit in the dark—for, had she a soul to keep her from getting lost, she never would have killed herself." So unnecessary an addendum that Dominia's throat tightened in hot displeasure and her batting eye welled up. "But the information about her existence is still available; her spirit exists yet. From that spirit, her body might again be derived by operation of the Higgs field, but it could only be derived in the place and time and way you wish it during the distortion caused by the Lady's possession of Miki."

"But I could have her back forever because of that rift."

"Yes," answered Lazarus, tiredly.

Those lips, soft, gentle, already so close: close as the honey of her hair, the feathery touch of her fingers. The General's mouth tightened. "Is there anyone else who can help her? Any other way?"

"In this world, this life? No. But there are potentials for future disruptions. And then, there's you."

"How can I bring her back?" asked Dominia, wretched. One of the women guarding the double doors slipped within to announce their presence. "How can I help her?"

"With patience." Lazarus folded his hands politely before him, his expression apologetic for his unhelpful response. "Trust me, please. Don't ever trust your Father. Don't try to bring Cassandra back on your own just yet. And don't forget about Valentinian."

XI

Gratia Plena

As the daughter of the Hierophant, and an (arguable) only child throughout most of her life, Dominia had been exposed to much grandeur. Yet, as those towering doors yawned apart to reveal the Lady's throne room, she felt her Father, never shy in demonstrations of wealth, would blush to see such ostentatious architecture. Almost. In fact, its gilded glory deliberately recalled that of the hotel lobby, which had been a garish masterpiece of marble and gold. This, somehow, was far more marvelous, and farther stretching, the path of crimson carpet that unfurled its length marking, after the halfway point, the width of a bridge crossing the low pool inset before the throne. The throne itself sat atop a platform, which, accessible only from the flight of stairs marked by the carpet and the theatrical curtain behind the massive seat, had the effect of stranding its sovereign on a beautiful island. Upon this glamorous throne sat a woman. Though shriveled by the profundity of her age and struggling to breathe, let alone sit up, she was nonetheless as bejeweled as her temple and richly dressed in fine, thin linens that clutched the wheezing bones of her ribs.

This, after all, was Trisha: the body of Trisha. Like trying to connect Valentinian to Basil (who sat, tail wagging, at the Lady's shriveled side) or the nymph to earthly Gethsemane, the buxom redhead's appearance refused to conform to that of the dying avatar. Indeed, to avoid looking too closely and having her visit with the porter ruined by images of cobwebs upon a patchy scalp, Dominia bowed as soon as she and Lazarus stopped at the foot of the stairs.

The Lady's voice was a choir of voices that contained most prominently that of Trisha, vibrant despite her body's age, and crisp despite its immobile lips. *Our prodigal daughter returns home.*

Trying to discern the source of the voice only derived the strange notion it emerged from her own central nervous system; she tried not to question it too deeply after that. "I wasn't aware I had been Your daughter before," she said, trying to be polite, then relenting in a wan smile at the Lady's laughter.

All children stolen by your Father were Our children, first.

As the General lifted her gaze to better admire her surroundings, she instead found her eye drawn irrevocably toward the Lady. It seemed some black hole vibrated in that seat, stealing all light, absorbing all information. In reality, this was a tiny woman. How could such a body contain so much power? How could this body, upon which Dominia could hardly bear to look, be in any way linked to the creation or destruction of reality?

You cannot stand to look upon Us because this body is old and wretched: and you, like all mortals, fear death. Perhaps more than most.

Embarrassed to have her mind read in front of the room (as she glanced away, she noticed Gethsemane standing stock straight before the nearest pillar, and found that each pillar now had a Bearer stationed before it), the martyr began to apologize, but the Lady's voices rose. *Some look into life and see only death. Man must see in three dimensions, because if he saw in the fourth, he would see nothing but his fate, which otherwise he can but intuit. Yet most do not see either life or death. They do not see at all. You understand that, don't you?*

Dominia assessed those priestesses waiting like the garden statues, faces unveiled and vestments different. These new clothes resembled the uniforms of those female martyrs who took Holy Orders and joined the Church, but with a higher white collar, and no sign of a hood. This lack of a hood allowed for another second of searing eye contact with Gethsemane, which inspired the General to say to the

Lady, "Some of us do not see death or life because we are not of this world, I think—not because we are not conscious."

Just slightly, the body upon the ill-size throne smiled. *Who is truly of this world? We have taken many forms. We have had many homes. We have borne many names and been born a hundred thousand times. Yet, We are not of this world.*

"Clearly."

You are not, either. Not anymore.

She hesitated. "Not entirely."

Do you think you were ever of this world, if you are able to become not of it?

"I suppose not."

None are truly of this world. Death exists only in the fears of mortals who lie awake in the dark of night and wonder if that darkness bears similarity to a future which is, in truth, incomprehensible. Do you dream Cassandra sleeps, to be roused by the life-giving kiss of her gallant trobairitz?

A white sag of sadness raced through Dominia's body: not to hear her wife's name or think of her death, but to think of her without a soul by which to navigate that after-space. "I cannot imagine how it is that she exists at all, now that she's dead."

She exists. She has trapped herself in an eternity of suffering. The reality was not delivered unkindly, but there was no kindness in reality. *By taking her own life, she has committed herself to repeating the experience forever, and shunned the possibility of redemption. But that does not mean that she cannot be redeemed. Come to Us.*

Sadness mixed with gentle horror as, degree by painful degree, the body lifted its right arm. Blinking away her eye's mist, Dominia glanced to Lazarus, cleared her throat, and reluctantly strode to kneel before the ruby-encrusted arm of the throne. There, her nose filled with the woman's breath, reeking to martyr faculties of damp dust and rotten age. In her struggle to be polite by finding some place to put her gaze, her focus fell to the mounds of jewels draped upon the avatar's visible sternum. From these, Dominia recognized in a half second that most beautiful and perfect of diamonds hanging amid her inferior siblings. As though they dared compare!

You worked so hard to avoid seeing Us that you did not even notice your bride among Our jewels. Take her back: you came all this way for her, after all.

With itching fingertips and anxiety caused by Gethsemane's warning that most could not even touch the Lady, Dominia felt only a heartbeat of concern before she once more caressed the cool surface of that diamond: the compacted ashes, hand-delivered by the Hierophant several weeks after the funeral. Nothing had mattered after her initial receipt of that diamond, and nothing would ever matter again. As she slipped the necklace over the Lady's head, the old woman's lips softened into a smile.

It was that thought that made all this possible, wasn't it? That nothing would ever matter to you again, not in this world.

Desperate to steer away from the subject, or regain some ground, Dominia held Cassandra to her heart and reveled in the relieving cocktail of dopamine and oxytocin. "Why don't You speak? Your body, I mean. I've heard Your voice will destroy the world, but will it? Why?"

Because Our body has been gifted Our true voice, which speaks only true words: and true words are truer than reality. Mortal bodies who hear them are not equipped to comprehend them here, and may go mad, or perish, depending upon the word spoken. True words can only be safely spoken in the Ergosphere, or in moments where that other place is in contact with this one. True words are the objects they symbolize; therefore, speaking these true words will bring their objects into being. Shall We speak for you the true word, the universal word meant when earthly men speak of "madness," so you can understand?

"No." The General's words were thin as she slipped the diamond over her own head. "That's fine."

Relief! That slight weight. Her wife bounced upon her heart and at passing speculation on the true word for "diamond," a revelation came upon her. She turned her widened eye toward Basil, whose tail wagged in giddy confirmation as she spoke. "True words—that's how you make fire! Or the playing cards! You're not *making* anything— you're speaking! Oh my God. Or—uh—" She laughed, feeling she'd committed some faux pas. "Sorry."

The Lady, not poised to take offense, chuckled in Dominia's heart. *Very good, General. Perhaps you will be ready for the whole truth, yet.*

"I'm ready to know anything you'll deign to tell me."

Yet you would not hear Us speak true madness, would you? While the General faltered, the Lady's legion carried on. *You are not prepared for all truth. Mortals so fear the truth that they would rather wander in the dark. We see you wish to protest: but you do not realize you have died many times, been lost in the dark many times, upon your death. Many times, you have died without a soul. Worse, you have often died with a corrupted soul. In the past, you have brought your wife's abomination into Our Earth and let it roam free, or opted to resume your place at your Father's side. Or you have forgotten it is by the grace of the magician you are here at all.*

"And will Cassandra have the opportunity to be here?"

She had one. She wasted it.

"That's bullshit." The General was shocked at herself but couldn't stop. "What about all the people who have ever died? People who didn't know anything and didn't have the opportunity to know anything? The illiterate, the isolated, the atheist? You're telling me all those people are condemned to wander around, not knowing anymore who or what they are, or where, or why? Is that just?"

Would We could craft it all another way, agreed the patient goddess, a kind of merriment stirring in Her body's milky eyes to the resentment of the General. *Would a goodly Redeemer sweep those souls together and set them right. But We are hardly more than one of the many columns in Our chamber—the lowly support of a palace made of Our same substance, though far grander in scale. We took no part in its building. We are simply here as its support.*

"Everybody loves to shuffle off responsibility," Dominia muttered, more to the diamond whose facets she stroked than anyone in the room. "Whose fault is it, then, that all those people are lost?" She studied the dog, who acted like an actual dog for the first time in their acquaintance, seated at the side of his mistress. "Valentinian's? God's?"

It is the fault of your Father, because that is the order he has chosen to maintain in his world. He has mastered the art of rendering his flock docile while keeping his neighbors too busy fighting among themselves to see how he steals, one by one, their own poor lambs. None of them have hope of surviving death, so long as they believe his is the only way.

"And it's somehow my responsibility to fix this?"

You are the Hierophant's daughter, and his only liberated child. Therefore, you are the only one in a position to accomplish his death. It is not necessary that you fix his world alone, however. You have already begun to collect many friends.

The General assessed the deity with a new brand of impudence that arose, perhaps, from the comfort given her by Cassandra's cold weight. "And one of those friends, you'll be keeping."

It is Miki Soto's destiny—her dream—to become Our avatar. She has never not been Our body. She had forgotten: recently, she remembered.

"So she has to stay here forever, alone, in this palace?"

With a stiff turn of Her head that was supposed to amount to a wry glance, the Lady suggested, *We are seldom alone, child.*

"Yes, but—"

Miki will not exist as you know her much longer. Not in this place. You will see her again, but not here. You already know that.

As Lazarus laid his hand upon her shoulder, Dominia softly asked, "Miki's not going to die, is she?"

Quiet Basil wagged his tail. The bearded mystic answered while drawing the General down the steps, away from the throne. "Her consciousness—her soul—will fly far from here, like the porter's."

"Then she'd might as well be dead." Misery tightening her throat, Dominia ground her thumb into the sharp edge of the gem and wondered if this trade had been worth delivering Miki to her end—or allowing Miki to deliver herself.

Without Miki's sacrifice, assured the eavesdropping goddess, *the integrity of reality could not be maintained. We are that which must have some presence, or else the world may not exist; yet, were We to reveal all of Our holy self, the world may cease to exist then, also. But the women in whom We live, child, live forever. Miki's voice shall be lifted among Ours, but her soul will fly freer than it ever has. And she will be given a rich treasure: something she has prayed for every night, imagined every second of her life. She will become a biological woman.*

What other promise could inspire such self-sacrificial religious devotion in a girl so materialistic she had almost cried over abandoning clothes on the train? Good thing they held off allowing her to—uh, absorb any of Lazarus's genetic material until recently, because if the body of the Ergosphere demonstrated the soul's personal truth, Miki would have discovered her femininity there and never returned. The whole world would have collapsed while she found her way to the City to party as the person she really was; or maybe she would have tried to find her way, and gotten lost. Far worse, in Dominia's opinion.

Yes. It is treacherous to navigate existence unbounded to materiality. Too many directions to go, too much to do, too much for the untrained mind to affect in themselves as well as in others. But that is for another night. This body is most easily exhausted, and how We long for one not quite so delicate! Be glad yours is so resilient. And gladder, still, of Our gift to it.

"What gift?" Even as she asked, Lazarus withdrew a silver flask from the sleeve of his kimono. Her attention, drawn to this, could not counter the finger he extended to flip the patch from her right eye socket; though she tried too late to jerk from the sudden intrusion, she could do no more than wince as the old man splashed the flask's contents beneath her eyelid and then, much against her will, past the upper lip whose swelling had abated mere moments before. The Lady's words muted the General's sputtering.

The Observer gives you Our water, which he has brought from the Ergosphere. It is precious: abide its workings. You shall need time for the restoration, and there is little before they arrive. Before, a treacherous snake gave you two false teeth: one to track your movements, and one to listen to your conversations. Now, your Mother returns your real teeth, which you gave up so long ago.

Response was impossible. As much pain as had surged through her at Lazarus's abrupt removal of her teeth, this pain was far beyond that. Not to mention totally foreign. The terrible, salivating itch began in her gums; its tear-provoking cousin emitted from her sinus cavity to consume the entire right half of her face in a quake of pain whose epicenter was her eye socket. As she thrashed free of the old man amid the terrible confusion of presumed betrayal, the General could not even reach for a weapon over the fiery screams of her nerves, and would only have thought to shoot herself to end the agony, anyway.

She touched her gums, home of that pain with which she dared interfere—and the hard buds of new teeth cut through the tissue to meet her touch. Mouth widening in astonishment, the General rolled the gaze of her good eye toward Lazarus while the Lady, with gentle amusement, observed, *How afraid she is.*

The mystic nodded. "Like a cat, at the veterinarian." Basil added a soft bark, a laugh.

Somehow, Dominia had ended up on her knees, and as she accepted the old man's hand to be helped up, the pain ebbed into numbing endorphins. She dared not—not just yet—open that right eye, for a strange but welcome pressure increased as an orb bloomed within that too-long empty socket like fruit from the branch of a tree. "This will be my old eye," she asked. "My eye from before? These are my real teeth?"

You already know. All information is present upon the surface of a black hole, just as all that you are is reflected within the blueprint of your DNA. Our waters contain your eyes, your teeth, because they are Our eyes and teeth. We have loaned them to you, spirit, to do your duties in the world. Everything you have ever received has only been a loan. In truth, you have no body. In truth, you have only one eye.

In truth, the Truth was an apt name for the Ergosphere, and it was one that followed her back to Miki's quarters. Truth could set one free, or be weaponized. Her Father was an expert at using the truth to collar slaves and sew doubt, as he had about Valentinian. The truth had killed Cassandra. The truth had driven Dominia from her home. The Truth, yes, was that her wife, her life, and her eye had been taken from her—and it all seemed fantasy when she looked into the mirror of sleeping Miki's vanity and her teeth reflected back. Those were fine enough that she laughed to see them: but when, with the easy pace of a burlesque act, she unveiled her long-absent right eye, it glossed in instant tears of joy to find itself back home. Her own eye. Not some artificial toy, some spy developed by the Hierophant. Her own flesh-and-blood eye.

Or the Lady's eye, she supposed. Lazarus had stayed behind to speak with Her; otherwise Dominia would have plied him with questions.

The only one she had to show was the dog, who had followed her back to the room, and over whom she now bent. "Look," she said, pointing at her prizes, then laughing softly. At the excited light in the dog's eyes, she worried he might bark, but the wise animal sat up to kiss her cheek and then, gently, paw the diamond around her neck. Again, the dog looked at her—now with more significance, though his joy was undeterred.

"Yeah," said Dominia, "isn't it wonderful?"

What else could she say when there was still so much to think about? Basil opened his mouth in that agreeable canine smile, then let the expression fade as he hopped upon the foot of Miki's bed. The Bearers, who slept in rooms adjacent, had made a cot for the General, and her things had been piled neatly beside. For a time, the General tossed and turned, the chain around her neck something to which she once more needed adapt—especially when she tried to sleep outside her normal circadian rhythm. Unconscious bliss had come with such ease in the Ergosphere, with the help of Valentinian. If only she managed to bring him back with her, as Lazarus had retrieved the water! Dominia had all but forgotten that short stop by the fountain—so early in their trip it seemed a century ago. Why was it possible for the water to come to Earth, or a *tulpa*, but not a lost soul? Why was it not possible for her to bring Valentinian into the world and save it, but also, for her own selfish interests, have Cassandra?

Sorrow tightened her throat, and the General relented. She slipped the diamond over her head to place it safely in her satchel. Although it was good to have her wife close again, thoughts of her and concerns for her well-being kept Dominia awake. Were Cassandra there, she would want Dominia to sleep more than she would want her wearing the diamond all night. As she reached within to tuck her wife into bed, the General's knuckles brushed something cold and hard that she did not recognize. For this, she traded the diamond, and withdrew her hand to see Valentinian's deck of playing cards.

As if those would help her sleep! They made her mind rove even wilder, fill with guilt and embarrassment; but, somehow, the hard rectangle of the pack was better than a sleeping pill, exuding from its place beneath her crossed arms a sense of safety. A reassurance that the magician was, in fact, not some dream. That reassurance evoked his voice, which she imagined chastising her: "How could anyone dream up somebody as great as me?"

Or did he actually chide her? Speak into her ear from the Ergosphere? She had felt the Lady's voice originated within her own nervous system. Perhaps all experiences with the divine, the otherworldly, were the same. It was all so strange; yet, thinking of the Ergosphere lured her off until, in the predawn hours, the General (who, for the record, was almost certainly struggling with undiagnosed PTSD from her many military experiences) awoke to the frantic shaking of Miki. This left the martyr thrashing about and so violently trying to clutch her perceived attacker that she tumbled from the cot to land face-first upon the floor.

Hilariously, Miki asked if she was awake. "Well, yes," she said into the antique rug.

"Then come to my bed and talk to me! I woke up an hour ago and I can't get back to sleep. Wait"—she gasped as the General righted herself—"is that your eye?"

"The Lady fixed it. And Lazarus. Long story. I'm surprised you saw it at all; I can't keep it open right now." Drawn to her feet and given a shove in the direction of the real bed, the martyr flopped upon it and somehow did not disturb the dog who snored in enviable peace. "Don't you want to try to sleep?"

"I've tried. I'm lonely! I'm scared." The human climbed back into the right side of the bed whose entire surface had been disturbed by fitful tossing. "You know how long it's been since I was scared of anything?"

"From what I can tell, I'd be nervous, too." Not that the martyr would ever do a thing like this. It was an unimaginable level of self-sacrifice: she was already being pressured into sacrificing the one thing that meant anything to her, and even the lives of all her people. To sacrifice herself? She couldn't picture it.

As both women ruminated, Miki's lower lip disappeared. "Will I still exist?"

The General's neurons dreamed of the porter's red hair tickling her neck. "I think you will." She told Miki about the hotel, and Trisha's appearance there; the prostitute wrinkled her nose in displeasure after Dominia had finished, whitewashing, of course, the "visitation."

"I have to work for eternity? As a desk monkey? I don't know if I like the sound of that."

"I don't know, she seemed to like it. I think she was the boss. Or she didn't care what her boss would think. And I wouldn't call it 'work,' what she was doing."

Although Miki smiled slightly at that, the smile was quick to fade. "What if it isn't like that for me, though? What if I lose myself completely? Like, what if I don't even know who I am anymore? I won't even know there's a me that's afraid…that's the scariest thought of all!"

Remembering how, as she wandered in a tiger's skin, the sound of Dominia's name on Miki's lips brought her to her senses, she took her friend's hand. "I'll pray for you," she said. "And you'll hear me, the way I heard you."

"You really heard me," marveled the human, unbelieving even now. "It's all so strange."

"Cosmic radio signals," Dominia suggested, positing a metaphor likely to be used by the man pretending to be a dog pretending to be asleep. Her head against the silk pillow, she said, "I used to worry death would be that way. That the final one would be a whole lot of nothing. Especially since I didn't remember the first one—I was afraid it would be like that again. Nonexistence. But now…I'm not sure." Darkly, she smiled. "Maybe it's wishful thinking."

All those people she had killed over the years! More nameless than named, but the named still too great in number for her sense of shame. She imagined them, all of them, wandering in the dark because of her. Those many victims of cities sieged, like the many starved to death in Tokyo before the last horrific blitz. It was all made up when, in reparations, the Hierophant donated the technology required to move the radio tower, and poured money into the Japanese branches of the DIOX Corporation as if he weren't just moving investments from one account to another. Everybody won: DIOX had a surge of orders for artificial parts following the war, which was around the time such items first came into mainstream fashion; the Hierophant, Dominia now knew, had his investment returned threefold; and the people of Japan, well, they earned the global right to kill or expel any flesh-eating demon discovered on their soil. They could suit themselves. The martyrs may have been expelled from Japan, but the tentacles of the DIOX company plunged deeper into the brains of the populace with each passing year.

Dominia had been the misdirection in his sleight-of-hand trick. While the Bitch of Europa turned her eyes on Hunters based in South America and Mexico, and the Family used this as justification to make their way south, DIOX products steadily slithered into the homes and bodies of everyone in the Far East to such extent that Dominia wondered if there was an electronic in the world to which her Father did not have instant access. She had killed many people, but he had control of so many more, and all of them were churned through his system of violence like grain in a mill. She was not a part of his mill, the General: she was his scythe.

But wasn't the fate of cut wheat, after the milling, to serve as the bread of higher beings? He had tried to convince her of that. Had tried to claim she was doing the right thing by leading his armies, by striving to please him. That futile striving led to the Black Night, an act of genocide that still haunted infamous Dominia. But that same futile striving led, also, to the moment when she began to question everything she had ever done in the name of her Father. This moment came a couple of decades before Cassandra, and was so simple it seemed nothing—was nothing, for certain, to the Hierophant. That nothing moment had been near the climax of the party after the Black Night, when a raucous feast was prepared with some of the slaughter and food was distributed for free to the rest of the masses. Dominia was several drinks in soon into the affair, which was why, perhaps, when she was finally able to get her Father's ear near the balcony, she had looked around through all the crowd and asked him, sincerely, "Are you proud of me?"

He blinked, as if either unprepared for the question, or unwilling to answer it. "For?"

For! She almost laughed. "For the idea—the South Americans are furious. They're already planning to strike Mexican soil, just like you want. You'll have your proper war. I thought it was a good idea."

"Perhaps it was—time will tell."

He turned away, and she, forgetting herself in all the drinks and the shock of his snub, grabbed his forearm. People nearby turned to look while she implored, "Hey! Can't you—" Now she did laugh, more a hollow exhalation that ended on a hopeful, high note. "Can't you tell me, just this once, 'Good job'?"

"Good job inspiring me to have all those people killed, Dominia. You didn't do anything yourself, you know—why, Cicero had more to do with enacting the operation than you. You may be my muse, my dear, my architect, my genius: but if there's a child I'm proudest of, it would be him."

Her mouth had fallen wide as her hand in that second. Now free of her grip, the Hierophant patted her cheek and said, "This is why we don't pressure our parents to play favorites, princess."

There went his back, into the depths of the party. There went Dominia's delusions about her place in the Family, and her hope that her Father might see her as something more than a grunt. All she had done, all the people she had killed to please him—all to accomplish an impossible task. To please an evil man who had kidnapped her from her home and trained her to throw her life away for him, acting like a doting Father but never quite letting anybody (except his precious priest) get any concrete approval.

Yes, a tiny straw, but the next night she filed her sabbatical paperwork, and the night after that she was on the plane to Quebec. What a stupid child she'd remained, for two hundred years! But that was testament to her Father's power. She couldn't blame herself when she had been so expertly trapped and brainwashed by him; Miki wouldn't.

Dominia rubbed her face, then turned over to see her human friend watching her with near-luminous eyes.

"I don't think you'll vanish into nothing," was what she settled on. The geisha nodded once, tucking her arm beneath her comically oversize pillow.

"I hope you're right. I'm so afraid! Maybe I'm egotistical." While the human laughed, her voice cracked and Dominia realized she wept. "After all, what am I compared to the whole world? I've seen too much of it to think I'm more valuable than all those places, all those people. All those people! My people." The General felt a strange electrical discharge, as if the Lady already welled in Miki's bosom; but her mortal tears kept the martyr grounded enough to reach for the human, to pat her, then wheeze as Miki threw herself against Dominia's rib cage.

"It's a lot of responsibility, isn't it! I feel so small. It's like when you're a kid, really little, and you think it'll be this way forever, you know—staying home with Mom, playing when you want. Even if she can be cross sometimes. Then, one day, you realize you have to go to school, and this is the *new* way it is—the way life *really* is—forever. Then school becomes work becomes volunteering for the board of your stupid HOA to keep yourself busy so you don't notice you're dying. I could see it, all of it, as soon as I discovered what the world was like, and I got scared then, too. Like I am now, but...worse. I put up such a fit on my way to kindergarten! I cried and cried. That was before Mom realized I was a girl so she'd hit me and say, 'Quit acting like a girl,' and, of course, I'd cry more. I was jealous of real girls! They got to feel whatever they needed. But I don't want to feel like this anymore, Dominia! I don't want to be so afraid. I wish tomorrow would hurry up and come."

Lowering her voice in case the Bearers listened somewhere (and, surely, they did), the General said, "You don't have to do this," but earned a hiccup of Miki's displeasure.

"I do! I've waited all my life for this. The world needs it. Me. And I can't stand the alternative, that nightmare I saw the first morning I was dragged to school. I'm going to die eventually, somehow, anyway. But I guess...this isn't really death."

Thinking of the fresco on her Father's ceiling, of that blue-clad woman, arms extended, attended by a choir of angels, Dominia said, "It's assumption. Immortality. Things can't be immortal here, so that which is destined for immortality has to go...elsewhere."

"Yes." Miki wiped away her tears. "Yes, I guess so. But...I don't want to forget." She hiccupped again, and laughed, squeezing shut her reddened eyes. "I don't want to forget my stupid mom. That bitch."

Laughing, Dominia kissed her friend atop her head. "I'm sure you won't."

"I don't want to forget you. Or"—her lips trembled—"you to forget me."

"Nobody," said the General, trying to stuff away her own emotions to tend to Miki's, "is going to forget anybody. Least of all you."

With a sniff and an emboldened nod, the human calmed at those words as she had been soothed by nothing else. From within the frightened girl, the regular, bossy version peeked out. "You better make sure you get it right this time, idiot." She flipped on her other side to back against Dominia for what was, at best, semi-consensual spooning. "Every time the cycle repeats, I have to go through all this fear again."

Yes, sad to say. Every time the unobservable cycle repeated itself, all of this would happen again. Dominia would remeet Miki every time the world was new, and every time, Miki would sacrifice herself. Most times, anyway. The General was sure there had been occasions where the girl prematurely entered her thought-body, or ran away with Dominia, or was somehow killed. And what happened to those worlds? How did they end? It was hopeless, surely. What a terrible thing to imagine, a hopeless world! And what a terrible burden to rest on Miki.

They had both been unfairly chosen to shoulder these tasks. By the arbitrary cruelty of the universe, Miki had been given the duty of maintaining reality, and Dominia had been given the duty of destroying it. At least, of altering it drastically. Of purging the world of her people, thereby ending it for them. Why was this not the task of someone better equipped? Of Valentinian, the Saint of Death? Perhaps all this was Dominia's responsibility only because of her originating decision: to choose between him, or Cassandra.

Now, it was the General's turn to lay awake. While Miki snored, Dominia turned and, in a bedside mirror strategically positioned across the room from its cousin, saw infinite selves engaging the same turn in an infinity of bedside mirrors. An infinity of Dominias: an infinity of wars, of sieges, of crimes against humanity. Infinite mistakes. How many times had she walked into that room and seen Cassandra blowing out her brains, the same crimson jelly of all the brains the General had bashed from human skulls? That same she'd bashed out of Benedict's skull, that day he'd come to her with the bright, sky-colored eyes of an innocent boy sent to war and said, "What a book, Tobit!"

He spoke while opening the steel plate installed in the door, through which she was expected to stick her arms to be cuffed for blood infusions delivered, insultingly, via intranasal drip rather than a glass. "You were so right. I got sucked right into it; read it all in one sitting! Well, kind of. I had a lot of duties last night, so I had to come back to it a couple of times, but—you weren't kidding! It was beautiful. Made a whole lot more sense to me than all that stuff about begetting..."

The poor boy. So excited to talk about that book. Probably even more excited to have some way to bond with his prisoner, to redeem himself in her eyes. Baffling, that desperation for approval. After her twenty years in Canada, she had been called back for a war that culminated in this, this moment, wherein she had a choice to make. Her own desperation for the approval of a hollow, evil person had put her there to begin with. Maybe that was why she did what she did, killing the private instead of just knocking him unconscious, or threatening him into silence. She saw a part of herself in him that she hated—a part of herself she wanted to kill. When his excitement over his opportunity to bond with her mixed with inexperience in just the right way, it kept him from fully ratcheting into place the cuff around Dominia's left wrist. It hung just a little loose as she lowered her hand; he hadn't done it properly at all, busy as he'd been talking about the angel, Raphael, who instructed Tobit in the use of fish whose organs could cure anything from demonic possession to physical blindness. That same miracle fish was the cause of Benedict's death in the end, when he opened the door and found that, in the seconds of its opening, the General had already jerked her slender fingers from the cuff, bending the metal to do it: he'd left as much give as a martyr needed, which was not much.

After six nights of being guarded by an overgrown boy, Dominia walked free while painted in his blood, and the blood of the two men who'd come to oversee her meal. Then she had gone on to kill every man in the ragtag encampment, silent as night, and had not thought again during the Nogales Rampage of poor Benedict, who ended his life twitching in her cell, short blond hair smeared in the same blood coloring her. The same blood with which she had manhandled his possessions in search of his gun and instead found a photograph of his mother, the town of his birth labeled on the back. She tossed it aside and took another man's gun because it was already in his dead hand.

She next thought of her jailer in Cassandra's hospital room, in the presence of the Hierophant. From that point on, Benedict's death was a trigger—the starting link in an inevitable chain of thoughts, which, like his endless "begets," led shame by deeper shame to the first human life she ever took under her Father's watchful eye as a teenager undergoing a rite of passage like any in her world: attending to the deaths of humans during Mass. Now, outside that world, her whole life was a horror.

As her thoughts reached a peak of sorrow, the dog emitted a soft "boof," eyes still innocently closed. Drawn from her unfortunate mental cycles to look at the beast, he appeared for all the world as if he'd barked at something in his dream. She knew better. With the same hand that stretched to pat the animal's side, the General wiped the tears from her face and lay back down in search of a few more precious hours of sleep.

XII

The Assumption of Miki

Those few hours of sleep Dominia managed proved vital. The ceremony was scheduled to begin shortly after the martyr normally roused; but, running on Miki's human schedule, she awoke at the stiflingly early hour of eleven in the morning. Truly back at war!

But, it was worth it. Worth it to spend Miki's last afternoon keeping her spellbound with stories of what Dominia had seen and done in that strange and sometimes terrible place where forty days had passed as a week's long march. Miki wanted to hear about the Kingdom, so Dominia tried to tell her, but she was at a loss to describe such a glorious place when, while seeing it, the General had lacked one eye, been sleep-deprived, and was overwhelmed by sensory bombardment after a long period of next to nothing. Dominia endeavored to comfort her friend, and to explain that, from what she had seen, the Kingdom was, well—heavenly. The human did her best to be reassured.

Not long after they awoke, they were brought breakfast: Miki received a platter entirely of fruits and vegetables, which meant that Dominia's thoughtful steak and eggs and (graphic) bloody Mary elicited the same envious cartoon eyes in the bride-to-be as they did in the dog. Although the General offered her a bite, Miki sagged.

"I can't. I gave up everything delicious forty-one days ago, when Kahlil and I arrived. I haven't even smelled meat since! But the Lady can't enter me if I've so much as touched it."

Vaguely, Dominia sensed this had something to do with the effects of protein on the spirit or soul inhabiting the body, but she could not articulate why or how. Somehow, it made her reluctant to sip her drink or finish the thick steak, which was, astonishingly, a natural side of beef rather than artificial. Not ideal—not human—but she was not sure she could bear to eat such a thing again, and not sure she needed to with the blood of Lazarus flowing in her veins. Whatever the substance, she was glad to eat normal, material food again—and the fine, buttery, almost sweet flavor of the otherwise intensely umami steak was a welcome way to start. Funny how mass quantities of beer paired with idle living made both cows and humans much more delicious.

Miki downed a big swig of her mimosa, then refilled the glass from a pitcher-size container; Dominia eyed the thing. "But booze is fine?"

"Shit, are you kidding me? It's required. I'm pretty sure the incense here is mostly cannabis, anyway." While Dominia thought about the cigarette the magician had given her, Miki shrugged. "Who knows what they'll be pumping into the air during the ceremony? Maybe pheromones." She tacked on a goofy eyebrow waggle, which made Dominia laugh.

They would probably require pheromones to get the General believing in anything scheduled to happen that evening. Though she may have been to the Ergosphere and met Trisha, the struggle to find direct correspondence between that world and the one she knew was as fruitless as expecting a dream to manifest in physical reality. Oh, sure, her Father's religion was also adamant miracles were possible: but his religion centered around convincing its worshipers that only the chosen—the highest and mightiest and very, very few—could hope to wield those powers of the divine that mankind called "miraculous." Now confronted with a religion focusing on the open display of divine miracles, the skeptical, spiritually jaded martyr wasn't sure how to react. Yes, she had been given her eye and her teeth, but lurking beneath the layers of mysticism was surely a scientific explanation: maybe exposure to the substance brought from the Ergosphere activated her genetic code or sent her stem cells into overdrive to recreate old missing parts exactly as they were. Whatever the explanation, the spiritual trappings over it made her uncomfortable, and left her dubious anything would happen at all.

Yet, when the time came to wrap up the stories of her Void march and leave the future avatar to her early-evening preparations, the General found herself reluctant to go. She waited for some protest from Miki; but her friend's face revealed no trace of that fear that, in the early hours, had awoken Dominia, and that was exhaled in one long sigh that left the human still and perfect. A dove, meditating in her nest.

"I guess it's time for me to start getting ready." A Bearer waited in the doorway. Miki laughed for no real reason and then, quieted, reached for Dominia, only to wheeze with surprise as the martyr crushed her with the force of her embrace. "Dominia"—the human made a noise like a hiccup, and turned her face against the martyr's heart—"thank you."

"Don't thank me for this." The General fought the trembling of her lips and moved to push away hair not there anymore, for it had been sheared off a month ago. She smoothed back what remained as she said, "If I were any kind of friend, I'd save you."

"Now you sound like Kahlil. There's nothing to save me from." Her eyes blazing, Miki turned her reddened face up toward Dominia. "I'm the one saving you."

As Dominia hurried toward Basil and those guards who were too excited to act authoritative, it was with one last kiss on the cheek for a girl who, strictly speaking, had caused nothing but trouble from the first moment she'd electrocuted the General into unconsciousness. How strange, to think they parted as friends! She could not even discern the moment they'd *become* friends. But the world was a strange place, and the heart, far stranger. The heart was open to as much change as it had love; and of all the people she'd ever met, Miki was most full of love for life and other beings. The only one with more—or the potential for more—had been Cassandra, but that capacity for love, if not shattered, had been damaged in two parts: the loss of Benedict, and the loss of Benedict's child. Yes, there were always the schoolchildren, but Dominia saw early on it would never be the same. Not the same as a child of Cassandra's own who she could love and raise and teach to be good, despite their surroundings. Despite what they were. And Dominia, meanwhile, felt for over two hundred years before her wife that she'd endured too much, lost too much, seen too much, to love another person in a full, soulful way. Cassandra's death confirmed it: what love she had was not enough, or, worse, was poison.

This scarcity of love in Dominia's heart made the love radiating from Miki that much more precious. The General had long since closed herself off from trust: from feeling. Once that brief golden window had closed to her for good, she thought of love as an organ—attached to her, but useless and dead, or perhaps entirely missing. A phantom limb. But here, led down the hall by a bounding dog intent on a direct path to the gardens, the General felt that dead organ pulse again. Alive with love for the world through which she walked: a donation from Miki's bottomless resources.

The gardens that night were a sight to behold, more than any other night for the past two thousand years. On first emergence, the exquisite statues seemed to have multiplied, animated, begun to talk and laugh and sing with all the gaiety of birds: only the priestesses, relieved of their duties and given run of the liquor stores for Lamb-knew-how-many hours by the time Dominia joined in. Though the General paused upon the threshold with an anxious glance for the faint veil of sunlight still sharpening the edges of Cairo's skyscrapers and cell-phone towers, Basil gave a supportive bark and charged out-side. Her body tense with the three-hundred-year instinct of pain, and the forty-/seven-day instinct of being swept into the heart of Sol, she crossed the threshold and found both her fears to be, at best, wastes of energy. If anything, she felt refreshed and alive—more than she'd felt in years. But the most remarkable effect of standing in the sun for those few seconds, in her own, real world, was the purity of it. In her mind, and her body. She didn't need to ask Lazarus or Valentinian: she felt in the base of her heart, as Cassandra must have felt those first inklings of pregnancy, that the normal food and bovine blood given her earlier, in concert with the sunlight, would keep her proteins from structural collapse. Perhaps a Lazarene martyr who chose to live at night still required blood. She hoped she would never have to test that theory, though felt as if, in the hoping, she had invited the experience by clumsy accident.

No matter. That was the sun, the real, earthly sun upon her face so long denied, and she was relieved that it sparkled through the trees, intent on sinking past the roofline of the courtyard; when she gazed toward the source of its light (as uninitiated humans were taught never to do under any circumstances, for fear of burned retinas), the boundaries of her body began to dissolve. The edges of her vision flickered with darkness, and against her skin rose the slightest vacuum pull—

Basil's bark tore her vision from the sun as if she had been but musing, deep in meditation. Had the orange trees spreading their leaves above not obscured the light, her untrained mind certainly would have whisked off to the Ergosphere. Ahead, the dog flirted merrily from woman to woman, taking advantage of his fuzzy appearance to receive the giddy embraces of perfumed arms and squealing kisses mashed upon his fur by so many pairs of painted lips that the white portions of his forehead bore the rainbow refraction of a prism by the time he halted at Kahlil. The young man's pensive study of the warrior Morrigan was interrupted by a pair of paws that, planted upon his back, shoved him forward. If he'd held a wineglass like everybody else, he'd have left both himself and the dog drenched. While the General tried to restrain her laughter so as to whistle for the border collie, Kahlil looked upon them both with bleak annoyance.

"Now there's a face I hoped I'd never see again," the man grumbled at the dog who'd shot him. "Tobias was right. If it's going to rain in Cairo, I'll bet I could tell you."

"Good thing that doesn't happen often. Other than that, you healing all right?"

Blandly, the man shrugged, then noticed Dominia's own empty hands. "You don't drink?"

Only all the time, as often as she could, for the past three hundred thirtyish years. "I've already had three or four this evening." Kahlil's vaguely impressed look transformed to one of religious scorn. "Just thought it was time for a break."

"How long ago?" On his asking, she was so baffled by the question that he had to repeat it. "How long ago was your last drink?"

"I don't know—they laid off a while, then brought me the last one about...an hour ago? I guess because they knew my time with Miki was wrapping up. Why, are we going swimming?"

"No, you—" Annoyed, Kahlil's voice dropped as he neared the General. "There's acid in the liquor." She almost laughed before he qualified: "Lysergic acid."

"What," the martyr practically shouted. "No, I've been drinking all day—"

And those first drinks hadn't left her quite like this. The lovey feelings; the hyperacuity rising over her; now that he mentioned it, she'd attributed that strange vibration in her feet to the sunlight, but she could place it now. Kahlil looked furiously up at her, a few curls of hair springing into disarray as his hands waved with his words.

"They started doping everybody two hours ago. I'm telling you, the women here are crazy. It's a cult! I *knew* they weren't going to tell you—I should have mentioned it yesterday when I saw you, but I...I had other things on my mind."

"How did you discover this?"

Annoyed to have to admit it, he said, "I looked around the place a bit, when I could shake them off my trail. They're up to no good; I've known it from the start. Then, last week, they were making a big fuss about something, and after I probed around with the girls I've been—hanging out with, and it turns out they have a lab to synthesize their own psychedelics. They have—basically gallons of it."

The phrase "gallons of LSD" may have been thrilling dirty talk to a certain breed of counterculture artist—she suspected it was to Valentinian, the way Basil's tail went nuts—but to the General, who still absorbed the fact that her brain currently processed its first molecules of lysergic acid since 1709 AL, the phrase was something out of a tahgmahr. Was this how the so-called miracles of the ceremony were accomplished? Where was the divinity in a base, drug-inspired hallucination? Oh, she'd dabbled acid and liked it fine, but then she came down and got back to her life like the rest of the world. Then, there were the bad trips, which made her stop for good: LSD, notorious for its self-insight, was not the best drug for cannibals dealing with the trauma of their first twenty-year war. It was one thing to try it a few times as a fortysomething kid. It was another thing to be given it nonconsensually as a centuries-lived General responsible for the deaths of hundreds of thousands of human beings.

"What would be the point of that?" The General pressed Kahlil even as his attention was drawn over her shoulder. "I mean, don't people usually charge for drugs?"

"It is a sacrament, General," intoned Gethsemane, who had approached from behind and now stooped to greet enthusiastic Basil. "Like the blood and flesh ingested in your ceremonies."

"Sacrilegious," admonished Kahlil, spitting on the ground. "The both of you. I'm ashamed to even be here. *Astaghfirullah.*" After one scalding glance of disappointment for the General, the boy marched back to the temple with a disgusted shake of his head. "*Astaghfirullah, astaghfirullah...*"

"God has already forgiven you." Gethsemane's call merited a nasty look from the man, who doubled his pace. Smiling, the Bearer rose to explain to Dominia, "The earthly mind is bound by laws that will be violated tonight. Because Kahlil has not engaged in the sacrament, he must sit out; these laws cannot be violated in the presence of a closed mind, for that closed mind would be destroyed. Tonight, the veil of the physical world will be torn to shreds and remade, and the witnesses must have the veil parted in their mind if they are to survive. Not all the women here are initiated into the truth of the Ergosphere, either; and these more than any require the sacrament, so their minds may justify what they see."

The Bearer took Dominia's hand. "Will you come with me, General, before the ceremony starts?"

Reluctant to follow anybody anywhere after being drugged, she gruffly asked, "Come where?"

"Everywhere." The girl tilted her head to press that soft, silk mouth— softer than that of the nymph's, somehow—against Dominia's lips. Annoyance giving way to arousal, the General embraced the Bearer's slim body until the human turned her mouth away.

"I don't know." The martyr sighed and held the woman, whose heavily lidded eyes were the physical quality that most resembled the Ergosphere's naiad. "My wife—and then there's you. There's danger in messing around with a martyr."

"Only if you feed me your blood, General, or if I lose all self-control, as I was afraid I might yesterday...but I am clearheaded today. Bearers need nothing of the sacrament. That makes me the best person to attend to you. Won't you come along? We must make sure you're full of joy before the festivities begin."

Full of joy—full of something! These people were alternately in touch with the source of cosmic truth, or a jet stream of cosmic bullshit. But Dominia was forced to admit: it was hard to hold on to grief, fear, and resentment when in the hands of the Water Bearer and her friend, lysergic acid, once they retired to the baths. Far from being the terrible, downright demonic trip once feared, the General relaxed more than she had in weeks—months! Since Cassandra's death, or even before. Each time the caresses of Gethsemane crescendoed in what Dominia found to be a more enjoyable purification ceremony than the day's prior, the General had the surreal sensation of being so relaxed it was as though she had no body at all: as though it had been dismembered, burst, scattered in pieces among the stars of outer space. The Void of space. That nest for the real center of reality, that antispace of the Ergosphere and the black hole around which it swirled. The cradle of all things: good and bad, life and death, Cassandra and Dominia. Her wife seemed so close, and so comforting, even as the General submitted to this near stranger. Each heartbeat pounding in her chest gave hope, seemed to say her existence was the only reason Cassandra lived in the first place, seemed to say nothing in this universe could exist without every other thing also existing.

But could a thing return? There would be opportunity for Cassandra, Dominia remembered while the Bearer anointed and dressed her. This time, the kimono was a woman's, and Dominia realized only belatedly (through a wandering mind that felt suspiciously as her Ergosphere *nous*) that the gown was that same Miki had worn the day before. Shimmering brass silk adorned with those long, midflight herons. As her consciousness mounted breathless heights, the General's body lifted her arms and showed the kimono's long sleeves to that hovering self. The patterned birds upon it appeared to move their wings. A still thing, given life. A single heartbeat, separating the dead from the living.

More heartbeats separated the dressing from the ceremony. Once both women had dressed and exited the baths, the Bearer led her by the lysergic-hot hand to the palace throne room: empty of the Lady, but overflowing with Her followers. Most crowded the edges of those pools flanking the path to the throne, but many more had been forced to fall back into the crowd. Still others were poised to contribute to the ceremony, each in her own special way. Overwhelmed by the suffusing fragrance of women, of lavender and frankincense and sweet plum, Dominia felt suspended upon the wavelike murmurs— the laughter, the weeping, the shrieks and moans of the crowd. The General squeezed Gethsemane's hand tighter and tried to laugh away the fright that crept in only because the drug left her, like a raw nerve, disposed to experience all passing sensations in triplicate. This was not always good.

Laughter, however, raised her up, and inspired more laughter. After a big, dimpled grin from the Bearer and a kiss that reminded her of Cassandra, Dominia forgot all her fear and became aware only of the intensity of the moment and its endless beauty. Basil bounded from the crowded women, anointed, the fur of his face having been washed only to be redecorated with the maroon lines of chalk or makeup. Guilt sprang as she leaned down to pet the dog and saw by his huge eyes that he, too, had been intoxicated by that evening's drug of choice—but, now more than ever, it was important to remember Basil was not just a dog: he was a man.

Yes. He was a man. Dominia's heart sank into a quicksand of grief when the nymph's counterpart pressed into her hands the playing cards along with Cassandra's diamond. She had never seen the Bearer acquire them. Dominia's hand tightened around the deck, its surface cool as that diamond whose pendulum swung against her wrist.

"Why have you come?" asked the Bearer of Dominia as the sound of the women diminished in a bobbing hush.

"For Cassandra." The General's words were weak: she knew it was not quite true even before the patient woman pressed her.

"Why have you really come?"

Lips parted, heart racing, Dominia lifted her eyes to see the red sky of night ("a sailor's delight," as her Father chimed) glowing through a glass ceiling she had ironically not noticed while having her sight restored. The question of why she had truly come barred from consciousness the beauty of that view. She felt on some mission for which she had been dispatched 331 years ago, which she had forgotten, or been made to forget. (Why—no! Thirty-two! Hadn't she passed her October Feast Night in the Ergosphere? Oh, spiteful Saturn and his ceaseless march.)

But wasn't that sense of mission the truth? The way it really was? Everybody in the room had a mission remembered to varying degrees: the not-so-simple task of living their lives. Last night, her destiny seemed unfair, but now, surrounded by these women waiting for Miki to surrender her body to the spirit of a pan-dimensional archetype with no static identity but for those it borrowed, many destinies felt worse than hers.

Of course, she had choices. Tobias had pointed that out. She could always turn and walk out. What was this silly cult business? It was her free will that was the valuable commodity, so why was she allowing herself to be railroaded? The thoughts swirled upon her as though from outside her: indeed, they felt so external, she imagined them in her Father's voice. Though normally the General might have struggled to free herself of the doubts he posed, the tangibility of the truth was self-evident while her mind was lubricated by the unfamiliar molecule. Thus, she could dismiss all his arguments against her selfishness, save one. That of how she missed Cassandra.

Yet Cassandra's life had ended in such suffering, and been one of such suffering even with its many moments of joy. To bring her back would be to force her to resume life from that most hateful apex of despair from which the only way forward seemed to be her own wife's gun. Was such a resurrection not the greatest of cruelties? Was it not possible that soothing oblivion, like sleep, served its purpose? That, to restore health and joy of living, the wounded spirit required ample rest before again enduring the material being in hopes of crafting a soul?

What did Dominia know of life and death? What was she doing, chasing this dream of happy resurrection—in logic's cold light, far less likely a success than the liberation of a dog and a man from superposition?

"Please." Her words for Basil were soft as a tear while the Bearer led them up the aisle to stand behind the throne. "Don't disappoint me."

Just once, the dog wagged his tail, then fell into solemn silence as the three took natural places with Dominia in the center and Basil to her right. To their flanks lay curtained wings, as though they were upon a theater stage. Dominia grew ill with a stage fright she had never experienced before. As if she had not, a thousand times, addressed centuries of men waiting to die at war! Her one consolation was that any eyes upon her were only upon her in passing. Most shifted uneasily from the throne to the doors, awaiting, as did Dominia, the glorious appearance of Miki Soto.

From her new vantage—still trembling, though less overwhelmed by her senses—the General studied crimson banners that had been unfurled down the columns. Man-height, thin iron braziers, like claws upon twisting staffs, were set nine on one side and nine on the other at even measure down the shallow pools. Their light prepared to support the room once night finished fading in. Those preparing women behind the columns were divided into band members, dancers, flower bearers, and still others who cared for covered boxes with contents Dominia could not divine.

The musicians were the ones who acted first, prompted by some secret sign or agreed-upon time to ring the room into silence with their cymbals. From the first iteration of their repetitive beat, they received perfect attention. Motion in the sweet, underappreciated periphery that she still expected to be a blind spot drew her attention right in time to see tiny, near-mummified Trisha carried upon an elaborate litter whose roof was a spiral of ornate gold and silver that spun high like the peaks of her Father's cathedrals. Four of the Bearers,

Gethsemane aside, carried her. Behind this litter walked Lazarus, who moved with as much, or more, poise than the women.

Though the cymbals continued, joined by the eerie sound of wooden *suzu* bells, they did so with new, muted reverence. Women stood on tiptoes for better looks at the Lady: as a result, soon the whole crowd pressed forward with such desperation it seemed the front row would collapse into the pools. By some strength, they contained themselves well enough to watch Lazarus help the Lady from Her litter and sit, gently, upon the throne. The beat silenced.

Dearly beloved, began that strange symphony of voices, *you are gathered today to celebrate Our rebirth: but you know it is more than that. This is the rebirth of the Earth. For all appearances, it shall be the same; yet, We will find it new. We will know it to be new. We will be new. And what of that part of Us that does not survive the transition? This body? Where goes the Queen Bee with her finest drones when she feels it time to split her hive? She founds a new hive, which must seem to her absented kingdom a wholly different world. Let us pray.*

The mass kneeling was audible, an action that seemed impossible to Dominia, given how tightly the women were packed. As the General belatedly followed their lead, the Lady led the prayer. The chant, as ever, did not keep the martyr's attention (particularly not under the swell of a drug that increased the excitement of her blood, the pressure in her body, as if she was, at any second, to be swept back into the Ergosphere), but she perceived it was intended for the sanctity and protection of the old world and the new. *Let the light of the sun shine upon its face when it is young and full of hope,* the Lady prayed, which Dominia didn't understand. How could a sun fail to shine on the face of a world where life already thrived? It must have been a symbol. Like Amaterasu, Miki's sun goddess, looking in the mirror. Like being upon the Earth, yet knowing—no, feeling—one was also within the black hole at the end of time. That one was eternal and mighty. More than a frail body.

As the murmur that had hypnotized Dominia into contemplation met an end marked by the rising of the women, the Lady picked up where She'd left off.

The planet is a rocket for the species, and the species is a rocket for the soul, and let no Man, by God, rent asunder the soul from the flesh. In soul, the flesh lives forever; in flesh, the soul is born. What is lost that does not exist? What is undiscovered that cannot be found?

The sounds of drums gently picked up, and Dominia found herself breathless as the Lady pushed Herself from Her seat with Lazarus's guiding hand around Her left arm. *The differences between soul and flesh are mere illusion*, She insisted, taking Her first step in two thousand years. *All that exists is light working in harmony, propelled by conscious will.*

Paused at the foot of her stairs, the creaking goddess eased around to face delirious Dominia. The General flushed as the room followed suit.

General—the voices boomed in her heart like the timpani of the drums and some fragile strings taught to rise at her announcement—*it is your will that today directs the rocket of this world. You have a choice to make. Tonight is a night for miracles. Tonight is a night for the occluded to be revealed, for a being rendered mere concept to be given flesh. You could ask for money or power from me, but your Father could give you those. Only I can give life. Which life will you choose?*

A sharp breath clutched Dominia's lungs the way her hand clutched that diamond. That same cold diamond that beat against her breast with each running step away from San Valentino; that diamond that contained the physical memory of her wife but only implied the spiritual memory; that diamond that could have the spirit imbued, and bring the body back with it, bring back her wife, her wife, her wife, oh, Cassandra—she was sorry. Dominia was sorry, Cassandra: but that was just the way things were. The General had to be the person she'd always wished she was. The good and generous person forever struggling to be seen as such, and not that selfish, murderous martyr, party to genocide and anthropophagy. She had to be the person she wished she could be for Cassandra. After all: What was the point in having Cassandra back if nothing changed? What was the point in any of this, if all of it happened again?

"The dog." She shut her eyes while a light came to Basil's. The border collie, in his thrill, tapped his feet upon the marble floor. "Take the dog and make him—make him Valentinian. Bring the magician here, into this world."

The General's head buzzed too loudly to admit the ripples of relieved sighs—the one or two cries of delight—among many murmurs of confusion. Only Gethsemane appeared she had known this would be the General's choice—Gethsemane, and Lazarus, who met the General's watering eyes, and nodded. As the Bearer stepped forward, herding the dancing dog, the animal paused to kiss Dominia's hand.

Halfway down the length of the pools, the woman and the dog both stopped, and the animal looked around, so delighted that not one scrap of magical dignity remained detectable in the beast. But this charming hound was a powerful sight when the music rose into true melody. The Lady and Lazarus waited at the path's termination while Gethsemane stepped aside, into the water, and the dancers swirled into motion on either wing of the grand foyer at the hall's distant end. As, in a floral hurricane of veils and ribbons, they crossed one another's paths, the tremendous doors swung open to reveal, more doll-like and perfect than ever, Miki Soto.

Tears renewed themselves in Dominia's eyes to see her, surely as they sprang from all the women in the room; though perhaps that was attributable to those many bright, scarlet butterflies released from the cloth-covered boxes—cages, the General realized—at the opening of the doors. Upon a twin of the Lady's litter, one attained no sense of her beauty's scale; but, when the litter stopped at the path, opposite the holy couple, and the future avatar stepped out, the room beneath the music became a vacuum of sound. One dancer stumbled to see the chromatic train of the splendid bridal kimono, which was embroidered with an explosive array of jade and carnelian flowers, cool turquoise mountains and swirling, hypnotic dirt paths that repeated beneath panels of violet skies dotted by glittering suns—the same suns that gave the stained-glass fabric the yet-uniform impression of gold. Even the sash seemed woven in the Void, or the Kingdom, and transported to Earth. Considering the weight of the deck in Dominia's hand, this may have been so.

But could that gown compare to its bride? Miki wore no makeup, and the human's long hair poured down her shoulders in a perfect ebony waterfall. There was no one who could more resemble that statue Miki had admired the night before. Enchanted by the sublime appearance of her friend, Dominia failed to notice, until both figures were a quarter of the way up their respective sides of the aisle, that the Lady's old body mirrored Her new one step for step. Now the General's attention shifted, and in so doing, she caught the exact second a rueful metamorphosis overtook the old woman. A flicker of hesitation sparked in Miki's eyes as she, too, saw the way Trisha's feet blackened. That blackness rose higher toward her knees with every step: but the new avatar emboldened herself, and her face hardened as the encroaching old body dissolved into something not of this world. Whatever it was, it provoked, amid the many women, a series of gasps that ranged from awed to flatly terrified. There was no going back now, but Dominia struggled with her urge to sweep in and save Miki. Instinct fostered the wish that things could be different. Maybe there had been some hidden other path, and she had failed to find it.

But, was there? Were alternatives fatalistic wishful thinking?

Perhaps it was possible. Already, the impossible had been made possible to her, so perhaps the future would reveal some method of salvation. Hand on her heart, Dominia dared step to Lazarus's side to watch with him. Dared, for with every step the Lady took, the entire palace—perhaps all reality—jittered and echoed like a misfed film. Was this the changeover of the film reel, following Valentinian's metaphor? The space over the dog flexed in a way Dominia mistook for a trick of the light, of her eye, of mere dust or ash from the torches. But that quiver of darkness fomented itself, then shivered and grew until it wrenched a tear in the delicate brane of reality to reveal that same naked Void that consumed the Lady's old body. It was wrong, Dominia realized, to call such a thing "black"; it was the absence, even, of that much. The absence of negative space. Black was a shade of white, and negativity implied positivity—even absence implied presence. This could not even be said to be absence. What was it? What *really* was it? Dominia emitted a short cry to see this extra-dimensional blot (truly extra-dimensional, for she sensed it was but the three-dimensional appearance of a fourth- or higher-dimensional object, like a hypersphere, or a tesseract, but beyond the comprehension of any mortal model) expanded its navy border ever nearer the dog. Gradually, with each trembling pulse of its surface, the tear revealed the head, then the shoulders, then the sanguinary vest, of Valentinian.

She discovered she gripped Lazarus's hand; for how long, she couldn't tell. The improbable image grew along with the space around it, and all light in the room—all light pouring through the glass ceiling—streamed into its vacuous mouth along with any lingering sense of time, reality, or causality. The women farthest from the (proverbial and literal) event horizon were frozen in motion, while others stuttered in and out of existence, and those closest to the scene, paradoxically, appeared the most real. Gethsemane was at times replaced by the tiny nymph of the Ergosphere, yet was still the human Gethsemane, and in this transposition Dominia believed she saw what was, arguably, the only true Gethsemane, which had to be a combination of both, plus all the other bodies to which the nymph had previously bound herself on Earth. Time compacted: there was no time, therefore all bodies were present at once. The effect was possibly the most beautiful thing Dominia's material eyes had ever seen, a burning beauty that ached her head and made her avert her stinging retinas to the dark Lady as She reached that two-dimensional tear in space. From the other side, Miki had done the same, and when the image of the Ergopshere failed for those fractions of seconds, her friend's openly astonished face appeared as through a window. The archetypal expression of astonishment, close to the rift as she was. All who watched the scene trembled, the atoms of their bodies threatening to buckle under stress of the shift like a martyr's deformed proteins destroying themselves in starvation.

From a distance, Miki opened her mouth, and Dominia was amazed her friend's voice emanated from that same no-/everywhere as the Lady's choir.

Are You death, the young Lady asked as the old one reached to embrace her. Miki, though frightened, seemed compelled to do the same.

Yes, answered the voices of the Lady. *And because We are Death, We are Life.*

With the tilt of her head, Miki's eyes fell closed, and the darkness of the Ergosphere accepted her kiss, returned it, wrapped itself around her and began to dissolve—or began, perhaps, to dissolve into her. The oversize bow tied in back of Miki's kimono fluttered in the pressure of the tear like the wings of those butterflies fleeing through the open skylight panels. Blood red, their wings: red as the sky into which they fled, and red as the waistcoat of the magician who, a flickering light between the merging entities, lifted his head to admire the lingering insects. The dark figure of the old Lady had almost completely dissolved, and Miki, doubled over, stood between the General and the magician with her mouth open and her gaze miles away. When she looked up at Dominia, those unseeing eyes glowed white. The astonished General met her gaze and was, yes, dazzled—dazzled, like Amaterasu consulting her mirror. This clear white light swallowed Dominia's body along with all noise and sensation until existence vanished in submission to higher Truth.

This was not the Ergosphere. Not the event horizon. Possibly. She could not explain what this was, for she had not even a dream body here; yet she knew this space, empty and eternal, contained both Miki and Dominia. Moreover, she sensed in this place they were the same, and she talked to herself. Perhaps that was just the spirit of the Lady, which was in everything. Somehow, in a way beyond hearing, she heard Miki tell her, "I guess this is goodbye for me, huh? In that place, anyway."

"I can't believe you have to go."

"We all have to sometime, right? But, I know what you mean." Stillness. "I'll miss you."

"And I'll miss you. I never could have—oh, Miki."

"Don't cry!" Although there were no bodies, there was the sensation of touch, like a hand on a shoulder. "Big, tough General—don't cry! You'll make me cry, stupid."

"Sorry."

"It's important I do this."

"I know. But...thank you. I could never thank you enough, Miki."

"You can try when we meet again." Laughter rang in the fading voice of Miki Soto, whose body appeared, perfect and female and nude as the one into which Dominia dropped, and around which clothes appeared, and space re-formed, and the flying soul of her foul-mouthed friend called, "So cheer up, you silly bitch!"

These were the last words the ears of Dominia's body ever heard her friend speak, and they made her laugh, albeit tearfully. This meant she was forced to cover her mouth when the tears dissolved into a gasp to find, as she came to her senses, the Lady's new body had swooned beneath the intensity of the transition and had been caught: not in the arms of the Bearer, but—at long last!—those of Saint Valentinian. His head lifted to reveal a grin for the many flabbergasted women, who had, for the most part, seen a dog blink into the shape of a man. Even those nearest, for whom time's flow had been least interrupted, surely had not perceived the sleight-of-hand moment the exchange was made. A dog and an old woman in exchange for Valentinian. Impossible.

Yet, the impossible was inarguable. More so when, once the new Lady was passed to those Bearers who hurried up the path, he turned to wave at Dominia.

"Hey, buddy!" As he called out, she was stunned to realize his voice was real. *He* was real. Real! Clear, more static than the magician of the Void where all was dark and shifting. With him, hope became real, too. Driven to tears, she sprinted down the aisle to throw her arms around her patron saint, her dog, her friend. The laughing magician embraced her. "I don't know how I can ever thank you," he said into her scalp. The General's grip around him tightened with her sob.

"Just help me, please. Help me restore Cassandra's life."

"I will." He patted her, then released her to call, "But, first, why don't we party! My God, I have a body! Physical thumbs! I could dance!" Cheesily, he hopped into the air and clicked his heels while Lazarus arrived behind them.

"Don't hurt yourself. The last thing we need is a magician with a bad back."

"What will happen now?" asked the General of the mystic. "Will you stay here? Is this your marriage, too?"

He has made a union with Our body to allow it to receive Us, as We have made a union with Our body to maintain the world. In the arms of Gethsemane, Miki's frame straightened, and its eyes reopened to appear, for all the world, normal organs. The body's mouth, as Trisha's, did not move, and never would again. Yet, amid that vast choir of feminine speech, Miki's voice displaced the previous avatar's as the most prominent. *Lazarus's wanderings must be ended. Those final souls who would follow him only by knowing him will soon be initiated into the faith*—was She talking about Dominia?—*so it is vital he remains within Our reach. Elsewhere on Earth he would be too easily swept into the hands of your Father. Until now, Our actions—yours, and his—have had the capacity for variance. The choice you made tonight has limited the possibilities of the future. Of those limited possibilities, the safest for Lazarus is to remain by Our side.*

"Lazarus was Trisha's—boyfriend," said Dominia with a glance to the perpetually exhausted-looking man. "What does he have to do with the Lady? Why can't he retire to the Void in peace?" Even as she spoke, she caught Valentinian's glance and thought of his Mandelbrot lecture.

His blood, said the Lady, taking Her final, unsteady steps to the throne, *is Our body. With it, all worlds will have the keys to the Kingdom.*

"So you'll ship him to Mars when you're done here?" she asked wryly. Miki's body smiled as it eased into its seat.

Another like him will rise there, and his key will be of a different substance than mere blood. The same old story will continue again.

"What about me?" The General spared an anxious glance the way of the magician. All those weeks ago, she had been certain this moment would be how and where her story ended. She would hold Cassandra in her arms and—what? They would live happily ever after? What had she expected? What did she expect now? The gravity of the situation settled in. Having forsaken her country, her people, her Family and their Church, she had been labeled a terrorist, pursued across the globe, had eyes removed and replaced, killed many and been nearly killed—and all so Lazarus could get shacked up in a polygamous marriage with an avatar and her goddess? So Miki could lose her life? So a dog could be made into a man who scrutinized her from the corner of her tear-filled eye?

"What about everything I've done," she asked, "everything I've been through? Where will *I* go?"

We have much to discuss on that subject, General. The Lady folded Miki's hands in the colorful fabric of Her lap. *We shall require an army. When We have one, We wish you to lead it.*

Astonished by the flat implication that the Lady intended to initiate war, the General had time to ask, "Against my Father?" before the first, not-so-distant explosion rocked Cairo. As power failed outside the room, Dominia, along with the rest of the women, became abruptly aware of the thickness of night that had fallen above. In the distance, sirens rose. The light-poisoned sky relinquished its hidden stars only to see them dismissed by the next rocket, which, screaming past, destroyed in a violent spew of dust some part of the palace only visible from Dominia's position by the emitted debris. Amid the smoke, the sirens, and the screams, the General recognized the noble constellation of Orion.

XIII

Prisoner of War

Were it not for the thousand battles in which the General di Mephitoli had fought, there would have been no comprehending the horror underway. Between the sickly-sweet waves of the drug that opened the cleft between materiality and consciousness enough to render both distinguishable, all emotions were amplified, and those amplified emotions bled through the room so swiftly that fear, like toxic gas, raced between the bodies from the first scream. Shadows poured into the room. Some had guns, some had blades, but all shouted, and the General was never too disoriented or too peaceful to recognize a battle. As Cassandra's diamond fell into its place against her heart, Dominia snatched up the nearest brazier, and Valentinian, amid the madness, asked Lazarus, "Are we doing this already?"

"Do all the drugs you do in the Ergosphere impact your physical memory, too?" was the mystic's contribution as the Water Bearers, with ceremonial knives secreted somewhere upon their persons, fell into battle. The demons, named by the scream, "Al-Saalihin," were soon revealed as but men. Perfectly killable no matter how great their number as they poured, like ants through a beehive, into the temple's throne room. This recognition of reality elicited an inappropriate laugh from the General as half the women fled behind the throne, and half, ill-suited for any fight, charged to meet the men. She experienced an instant shift of priority, from defense of Miki—no, the Lady—to handling the threat. As she sprinted for the fray, Valentinian's distant laughter rang around the words, "Go get 'em, tiger."

Oh, did she. With animal grace surmounting that of the image into which the dreaming Void transformed her, the General covered the length of the marble aisle, pushed past women who arranged themselves to block the way, and began freeing space in which to fight by sweeping the brazier like a spear whose claws penetrated the breast of the first man she met. This action earned not just her first kill of the night but also a weapon: a vibroblade more eager than ever to cut down man after man. They forged a brief, unique relationship, the General and that blade, as the brazier fell out of her hands and the handle of the sword, in. Thereafter, the shimmering metal swept up, left, into another man's gut and through his comrade's hip bone like butter in such a slick, smooth, easy way that the martyr's drugged mind felt precious more than lurid fascination. The muted voice of her horrified conscience reminded her of the wish made to Gethsemane: but there was no time for hoping these men were willing to talk. In a free moment, she withdrew her gun from the sleeve of the kimono and emptied its rounds into the hearts and heads of three soldiers, and she wished she could apologize. Maybe that was just the acid talking.

Most of the women (indeed, most people) could not handle the mere concept of a sword fight on LSD, and certainly not amid a storm of gunfire. The General was not most people. Fighting had been her life for a longer period than memory served. On a mental front, she had spent three centuries fighting with her Father and Cicero. But it was the physical dance she always loved, and how well she knew those steps! By their nature, insurgents used unlocked guns; her own beloved weapon swiftly out of bullets, the General dropped it to snatch the first abandoned rifle she found. With it, she laid down a line of black-cloaked men, which allowed the Bearers to collect more guns from the wreckage. Gethsemane, trailing past, tugged her vulnerable consciousness briefly after and cost Dominia a nice scratch in the face. Even so, that same drug that distracted her produced a kind of tunnel vision, slowed time, and illuminated to her every intended movement of her opponent's paltry human muscles better than even the DIOX-I.

Indeed, it felt not dissimilar from those times in the past, when prayers to the Lamb invited his spirit into hers to guide her victory. (The place she saw when he came into her—all that time, that must have been the Ergosphere! All her life, imagine! Yet never once had she known of that space, not in over three hundred years.) The flow felt more natural than running, more thrilling for the intensity of her connection to the sorrowful aspect of her duty.

After all—was it not that bleak, wandering Ergosphere to which she sent these men? Or were there those among the Hunters who had somehow, like Akachi, acquired Lazarus's blood, so their souls would fly at death to their eternal resting place? Would that be the Kingdom? Most of them thought it was Jerusalem or Mecca. Once upon a time, the fringe religious groups who were the forebears of the Hunters had placed symbolic emphasis on only the earthly city of Mecca, as had those more centrist followers of Muhammad who had drifted into the human conglomerate known as Abrahamianism. Most of these good Muslims still placed emphasis on Mecca, like their ancestors; but the Hunters, who also called themselves mujahideen, had shifted emphasis upon the movement of the Holy See of the Catholic Church from Mephitoli to Israel. This was not for a religious reason but a practical one: they recognized the Hierophant's specific interest in claiming Jerusalem and smiting the final tatters of what was once the most powerful faith in the world in hopes of absorbing the rest of its followers into his flock, and justifying his control of human souls. What he really wanted more than anything was what Jerusalem represented, and this Dominia knew better than anyone on the planet. What he really wanted, what he dreamed about at day (if he ever slept, which she doubted), was the night the Holy Martyr Church could finally claim it *was* the Roman Catholic Church, and nobody would bat an eye.

That night had not yet come, suffice to say. The word "mujahideen," which had once meant "jihadist," now meant something akin to its own brand of faith—one distinguished from the Abrahamians largely by the feverish psychopathy its members vented on martyr and human alike. They did not want Jerusalem for any particular religious reason. They wanted Jerusalem because her Father wanted Jerusalem. But perhaps they really craved the city for the other reason her Father desired it: all those souls, believers who took their faiths too literally and flew to the Ergosphere's interference pattern variants of Jerusalem or Mecca. Claiming either one of those would have disturbing implications for the Hierophant's spiritual power. Who knew what he would be able to do with, or to, all those souls? And who dared think he'd stop at Jerusalem, without going on to take Mecca? Then, one by one, all the Eastern countries, and their holy cities? The Hunters convinced themselves they did a service for mankind by keeping the Hierophant out of Jerusalem, and that was true to a certain extent, but the sad fact was that Hunter interference in and around the city was the cause of violence and turmoil. Was the suffering of the living worth the protection of the dead?

One of the Bearers screamed for her sisters to halt: all the women obeyed, which produced the uncanny effect of stilling the entire room—save for Dominia, who was midway through decapitating a man while deep in thought. Now, she returned to herself with some surprise for the carnage produced by the blade and her body while she ruminated on the nature of Hunters. With another glimpse of that elevator conversation, she regretted her lack of awareness, and turned with a surge of disdain to see Dr. Tobias Akachi standing behind the throne, one hand upon the Lady's shoulder.

"There." The dentist's teeth illuminated a room long-since dimmed by the crashing of its standing braziers and the disappearance of the sun. "You know, I do a bit of teaching now and then. When my pupils are unruly, I find the best way to attract their attention is to stand in perfect silence! They always look up, soon enough."

Dominia made a fast move forward until his pistol was against the Lady's head. As the martyr froze in place, the dentist carried on, "And when they continue disobeying, the second-best way to acquire attention is by threatening something they cherish. Put down your weapons, Miss Mephitoli."

"Do as he says." Lazarus's body was tense, but his words were so calm and gentle that one might not have expected the mystic to be surrounded by (merely incapacitated) bodies.

"How did he get up there?" asked the General, shutting off the vibroblade and lowering it to the floor. She was more reluctant to relinquish the gun when she had misplaced her precious antique somewhere amid the fray.

"I was given a private tour. This place has an elaborate series of escape tunnels, but they are not convenient routes by which to bring an army. Why, it is not even wise for all those fleeing women to use them now. A few men behind and a handful waiting at the end could cut them down like wheat!"

"Don't," demanded Dominia as the dentist laughed.

"It does not matter where they go today. We will see them again eventually, I am sure. Tonight's number of casualties is already high enough, don't you think? Why, I do not even wish to harm your false idol, but truth be told, I do not care one way or the other."

Now, the Lady's voices rose, Her lips unmoving as She said, *Let your finger be quick and your shot true, lest We open Our mouth and share Our true voice.*

"I suppose we *are* in something of a standoff! My death would be a worthy fee for killing you and sending your vile putrescence back into that unclean place from where it comes: besides, there would be someone to take my place, whereas I have read that if the Lady were to die before Her disease was passed on, there would no longer be a Lady on this Earth."

The goddess did not speak, did not move, and Tobias smiled in a vile way. The General, emotions tipping into panic with the drug in her blood, demanded of Lazarus, "Where's Valentinian?"

"The magician was here?" asked the dentist. The question made Dominia sick, but not as sick as when Lazarus looked on in pointed silence. After assessing the room, Tobias emitted another, lighter, laugh, perhaps of relief. "Well, if he was ever here, he does not seem to be now. He can never resist coming when called. Too great a lover of attention."

As the General's head whipped this way and that, no sign of the crimson waistcoat was found. The Bearer spoke of the drug as being necessary to ease a gap in reality. Had he ever been there, or was it all some hallucination at the peak of an acid trip? Or—worse, had his manifestation been dismissed by the presence of destructive interlopers? Whether or not this was the case, there should have been a dog—right? Where was Basil?

"There may be no magician to help you find the easy way out, General," continued Akachi, tightening his grip on the shoulder of the Lady. A low hiss rose from one of Her nearest Bearers. "But I am happy to offer a trade. These ladies up to their knees in bloody water may have their mistress—may abscond with Her far and away down that tunnel, if you and Lazarus come along without a fight."

"Come along to...?"

"Jerusalem," answered that ever-smiling leader of the Hunters, a man more openly jolly, and perhaps consequently less trustworthy, than even the Hierophant. "You and me and Lazarus and my men."

"For what?"

"Don't you, who have been forced by circumstance and love into flight from your oppressive country, wish to see your Father overthrown?"

"Not by the Hunters."

"That is a decision based on emotion, and not on logic. What does it matter to you who eliminates the Hierophant, so long as he is eliminated? I would think that, particularly to a martyr, it is all the same. Are we humans not insects to your kind? Or perhaps cows are the better analogy."

Though mere moments before, the General had thought of the scene as one between bees and ants, she could not help but find one insect preferable. The Lady and Her servants appeared concerned with eliminating the Hierophant because he and the martyrs presented a long-term threat to humanity, the planet, and, frankly, the universe at large. Her concern was with the balance of things, and the idea that consciousness should be given an opportunity to develop without oppression by its many enemies.

The motives of the Hunters were totally different. Although they spoke of religious liberty and piety, they were violent hate-mongers, and enslavers of women. To them, the Hierophant was an obstacle in the way of their own power. They were envious little men. He had wealth unending, whereas they had what they pillaged; he had stockpiles of weapons, as opposed to those secondhand guns Hunters acquired via back channels; he had the adoration of his people, crowds chasing his Void-black cars down the street and shoving their own family members out of the way for a chance to kiss his ring. The Hunters had been reviled since before the Hierophant had even come to power. They would have received much from her Father's death, and everything on that list was something no one wanted to see them touch.

Akachi's willingness to bargain for the life of the Lady (a valuable commodity, arguably a kind of superweapon, and, if nothing else, a bargaining chip for the Hierophant, who wished Her dead) was miraculous, though the General suspected this was motivated by the three most notorious Hunter disdains: women, religions not their own, and Red Market prostitutes. To be sure, there was some relief on the dentist's face when the General consented she would go, and he was no longer required to touch the goddess; but that might also have arisen from instinctual fear to lay hands upon the radioactive container of the Void. No matter how the blood of Lazarus altered the body's genes to make them less sensitive to its effects, even Dominia had hesitated: if nothing else, she had to give Akachi, a mere human, credit for his courage.

"Very good, Miss Mephitoli. I appreciate your level head. Most would have made a much stupider decision!" Chuckling, Tobias stepped back from the throne and allowed the Water Bearers to rush up. They slung their Lady in their arms with little more than a glance for Dominia on their way toward that back tunnel: Gethsemane, who led the way in this effort, let out a cry of surprise and the word, "Why?" to someone discovered in the shadows.

With reluctance, Kahlil edged into view. Dominia, her expression (and even her vision) darkening, understood how Tobias had managed his private tour. "Did you really think this was the right thing?" the General asked him, her tone as pitch as the world around. The boy evaded her gaze and tacked on an irritating shrug.

"Kahlil has been a Hunter since he was a child! He told me during our brief chat in Kabul that his father was one of us; isn't that right?" Laughing, Tobias meandered to the young man and clapped a hand upon his shoulder. "Though I imagine his father would have acted faster than he did... It took him such a long time to contact me. I was starting to get worried. But, one must trust the human soul in the end. He has a moral obligation to help the human race shake loose the blight of the Hierophant, and he knows it."

"Did you know about Miki?" Dominia demanded of the dentist. "Before you positioned yourself with Kahlil?"

"Hunters only use specific medical-care providers... It was not difficult to have the boy assigned to me. He is far from our only source of information about the goings-on of your Father's world, and the Red Market. Our intelligence indicates Miki has been groomed to sell her soul to these harpies for half a decade. Documentation regarding the search for the Lady's new avatar goes back further, almost a century. Your Father may claim to be psychic, or have his sacrilegious Lamb, or demonstrate immortality beyond the lifetime of even God's universe: but all I need is a cup of coffee and a morning to review some print-outs, and I know the plans of all my enemies by the time the sun is up."

"And you?" Again, Dominia stared down Kahlil; now she got him to speak.

"I wanted to save Miki," the young man said, his tone miserable. "But they came too late."

"On the contrary. Just in time. But, you have always had a bad habit of putting women above the cause, eh? God's coincidence brought her in to me, rather than forcing me to do backflips to get her number out of you"—Dominia's mind cycled through all the background coincidences that had occurred in Basil's presence and, perhaps due to his absence in her time of need, blamed the magician for the broken tooth that had brought Miki to this hateful dentist—"but I suspect you, Kahlil, were a pawn in the Red Market's game from the start! She began using you the second you met, in hopes of becoming the leader of a cult! That same cult assigned her to you long after the first time you engaged their services, didn't they? Because they learned your value."

At the boy's speechless expression, the man ranted on. "They intended to use you to get to me. They knew who I was and wanted to see me killed—wanted to use Miki Soto to gain intelligence on my security, or blackmail me. But they did not understand that I know their ways. They are not some innocent ring of prostitutes, whose morals are already of question. They are sacrilegious cultists—heretics, Kahlil, who wish me dead. In fact, seeing this carnage now, I suspect they meant to kill me this very night. But"—Tobias grinned—"they failed, because I had you."

"I just—" Humiliated to speak before the room on this strange web of conspiracy, Kahlil turned pleading eyes to the one person capable of understanding him: Dominia. "I tried to be her friend."

For once, Akachi's voice was solemn. "And now she is dead."

"Yes," said the boy, softer, his head turning in the direction of the escape tunnel through which the Lady was carried. "Now she's dead."

Tobias nodded sadly and, from his cloak, once more withdrew his gun. "I think it's kindest for me to send you with her."

Though, at the first flash of black metal, the General charged, a martyr was not faster than a bullet without entering the Void. Over the next year, hardly a twenty-four-hour cycle would pass in which, like the tragedy at McLintock Farm, Kahlil's death would not replay itself. In those moments, she would demand to know of herself why she had not learned enough by then to slip into the Void in a wink and cross that room in the second it might take to save his life. Why had she not already two thousand years, infinite years', experience of the sort had by her Father, which taught him to slip in and out of the Ergosphere like it was a coat? Somehow, it seemed her fault, that gap, though she knew this false every time she remembered the shock in the boy's exhausted eyes—as if death had woken him up, right before putting him out forever. Hail, Saint Valentinian. The shock on Kahlil's face would never leave it, much as that image would never leave her mind: it clicked into place next to Benedict's savaged body, where it lay with the McLintocks and sweet Cassandra in the section of her brain devoted to only its most haunting traumas. While the General froze with her hands in the air at the pointing of a hundred guns, Akachi shook his head.

"I despise traitors to the cause of humankind." The dentist holstered his gun. "And I cannot stand the thought of an organization of men who do not know what they want."

"You're a real bastard." Tears filled Dominia's eyes to see that same blood that coated her now oozed from Kahlil's dark curls. "He was a kid."

"The most dangerous kind of kid: one with information about us! As readily as he sold out the Lady, I do not think he can be trusted; at any rate, he has made it clear his loyalty is not with me, but with a dead woman."

"Miki lives. She lives in eternity. And Kahlil—" She had not seen him there, but, blinking rapidly, she insisted, "He's there, too. I don't care if he wasn't a Lazarene. I'm sure he had to be there. He was just some kid—oh, you *bastard*."

"Then perhaps you can come along with me, Miss Mephitoli, and tell me about it."

A pair of Hunters restrained her arms while a third attached one of the silver shock collars that were, in her native lands, a capital offense for humans to possess. The dentist made his way down the stairs to smile into Lazarus's face even as the mystic experienced the same treatment. "I think, more than any secret resentment or love, Kahlil came to me because he saw this was inevitable—because the good Lord chose to work through him, to give his soul a chance at redemption. The state of the world is not a sustainable one. Your kind have seen to that."

"Then why not join forces with the Lady?" asked the General. Behind them, men shouted for the women to clear away from the doors.

"Because the moral element is the only thing that elevates humans above martyrs." She had been taught similar things about martyrs, but did not respond as the windbag carried on. "The Whore's Market demands of its women a relinquishment of morals that is irreconcilable with the state of humanity. At best, they require reeducation. At worst, they are unsalvageable objects."

"What happened to all that garbage about the burden of sin being on the John, not on the prostitute?"

The cherry-picking dentist chuckled, his tone dark. "The sale of a body is one thing, but the worship of a golden calf is another. The Market would see this world turned into a global Sodom and Gomorrah; She speaks of balance, but we are those who wish to maintain the balance set in place by God."

"I've heard Hunters keep sex slaves." Her lip curled. "At least martyrs don't rape their property. Not in a way that's socially or legally acceptable, anyway—your kind seems to love it. Is that part of your balance?"

Infuriatingly, Tobias spread his hands. "It is the nature of the Abrahamian religions, and of God, to allow the keeping of slaves. We are all God's slaves, General. That is a point on which your people and I can agree."

"Then what distinguishes humans from martyrs?"

"God did not allow the existence of martyrs. That was a mistake made by man, for which we are rightly punished: but as we caused the problem, so, too, is it ours to solve."

She would have liked to argue all night, but the General was pulled down the hall to see, with a streak of pain, that men defaced with chisels those elaborate tableaux lining the halls. Where was the magician, for God's sake!

"Is this honestly necessary?" She related more to her Father every second, felt him bubble up inside her like tar as the slumping effects of the drug tightened her skin so her anger was quicker to rise. "Do you need to destroy beautiful things while taking innocent lives?"

"There is nothing beautiful here, General. Only sacrilegious icons of a false god that must, for the spiritual sake of humanity, be destroyed. Though, if you are going to react so strongly to mere carvings, it is a good thing we got your collar on before we reached the garden!"

Pale with indignity, the General turned helpless eyes toward Lazarus, who did not say a word. As they were dragged outside by their captors, bile rose in her throat. One at a methodical time, Hunters shattered the garden's statues to acquire the encrypted drives that, as Miki must have (stupidly, stupidly, oh-so stupidly) spilled to Kahlil, contained data on all of the Red Market women at a global scale. "In all fairness," the dentist said, "your teeth were beautiful works of art that were nothing to destroy. They were not even given a chance to do their jobs! But a blip on my radar and a few moments of chatter to mark your arrival to Cairo was all I needed. Good thing Miss Soto felt so comfortable with Kahlil. Or feels, rather—one had ought not encourage children to play pretend, so far as I'm concerned. 'The Lady.'" Tobias laughed, as did one of his men. It was this man who the General murdered by snapping his neck, a hollow kill to vent her fury for the annihilation of all this beauty that left her feeling worse. The dentist tightened his hand, and the switch secreted in his palm shocked not just Dominia but Lazarus.

"Behave yourself, please, General. Tranquilizers don't grow on trees, and it is not a short drive to Jerusalem."

If she clenched her jaw any harder, she might have bitten off her own tongue. After the statues were brutalized and the stocks of the palace pillaged with nary a police officer or military official in sight ("Because they understand we do them a service," the vile dentist explained), the martyrs were dragged through the front entrance and to the assortment of waiting T1-63 Rs. Dominia and Lazarus were pushed into the back of one along with three of their armed captors; Tobias remained outside with a mocking salute.

"How I would love to stay and chat, General—but that would be asking for trouble! Never fear. I'll be right behind you."

The vehicle's doors slammed shut, its engine roared to life, and, in a profusion of smoke and disappointment, the *tanque* set off on a course for Jerusalem. As good as alone for all the English the remaining three Hunters chose to speak, Dominia addressed the mystic.

"Why didn't you say something about this?"

"Are you going to ask me that when you stub your toe from now on, too?"

She managed a scoff to communicate but a molecule of her thundering astonishment at his attitude. "People *died*, Lazarus. I'd think that would bother you."

"And of all the people in that room, who killed the most? You, no question. If I had a problem with death, I'd have a problem with you."

Fair enough. Still, she couldn't take responsibility, lest her thoughts writhe into that sorrowful anxiety that, vibrating across her mind, almost paralyzed her now that her expertise in battle was restrained by the collar. Without that expertise available, the drug had nothing on which to focus her consciousness. Its effects were now free-floating and unpleasant. Far better to find someone else to blame. Far easier— and more relieving—to rail against the absent magician.

"Where is Valentinian? He was here, right?"

"Yes." An approving smile lifted the edge of Lazarus's mouth. "Yes, he was here. Thank you."

Though that settled her a bit, it didn't stop her. "Well—where the hell *is* he? You mean he just buzzed off when things got hot? What good is a magician if he disappears during battle?"

"What good is a magician if he's been stabbed to death?"

"Oh, he's not going to be stabbed to death; he's a martyr." With a wave of furious dismissal, Dominia crossed her arms and pushed herself farther into the corner to distance herself from their captors. "Not only that, but he's supposed to be a great magician! A bona fide Saint! Why couldn't he have stuck around and magicked us some armor, or a weapon, or—oh, no!"

The memory of her gun arose with that same bitter disappointment that always spawned on the recognition of a lost object. In it lay echoes of that horror, that shame, when she found it absent along with her wife. Now, Cassandra was with her, a cold crystal at rest upon her heart; and the gun, a priceless treasure many centuries older than its owner, and a tool on which the General relied for ages, was lost. But, it had been lost before. Anything was possible, some hopeful part of her reminded the rest.

That rest, bleak and annoyed, shouted the optimistic sliver down until it was no longer clear whether it existed. Despite the Lady's speech, things lost never seemed to return. Those who absented themselves tended to remain absent.

"Look"—the mystic rested against the black headrest of the vehicle—"I know it's a tough day for you."

"Excuse me?"

"An understatement, I know. But someday you'll feel about these memories the way I do about them now, so try to hang on to that. It's not as long of a drive as Akachi thinks, you'll come to agree. And, we're not actually having to drive it. Or walk. Again."

Speaking of walking. "The minute they let us into the sun, we'd ought to make ourselves scarce."

"Wouldn't that be nice? But these things auto-shock if they lose contact with the skin before they're shut down. That means when you start to disappear, it shocks you into staying. Even if that weren't true, there's no point to our vanishing, because Akachi will follow us. Hell, he's already there. Consider this. Subjective time here is best measured by steps taken in that other place; as we already discussed, different directions lead to different...fates, effectively. Like, imagine each fate's juncture point as an invisible peg. You trail a string behind you—"

"I fucking get it," snapped the General, sick of having things explained to her by the magician, let alone anyone who wasn't the magician.

"Sorry. I know, I just need to make sure you're with me, because it's important to understand that, as soon as our position is observed, there's no going back. Until then, you can alter the weaving by backtracking to your starting point, or returning to a previous juncture and taking a different route. When you get to reality again, it's like nothing happened—no time passed—or what happened was something different than what would have otherwise occurred—alternative time passed. This is even true if you travel in a group. But during this period of alternative time in reality, if another soul enters the Ergosphere with his own string attached to him from his own starting point, there is the possibility that he will meet another, or a group of others, along his journey. Then, the strings get tangled. Observation means that the positions of our...molecular souls, say, are now locked in. You know, like a waveform collapse... Sorry, I don't mean to overexplain." He saw the look on her face, though, in fairness, its tension arose largely from the simple act of trying to conceptualize this business in a firsthand way. The LSD helped her understand it in an emotional, visceral manner, but trying to intellectually recount and understand it felt like trying to retain a thought in the Ergosphere. It grew easier as Lazarus continued. "Anyway, from that point on, going backward in the Void to your apparent starting point will only take you back to your geographical starting point; it's all forward in linear time, unless you return to the initial point of observation."

"Assuming you don't get tangled up in anybody else's thread before then."

"Exactly," said Lazarus, as another nasty epiphany churned the General's stomach.

"Is that why my Father checks in on me every night? Because he's—solidifying time to make sure we can't go back?"

Perhaps it was the drug, and the way it cleft the Void, the darkness of the *tanque*, and the General's spirit; perhaps it was years of indoctrination. All the same, Dominia heard her Father's voice in her head; she seemed to sit in his dream-study while the disfigured *tulpa* thrashed in the shadows behind his chair.

"Certainty of an educated decision"—her Father spoke in words she had not heard him say during that moment, which made it seem more than mere memory—"is the hallmark of intellectual maturity. Certainty of a rash decision is the hallmark of stupidity. Uncertainty of any decision is the death of power. I try only to empower you, Dominia."

"That's basically what he's doing, yeah," Lazarus continued, oblivious to either a vivid figment of her imagination or a genuine connection to the Void. Perhaps due to the molecule, the latter seemed probable to the General. Indeed, she sought to feel herself in that chair, finding it preferable to the seat of the *tanque*, and tried to stoke her imagination like a sun into which she was tempted to step could she but find a way: yet it appeared for all the world that it stepped out of her. There was her Father in the empty seat beside Lazarus, hands folded between his knees as the mystic said, "But your Father has many motives besides that."

"Like what?" asked Dominia, focused on that figure who, in turn, set unmoving black eyes upon her. More than imagined, perhaps?

"Like luring you into his service. Getting you to betray me."

"How easily you could kill them all, Dominia," said the Hierophant, or his figment, or the General's own bitterness given by her mind a most appropriate shape. "They have no idea."

"How could he hope to do that? He can't give me anything I want."

"He can give you what you think you want, or what you think is good enough. What looks like what you want, what seems like what you want."

"Take the gun of the man to your left and shoot the one to my right, and by the time the fellow over there hits the button, you're upon him. You can fight through the pain long enough to see him dead."

"What do you think I want?"

Lazarus did not answer.

"Then, it's a simple matter of the driver. And if the mystic tries to stop you, kill him, too."

"What?" she asked sharply of the fancy. To cover herself, she turned her scrutiny upon Lazarus. "What—what do you think I want, please?"

"I think you want to be happy for once," said Lazarus.

Dominia's mouth opened in a jolt of emotional turmoil. Ashamed she had been angry enough to let him in and hear his ill thoughts of her friend, the General glanced to the place she imagined her Father.

The seat was empty.

XIV

O Vas Nobile

Though the figure vanished, and the LSD wore off six hours into the drive (following a miserable, sweaty, three-hour comedown), that was not the last Dominia was to hear of her Family over the next week. Quite the opposite: having been out of the news loop for what was technically over a month, much had happened beyond her awareness. This became apparent when, around the time the acid relinquished her state of mind but not the impossibly tight muscles of her neck, the driver flipped on the radio and tuned through the stations as if prompted by the rising of the sun. As the man said something in the (at the time, dying) language of Farsi, Lazarus snorted, and Dominia glanced at him out of—not curiosity, so much as obligation. The curiosity ship sailed with her last bit of energy.

"Tobias told him to make sure you hear the news," he explained. As the General rolled her eyes, the driver settled on a station whose distinguishing feature was its use of English. Specifically, a familiar, nasally form of English, spoken by her useless baby brother, Theodore del Medico.

"And just who are these people complaining about my administration, anyway?" he asked a boisterous crowd, having (apparently within days of his term as Governor of the United Front) dropped all pretense of being a professional in favor of off-the-cuff banter with his audience—flavored by a dash of fearmongering. "I'd say they were humans, but it's not just humans, is it, ladies and gentlemen? After all, there are humans here—the good sort, you know, who can see the bigger picture because they were raised in the Front and understand its culture. No: the problem comes from the west—or the Far East, if you'd rather—and brings with it habits, customs, needs that threaten to divide us as a people. And are we not one people, citizens? Are we not United? One nation, under God, indivisible!"

This was a violation of her rights as a sentient being. Theodore's voice was an audible war crime so piercing in its obnoxious emphasis that it was close to impossible to block him out. Last time, when she heard his voice in that holo-vision, she had managed the feat of tolerating it; but now, with her mental faculties burned out from nine hours of high-speed whirring, she couldn't find anything else to think about—certainly nothing preferable—and was forced to listen as the resounding applause of the audience reduced again to her baby brother's drone.

"There are those who have condemned my treatment of these illegal aliens as too harsh, but I say I am not harsh enough! They point to the news stories about kids in cages like I'm some monster, when the reality is these people come to our nation half the time specifically to destroy it, to rend us apart and foment dissatisfaction among you good and wholesome citizen. We are *protecting* their children, and we are controlling *them* by funneling them into registered neighborhoods—while still doing them the decency of allowing them to live here, mind! But that's never good enough for a group as entitled as that.

"They would have you think your nation, your government—your Holy Father!—doesn't care for you. They come to take food from our mouths and money from our wallets all so they'll be ready to rise against us on that fatal night. Some extremists, I have heard, even wish to"—his voice dropped—"euthanize the children of martyrs! Some of these immigrants might be good people"—this was added in such a half-assed way that Dominia and Lazarus made eye contact before the former rolled her eyes—"since China, India, and the Risen Sun are so tightly packed, along with the rest of Asia; but far more of them come farther, from the Middle States, or have been indoctrinated with the values of the Hunters' South American branch. We can take no risks. Our Adaptation Centers have already reduced crime and improved the living conditions of our true citizens beyond measure. It is our hope that by isolating those individuals who we believe to have come to sew dissent, we will sort out the good apples and set our future citizens on the path to right living."

Yes, having one's children taken away while one is made to labor on a fodder plantation will do that. Especially when said fodder is sent to the same concentration camps (sorry, "Adaptation Centers") where the children were staying. If they were (un)lucky, some compassionate martyrs were browsing the aisles right now, looking for a son or a daughter the way humans looked for puppies.

Once, when young, she had believed all that about dissenters, or lunatics planning to euthanize martyr children (though, in fairness, that was a genuine concern on occasions when Hunter cells found balls enough to attack a lesser town with a small martyr population). She had also once believed, quite wholeheartedly, that all humans were scum. Food at best, half-formed martyrs at worst, she had perceived them for the first 150 years of her life as filthy animals full of hate and resentment. But, over a long period of time, she found her opinion changing, and this was before her encounter with Benedict. Her nagging sense of wrongness about her lifestyle culminated in that moment with her Father's total disinterest in even paying lip service to his appreciation for her. He would say or do anything to get her to obey him, believe in him, kill for him—except respect her. She recognized with that simple brush-off—still recognized, every time she thought of it—that she was as much an object to him as every human he had ever killed, and he would kill her the way he had killed all his children. The way he had enacted so many deaths.

That's the kind of realization from which it takes twenty years of cold isolation to recover. By the time the General met Cassandra after a final, four-year spray of battles, she had been ready to eschew her speciesist perceptions forever.

Yet, it was so tempting—*easy*, too—to consider falling back into the trap of old, bigoted beliefs. Locked in a rumbling box with the same

Hunters who, during a religious ceremony, invaded a palace, killed a score of unarmed women, and destroyed every work of beauty on the property, it was hard to remember there were good humans in the world. But—poor Kahlil's face emerged behind her eyes countless times. The issue of the Hunters was not an issue of humanity. The hacker had been human, and so were the women cut down in the throne room.

Was this the natural state of humanity, this struggle of mankind against mankind? Or was it perhaps the state of consciousness, which struggled between the species for fear of those foreign traits that rendered unrecognizable its own divided identity? Problems of race, gender, religion, and geographic location had plagued humanity since the dawn of time. Consciousness could make an argument of anything just for the sake of having an argument.

The radio prattled throughout the drive, occasionally relenting to Arabic and Farsi stations as the men checked the weather or took advantage of a break in the English broadcast to listen to a few songs. She hung on to those details because they made her think of the men as people, rather than things or animals, which was how her Father had conditioned her to think of them for the majority of her life. But, ah, was it not tempting—would it not have been easier—to cut their throats, as she had cut the throats of all those crude men in the temple?

No—that was the Hierophant. When she peeled her Father's conditioning from her honest opinions, the General uncovered, to her surprise, a wellspring of shame: as if she'd lifted a rock to allow the expulsion of some boiling geyser. Those men she'd killed may have been wretched—may have joined the Hunters knowing their lives would meet a bloody end at some martyr's hand—but Dominia could no longer shake the notion they had once been children, with hopes and dreams and mother and fathers. They were not always cruel and evil. No one was born a rapist, were they? But, if the world happened over and over again, was it not true that the seed of evil lay dormant in the growing mind, perhaps expanded backward to the newborn, the way the newborn expanded forward through time? Then there must lay seeds of good in equal measure. Why should Dominia, mere gardener, have blamed herself for turning over soil that decided to germinate asphyxiating weeds, rather than sunflowers?

How difficult to find consolation! Perhaps it was the acid. Perhaps, even more, it was the ceremony. The difficulty may also have rested in the notion that she once again had two eyes. Did she deserve them? And her teeth: By Elijah, what made her special? She had killed many more than those men had, and been crueler, too. She liked to look down on the Hunters for their misogyny, but Dominia had been, at times, a misogynist. Her soul was not clean of striking Cassandra any more than Cassandra's spirit was clean of striking her.

Was it the Hunters who were so repellent? The humans? Or was it all those undesirable traits of herself that the Hunters forced her to see by reflection? Their behavior was the logical conclusion of her own. A caricature. Was she not as bad as her Father, playing his game of Holier-Than-Thou?

"I wish you would tell me where that fucking magician is," she snapped at Lazarus somewhere during the fourth rebroadcast of Theodore's speech. This time it was with Arabic translations at which the Hunters jeered, nudged the General with their rifles, or, most appallingly, spat at her feet. "Not all humans," she reminded herself in silent ad nauseam until her irritation found outlet on Lazarus. The old man hardly opened his eyes, being exhausted as she and still just as sleepless due to the stimulant effects of the drug.

"I can't. Takes all the fun out of it when the rabbit pops out of the hat."

"But he's coming back?"

"I need you to have faith."

"And I need you to stop saying that."

"Well? It's true. I know, inquiring mind. You're desperate to know everything all the time. But the fact of the matter is that, sometimes, you can't."

"Is he in the Void?" she pressed, which elicited from Lazarus a groan.

"I don't know. Maybe."

"The Kingdom?" When he didn't respond, she kept going. "If he's in the Kingdom, I can find him. I'm sure that—"

His eyes opened, words as contorted by annoyance as his face. "Look, kid! I don't know where he is. Now that you've put him on Earth, he's got work to do. So do we. Having a shitty attitude isn't going to help. Jesus! How can somebody take acid and see something like that and just be so—pissy?"

"Oh, I'm *sorry*! Maybe I'm rattled after having had the whole thing interrupted by a bunch of fucking—" The humans were staring; the word she had almost used, "bits" (a reference to early asteroid mining), was a derogatory term understood across most languages despite its archaic origins. She closed her eyes to do some deep breathing before continuing in Mephitolian.

"I am having a challenging year. And this week has been, in particular, very hard. So please, Lazarus. I'm trying. I don't get the so-called benefit of having lived this before."

With an exhalation of his own, Lazarus squinted through the slit window. "I know. I'm sorry. I do have trouble remembering that sometimes. You have no idea how tired I am of all this."

"As tired as I am?"

A small smile touched the corner of his mouth as he looked back at her. "Maybe not." Blessedly, the *tanque* screeched to a halt. "Look, Dominia: I need you to keep this in mind for me. Valentinian has a lot to do, and not a lot of time to do it, which seems sort of weird, but it's true. If he spent his time here helping us, when you can help more adequately than he could—I mean, not only would that be a waste of resources, but certain things that need to happen might not be able to happen. I need you to believe in him, and I need you, whatever happens, to also believe in me."

"'Whatever happens,'" she repeated lamely, the words rolling over her tongue with distaste as the black doors of the *tanque* were thrown open. Light exploded in with such immense fury that she did, just for a second, feel it in her soul like the chilling dissolution of the acid. But Lazarus was right: she was hyperaware of her neck, of the tension of the collar around it and of her own furious desire to stay and throttle every man around; those things, like leaden weights, restrained the coming of the Void. Just as well. She didn't want to risk bumping into that useless magician, anyway. He needed to do what needed doing, she supposed—whatever the hell that was—but she was no less sore about the matter. It felt not unlike her parents' abandonment, and because of that, Dominia did not allow the hope that she could be saved by anybody but herself.

And then—then there was another small detail that, as she was yanked from the van, encouraged her to force awareness of the Earth beneath her feet and focus her consciousness on staying grounded despite the intensity of the vibrations in her body: as that darkness of the Void trembled in, so, too, had a strange series of terrible screams. In her periphery, there writhed gray shapes that could not assemble themselves into a form before her because she had not entered that bizarre, quasi-imaginary space. In those seconds in which she was exposed to the clamor, however, her mind tried to make sense of it. Amid the screams, she was able to discern, in languages her physical ear could not understand, a spray of agonized questions—"Where is Jerusalem?" "Where is God?" "What has happened to me?"—before her body was set before smiling Dr. Akachi.

"Hello again, Miss Mephitoli! And good Lazarus. I trust your journey was not too uncomfortable? It is not complete yet, I admit, but I expect—or hope—that you will find the last leg more bearable, being, as you are, with me."

"If only my Father were here! Then it'd be a real party."

"Be careful what you wish for, Miss Mephitoli! But that is unlikely. Our nation's defense is top of the line, and our base camp changes its many locations often, even in the course of one year, to evade his attention. Oh, every now and then he gets a valid piece of information, but I do not expect he will ever be able to find all of us. Certainly not at once. I suppose we are rather like cockroaches that way!"

"Your words, not mine." She squinted across the desert as her long-time dark-adjusted eyes adapted to the light. All around swelled the (oddly comforting) sensations of a ramshackle military encampment: trucks rumbling hither and thither, men practicing their shots in the clear morning air, boots on the ground, and the overall clank-and-clamor of energy. "It's a lucky thing I had you remove my DIOX-I, huh? For you, I mean."

"Oh, goodness, no! Lucky for you. After all, had you not volunteered, I planned to yank it out when next we met!"

The more merrily he laughed, the more Dominia wished to grind his face in the dirt with her uncuffed, perfectly free hands: but she knew that he—and one or two others with auxiliary remotes—hoped she would do exactly that. Instead, as was apparently in vogue, she spat upon the dirt. "I'll keep that in mind when I get you alone."

As the handful of nearby men who spoke English laughed along with the dentist, another pair pulled up in a light utility vehicle: unarmed and intended for reconnaissance or speedy transport, as opposed to the heavy-duty operations of a *tanque*. While the men climbed out, Akachi said, "Then you may be excited to know you are about to have an opportunity to do just that! There is something I would love to show you."

That was never a good thing. Time to find excuses. "And I'd love to come along, but this sunlight—I know the collar is keeping me here, but I feel like my body might fade off at any minute."

"Oh, Miss Mephitoli, of course! Never fret: we have a very advanced piece of technology to keep the blue light from your eyes and prevent you from being swept away to the end of time." Turning, the dentist said something in Arabic, and the man to whom he had spoken produced a pair of sunglasses. He handed these to Dominia with a shit-eating grin.

"You know"—she turned the glasses over before putting them on, as if in search of their anthrax coating—"if I didn't have this collar, I'd kill you with these." But, it was true. The sunglasses did stabilize her. Akachi was getting in the truck; with a helpless glance in the direction of Lazarus to find him silent, she asked, "What about him?"

"Lazarus will remain here at camp with my men."

At last, Lazarus spoke. "I can't do anything for your men."

"Now, that is simply not true! But, you need not fear. I know your blood is the most precious commodity this Earth has to offer. Gold, diamonds, coal, oil: all good as lead next to the blood of Lazarus. Killing you—as, say, desires the Hierophant—well, that is a shortsighted idea!"

"Not as shortsighted as giving my blood to people who shouldn't have it."

"Now, I think it is fair to say that if someone drinks your blood in this world, they have earned it! The good Lord would not have made the action capable of happening in the future if it were unacceptable to Him in the past and present. All things in the world of men are precisely as they need be at the given moment: all the damned are damned and all the righteous are righteous, and nothing can be done to deviate these game pieces from the colors God wills them to take."

Now it was the mystic's turn to be annoyed. "That's right. I forgot about your position on free will. How it's all an illusion. You think that because you don't have any, yourself."

"How fascinating it will be to talk to you, and learn what else you've forgotten about me!"

"Well"—the mystic stared down the dentist who was, in the end, little more than a human—"I remember how you die."

For but a second—a sweet, gratifying second Dominia drank like the Hierophant's wine—Tobias's mouth opened without a sound. The eyes behind his sunglasses even widened a hair. Bit by bit, he recovered and tried to laugh as though it did not bother him. He settled on an uncharacteristically tight smile. "Perhaps I will make you tell me about it so I can dodge this fate, eh?"

"How can you?" asked Lazarus, so dryly it was the General's turn to laugh. "You think free will is an illusion."

Again, that mouth opened; one of the English-speaking men glanced at the talkative dentist with his eyes narrowed until Akachi turned to him with an Arabic snap. As he and a few other men collected Lazarus, the dentist told him they would speak later. He leveled his gaze with Dominia's.

"Now, please, Miss Mephitoli, tell me you will accept my invitation of a drive. It is not long. Only a few hours. I think it important you see Jerusalem."

"Yes." She glanced at Lazarus as he was dragged away, her ears filling with the memory of screams. "I think it's important, too."

In mild relief, the dentist smiled again. "I am glad you agree. I am sorry—I did intend to remove your collar as a sign of respect, but I am afraid"—that laugh was yet a little warbling, a little unsteady— "your friend's commentary does rather have an effect on a man's mind!"

"Probably the smarter choice," agreed the General, tapping the metal device and fancying for the sensitivity of her cells that static built within them. Perhaps that was part of the reason for her foul mood. "But it is incredibly uncomfortable."

"Well, in the long-term we can discuss removing it. I suppose it depends on the changeability of your mind."

As the dentist patted the empty seat of the vehicle, the General evaded a man who intended to drag her over and made her way to the passenger's seat. With that ever-cheery mien set in place, Tobias resurrected the engine with the push of a button and advised her, "Be sure of your seat belt!"

How difficult it was to avoid saying anything to him! But, engaging him in conversation was a trap. The Hierophant had his way of goading people when in an outrageous mood, but it was Cicero who exhibited this quality on the regular: yet, even he, who had not so much as spared a teenage student from his taunting (the bitterness of youth's lost battles no doubt stoked the flames of future battles won, for whatever that was worth), failed to approach the soulless nature of Tobias's so-called cheer. Her relatives' laughter, even at the evilest of circumstances and the blackest of jokes, had seldom been anything but pure; and, in the case of the Hierophant, it had often been the gay laughter of a man who, one needed grudgingly admit, was of extraordinary intelligence and no meager stock of wisdom.

Tobias's laughter was patronizing. This was a man who believed the world was a pit of fools, and not in the harmless way Miki did. The Hierophant's laughter was the laughter of a man who waited for the world to teach him something new, and reveled in it, greeting each new piece of information with an excitement comparable to a child's. Akachi's laughter was the hollow sound of a man who waited to die, because he thought he already knew everything and scorned the notion that he didn't.

"So"—Dominia couldn't resist engaging him for the entire two-hour length of the drive—"how do you think you're going to die?"

"Trying to get into my head, are you, Miss Mephitoli? Good. That means I am already in yours. But, if you must know, I expect I will lose my life in a battle of some kind, like so many of my men. I can only hope by the grace of God that it will be a battle in His name, which glorifies Him and secures my place in the afterlife."

"You know what the afterlife is, though, right? Souls? The Ergosphere?" Burned out from the LSD, which had never quite elevated her drug experience from "vaguely uncomfortable" into "psychedelic trip," the General could not explain what had been so comprehensible when in the Void or influenced (however mildly) by the foreign molecule. Instead of trying to grope her way through an argument whose firsthand meaning she had lost, she settled on, "You're already saved, through Lazarus's blood."

"Blasphemy! That is pure and simple blasphemy. I forgive you for saying such a thing, but I must ask you to refrain from insisting on it in my presence. It is offensive to my spirit, Miss Mephitoli."

Was it possible for a person who had drunk of Lazarus's blood to be so corrupted their soul no longer sensed the truth? Or was he right, as he went on to insist, "The mysteries of God cannot be made known to us in this life. Once upon a time, the true Church kept the mysteries of Christ for Man, and by meditation on these mysteries and the acts of the sacraments, the soul could hope to transcend purgatory after death. Men of all stripes have meditated on this subject in all ways, and on achieving revelations from small to great, unique genetic markers are activated. The blood of Lazarus activates all these markers, along with many others whose uses we cannot yet explain. The Lord may allow the consumption of blood by the masses for now, General, but the cults that imbibe it are becoming as dangerous as the so-called Church of your Father. Soon God will see fit to smite them for their insolence. Then it will be a return to the old ways, when humbled human men and women understood that the mysteries of the divine should be kept for the afterlife. For mankind to insist that they are intelligible is not only blasphemous: it is dangerous!"

"Aren't you the guy in charge of the organization who says murdering martyrs is God's will? Aren't you talking to me about God's will and intentions right now?"

"There is *only* God's will, Miss Mephitoli, which is revealed over time. Not yours or mine. Even the will of your so-called magician friend is but a dream!" The General clenched her teeth at the thought of Valentinian but tried to find solace in the obvious anxiety he caused Akachi to provoke these semi-frequent mentions. "I find myself thus, and thus, it is God's will. Just as it is God's will you should be here with me; just as, I am sure, it is God's will you will come around to seeing things my way."

"Dubious" didn't begin to describe the General's attitude, or even her facial expression as, during the long, dusty drive to Jerusalem, Tobias proceeded to lecture her on everything from the inherently sinful nature of martyrs to the barbarous war crimes her kind had committed. "You, yourself," was a phrase which oft punctuated the monotonous drone, and it was, truth be told, the only thing that kept the General awake after the first hour. Now she was truly over the effects of the drug, worn from her battle, and growing famished. Not to mention drained by the unfamiliar heat of the sun, which, while no longer fatal, had already left her so sunburned she seemed to have laid her face on an iron.

The slightly worse part was the traffic as they approached the city. The highways snarled across one another to account for a populace whose size had grown completely out of bounds of the original, meager imaginings of its long-dead planners. In fact, the boundary of Jerusalem, she heard amid all his rambling, had technically been reached an hour into their drive. If they wished to hit the center of the city, it would, at this time of day, take three or even four hours. This was not an uncommon problem in that night and age: Dominia's long-missed San Valentino had, in the United Front's ancient nights, been a conglomerate of several cities that had merged together over time, proximity and environmental pressure—not to mention social laziness. It was easier to refer to the massive areas as one sprawling unit and the individual, former cities within as secondhand townships when one didn't know the area or didn't care. Had the General been driving Tobias on a courtesy tour of San Valentino before murdering him, for instance, she would not have bothered pointing out the boundaries of the counties within, like where San Francisco let out to San Jose or where that became Modesto; nor would she even touch the small boroughs within those. This was in part because he would not retain the knowledge posthumously, but mostly because he had no frame of reference for it. Maybe if he'd read Steinbeck. Doubtful.

However, Tobias did not show similar courtesy. He was too in love with the sound of his own voice to be stopped from naming every part of his city in agonizing detail, and explaining, until her slumping head was barely supported by her hand, how his cell was encamped in an area not far from what was once called Be'er Sheva. Once a jewel of its nation, it had been rechristened by the predominantly Arabic-speaking Hunters "Bi'ir as-Sab" and, from what Dominia could tell, had been trampled by the terrorist presence like the carpet of a Front farmer who wore his shoes indoors. As Tobias began to explain the city's name meant "Seven Wells" (or "Lion's Well," depending), Dominia groaned in frustration.

"I know! I know about Be'er Sheva. I've read the fucking Bible. Somebody swore some oath over water there, or something. Jacob had his vision of the ladder when he left it."

"That is good! Then you will understand God has been here since the dawn of time. Since long before the state of Israel, and the founding of Jerusalem! His design is such an intricate one that He understood someday Jerusalem would explode to stretch as far as the Seven Wells, you see? That is why this country has always been holy, has always been contested."

"'The Promised Land,'" suggested the General dryly, unwilling to humor the hypocritical rantings of the most boring man on earth. "Yeah, I get it. But what about your spiritual promised land? Is this all there is to you? Earth, then death? And what's going on with death, then?" Somehow she'd not only gotten into a religious debate, she'd revealed to herself, by total accident, that she was developing beliefs of her own.

"Only at the true end of the world, upon the second coming of Christ, will the gates of Paradise open. For someone who claims to have read the Bible, I am surprised you do not know that! But that mistake you have just made, that dangerous mistake, is why I have brought you here.

"I am not an unfair man, Miss Mephitoli. Unlike your Father, I do not believe in punishing the ignorant for crimes they have not known themselves to commit. Quite the opposite. Minds can be changed, because they are only human, and God's truth is law! The highest law is not intelligible to Man."

"The poet William Blake once wrote it is impossible for the truth to be communicated in an intelligible way without being understood."

"I cannot say I have read his work"—of course not—"but he sounds like a heretic."

"Oh, by your standards, he was."

"My standards are God's standards, Miss Mephitoli. The only standards."

"And how do you know what standards are God's if nobody can know the highest truth?"

Tobias took an exit ramp, and they eased into the city in some long-neglected factory district—though, in fairness, what she had seen thus far looked much neglected already, war-torn by the Hunters' thousand-year, on-again-off-again occupation. "His law has been handed down from generation to generation in the form of His book."

"Yeah, thank God we've preserved all those rules about mixing fabrics and selling slaves."

"Indeed! Or else your Father might be at as great a loss as I. How do your people treat human beings who kowtow as 'Renfields' and other forms of servant but as slaves? And these consent, unlike the trafficked or encamped."

The most repugnant person on the planet, Akachi: lecturing her as if she didn't know. He turned the corner into a (fairly harrowing) area of town from which everything was obscured but the towering factories, defunct and appropriated, blotting out the sky to prevent a good look at the breadth of ravaged Jerusalem.

"Will you follow me?" He asked as though it were really a request when they stopped in the dusty parking lot of a seemingly abandoned building. Grinding down her irritation somewhere far beneath her feet, Dominia obeyed only when, to her astonishment, he threw open the doors to reveal the testing facility of a superweapon.

Over the stomping of metallic feet sprinting in seven seconds from one end of the soccer-field-size building to the other, the proud dentist announced, "This is the world's first musculature-unifying suit: the ALIF-8."

"An exoskeleton." Against the northern wall stood an uncanny rack of empty suits that, at eight and a half feet with back legs poised to thunder across the ground with an almost-feline gait, recalled in some ways the articulating mode of the T1-63 R *tanque*; in others, the odious movement of the *tulpa*. As the in-testing device pummeled an already brutalized punching bag, she observed, "I'm surprised it took humans so long to produce something like this. Or surprised it was your kind who developed it, instead of a respectable government."

His eyes, visible as his lenses faded from their sun-exposed state to their indoor one, curled with glee. "Not for want of trying! I am told that, similar to the problems of space flight and the initial visions of the Light Rail, development on most such weapons halted as your Family rose to power."

"Same reason artificial intelligence capable of anything beyond brewing coffee is illegal in Europa and the Front. Can't have anything that might be used against him. Not unless he's developed it, himself, and can maintain control with the flip of a switch."

"Quite right. But now, the only thing preventing countries across the world from developing such technology—aside from the spies and lobbyist traitors he has slipped into the human populations—is slothful fatalism. We are all dying. The planet is poisoned by us; the species is held captive by martyrs. Why not submit to the idea and enjoy our debauched lives while we can? The average man is too busy enjoying himself to contribute to the human race, and those still motivated by the thrill of scientific discoveries are too afraid of provoking your Father to engineer any new military technology not meant for defense.

But, you see, we Hunters have time on our hands, and there is no one to tell us to stop doing what was do. And we are certainly not afraid of your Father."

When, in a brotherly way, Akachi draped an arm around her shoulders, the tensed martyr allowed herself led on a stroll toward the exoskeletons. Closer, its structure was such a mass of wires, hydraulics, and metal bones that it resembled a skinned metal being, as though it were organs, flesh, and—well, a torso and head away from a living entity. "As a military woman, I knew you would respect what you are being shown. I can see you do, I can see it in your eyes! You know what devastation these things could wreak among your people."

Not untrue. The General leaned into the nearest suit and studied a graphene-encased battery pack tucked away within, its power source both surprisingly mobile and only accessible from the front, through the body of the human controlling it. The back was defended by osteoid plates of steel armor, and all pieces were designed in a way that, taken from the *tanque*, made it impact resistant: not even a fall would destroy them. "Martyrs may be swift and sometimes so gifted they seem capable of unholy magic—but, wearing one of these, I could break your hand with a twitch of my own!"

Across the room, a brick shattered in the hand of the testing unit, and the General tried not to roll her eyes or smirk at the image of Tobias choreographing with his men those actions he thought the most menacing. "So I'm supposed to be scared? I'm not leading his army anymore. It's not my problem."

"No, my dear, you are not leading his army. But what is a general without an army, eh? Not much more than the average man or woman!"

"Trying to appeal to my vanity to get me to fight for you?"

"Yes: and to acquire information! I do not expect you will disagree. Your Father took your life! Your life, and your wife."

"Let's not," said Dominia, words arranged through tight lips, "talk about my wife. All right?"

"Just as well: I have one more thing to show to you."

With his unpleasant smile still stupidly in place, Akachi crooked a finger to indicate Dominia should follow him to a door on the left.

This door, in turn, led through a series of others, and the General was forced to stop many times to wait for the dentist or his men to unlock them. As she endured all this, he prattled on, and by the time they reached their destination, she was sickened: not by his words but by what she saw.

"Exo-suits are well and good, Miss Mephitoli, but there are still many problems with the logistics. For instance, one cannot easily smuggle these weapons into any old place! Your Father's favorite city, Elsinore, is a good example: it is enwalled and defended by land, sea, and air, to such an extent that there is perhaps no city more impenetrable upon the face of this Earth. How, then, is mankind to cure the infection of a source that cannot be reached? This problem has plagued me for many years, Miss Mephitoli. Ever since I rose to power. But I mentioned my solution before. When the body cannot send its white blood cells to fight a disease, an infected tooth, or any other trouble—when these white blood cells are simply not enough, what can be done? What must be done? One night, I awoke with a revelation! When the body cannot cure itself, the body goes to a doctor, a dentist such as myself—and what does that doctor usually do? He gives it an injection. He takes an external thing—in this case, the medicine—and injects it into the body. Or perhaps, as in my case, he comes to remove a thing, as if out of nowhere. Like that"—he snapped his thick fingers—"the body is able to once more fight its ailment. We are the medicine, General, but can you guess the doctor?"

As she refused to humor him, and he threw open a door to an external walkway whose bright glare made her grimace even behind her sunglasses, he answered, "Lazarus. His blood is the needle that transports us from one location to another: using that, I realized, it was possible for us to take our weapons into your Father's city."

"How is that? You can't even control how you appear in that place, let alone what objects are in your possession. I'll bet if I went there right now, I'd still have my gun, and that's somewhere on the floor back in Cairo. You can't seriously expect the ALIF-8"—she got the joke as she said it aloud and interrupted herself with a snort. "'Elephant'? What a stretch."

The gratified dentist laughed and annoyingly jostled her shoulders. "Too few people get it here! They just hear the Arabic letter—but, you were saying?"

"I just mean, you can't expect this to work."

"It is true that if I entered the Ergosphere with the suit on my back, it would not follow me. But that proved a solvable problem. Do you understand the chemical process occurring when you step into the sun and are hastened by the Ergosphere?" For a change, he was going overexplain something useful.

"I know some. The CRY gene has been activated and lets us see electromagnetic fields." The General forgot to hate Tobias while infected with scientific enthusiasm. "That's what allows flies and birds to perceive them regularly, right? Magnetic fields of some kind, at least."

"Very good, Miss Mephitoli, very good. Yes, you are seeing electromagnetic fields: others, and your own. I have heard it said that some old men who have traveled back and forth many times can even see them here, just like the birds and flies. And—"

"What I don't understand"—she interrupted him, eager to learn while in the presence of someone willing to explain anything—"is how this function is possible. This is a new sensory experience you're talking about, and in order for the brain to interpret a sense to the mind, it needs an organ—openings in the bone. What organ is it here?"

"That little bundle of nerves in your center, your solar plexus! Didn't they tell you?" They had, in fact. While she almost laughed, he led her to the final room, which consisted primarily of a metal detector. "Your entire body is the opening: your torso, your ribs, the gap between your rib cage and your pelvis. Your body has reinterpreted its relationship with itself, with your mind, and with light. When your newly sensitized CRY genes are exposed to sunlight, energy is carried through the nerves and increases the vibrational frequency of the body, which increases the vibrational frequency of that light. The more directly one looks at the sun, the more energy is transmitted, and the frequency heightens until the absorbed light wavelengths increase past those of x- or even gamma rays. At the peak of this self-generated radioactivity, molecules of the body effectively slip between the Plancks of reality and into the Ergosphere at the end of time, because such high physical vibration and perception is not compatible with material existence in the Lord's world. This is why the process is possible at night—moonlight is still sunlight— but disorienting. It is weak. Much like your half-formed martyr blood, which is an inferior poison beside that of Lazarus. Without Lazarene blood, your martyr molecules, also, are growing excited, but because your CRY gene has not been activated, the increased vibration serves to destroy your body from the inside out in a matter of minutes."

Due to her metal collar, Dominia was guided around the metal detector, although a number of scientists and research assistants stood in line for a routine morning inspection on their way to the office. "If an organ could manage such a thing for an organic body, why should it not be possible for an artificial object? We have machines that hear, and see, or substitute for the parts of us that do those things for our mind. Was it not possible that we could develop a device that excited the molecules of anything, everything, to that same extent? Was it not possible to use the blood of Lazarus to transport even basic matter from one location in space-time to another? After all, that is why it is possible for us to enter the Ergosphere at one location of space-time, and exit it a different location: at the end of time, the black hole envelops and contains all things as the throne of God, and therefore all things are in the same location. A hologram. It is all a matter of tricking the objects—and the hologram—into confusing two separate points in physical space for even a Planck."

As that aforementioned sickness settled upon her empty stomach, Akachi's men dragged open a heavy, lead-lined door to reveal another vast warehouse. Unlike the crowded lab of the ALIF-8s, this room's focus was singular as that of any church: beyond her breath condensing in the cold, her eyes were drawn, not to an altar, but to a gargantuan metal chandelier that, enrobed in wires and panels and glints of golden coil, hung above a similarly ornamented doorframe.

"Congratulations, Miss Mephitoli," said the smiling son of a bitch. "You are the only woman yet to lay eyes on humanity's first teleporter."

All the horrible implications thudded down as he drew her close to the object. The wires around the frame of the vast door twisted like sinews about a glass pipe that ran with auburn fluid she could only assume to be blood. Its color was echoed by that of the apple that sat innocuously upon the threshold. "It has been many centuries since it was difficult to recreate the cells of a specific individual from only a sample. I think your Father has not done this for the martyrs, not because Lazarenes with their blood vials are difficult to catch, but because he does not want to reveal the source of his power. But I have my own source." Tobias drew from beneath his cloak a chain upon which dangled a glass bottle, forever stained rust red. "And it only took a few flakes for us to create a mass supply of the most valuable resource this world has to offer. The travel is not at a superluminal pace: the one regret! This means, much like when we enter the Ergosphere, we lose time. But it still affords a kind of movement that is nonlinear, and far faster than transport by walking from the perspective of those on the journey—not to mention, far more discrete. When the device is fueled and its artificial CRY organs are stimulated by a burst of photons and the carefully measured decay of a radioactive isotope"—he waved a hand and, in the first demonstration by which Dominia was genuinely impressed (and secretly terrified), a doctor threw a switch that blasted the doorway full of flickering light that vanished faster than it appeared, along with the apple—"entrance to the Ergosphere is possible for even an inanimate object."

"But how does it know where to come out?" Her throat had dried at the sight of the emptied doorway, but that may have been the same brief radioactive exposure that stung her eyes. Hopefully the blood of Lazarus had rendered these humans resistant to the radioactivity. "A conscious being who enters the Ergosphere decides where to leave it and looks at the sun, but an object can't do that."

"No. But if one possesses a pair of finely tuned, ultra-accurate quantum computers"—so that was the chandelier—"and activates one, then activates the second at a time proportionate to the distance it takes to travel the Void from the first teleporter to the other, those two locations could be said to be physically the same when the calculations are made to the Planck. Both the same black hole. It was a matter of finding men cleverer than I to research all this, and to teach the doorway to match the coordinates of its photons to those of its specific partner, rather than any other doorway that might, by some happenstance, be active at that same Planck; the ratios of time and distance, I am told, are key in this. And we may thank your Father for the radioactive material the world has dumped on the fair continent of poor, abused Australia, because that was his donation to this project! In a way, you could say it is not the universe or the entity that is being tricked, but the doorway. It thinks its other side is far away! Were you and I to step through and join the apple, we would find ourselves several hours in the subjective future, in my favorite city in the world: Tunis."

"Carthage," she said, frowning. "We have a lot of intelligence about African Hunters assembling there, but the Hierophant's spent the last three hundred years politely avoiding the entire continent while warring with everybody else."

"Because he understands that, were he to go to war with a single country on the continent of Africa, China and most of Asia would leap into the fray. They cannot allow martyrs more land than they already possess; moreover, possession of Africa as well as Europa would allow him to slip a noose around the Middle States in a matter of decades. The right move is to head him off at the pass, as they say."

"You're planning an assault."

"Malta has been a sensitive city ever since your Father claimed it," he said, referring to an island that, like Venezia, had been retrieved from the greedy sea by her Father long after climate change deepened her waters. "Though it trades with human states, it is notoriously overfull of martyrs, and defensive when it comes to outsiders. It will not take much to begin a conflict there: one that will see us invited to Europa's proper shores."

"Then you'll ride your ALIF-8s through the Alps, playing Hannibal Barca."

"Hannibal made a few fatal mistakes: namely, being set against Scipio Africanus, rather than trying to reach him man-to-man. That is why I brought you here today, Dominia. I do not need to elaborate on the implications of this device. We have learned to set them up quickly, and a team of twenty engineers can now produce a working doorway, given the right prefab parts, in roughly twelve hours of assembly. The only problem is one of defense, and ensuring that the second teleporter is not interrupted in its future calculations: always a sticky wicket with teleportation, as science fiction taught us, but that is the nature of the beast! I think the risk is worth it. An endless army of men with guns, bombs, and ALIF-8s funneled through could destroy anything found upon its other side. And there is no reason for you to face them, so far as I can see."

"I don't intend to face them." Her voice was dark as her expression. "But I don't intend to lead them, either."

Irritation strained the dentist's mouth; for emphasis as he spoke, he slipped the glasses from his eyes, using them to gesture like a pointer. "So you will sit and do nothing against your Father? You cannot think this should be sustained!"

"You can't think the world is better off with your Hunters in control."

"You make my ends sound like some vain, cartoonish plan for world domination, my sister. Look at yourself!"

With childlike stomps, he stormed to a nearby table, removed from its cluttered surface a television remote, and flipped on the nearest of several two-dimensional televisions mounted to the walls of the room. The display arranged into a face Dominia knew too well, distinguished from that of the Hierophant's by age, its lack of composure—and its missing right eye, replaced by a custom DIOX-I making no efforts to disguise its nature. The implant, of crimson pupil and black sclera, whipped in all directions regardless of the position of its adopted brother.

"This was recorded yesterday." Tobias rewound the video of El Sacerdote standing at the pulpit of a cathedral in the heart of Mephitoli.

"Sacrilege," Cicero snarled, having abandoned the cultured, European priest of peacetime in favor of a preaching persona closer to the fire-and-brimstone brand on which humans and martyrs of the Front both thrived. "I have heard from the Lord and the Lamb both that there are those among the flock who have the temerity to question our teachings; those who have been, by their own, weak wills, swayed to such extent they now doubt that most evident truth that we martyrs hold so dear. We are God's chosen people, my faithless children, and let you all have no doubt—although I know so many of you, cowards that you are, surely will. Let not the actions of a pathetic terrorist, that coward of all cowards who ran from home to consort with enemy forces, dissuade you from your basic knowledge of the truth! That it is *you*, children, who are on the right side of God, of the Lord, of Christ, of history— you, and not the traitorous bitch who tore out the eye of your own hapless priest! Your own humble servant of the Lord! Will you, children, be so fearful and selfish, so base and animal—so human"—hisses arose— "that you will let the actions of one fool criminal decide the fate of an entire country? Or will you remain as one, a noble cause beneath the eye of God, so when He looks upon the Earth and sees His people standing together, He will know without fail that same truth those few, most virtuous souls among you have always known: that it is the martyrs who are righteous? For it is the martyrs who shall inherit the earth. It is the martyrs who are the true children of God!"

The General only realized she clenched her teeth when she caught Tobias studying her face. She shot him a withering glance that inspired him to correct his attention and redirect it to the rant of the near-foaming Eternal Son. "Who among you will be counted as the righteous in the coming nights? Who among you will be damned to an eternity of despair for your faltering hearts, your traitorous nature?" Voice lifting above the growing clamor of his parishioners, Cicero beat the edge of his pulpit with force that would bruise a human hand for several days, rather than the several minutes of his martyr's flesh. "There have been other generations of my Father's children, many before Dominia. I have seen them, and of them all, only I am left standing. Why? Because I alone have remained ever faithful to my Holy Father's will. Because I, his Eternal Son, lean not upon my own understanding, but trust in the Lord with all my heart."

"Filthy, unholy garbage," muttered the dentist under his breath, withdrawing from his pocket a rosary (a simple two-barred cross of the human sort, rather than a crucifix with a second crossbar dividing a horned circle as was the symbol of the martyr church). He toyed with its beads as Cicero, returning to Earth, smoothed his blond hair.

"There have been other whelps put down before Dominia. There will be many, I expect, in her wake. But let her be the first in the lifetimes of many martyrs I see here. My Father has authorized a bounty of five hundred million dollars for the life of Dominia di Mephitoli, whether her killer be human or martyr, foreigner or citizen." As the crowd's fervor scattered into a series of gasps, the General lowered beneath Tobias's watchful eye into the chilled metal of a folding chair. "Should she so much as show her face again, it will be the last time she shows it anywhere. Yet even if she does not return home (if hypocrites can be said to have a home), she will know no safety, for my Father waits ever vigilant for news of her resurgence. It will not be long, now; and when she does reemerge, we will be ready to destroy her. Let none disrupt this tenuous peace we have built with the human world and live to revel in it. Let none lead astray the souls of the Lord and ever find safety or comfort again. Let us pray, children: pray that the disgraced Governess is caught and killed for her crimes."

As a few cheered but more audibly knelt to pray, Akachi finally did Dominia the courtesy of pausing the recording.

"Do you see what I tried to tell you?" he asked her, in a way so gentle it was, from him, utterly patronizing. "I wish I could be more delicate, but I must be blunt, General. It should not matter to you who displaces your Father, because you are already a nonentity. As good as dead."

"Then I'd might as well throw my life away to kill you now, hadn't I?" She didn't move, whatever she said, too drained physically and too emotionally adrift to prove capable of violence. Tobias seemed to sense that, and made no move, himself.

"What a waste that would be! You cannot let this news sour you, General. I am doing you a favor. I am liberating you by pointing out the truth! Now, you are freer than you have ever been. All your previous self-definitions are lifted from your shoulders. That we should all be so free! But think of all you can do with that freedom. Think of the wrongs you can right, all the deaths and martyring you can prevent in the future."

Akachi touched Dominia's forehead, which startled her, as she had covered her eyes; but when she gripped his arm, it seemed in a black and terrible instant as though she had arrived again in the presence of the black sun. The factory fell away and all around them were the howling, writhing bodies of souls that tore at their hair, screaming and weeping and pulling at the sallow skin of their faces. Smearing their flesh with black ash and dirt, they were the only things in sight (waves of sorrow, a sea of sack-clothed screamers) as far as Dominia's one-eyed soul could bear to see.

Akachi shouted over the din, "This is what your Father has done! These are all those souls he's led astray, human and martyr. The Kingdom of God is unknowable in this life, Miss Mephitoli! Those who think it is will find themselves trapped forever."

"That's not true." Bolstered by thoughts of the Kingdom, she wheeled out of Tobias's clutch just as a wheezing figure at her feet made to grab a boot that was simultaneously the bloodstained hem of that regrettable kimono. As the circuit between their bodies was interrupted and the vision disappeared as it had come, the General insisted, "Surely those people are just lost. Trying to get into the Kingdom and not knowing how, regardless of their religion. They can't all be my Father's fault. Or—are those soulless beings?"

"Worse: they are beings with corrupted souls. Befouled souls. Your Father has forced them to misunderstand. How long they've suffered! And how many more will suffer. They cannot present themselves before God when mired in the lies of the Hierophant. And how many have you, yourself, put into that abominable place!"

Trying, somehow, to justify away her guilt, the General insisted, "Surely it's not so different from being lost in the Void," but she knew after she said it how wrong she was even before Tobias shook his head. The sub-radio frequencies mentioned by the magician and by Lazarus—that must have been what they meant, that altered, hellish zone of screaming souls.

"One does not have a self when lost in the darkness there, for there, one is part of the true mystery of God while also being separated from any notion of the divine. That is why one is anything there, and nothing; and it is also why there is no suffering there, because there is no knowledge by which one can suffer. But in that place in the Void that is called Jerusalem, an unholy trap, souls congregate: aware enough to never forget their suffering and what they have done to find themselves thus, but never aware enough to liberate themselves. That is true hell, Miss Mephitoli, and your Father is the Devil who puts them there."

She was tired of arguing about her Father's hand in it and opted to communicate her resentment telepathically. She imagined sending Tobias her hatred through their overlapping electromagnetic fields while she demanded, "And what do you expect me to do about it?"

"You know your Father's military better than anyone on Earth, except perhaps your brother. You know the plans of his cities and fortresses, the weaknesses he hides and the things he most cherishes. You know the ways of martyrs and can offer a beacon to those wise enough to repent before they die. The only question I have is: Will you repent, yourself?"

"I won't repent for being what I am," insisted the General, her eyes landing on the blonde female in the background of Cicero's speech. Innocent Lavinia, who was not by any stretch of the imagination there through choice of her own. "And I won't tell you that martyrs need to repent. You want to talk about repentance? What about you? What about all the people you've killed, sent to the Very Low Frequency perception of the Ergosphere? Because I get the feeling you've misled as many as my Father. You're as bad as him."

The humor had fallen from Akachi's face some time ago, but his expression grew particularly hard at that. "So you will roll over and accept you are dead, and your life is at its end? That there is nothing you can do to save yourself, nothing you can do to save anyone else? Martyrs really are less than human. They lack all the human spirit of hope and striving."

"Martyrs are more human than you. We kill for food. You're a bigot, a rapist, and a liar worse than my Father. He doesn't try to pretend he isn't evil when you get him alone in a room. He doesn't shoot a loyal man before an audience, then delude himself about his moral compass. The sad thing about you is that you think you're good."

In the face of her disdain, his words began to stumble, and all his blustering was revealed for what it was when he was reduced to petty schoolyard insults. "Well—well, we will see if you don't change your mind when we begin collecting Red Market whores for reeducation and repurposing. For all the time you spent with them, perhaps you are considering becoming one."

In lieu of comment, she spat in his eye, and was promptly given by her collar such a jaw-seizing, brain-frying shock that she immediately lost consciousness. Too bad: the General would have appreciated the horror on his face.

Though she regained consciousness halfway through the drive back, Akachi was, oddly, no longer in a talking mood. This, she gathered from her own gag and handcuffs, and from the way he spared her a repelled glance as she shifted in her seat. The silent treatment was immeasurably preferable to the dentist's so-called conversational skills, however, and the first scrap of rest she'd received in too long seemed almost regretful to leave behind.

"Every time we meet, Miss Mephitoli," he said as they reached the base camp, "you prove you and your kind are animals. A damn good thing your saliva is not a carrier for your disease like the rest of your fluids, eh? Camels and reptiles spit, General. Fish. Civilized beings do not. They possess self-control. With this, you cannot argue. I will prove it. Perhaps when you have humiliated yourself again, and proved me right, you will manage to rejoin civilization."

As Akachi parked the vehicle and threw open his door, Dominia was dragged from her side by a pair of burly men covered in the sweat and dust of their nomadic military life. Above the noise of the camp, the dentist shouted Arabic orders. This resulted in her being shoved the direction of a tent that was a cover for a bunker set deep in the dirt. The flimsy ladder down which she was forced to maneuver with wrists still cuffed gave way to a claustrophobic cellar, whose penal nature she divined not by its subterranean position but by the chains mounted in the bricks of its grudgingly added walls. A voice cried out, and one of the guards whipped off the cuffs while the other held the barrel of his gun against her head.

"Don't bother calling us unless you've killed him," said one man in thickly accented English.

"Killed who?"

Her captors retreated up the ladder, so the only one left to answer was the voice of her fellow prisoner: a voice absent long enough it momentarily registered as a stranger's.

"Dominia," it asked, "is that you? Oh my God! Oh, God, please forgive me! I didn't want to do what I did."

In the darkness of the corner, the General bent over the wincing shape. As her eyes adjusted to the dark, she recognized blinded René Ichigawa, who, arms over his head, wept and waited to die.

XV

A Rat in the Cellar

While far from a connoisseur of men, the General had aesthetic sense enough to know what an attractive one looked like. With his pointed, weasellike features and bony frame, the former English professor always appeared too untrustworthy to join that category, but now the poor fellow was genuinely repellent. The sharpness of his features was emphasized by his malnourished state and the dirt that had, over time, caked the corners of his grotesquely crusted eye sockets to seal them shut. Gagging, Dominia tried to redirect her gaze, but there was no better place to let it sit upon him, for his wristbones poked like daggers from his flesh and his belly protruded in a symptom of true starvation.

"My God, René, have they been feeding you?"

"The past few days. Mostly"—his voice dropped to a whisper—"I've been eating bugs. Oh, God!" His lips trembled into a tearless sob while he admitted, "I hear them scuttling around. That's how I find them. They get in through gaps in the bricks—these are only here for the chains. I don't even think the ceiling is supported, is it? It could collapse anytime!"

The five-foot, claustrophobic ceiling that forced its prisoners to sit upon the ground once they had descended the ladder was supported with one courtesy beam, but the General hardly blamed him for not knowing. His short chain kept him trapped in a foul-smelling corner arrayed with straw and newspaper. At least in Nogales she'd been given a toilet!

"René," began the General, but the man raised his voice in a series of terrible cries.

"Please, Dominia, please! You can't kill me, oh, God, I'm so young. Do you know how young I am? Forty-five! I still have another fifty years to live if I don't have any engineering done, and now I have to live them blind—but I still want to live them! Please, please! You have to forgive me for the train, and before. You have to forgive me, please! I didn't have a choice."

"Would you calm down? I'm not going to kill you." In fact, so many injustices, petty and profound, had occurred since René's betrayal on the train that she had almost been glad to see him until he'd reminded her of his crimes. Even so, she pushed her irritation aside, because Tobias no doubt hoped she'd ruminate on the betrayal to a breaking point. "That fucking dentist is trying to make me repent by proving some point."

"What point?"

The blood of all those men lying dead in the temple still stained the General's kimono: and the hot metal of Benedict's type O still filled her mouth, vivid enough to make her stomach ache with knowledge of its emptiness and its separation from the now-vital sun. "It doesn't matter, because it's not a point that's going to be made. We're going to find a way out."

"I don't think there is one." The blind man whined on while Dominia, severely stooped from her full height, felt the walls, the corners, and the dirt-embedded stones. "I don't even know how long I've been here! Two weeks? Three? It's so hard to tell."

Thin as he'd been to start, that meant the cells in his body were breaking down his proteins, or had been until the Hunters started feeding him again; funnily enough, he was now enduring a prolonged version of the experience had by sun-exposed martyrs. "How often do they bring you food?"

"I think it's once a day, but it was twice today. Oh, God." His voice quivered like a preteen's. "They're trying to fatten me up, aren't they?"

"Then they're doing a poor job of it." Grimacing, the General yanked a brick out of place from the wall and frowned at the dirt behind. "We could always tunnel out."

"*You* could," said René with a jerk of his chain. "I'm stuck here."

"I don't have time for your fatalism, René."

"That's easy for you to say! You're not chained to the wall like a dog. Oh, Christ, when I was little, we had a dog. I loved that dog! But my mother always kept him in the backyard and never let him inside. Is this karma? Is this what I get for letting her treat the dog that way?"

Though on the verge of saying the notion was ridiculous, Dominia found herself there again: abandoning Basil in the back of the *tanque* while she pursued René in effort to board the Light Rail. Valentinian had abandoned her, just like she'd abandoned him. Her incredulous mouth fell open. The real question was whether she was more appalled by her own actions than she was furious at the magician. In that fury, the martyr stormed to René's side, and while the man flung his cowering arms over his head, the General tore the chain from the shoddy brick in which it'd been anchored.

"Oh," said René, groping for, then picking up, the now-freed end of the chain. "Well—thank you."

"You know, Tobias tried to intimidate me by having one of his exo-skeletons crush a brick, but I'm starting to think the Hunters just make shitty bricks."

"Maybe there *is* a chance," decided the mercurial professor, clasping his hands, then running the chain through them as he might a necktie. "But what will we do once we're out of here? You've seen the camp."

Her knee-jerk response was the same as in Nogales: murder the guard, then sweep through the camp as silent and bloody as the incarnation of Saint Valentinian. Well—poor turn of phrase, considering how sore she was at the moment with her patron saint, but one got the idea. "I don't know," began the General, with utmost caution. "Maybe, say…you distract the guard and I knock him out? If we find weapons on him, we kill him and take them."

"No! We can't hurt the guard!"

"He knows what he's getting into," said Dominia as, conveniently, the trapdoor was lifted and the minor glow of interior light showered in alongside a powerful flashlight beam.

"René!" The instantly recognizable, vaguely girly voice of Tenchi Ichigawa took the wind out of Dominia's scheming sails. "I brought you something extra today!"

"Oh, no," she groaned, while, his expression grim, René asked, "You see?"

"Who are you talking to down here?" asked the portly sailor. On turning at the bottom of the ladder, the beam of his miner's cap swung across René's unresponsive face and into the General's wincing one. With the delay of a second, Tenchi shrieked and lost the food on his tray as he pressed himself into the farthest corner.

"Oh! Oh, Mephitoli-san! Oh, *Kami-sama, tasukete kudasai*! Why didn't they warn me!"

"Because they're hoping I'll kill you, too. They saw how I let you go on the *Jun'yō*, and they're wondering if I'll do it again now that I'm starving and you're between me and freedom." Frankly, if either human was likely to whet her appetite, it was the porcine one, and not his skinny mustelid cousin. What a good opportunity this would be to test her self-control, along with her certainty about her need of direct sun! She tried not to dwell on the thought and found home in annoyance, demanding, "What are you doing here?"

"I—the same thing I was doing the last time you saw me." The trembling man held the plastic food tray like a shield over his heart. He seemed ready at a second's notice to spring back up the ladder to which he looked with increasing frequency. "You know—serving... the resistance..."

"Tenchi!" The chide provoked such a wince in the man that the martyr almost laughed and strained to drop her tone from a drill sergeant's bark. "You can't seriously think that the Hunters are in the right here. Don't you know about them? They go from human town to human town, conscripting the men and using their daughters and wives as sex slaves to recruit more men. Some cells even try to 'reform' women like me through rape. Any human who doesn't practice an

Abrahamian faith is liable to be literally *stoned* to death in some of the crazier cells. *Stoned.*"

"In the year 4042," added René. This elicited a dirty look from the General, who swiftly remembered he could not read it and told him, "What are you talking about? You were a part of the Hunters before my Father got to you! That's why they put you here."

"I was a free agent who was used and abused by both sides," insisted the sore man, crossing his arms and tsking at the jingle of the chain. The noise attracted Tenchi's attention.

"Your chain! What happened?"

"I happened," explained Dominia.

Full of terror, the chubby man remembered himself and drew back the step he'd just taken into the low room of the dungeon. "I'm going to get in trouble for this."

"Good! I hope you do." Her sleep-deprived, miserable irritation needed an outlet, and she unleashed it on the man who'd been hand-selected to taunt her through no fault of his own. "I can't believe you would be a part of this, Tenchi! You seem like a nice guy. You can't know everything these people do and accept it without examining the implications of what it says about you. You're supporting violence and theft from other humans, and you're directly aiding that human suffering by being here. And for—what, some stupid war you're going to lose? Have you ever even been in a *fist*fight, fisherman?"

"Did you see the suits?" asked Tenchi meekly.

The General snapped, "Yeah, and I'm not impressed. Your shitty dentist boss can take the suits and his teleporter and shove them up his—"

"I think they would give us a chance in a conflict..." As though remembering why he was here, Tenchi looked at the platter in his hands, collected the few scattered packages of food, and slid it across the floor toward René. The blind man leapt at the sound, groped across the dirt, and, with fumbling, desperate fingers, tore away the cellophane. As both Tenchi and Dominia grimaced at the sight of the starving man cramming his mouth full of ration-grade honey cakes, the General waved a hand.

"You've let them make you party to treating your cousin like this."

"Oh, no! If it weren't for me, they would have killed him outright. Everyone was upset when he showed up without you, and with those eyes. I'm so glad I was there! I begged the guys—I mean, begged, it was kind of embarrassing—"

"*Really* embarrassing," glutted René through a mouthful of nuts.

"—and Dr. Akachi said, 'All right. If he can survive until Dominia arrives, your cousin will be free.'"

"They just didn't tell you he was going to have to survive like this. Tenchi, why would you trust them? Honestly, I'm baffled. I'd think you knew better after staying in the magician's City."

The General realized she'd made a chronological gaff only after Tenchi's brow furrowed. "City," he repeated. "Magician?"

Vaguely, she remembered Gethsemane warning the sailor against revealing the future to Dominia. "Nothing. Never mind." Hopeful she would not slip up and kill him in the future, and that the portly man could be turned away from his so-called brothers-in-arms, the General pressed him. "But how can you accept being a part of this? How can you think what the Hunters do is an appropriate price to pay for overthrowing my Father?"

After a few seconds of thought, the sailor shrugged. "What other choice does a human man have in this world? Especially if he wants to help people in the Front, or do something to contribute to the dissolution of martyr dominance. I mean...it's sort of your fault."

She would have loved to argue, but, in a sense, he was right. The Battle for the Reclamation of Mexico had initially been won by the South American Resistance Army, but it was a costly victory that had shattered most of their best forces and caused other troops to be funneled from the Western Front. This had meant that, when Dominia freed herself and slaughtered the entire camp, then turned around to call in reinforcements before freeing what few captive martyr officers had been claimed from other victories, the two groups cut a bloody swathe across the remaining human militias and left them destroyed. When Cicero's unit met Dominia's in Tucson, he found her and her ramshackle group of six martyrs holding down a building that had once belonged to the Resistance and had been, long before that, a bank. In those sweet moments when first she saw her brother again, the martyrs were in the process of trying to break into a heavy-duty vault to acquire the humans within. How helpful Cicero had been at that moment! How good it had been to see him. They met outside the ruins of a nearby mosque whose crumbling façade was still emblazoned with the English block letter phrase, "HAPPINESS IS SUBMISSION TO GOD". In that reunion, he was more her brother than he'd ever been, or would ever be again. She's screamed with delight to see him! She longed for that moment, oddly, for although her nights at war were not good nights—that war more than any war she'd fought—they were nights when she had the illusion of Family. Love from her Family.

Her Family had been all that mattered to her then, even after the Hierophant's snub. Perhaps that was why the image of Benedict stuck so deep in her unconscious craw, though it had been too simple to murder him and every other man nearby. Perhaps that was why it bothered her so to see Tenchi now, led by fear and ideal into the service of a cause so backward it was downright evil. She saw in the sailor too much of her old self, cutting into that bank vault and murdering a room of trapped soldiers with Cicero's help—and feeling it was fun. That was the last time she had fun killing anybody: even by that point, death had lost its glow.

And now, well, violence wasn't even an option. She could not bring herself to kill Tenchi, and for whatever sorry reason, after he collected René's tray, she allowed the tubby man to depart. She would need spend at least one night in this wretched place. But, ah, how quickly one night turned to two! Particularly as, to its credit, the cell served as a very fine, very dark place for a martyr—who had been given a psychedelic drug, forced to engage in a battle, dragged on a six-hour road trip, then made to spend another two hours driving in the sun before being electrocuted, and who was *still* not able to enjoy unconsciousness for more than an hour or so—to sleep, sleep, finally, sweetly, sleep. O sleep, O gentle sleep! Nature's soft nurse, as wrote the Bard. There was no energy left in Dominia for her mind to connect to the

Ergosphere and provide her a dream—except, on waking, the memory of one: Cassandra, standing outside the City's marketplace, where the General had met Tenchi. She got so far as to touch her wife's hand, to kiss her orchid lips, before awareness of that dream faded off again.

When Dominia awoke so refreshed she felt like a whole new person, it was, by René's reckoning, some twelve hours later. "Not that I have a way to tell," he added miserably. "I base my guess on how hungry I am."

"I'll buy you a grandfather clock when we get out of here." Dominia sat with her back to the wall and her legs straight before her. As she bent forward to stretch before she exercised (much as one managed either in such a cramped space), she asked, "What did you think they were going to do to you when you showed up empty-handed, René? Say, 'Oh, that's okay?' Especially when you confessed the truth about your eyes, if that's how it happened."

"It is," he confirmed with a sigh. "I don't know. I was desperate! I was terrified the whole way to the Hunters, sure that any minute you would change your mind and come to kill me: or that Cicero or your Father would swoop me up again."

"Did they really send you to me, René? What was the Hierophant's plan with you?"

Apparently, René was supposed to spy on Dominia and stay with her to provide a consistent location to the Hierophant. Had things gone to plan, he explained, the Holy Family would have followed them all the way to the Hunters, and then to Lazarus. "He and Cicero came to me because he knew my cousin's connection to the Hunters, and threatened to kill me for it, saying I was probably a spy. But he thought we could make a deal, too."

"Why you, specifically? Surely there are plenty of humans he could have used."

"I don't know. A lot of my colleagues were busted before I was approached, which must be how they got my name. I think he spared me because of my education."

Entirely possible, or even probable. The Hierophant had a profound love for all art and music, but Western culture was his soulmate, and those involved in its preservation and transmission were, to him, salvageable. It was the same reason why Dominia had been introduced to the human from the start. When, three months after Cassandra's death, the Governess managed to look another person in the face without finding herself on the verge of tears, she forced her hollow body to attend a party hosted by one of Cassandra's artist friends. The whole thing had been twice as depressing as it sounded on recounting (exactly as depressing as she had expected at the time); but it seemed worthwhile to stretch herself, even as she, antisocial and avoidant, skeptically allowed the human to be introduced to her while she brooded about her exit in the corner of a black sofa.

"Dominia," the well-to-do friend had been saying, "Dominia, I have somebody here I think you *must* meet, and he's said he wants to meet you, too—pretty *bold* for a human, I thought, but, oh, what a *riot* he is! This is René Ichigawa. He's a professor at Berkeley and just *too* funny. You'd think he was a martyr if I didn't tell you!"

"I'm a poet, too," he'd been swift to add, as all poets are.

"It must be hard to be a human and an artist," Dominia remarked. René had laughed.

"I think it's harder to be a martyr and an artist. What struggles do you have to write about? Not even mortality oppresses you. A martyr will always have his home, but a human might be eaten tomorrow. That means I have to write like I'm about to die, all the time—and that means every new work I create is the best work of my life."

By that standard, Dominia was ready for her magnum opus. Tobias had a fair point when he said she was dead, thus liberated. This truth was comforting and depressing. Yes, she could go anywhere—in hiding. Yes, she was free—to live a lie and forever await violent death. She supposed she could just disappear, move to the City, but that required her to get outside, if only in moonlight, until she found better means. If only there were someone to help her. Say, a mystic, or a magician.

The magician, she almost understood. He had things to do, and was probably also passive-aggressively teaching her a lesson about abandonment. But that Lazarus had been in this camp, yet not tried to break her out, was a matter of mild concern. The idea of having come this far only to have something happen to her most valuable companion was an infuriating one, and she tried, to no avail, to get information out of the younger, rounder Ichigawa when he came the second day.

"You haven't seen a bearded man, have you? Martyr, older, maybe still stuck in a kimono?"

"I don't think I should talk to you about what goes on in camp," answered the dubious man, who sat just inside the squat dungeon to eat dinner with his cousin, ready to scramble back at a second's notice if the famished martyr got any ideas. "Nobody's gotten me in trouble over the chain because I don't think anybody's willing to come down here, but I know that if I say anything about anything, it will haunt me."

René brushed off his saliva-dampened hands, having finished a plastic tray of repulsive mashed potatoes, sad vegetables, and saltine crackers. "Here's a question for you, then! Why's the boss such a hypocrite? I heard him crying about the debauchery of Western culture when he was yanking out my DIOX-Is, but what should I hear while I'm being dragged to my new hole? Mozart!"

"I like Mozart," said the sailor defensively. René raised his hands in agitation.

"Don't we all! That's my point. These religious nuts try to condemn basic human qualities like a deep love of music, then fall into their own traps because they can't resist them! They just want an excuse to fuck up, the masochists."

The notion made Dominia laugh, recalling, for fleeting seconds, dear Miki. That first proper meeting in the dining car. As her smile faded with sudden longing for her friend—and pain at the knowledge they could not meet again on Earth—the General cleared her throat. "The Hierophant and Dr. Akachi could put aside their differences if we just got them together at a concert. My Father loves Mozart, too."

"See," insisted the blind professor. "Everybody loves Mozart."

There was something therapeutic about being able to talk to more than one person at once, but it was also relieving when Tenchi finally ascended the ladder. Tobias wasn't entirely wrong: the fat Ichigawa cousin was a tempting target for her appetite. With the bone-deep hunger of a martyr instilling itself back into her body on the denial of sunlight, the craving for human flesh was stronger than ever. Blood received from René could keep her alive, it was true, but nothing would offer the satisfaction of an actual meal quite like a shank of human flesh. The idea was almost impossible to ignore once she got it into her head. Everything in her sought to rationalize, say, borrowing one of Tenchi's fleshy arms. That wouldn't necessarily kill him, would it? Easy to replace, too. But, no. It wasn't right. Not knowing that he was in the City, and not knowing it was what Tobias wanted.

More than any problem with Tobias, Dominia could not stand to slip back into the roles of the old person she'd been; she could not relive Nogales, no matter how simple a way out violence formed.

"You look bad," Tenchi told her on the third night, sucking chocolate pudding out of a cup. How he acquired it in a camp where even basic rations were surely precious, she did not know.

"No shit." The General rubbed her forehead to work away its ever-growing throb. "I'm starving, Tenchi."

After a thoughtful moment, the fat man rolled her the apple that had formed a neglected splotch upon his tray. Dominia almost snorted, almost told him, 'That won't do any good,' but when her mind revived in a flash the image of Benedict, she bit her tongue and thanked him. It was the illusion of sustenance, she supposed, something to keep her stomach from dissolving its own lining. But it wouldn't help her shaking, and in the long run, it would increase the damage of starvation, because calories her body expended in digestion would be replaced, but the food wouldn't provide her body with the protein her dysfunctional cells required to maintain their own stability. She'd end up malnourished, like a duck fed bread instead of seed.

As, night by night, René filled out, being given more food than the scraps he'd received on his previous schedule, the General felt her muscles growing not only weaker but harder to control. Sit-ups had become a chore at an alarming pace in the dungeon, and push-ups grew out of the question as her hands lost the ability to manipulate objects. Part of the problem was her age. As a young woman, she could've gone without eating for a longer period of time; but around the age of three hundred, most martyrs experienced an increase in metabolism that was regularly attributed to the increasing instability of their cells. This was not a problem so long as one kept oneself surrounded with food or regularly attended Church for the blood of the Lamb, which was why martyrs had popularized cities to an extent surpassing even humans. It was also why, as the martyr population expanded to uncomfortable sizes, humans across the globe grew more nervous. Some even sought to donate their children to martyrdom (another popular cause of illegal immigration into the Front) as though to circumvent the problem altogether—or, in all likelihood, spare their own lives.

What a horrible thought that had always been to Dominia, who had been martyred not only without her consent, but without her knowledge. The way it happened was horrible, but also gentle. Morgan had been fortunate: too young to comprehend what it meant to be a martyr, or, say, know the symptoms of the disease that heralded its transformation. Thus, so far as she had been concerned, she was just a girl sick at home, like a hundred million other girls, future and past, sick at home. It had been scary, especially because her parents had been so upset yet so silent about what was going on. But, in retrospect, it was a kinder fate. Those last few days, her father sat with her and told her stories about the family genealogy so she wouldn't forget. Her parents were from the Front; her father was shrewd with investments despite his rural background, and they'd struck gold on stocks related to then-recent Martian terraforming developments. That same acuity with investments—and disdain for taxes—would someday attract the Hierophant to their door. Give him an excuse, anyway.

Dominia was from Mephitoli, but little Morgan had been named after an American ancestor who was herself the daughter of a North American and a South American. That North American line, further back in time, well—they really *had* been from Meph(Italy) if you picked the right set of ancestors. So, they'd moved there. But with every member of the Front at that point in time a mutt of lineage, they could have justified moving anywhere when Morgan was on the way. If only they'd picked the German ancestors, the Irish, even the Polish! But Poland, like every Slavic state, was martyr country in excess of even Mephitoli;

Morgan and her family could have been murdered and eaten before she'd learned to walk.

Which was the worse fate? She had gone to sleep one day and died, like so many of those other girls sick at home. But, like a proportion far fewer than even that number, Morgan rose from the dead to find herself with a new Family, a new room, a new life, a new name. A new genealogy, to replace—or supplement, she preferred to think—the one her father had spent her last days teaching her. It was traumatic at the time, but naturally there wasn't much choice in the matter, and that made the trouble far easier than the struggle undergone by a martyred adult. Being powerless simplified the pain as much as being, in the way of children, unconscious to the horrible details of existence.

She shuddered to think what Cassandra had endured. In Dominia's current opinion, an adult's decision to become a martyr was sign of mental illness. Before Cassandra, she'd romanticized it. After the suicide, Dominia understood why her Father impressed upon his people the importance of martyring children, and enforced the taboo nature of human-martyr relations.

All this was why it was so disorienting when Dominia, awoken by pain in her ankle, looked down to see the metal plate of René's chain, its sharp corner darkened by rust. Or—no. That was blood, certainly blood. Certainly *her* blood. And its source, no doubt, was that to which René had alarmingly attached his lips. Ravaged by hunger and torn from dreamless sleep, the General hardly understood what these images indicated until the pitiful professor, caught in the act, scrambled away, wiped his bloodied lips, and cried for the umpteenth time, "I'm sorry!"

Perhaps it was all just a shock because, in the past three days, the General and the professor had exchanged surprisingly few words. What words they had exchanged had often been literary quotes. Between the two of them, they were able to remember a satisfying amount of *Macbeth*; and Dominia regaled him with her own recitation of "The Raven"—in her opinion, more soulful than Cicero's. This had been most of their relationship, to be frank. After the bootlicking would-be-Renfield had forced his calling card into Dominia's hands (at the time, she thought it the action of your typical martyr-chasing human who could nonetheless come in handy as a future slave/tool/meal; now she understood it as the action of an inept spy), the Governess found him soon trying to make an appointment with her office, ostensibly to petition for an artistic grant. In reality, once he had her ear, he passed her a book.

"What is this?" she had asked that hot July evening, bending to view the pages through which she flipped with one hand while unbuttoning, with the other, her stifling suit coat. "The focus of your grant? I expected it to be artistic, not scholarly."

Perfectly cool—no doubt trained in this, or vetted for this quality, by the Hierophant—smiling René stroked his trim goatee. "This, Governess, is something that could get me killed. But I don't think it will, because of what it means to you."

"And what does it mean to me?"

"Having your wife back."

She could have crushed the spine of the book like it was René's bony one. Indeed, she had been forced to set the volume down. "What would you know about my wife, human?" she asked him, her tone razor sharp.

The professor had not batted an eye. Instead, he proved the first to say what so many others along her journey had said in response to that same question.

"I know you loved her very much. Otherwise, you wouldn't..." He tapped his chest to indicate the diamond over Dominia's heart. "But I think you wear—her because you know there's hope."

She nearly laughed, but there was nothing funny about Cassandra's invocation by this know-nothing human. The Governess had thought seriously about killing him. Maybe she should have. In some universes, perhaps she did. Instead, in this one, she had flipped back through the book and found it to be a foreign holy text in an unknown language. There had been drawings that, at the time, had meant nothing to her, but had depicted a temple full of women, the arrival of a man, the sacred marriage of that man to one of the women, and that woman's ascension as a goddess. It had impressed her so little that she did not internalize any of the images well enough to remember them concretely: any, except for the image of the old goddess shedding her skin and fleeing, naked, upon the back of a tiger, ready to fly off the page and upon Dominia's desk.

"Why don't you try to explain," she had said, "and I'll try to decide whether to kill you."

Then, René told her the story of Lazarus. Not the Lazarus Dominia knew—the imaginary figurehead of a bunch of lunatic cult members. The real story had been so garbled by time and her Father that, even in its accurate tellings, it was Lazarus's blood that was capable of raising the dead; or perhaps it was something he did in a magical way. On that matter, René had never been clear. But as Dominia had pressed him to know why she should believe this was not a lie, he had said at the time, "Because I wouldn't mind drinking his blood if some of the things I've heard are true—and I would never drink a martyr's blood."

"I'm sorry," René screamed all of three months later, imprisoned with Dominia in the dungeon beneath the Hunters' camp. "I'm so sorry, Dominia, I never wanted this, but I can see you in my dreams—I see hunger in your eyes! I see the way you look at me when I sleep and I hear the way you breathe near me when I'm awake; it's only a matter of time before you can't help yourself anymore."

"René, what the *fuck*!" The level of violation was impossible to describe. Recoiling against the opposite wall, the General felt her skin crawl on a metaphorical level to join the physical sensation of the slow-leaking wound at the base of her ankle. "Why would you even think this was a good idea?"

"Because my flesh will be no good to you if I'm a martyr! No matter how hungry you are, you'll never think of eating me. Hey— maybe we can eat Tenchi together!"

"Oh, Lord love the Lamb, René, would you listen to yourself?"

"I didn't know what else to do," the man cried, looking for all the world like a bearded, blinded child. "I couldn't just sit here waiting for you to kill me."

"I wasn't going to kill you, but now you're definitely going to die. Frankly, I should put you out of your misery, but—shit." Furious, the General tore a rock from the dirt behind her and hurled it into the bricks not far from René's head. He winced. It was cruel, but satisfying, because it was the most cruelty she could afford to inflict upon a man whose death would mean a victory for the principles of a thoroughly unprincipled man.

"Please, Dominia, don't hurt me. Now I can help you get out!"

"You still won't be able to see, you know."

"But—but I'll be able to fight."

"You'll be able to blindly charge off into the night, trip over your chain, and get shot like any other idiot."

"But I'll be faster, right? And stronger?"

"You'll be incredibly fucked up and disoriented and probably won't be worth anything until you've had a meal—and I'm not letting you eat Tenchi. Fuck! What are we going to do?"

The choice had been stupid, burdensome, and now firmly set the responsibility of René's life on his nonconsensual creatrix's shoulders. Although she could easily kill him and avoid the whole issue (and get herself a meal before her proteins altered his), that wasn't an option. She would have to use the situation she'd been given. It wasn't all bad.

"Okay," she said. "Okay." Then, smoothing her hands over her face and back through hair cropped so short it resembled René's former professor cut and not his increasingly floppy, unkempt prisoner's mane, the poor General tried one more, "Okay," before laughing at herself. Her hand touched Cassandra's diamond.

Nobody had more than one chance to do anything in life. She had to remember that.

"Here's the deal, René." The General found some small satisfaction as he responded to her movement toward him by wincing against the brick wall. "Just relax. I won't hurt you, but it's important you know you are going to die."

As she sat beside him, he leaned away, but she caught his filthy hand and squeezed it until he squeaked her name. "It's going to hurt. You'll have a fever, and probably the shits, and those will mostly be blood. Your organs will feel like they're on fire—like somebody's just… reaching a hand into your body and squeezing"—she tightened her grip on his hand—"twisting your spine and tangling your intestines."

"Jesus, Dominia, do you have to tell me this?"

"You're going to die in this cell, floating in a pool of your own bloody sweat and bile vomit, because you chose to do this to yourself. And when you're dead"—her eyes burned like Valentinian's fire, so bright even the blind professor might have seen them—"I'm going to use your corpse to get us out of here."

XVI

The Price of Information

The positive aspect of René's adulthood: the protein's malformation spread faster through the body. The negative: it was much more violent than anything a child experienced. For the fortysomething English professor, the illness took three days. Dominia had been concerned more time would elapse; she would have been in dire straits herself, were that to happen. On the sixth day of her captivity and the third day of René's illness, as he shivered in the corner, covered in sweat while trying to maintain a conversation about Shakespeare's use of alchemical symbolism in his late romances, the General opened her mouth to point out how the use of alchemical metaphors stretched back to the cradle of civilization where lay the Middle States—

René was patting her cheek with a clammy hand and saying her name, as if he'd leapt across the room like the Hierophant. She barked out an irritable series of "What, what!" as she slapped his dirty palm away.

"I think you were having a seizure—you took a breath like you were about to speak and started choking. You were thrashing. Are you hurt?"

Yes, actually: her head throbbed, but she was still straight up against the wall and hadn't gnawed through her tongue. Best to accept the seizure had happened without making a production.

That same afternoon, René Ichigawa died without fanfare in Dominia's reluctant arms, and the General was concerned the martyring process that had killed him so hastily would complete his resurrection before Tenchi's next visit. Though the captives had gone to some lengths to hide René's state of obvious illness from the portly sailor, he had noticed his cousin's far sweatier condition on the second night. The third night, René had been too weak to stay awake for his cousin's visit, so Tenchi left the tray of food at the bottom of the ladder and hurried back up. He must have seen the intensity of hunger in the General's eyes, their blue tones reduced to mere shadows that matched the ones carved into her face by starvation-emphasized cheekbones.

The changes were subtle now, but she had already lost muscle mass, and this was a definite concern. She was not sure she'd be able to control herself well enough to maintain their charade. Once, on the ship, she felt a sense of pride about her self-control, and look how that ended! Even if it had been Cicero's fault, she had to admit she'd been well fed the rest of the voyage. Those last few days of sailing came upon her now with alarming fondness. It was possible that, when placed in front of more than one or two healthy, beating hearts, the General would prove Tobias right: snap as she had when given the chance to free herself from Nogales. And that was with courtesy bags of intranasal blood!

The worst part was that none of this would have been necessary if the magician hadn't vanished. If he was so powerful, he should have appeared in her cell to whisk her away at a moment's notice. Turn all the jihadists into statues, or transmute Dominia into a flea small enough to crawl through the crack where light trickled from the trapdoor. He could create a miracle—that son of a bitch could do it, no matter what anybody said—and he was nowhere to be found.

Yet—wasn't it a miracle that René had not woken to his second life the next time Tenchi whistled down the ladder? Who was she to distinguish between miracle and coincidence, fate and good timing, when she'd seen firsthand all space and time were one? With haste, the General gouged her hand on the edge of that same loose plate René had used to steal her blood: this, she smeared across her own mouth, then across René's throat and the front of a dirty shirt pre-stained with bloody vomit and bloodier sweat. The importance of gory freshness, however, was key. And it was more important still that Tenchi catch her in the act, so when the beam of light fell across them, she could look from where she hunched over René's corpse and absorb the sailor's girlish shriek in deliberate imitation of her Father's dignified calm. "René is dead. I'm sorry. Please get the other guards, and Tobias. I'd like to talk to him."

"Oh, René!" With a cry of terror, the fat man scurried up the ladder at a speed faster than the General would have expected him to even walk.

Now came the hard part. Now, she composed herself. Now more than ever, her Father's blood flowed through her veins, and she reviewed all the times he reacted with perfect ease to outward annoyances (those disruptions by boisterous children in Mass that so bothered fastidious Cicero, for instance—why, more often than not, the Holy Father was cajoling them into outlandish behavior to get his Eternal Son's goat). Wasn't this that certainty of an educated decision with which his specter claimed it sought to empower her?

"Specter." The word made her frown. Her deprived mind scrambled between subjects even as the trapdoor reopened. Was the root of "specter" not "spectrum"? Perhaps she had seen her Father after all, manifesting in her electromagnetic field: her own thoughts about him, summoning him, inviting him the way he invited her each night into his dream-study. One English voice amid several Arabic shouts told her to face the wall. Her mind was elsewhere. A thoughtform, or his true spectral presence non-temporally in her field, mistranslated into the visual cortex. Hallucination by definition, supernatural by speculation.

Whatever that image was, it had been right. Even as she faced the wall, she felt in perfect power. Perfect control of the situation. She controlled the most valuable asset of all. Not freedom but knowledge. Knowledge bought freedom. Tobias had plenty of freedom, but he lacked the knowledge that René would awaken. He did not realize he had been duped as he made a personal appearance in her prison, one man shoving a gun into the back of her head while the dentist checked the pulse of her dead cellmate.

"So he *is* dead. Now you understand what I was saying, General? You cannot help yourself. Moreover, you are so bound to instinct you cannot use reason! Every day I have sent you a fat, tasty pig of a man, and you chose to bleed this skinny rat."

"His death came out of more than hunger," the General explained, calmly studying the roots pricking out of the dirt wall's surface. "It was owed to René, for what he did to me, and for getting in my way. For getting in the way of our association, Akachi."

"Ah? Now, what would you mean by that?"

"I've thought about the ways I could say this: the problem is, I hate you, so I have a difficult time putting it politely. But you've forced me into a corner. Almost literally," she added, sparing a soft laugh for the wall against which her nose was pressed. "There's no animal so vicious or stupid that, given a long enough time to think and the words to think in, won't come around to doing what it can to save its own life. I don't agree with you, or your cause. But if René had done what he was supposed to—if he'd come here with me, become initiated by your group, and given me a chance to consider an agreement with the Hunters without duress—none of this would have been a problem."

"This all sounds convenient, Miss Mephitoli." Dominia was grateful her face could not be seen from this position. "How do I know you are not going to get aboveground and begin killing my men?"

"Besides the rifles, you mean? Because I would already be aboveground and killing them, if that were the case. Tenchi would be dead and so would these fu— fine fellows pointing guns at me."

"Look how you tremble." The dentist took up her hand so abruptly that she started away. "Your meal did not have much meat on him, eh?"

"That should tell you how serious I am about working with you," she said, every word more cautious than the last. "No matter how hungry I am—no matter how many men I could still eat—I refrain, for civility's sake."

Chuckling, Akachi patted her shoulder and said, "Perhaps there is something of a person left within the animal." In Arabic, the dentist delivered an order, and the man with the gun to the back of Dominia's head steered her toward the ladder.

"Where am I being taken?"

"For a meal, and new clothes! I would like to speak with you again, now that you are feeling reasonable. Perhaps we can forge an agreement! You, and Lazarus and I."

Her heart skipped a beat at the thought of seeing a friend who frequently evaded her mind during her duress. If she had thought of anyone, it had been Valentinian, and only in the most malicious way possible. But it was hard to think when one was starving and the cells in one's body (and brain) were losing the ability to keep themselves shaped. After six days' imprisonment in that wretched tomb, the General's brain screamed at sensory stimulus. The cardinal light of the setting sun so blistered her sensitive eyes that she tried to cover them and could not because of her captor's grip. She cried, instead, to think how weak she'd been made by her hunger, and how tight her skin was under the touch of her captors, and her body's urge to be free of her collar. How she wished to leap off into the remaining sunlight! The overwhelmed General lowered her head toward the dust as, in surprising numbers, men emerged from their small tents to view the passing martyr. Somewhere, Tenchi wept.

In the suffocating heat of the medical tent, which reeked of putrid wounds and sweet antiseptic even though it had been some time since the unit had seen combat, Dominia was handed a hot blood bag along with the promised change of clothes. After inhaling the ration (and snatching another from the nearby refrigerator when the guards were busy arranging René's body on a stretcher at the behest of the medic), the General loosed the stained brass kimono and redressed, ignoring the eyes that struggled to avoid her—and in this case had religious, medical, and prejudicial reasons to do so. They could get fucked, so far as she cared: she'd seen too many naked idiot men snapping towels at each other's repressed backsides to help but feel by the age of 331 (no, remember, 332, can't forget), that nudity in such a scenario was about as sexual as a mud puddle. That was her own opinion, at any rate. Some people no doubt found mud puddles sexy. She was getting damn tired of this world, Valentinian.

The clothes she had been given were not unlike the Hunters' own "casual" outfits—a shin-length gray kurta with a thick black bar running down its front and a pair of white pants for beneath. At the instance of the English-speaking guard, whose vocabulary on this subject was limited but who managed to cite "religious reasons," she donned the black kufi and wondered at the point of it since it was the same black as her hair. Better that than a hijab, she supposed, when it came for vision in battle, but greater head covering would have (perhaps falsely) reassured her she couldn't be whisked off into the Ergosphere due to her own inexperience. However, to her relief, they emerged from the medical tent to find the reddened sun had relented to plum night. She looked for the moon, and as she saw it remembered that trying to enter the Void in earthly night would only deposit her into that place's more terrible low ebb. A night in which the soul barely existed. It was not worth trying—not that way, anyway. If push came to shove and safety required a regroup in that other, more nebulous space, the General would need another way to enter the Void. Not to mention she'd have to find a way back out, if she were to do so before the sun rose. Her Father managed it. If only she had someone to ask. Oh, Valentinian! Where was that sorry bastard?

Not many steps from the medical tent, she detected the distant sound of music and realized with an uncanny shock of synchronicity that not only was René right—it was indeed Mozart that Tobias arrogantly played in the middle of a camp full of men ideologically opposed to most forms of art—but tonight it appeared to be that very Requiem that had lit her drunken soul so long ago. Then, as now, she had been separated from Valentinian. Those haunting voices, ah, how well she knew their notes! Lavinia performed the same in concert, with Cassandra and a choir of other, lesser, singers, after the latter revealed the beauty of her singing voice to more than just Dominia and rooms full of lucky schoolchildren. The Hierophant insisted on making a Christmas gift of lessons for as long as the Governess's wife desired, then enthusiastically organized the concert not more than a couple years later.

That had been a fine morning, and it had been good to see

Cassandra so happy. So close to their sister. Perhaps that unconscious memory coaxed her into selecting the piece when visiting her Father's empty study. Ever after, all versions were inferior, but this variant was fine enough, and proved comfort when the quality crisped upon being pushed into Tobias's tent. No song, however, was comforting as the sight of Lazarus, who read, markedly collarless, beside a generator-powered lamp.

"Kiddo," he said as she hurried over to embrace him, the reality of a person friendly to her. Truly friendly, and not a user in the way of René. "You all right?"

"I wasn't sure what happened when I didn't hear from you after the first day, but—I was so stressed and hungry I hardly thought of you. I'm sorry."

"I'm fine; you never have to worry about me. Well. Not anytime soon, anyway." Weakly, the old man smiled, then frowned and tipped up her chin. "Same old story for the past four iterations...still got your collar on."

"Is it supposed to be gone by now?"

Tobias provided her answer as he entered the tent. "A funny question to ask. In point of fact, I toyed with the idea of having my men free Miss Mephitoli in the medical tent, but I decided it was better I do it myself. If she made it this far without changing her mind, I thought that a good sign. Before it was different, eh? You see"—he elbowed Lazarus in an obnoxious way before pushing the cylindrical key into Dominia's collar—"God inspired my choice, to teach you a lesson about how much you know!"

As the martyrs made withering eye contact over the dentist's head, the latch clicked free and the collar swung open. At the liberation of her throat for the first time in six days, Dominia enjoyed an inhalation so pure, so sudden, it elicited a head rush that bled the room of color. The General laughed at herself and touched her neck while the dentist said approvingly, "Isn't that much better! If you are willing to be a reasonable woman, I am willing to be a reasonable man."

"Does it require a lot of cognitive dissonance to believe the reasonable thing was killing René?" Dominia rubbed the impression left by the metal, wincing at the bruising that could now begin to fade.

"It is always reasonable to kill a traitor. Even Judas Iscariot agreed with that point, my friend; that is why he hanged himself in shame. René Ichigawa did not possess that level of self-insight, but you came around to it, yes?"

"I suppose that's one way to put it."

"Hunger was a motive, too, I'm sure." Tobias chuckled as he sat near the stereo. "My man outside the tent tells me you made short work of your ration. Are you still hungry? Shall I fetch the other Ichigawa cousin for you?"

"Why are you so eager to see me kill them? I thought Tenchi was one of you."

"Tenchi is one of those Hunters who is only a Hunter in the loose sense of the word. Think of him like Kahlil—that young man could have turned a toaster into a cell phone, and in fact I believe he did, to contact us with information about the Cairo ceremony! But that skill made him dangerous, as did his so-called moral stance. Tenchi is much the same. He is useful insofar as his sailing connections are concerned...that means he provides us with transport to the Front, and, for refugees funded by our cause, transport out of it; but there are many other men who are just as useful as he, for the same or similar reasons. And, of course, men of his use will grow defunct as we are able to establish teleporters. I am not eager to see you kill him, or anyone else. But I am eager to remind you that I, who need not kill to eat at all if I do not wish, am superior to you."

At the narrowing of the General's eyes, Lazarus said, "Tobias, please. We've discussed this."

"It is true we have made progress," the dentist agreed, "and more progress will yet be made. But I can see in your General's eyes, my brother, that she has not accepted my authority. And she will need to, if we are to defeat her Father."

"What about me?" She glanced at the entrance of the tent, then focused on the dentist. "I mean, Lazarus is integral to your plan and has uses even after the Hierophant is overthrown. But what's supposed to happen to me after this is over?"

"A wise woman, thinking long-term. You will be allowed to live."
How gracious! "But you will need agree to live elsewhere, if you
understand what I mean."

"I'm not entirely sure I do."

"There are options. Perhaps you would like to retire to your magician's sacrilegious Kingdom, eh? I do not think it will be a good
idea come Judgment Day, but that is between you and God. Or, if
you would continue this life, doing penance for what you have done,
I suppose I could see to your deportation to the Mars colony. It is
only Earth that belongs to mankind; we are to be her custodians, not
those of Mars. Martyrs may do with it what you like. Indeed, it seems
even suited to your names!" He was pleased with that, and missed the
second withering glance Lazarus and Dominia exchanged while he
chuckled to himself. "Martyrs from Mars. Better than 'Martians,' don't
you suppose!"

"So my choices are 'get out,' or 'get out.'"

"Or die."

"Reassuring."

Brow furrowed, Tobias leaned forward. His body, pressing into the
arm of his chair, outlined the gun hidden beneath his clothes. "Have
I told you the full story, Miss Mephitoli, of how I, mere dentist, came
to be leader of these violent men?"

Bracing herself for a windbag monologue, Dominia offered a tight,
polite smile not unlike the one Lazarus presented. "No, in fact, you did
not ever tell me that. You said you were going to be a...'slave.'" Rather
a harsh notion, though not inaccurate if the martyr in her could admit
it. All the same, Akachi continued without note of her reticence, pulling from beneath his shirt that hidden chain she had been shown in
the warehouse. The stained vial glittered in the low light.

"We both keep something valuable around our necks." The dentist
chuckled. "That is why I did not allow my men to take your wife from
you. Did she keep you company in the cellar?"

In that cellar, Dominia had thought of Cassandra less than ever,
perhaps because all hope of her return was dead and gone. Now, the
General waited, stone-faced, and the dentist sensed his overstep but

did not acknowledge it as he continued, "When I first came to the Hunters, I was barely more than a boy—barely better than your fat friend, Tenchi, eh? A bit thinner, but just as wide-eyed. I plied my services as best as I could among the men, but how hard it was to get respect! How hard it was to get them to see my ideas. They had so many resources, and what were they trying to build? More drones! More rockets! Stupid." Akachi waved his hand in disgust. "That is what your Father wanted from them, wasting time and energy on toys. The better plan was to create a more effective weapon. One that put mankind on the physical level of the martyrs, or higher.

"No one would listen to me. I was just some grunt, some child fresh from dental school who had never seen a battle and could hardly handle the sight of blood when it wasn't in a mouth. But then I was deployed to another unit, because, well!" He grinned. "A dentist always seems useless until the abscess, eh?

"The man on whom I had been brought to work was an important fellow. I did not realize how important until, under gas, he began talking before his procedure. Talking and talking, about how he had long ago acquired the blood of Lazarus from a man greater than him; he was not sure he deserved it anymore, which was why he rambled at the lightest touch of my drugs. When he was out enough for me to get to work, I noticed this." He lifted the red ampule. "I had heard the stories. I could not resist the promises of power. While my patient was unconscious, I stole a drop. Soon after, he was killed, and, because I was, at the time, learning how to navigate that unholy place, I went to the site of his battle by a shortcut through the Ergosphere and claimed the vial. But it was not the symbol they cherished on my return: it was the man. Why? Because the Hunters are a superstitious and changeable people, and all superstitious and changeable people are especially so when in the presence of the divine. By the grace of God, I appeared before them out of thin air, as had their prior leader. Their following me was more a question of my divine selection by the Lord than of respect for the blood of Lazarus. A question of my power, and their hatred for martyrs."

"And you expect them to listen to what I have to say, if I serve you?"

"*If* you serve me, yes. If you serve God. They will not listen to you

if you are not a servant of God, Miss Mephitoli, but I see in your heart you possess the ability to turn your life around. All you need do is give me information."

"About?"

"About your sister, Lavinia." The request was so bizarre, so sudden, the General only laughed in bafflement, and Tobias did the same, though in a tone more mocking. "Now, General, do not think you can play games with me. I know Lavinia is invaluable to the Hierophant. I know he keeps her locked in his castle as though she were the most precious of gems. I would like to know why."

"She's an incredibly powerful woman with the temperament of a girl," responded the confused General. "He infantilizes her and keeps her helpless, because she's his favorite, and he's creepy."

"Please, Miss Mephitoli." The humor faded from his face. "Do not hide behind the charade of sibling rivalry. Your Father keeps no one closer than those who are most powerful."

"I told you, she is powerful. It's just—"

"If her memetic abilities were the only issue, would she not be ever by *your* side, provoking enemy forces to dance, or inspiring the women of besieged villages to drown their children? Had I a weapon powerful as your little sister, I would see her used. Instead, he keeps her on a shelf."

He had a point. Still, heels dug in, the General insisted, "Aside from what you're describing being a war crime, I don't know anything about that. He spoils her and keeps her isolated from the world for what he claims to be religious reasons. That's all I can say."

"You know something." Accusation, not speculation. He was an idiot if he thought she'd reveal anything she did or didn't know after three hundred years of intense practice at closely guarding Family secrets.

"All I knew was the black sun business. His promise that martyrs would walk in the day. I didn't know anything about Lavinia. Are you sure you're not jumping to conclusions?"

Fury twisted the dentist's face as he snapped, "Do not patronize me, General. I know when something is wrong and will not be persuaded otherwise. You know more than you are telling me."

Dominia was growing concerned this plan would take her down a longer route than anticipated—she might have to play the long con, until there cracked an opening by which she could escape into the Void or the desert. But, almost early as predicted, a terrible scream rose in the distance. Two more; a peal of bullets; silence, beneath the rising cries of "Dies Irae." As if from nowhere, the gun appeared in Akachi's hand, and he strode for the door with it aimed at the General while demanding, "Stay there."

"It's no use," said Lazarus. "René has been martyred. If he gets a gun he'll shoot up half the camp, eyes or no."

"Sounds like he's already got one." Dominia studied the untrained length of the next burst of gunfire. "You might want to tell your men to hurry."

"Lying, traitorous bitch." The snarling dentist looked as if he considered shooting the General but decided against it—wisely, from the way Lazarus was poised. Instead, baring his teeth and shouting in Arabic, Akachi dashed into the chaos of his rushing men to deliver orders and make them of one mind.

"We have little time." Lazarus hurried to bash open Akachi's weak desk and reclaim the flask containing the Ergosphere's waters. "Book it back to the medical tent and get a weapon before it's too late."

"Too late for what?" asked the General, distracted by another rush of footsteps outside the tent. No answer. Dominia, frowning, turned back, and said Lazarus's name only to discover she was completely alone. Again, she said his name, and again it only emphasized the point that there was no one to respond. These useless holy men!

She emerged from the tent in which Mozart's tubas blasted to find the camp had, in the space of seconds, been deserted. The astonished General hurried back along the route by which the Hunters had led her, finding the medical tent not by its size or her memory, but the body outside and the aroma of fresh death within. Her stomach snarled; she stepped inside to see René, assault rifle forgotten on the floor as he crammed hunks of meat from some soldier's torso into his blood-covered mouth.

His head lifted as she stepped inside. "Dominia?"

"Yeah, René, I'm here."

"My God, Dominia! I feel so good! I feel—" He laughed through his full mouth and swallowed its contents with a belch. "Would you believe I *smelled* you coming? I didn't even know I knew what you smelled like!"

"I'll try not to be haunted by that sentence." Dominia snatched the rifle. "Stay here. If things get hot and you hear it getting bad outside—just hide under a bed, or something."

"Roger, General," chirped the feasting martyr, who pulled out a slippery chunk of pancreas. "Oh, Dominia, this is great! All this time I thought it would be such a horrible thing, but...human really is delicious."

"We wouldn't eat it if it tasted like shit," she said, half laughing on her way from the tent before she fell into the camp's fog of silence. The tents themselves held their breaths, braced against the rising wind as Dominia was braced against whatever these humans could throw her way. They were, after all, just humans: but they did have tools.

The answer to Dominia's first question—where had everyone gone—came when she experimentally cleared, gun first, the square tent beside that of Tobias. Not unlike the tent covering the prison where she and René had spent the last week of his human life, this sheltered the entrance of a tunnel. Now the General understood, not only why her Father never bothered bombing Hunter encampments or otherwise engaging them militarily on their own turf, but how appropriate it was that her instincts likened them to ants. Beneath the ground rested an elaborate network of bunkers the Hunters had dug and outfitted as suited their needs—perhaps centuries old, at that. Small wonder the bricks had been so quick to turn to dust in that cellar. Perhaps it had once had four brick walls, and prisoners had, over time, destroyed the other three.

How many such Hunter colonies were hidden across the Middle States? There had to be enough to keep the various cells cycling between them, plus a few extra, "just in case." It was an astonishing thought on which she had no time to dwell. While gazing into the black pit of the tunnel, the ground pulsed in echo of her heartbeat.

This was no fancy. This was something that moved. Something rattling the earth so violently that the General sprang into the open to put space between her and the four-armed, drill-outfitted ALIF-8 that spewed from the dirt like metallic puss out of an earthy wound. The two empty metal hands with which it pushed away clots loosed by its drills now lifted in fists to protect Tobias's fury-narrowed face.

"I cannot begin to express how disappointed I am to know it has come to this, Miss Mephitoli!"

An experimental squeeze of her trigger elicited no reaction in the suit, with a few projectiles of the spray coming close to its pilot but springing off a fist. When the thing crouched, as it now did, mere shards of flesh were revealed to an assailant; and when it moved, so, too, needed move its target. At the slightest hint of movement in that steel haunch, the martyr ran, arms pumping and gun bruising her chest. Cassandra's diamond crushed her skin, emphasizing the pounding of her pulse as the thing sprinted even faster than had the warehouse model. Above the impossible symphony of noise, Akachi's voice proved the most grating addition.

"You have made the choice to throw your life away when you could have been invaluable to the cause of the one true God. You could have saved your soul! But the Lord has seen fit to end your life. Others may think you are valuable—the Hierophant, the magician— but that is all the more reason why you should be killed. I only wish I had killed you a week ago, when first you fell into my hands! What a fool I am, trusting a martyr."

Between its broad strides—leaps—and the General's unfamiliarity with the area, the suit gained more ground with every step. As a drill impaled uncomfortably close to her back and was used by the thing to vault over her head, Dominia lifted the rifle, squeezed the trigger, and released a hail of gunfire that necessitated Tobias waste precious seconds protecting his face. In those seconds, the General skidded around a sharp right turn and made an immediate left around the next tent. Behind her thundered the suit.

"It is too late for me to spare your life, Miss Mephitoli, but it is not too late for you to enjoy a painless death. You have a gun—why not be like Judas Iscariot, eh? But, I suppose you are not capable of that degree of dignity—only of pretending you are."

With a tearing clamor, the suit charged through the tents around which the General was forced to navigate. In so doing, the ALIF-8 cleared a path like a goring bull flattening a fence for which it had never had respect from the start. It got so close behind her that her only choice was wheel around, drop, roll, and shoot blindly, then scramble back in the direction of the desolation to take advantage of the machine's one apparent weakness—the time it took to turn its unwieldy frame. What she did not account for, though, was the mobility of its arms, and one of those snatched the gun from her grip before she outpaced its reach. In the wreckage, she searched for something to replace it, and found, unsurprisingly, no weapons kept in the tents. The best she could find was one of the steel poles, which might serve as some semblance of spear.

"This is a tragic and humiliating death for a general such as you." One drill impaled the dirt near enough to Dominia's foot that she felt its oscillations. "Do you not wish to die with honor? Or can honor even matter to an animal?"

Something was wrong, amid all the whirring of drills. One ground at a louder, more rattling pitch, and as a steel hand caught her in an open-palmed slap that knocked her on her ass, she realized a tarp was tangled in the left drill. As her vision cleared of its black and red to reveal the mechanical man standing over her, the General showed her teeth.

"I don't know"—she slipped the pole beneath the collapsed cerulean tarp of the nearest tent—"why don't you tell me?"

Jerking the staff up didn't flip the tarp over the head of the dentist as she'd hoped, but it did drape the right drill, which had been so close to penetrating her guts that if she thought about the closeness of her call, it would ruin her ability to fight. Luckily, she survived. Even more luckily, Tobias required delay to wrench, with a metal hand, the ever-more-tangled pieces of fabric from a drill that only mucked itself up worse with each attempt to shred the tarp. By the time he'd extricated the piece giving him the biggest problem, the General was behind him with another, this tarp falling over his head and provoking a snarl of agitation. As, in the distance, Rex tremendae cried its opening chords like the heralding of an earthquake, the General used the pole: first to vault upon the covered back of the thrashing metal beast, then to impale it many times through the fabric of its prison. Now and then, the pole bounced off the plates of armor, but there were those sweet moments when it slipped between two metal joints to plunge through the oil-soft tangles of hydraulics that responded in hisses and pops too satisfying to believe. One last stab elicited a violent seizure in the left arms of the machine, which, frozen, proved so unbalanced that the blinded thing lost all equilibrium. It careened to the dark, dusty ground while the General sprang from its shoulders to land upon perfectly balanced feet.

"It's over, Tobias." With the tip of the pole, she nudged the still-whir-ring, twitching mound of metal and fabric. "This is why you don't use a prototype for battles."

No quip returned. For a hopeful moment, it seemed he was dead. She stepped nearer. "Listen to me: I don't want to kill you. I will if I have to, but I'd rather you let Lazarus and I go on our own. Where, I don't know. But we'll figure it out."

Again, no response. Now, with dread where once the General might have felt assured victory, Dominia removed her hat, then knelt to draw the tarp from the oil-oozing ALIF-8.

It was almost a surprise when Akachi's seat was empty. Almost, but not quite. Somehow, she had known: been unconsciously tipped off by the sag of the tarp, or the way the machine stopped moving, rather than continuing even a slight struggle. But, no. Without sunlight; with-out moonlight; without smoke, mirrors, or anything else Dominia had seen, the dentist had vanished into the Ergosphere.

Blood boiling with fury to find now even he felt justified in leaving her behind as it suited, the martyr snapped the metal pole over her knee and was about to use its point to stab the monstrous thing as though pinning a butterfly to a board. Yet, before penetration, her hand stayed. In the distance, after all, speakers played Mozart's Requiem. And, with a sudden, openmouthed shock, she understood what to do.

The attention of the General's soul mounted the vibrations of the music.

XVII

A Thousand Twangling Instruments

Perhaps, when using music instead of sunlight to manifest in the Ergosphere, she had expected to arrive in the doorway of her Father's study. Tobias was exactly hypocritical enough to use the Hierophant's thoughtforms as a nighttime entrance in (and maybe out) of the dangerous Void. But she had somehow forgotten she would appear in her old leather jacket, had not expected to find herself one-eyed. Even with her gun in its holster, to inspire that surge of love-hate!

And she had certainly not been prepared for the sight of herself engaged on the floor with the *tulpa*. Farther in the distance, the shrill screams of Jerusalem's writhing damned rose beneath the Mozart. She had not noticed it before, perhaps because her ears had not been tuned to hear it. Not been prepared, as she had been prepared to see her Father.

"Why, Dominia"—the Hierophant glanced from where he read in his seat, back to the obvious proceedings—"what an unexpected pleasure!"

Brow furrowing, the General opened her mouth. Confused as she was, she spoke only with struggle. "Haven't I already been here?"

"Part of you has, in a sense. That is the trouble with overindulgence." Wearing that innocent look, he sipped his own waiting glass of red wine. "Very difficult to become drunk and maintain a firm sense of linear time. The most common mistake of the conscious mind is the delusion that it observes all it does within the expected chronology. One assumes minute to minute we experience just the present. But in dreams, my dear, the past and future are as present as now; even in reality, time is only a suggestion. A mere condition of conscious existence."

Perhaps it was that muddying of distinctions in time that so distracted her. Whatever the reason, she lost track of why she'd come. Indeed, to be once more immersed in that boundless space of the Void was treacherous in ways she'd just begun to understand. Separation between then and now—that self on the floor and this self that sat in the empty chair—was impossible. Pleasure yet throbbed, lust yet boiled high in her blood; but no sorrow burned for Cassandra, because she was sure that thing was not Cassandra. Barely, she clung to the sound of the music: to the spinning record she drunkenly pulled off the floor-level shelf.

"I came here through the music...I didn't know I could."

"You are always welcome in my study, dear girl."

"No, I mean—I didn't know I could travel through music."

"There are a thousand secret ways into this place scattered across the world, but none so fine as music. Art lifts the soul as wind, the wings of birds, that we may climb to heights unknown by the paltry body." With hand adorned by his gold piscatory ring, the Hierophant caressed the record player's wooden edge. "Mozart, Bach, Rossini, Wagner, Sullivan, Homer, Shakespeare, Waterhouse...do you know what you and Mozart have in common, Dominia?"

"An early death," she almost answered; but the question was rhetorical and, given the way he smiled, he might have heard her, anyway. "You are both fine artists." He answered himself with a joshing wag of his finger. "The art of war is fine as any other: the martial arts that rule the body write poetry in physics. Every fatal battle is a sensual dance between souls who have agreed, without their body's conscious consent, which one of them shall die."

A battle. Yes! That was it—why she'd come. The battle with Tobias. The General's mouth opened in a frown of distress. To think she could forget! She locked eyes with her own, panting self on the floor beneath the odious thing. "Which one of us agreed to die tonight?"

"Between yourself, and the Hunter?" The Hierophant's eyes sparkled like onyx gems set in the pale olive of his face. "I think you both know the answer to that."

Outside, the night of the Void had almost completely fallen. In reality, not much time had passed because she had not moved save for the steps it took to reach the empty chair—although even if she walked back to the doorway, the fact that she had come to the Ergosphere for a Planck was now indelible. The Hierophant had seen her. But he also must have observed Tobias, so she asked him straight, "Have you seen him? The dentist? Tonight—my tonight, if you can tell one from the other."

"I can, because I pay careful attention. Yes, I have seen the dentist flee into the dark tonight. I have known him to use my study coming and going ever since he stumbled upon it in the daytime and recognized I came and went, for the most part, by way of artworks. I believe he finds the process easier than traveling by sunlight or actually educating himself on higher, spiritual matters, for the man has a poisoned and petty soul, and cannot make himself confront it in the bright eye of day. But, God will force the confrontation at his death. Can you see, my one-eyed child, how he sealed his own fate by condemning others to it? By spreading superficial and incorrect faith among his men? Say what you will of our Church; *I* practice what I preach. For the most part." Behind his lifted glass, he winked.

Too true. Granted, she believed her Father because she wanted to—but the Hierophant had a point that alleviated the last of her doubts about the VLF manifestations of Jerusalem, Mecca, et al. Tobias and the Hunters were just as responsible for those trapped souls as her Father. Every false leader of every false spirituality from the beginning of time was responsible for those souls: any superficial cult that did not provide sufficient frame of reference for its followers to navigate the afterlife. From that perspective, Tobias and the Hierophant were both just as evil—and she knew which manifestation of evil she preferred to deal with long-term. "Will you tell me what I need to do to kill him? How I catch him? What happens if he leaves the Void before I do?"

With the twitch of a lip longing in palpable way to reveal the answers she sought, the Hierophant seemed bound to refrain. Instead, he allowed his eagerness to be betrayed in the way he leaned forward, hands folded between his knees. "What you and the rest of your fine artist brethren all have in common, my girl—what you and Mozart have in common—is the ability to absorb those universal elements that make your particular art form grand. In all his journeying across the face of Europa, Amadeus consumed every scrap of music he found, and analyzed that spark within that made each piece transcendent. Through those sparks, he built a mighty flame."

Above the distant screams of the lost souls, the General heard the rippling trumpet of an enormous beast. An elephant. She lifted her head in the direction of the sound as the Hierophant continued, "The great artist lets nothing come between him and his work, and uses every smallest stimulus as fuel for the fire. Even sexual fantasies are, to the artist, fuel for inspiration, rather than the millstone they present around the necks of the uninitiated."

With a shock of recognition, Dominia's attention returned to her Father's mouth, whose remembered words she emulated with her own, with the same timing, cadence—everything—as him. "Sexual fantasies," the Hierophant and the General spoke together, in proper context, "are a misapplication of the creative libido down into the sexual drive, rather than upward, toward God."

At her wonder, her Father smiled, and continued as he had before: though now, his motions were different, and it was she who rose, slowly, from her seat. "The average man is incapable of salvation because he is so wrapped up in the material world that he cannot see his own lust for flesh is truly a lust for a higher power. The average martyr, even, cannot be saved, and the best he can hope for is a close connection with his community in the form of the living Church."

Her boot steps echoed across the chessboard floor, a beat to the Hierophant's words as she crossed to stand over herself and the horrific doppelgänger. Every second, it looked less like a person. "When we find our lover manifested in the flesh, we derive from them a surge of inspiration because the soul is liberated from the surly bonds of lust.

Our fantasies are revealed as the poisonous wastes of time they have always been. Idle hands are the Devil's playthings." He lifted his own, suddenly full, glass in toast to her.

"That's why we need art," agreed Dominia. The distant instrument of that animal spurred her first step off the lighted island of the study, into the black abyss.

"Yes. Yes, my girl. That is why we need art. That is why we need you."

Drawing her gun, the General glanced over her shoulder one last time. Her watching Father rose to see her off to the hunt. "Was it you in the *tanque*?" she asked him, studying the face that so studied her. "Really you, I mean."

Thinly, he smiled. "'*Wenn du lange in einen Abgrund blickst, blickt der Abgrund auch in dich hinein.*'"

As expected. Gun in hand, the General plunged into the inky dark, muscles coiled for her kill. If at any time in the future she had even the slightest probability of crossing paths with that which she sought—that beast, Tobias, who led her so astray she stumbled by accident into the Kingdom—then it was already impossible for the dentist to escape alive. And this place was all about probability, right? That he was at all audible seemed evidence of her victory, which pumped her dream-fast muscles into an altogether more uncanny pace. The rush of such running—nearly flying—filled her with delight, and the darkness whipped through and around her, over and under her. She nearly leapt for joy, heart racing, body light as it had been when first she'd learned to love the art of battle. Yes, yes—it was an art, was a joy to her. This, she could never deny. As a girl initiated into the Church, she had disliked the killing of even criminal humans for the Noctisdomin Mass, but had always loved a good boxing match, always thrilled at the satisfaction of a well-implemented strategy. She had been reluctant to free herself from the Hunter's prison by means of violence, but violence was the oil paint with which she had coated the world's canvas to produce the painting of her life. Tobias thought a human's ability to survive without violence set it as a superior species, but, in the dark, the General did not see it that way. Was it not said, after all, that the tiger was superior to the elephant when it came to the food chain?

When Dominia skidded to a halt and listened above the dreamy silence of her thought-body for the sound of the beast, she feared she was lost. What she wouldn't have given for her compass! Or for more warning as, with a terrible bellow, the freight train–animal thundered from the darkness to run her down or gore her with tusks not so different from the dentist's drills. As she had when fighting the exoskeleton with the assault rifle, the General aimed, but realized before the second charge it could do no good against an opponent such as this. In the Void, death meant waking up to reality. Once she killed him here, she'd have to catch him on Earth; and he could just as easily slip right back into the dark night of the Ergosphere. An endless struggle.

After holstering the gun, the General braced herself to meet the animal head-on, hands against goring tusks, because no matter what that putrid dentist loved to say, an animal was no match for a martyr. A martyr, though not an animal, had an animal within: as the elephant in her grip transformed with an alien shriek and a twisting explosion of particles into an eagle, and her hands were crushed by the piercing grip of the raptor's golden talons, the General found within herself the claws of that great tiger. Snarling with hunger, the predator leapt to latch fangs in the throat of the screaming prey. This feathery mane soon became a furred one, and the molten blood of a lion filled her mouth, swam up into her brain, became therein the poison of a thrashing serpent that she resisted—that was simplicity itself to resist. Her own knowledge of the Ergosphere far surpassed Tobias's, if only because she so humbled herself before the experience that she acknowledged she knew nothing. It was the tiger within her that beat back feather-wingéd lizards and lion-headed serpents until Tobias, who had tried to be so many things he had forgotten what he was, crawled across the ground, laughing, mad: half man, half writhing, bloodied beast.

"Will you kill me, General?" asked the dentist, his bright teeth glowing. "Will you kill me, and send me back where I started? Have you not learned what it is to die here! Nothing, nothing at all—it makes what we have felt here a dream, barely remembered."

Being addressed by her title brought her back to herself more clearly than the sensory stimulus of seeing her target as a partial man.

The gun had somehow found its way back into her hand, and now, free to have the conscious experiences of a humanoid, Dominia realized there must have been some source of light for his teeth to glow. She turned, and in the distance, there it was: the fountain.

"Of course," she said, her focus caught completely. "Be'er Sheva."

Before she basked in the glory of the implications, the beast behind her sprang and knocked her face-first upon the dirt. With clenched teeth, the General suffered her face to be slammed into the ground: ground scattered with life from that holy fountain, whose waters Lazarus used to reproduce her eye and teeth. That water—the same water, as all water—that was the Lady. That same water tended by the Bearers, through which one accessed the magician's Kingdom.

As Dominia's head was slammed back down into the ground, something snapped behind her eyebrow and she tried to remember it was only a dream. Still, she felt terrible, and the blood obscured her uncovered eye so that, when he turned her over, she was almost completely blind. His hands were around her neck, and they were attached to human arms, but what was beneath his waist seemed half a lion's haunch and part of a snake's long tail, with one eagle's claw that struggled to find uncanny purchase on the ground. "Maybe I send you back, eh, and am right there waiting when you arrive, ready to crush your skull! Then I get the satisfaction of killing the greatest martyr General twice in one night."

"Nice fantasy," she would have said, but it was hard to speak when choked by hands strong as a martyr's in the dream-space where so many things were equal it was hard to tell one object from another. But, better than saying it, she thought it. In a snap, the word "fantasy" recalled her Father's words: "The great artist lets nothing come between him and his work, and uses every smallest stimulus as fuel for the fire. Even sexual fantasies are, to the artist, fuel for inspiration."

Of all the tools at her disposal, one had been available since the start of her journey in the Void, but was single-mindedly eschewed. Now it possessed a higher purpose. The General's eye closed. Cut off from the perception of blood as well as the Ergosphere's aether, the Higgs field, or whatever it was her brain believed she was breathing, her mind began to fog over just as she reached out for the *tulpa*. Oh, sweet duplicate of fair Cassandra, so cruelly maligned. Did not the doppelgänger want her love? Could she give it if she were dead?

Could she give it, *still*, if the *tulpa* shared her body? Was it not better for the nebulous shape-thief to have a body separate from her own? A gateway into the real world, where it could receive all the love Dominia might offer?

The General must have been seconds from death when the deformed, burned, defenestrated, and bleeding future of the monstrosity erupted from the fountain with a terrible scream. Its ability to hold Cassandra's shape after its ordeal in the Kingdom had reduced to a horrific series of mouths: each opened to reveal her lover's face within, mouth after mouth, an infinity attached to arms that stretched forward, all screaming Dominia's name. This attracted the attention of the dentist just before it leapt on him with such force that both were knocked clear of gasping Dominia by several meters. Scrambling up, the General retrieved her gun, then limped to watch as the unwatchable thing swallowed Dr. Tobias Akachi, starting from the feet.

"God, help me," he cried. The mood she was in, the General found no humor in the plea.

"You said you became a Hunter to escape being a slave to the martyrs, Akachi. But you said it yourself. You're still a slave; and your master doesn't give a damn about you."

As the doppelgänger reached his neck, his eyes rolled up into his head, and by the time its teeth crunched apart his skull, not only did the thing bear a closer resemblance to Cassandra: it had put the leader of the Hunters out of his misery. The *tulpa* lurched to its feet, hand wiping its mouth, and smiled warily at the General.

"Dominia," it said.

Amazed her gambit had worked, the General did not speak. She extended her arm. Its face lit in so real a mimicry of Cassandra's, it elicited the same physical elation in Dominia. As the thing fell into her embrace, near crying for joy, she cradled it, her cheek against the top of its head.

"Thank you for coming to me."

"Love you, Dominia." It turned its whispering face toward hers and tried to hide the hollow nature of its eyes with a deceptive smile, lips parted to betray a glimpse of satin tongue. "Love you, love you."

"So you'll be able to come back to Earth, now, in place of him?" The General tipped the thing's chin up.

"Uh-huh, Dominia. Love you forever, Dominia." How dotingly it smiled up at her. The counterfeit's hot body ground against hers with the promise of mindless, eternal devotion.

"Good." She lowered her head to meet the thing's kiss while lifting her gun to the back of its head. "Thank you."

The sensation of the dream suicide was impossible to describe, perhaps because it was all such a terrible implosion that it snapped her back in time and space like a rubber band. In an infinitely small parcel of experience—a Planck, she supposed—she whirled back through all her interactions in the Void to the point in reality where she entered it: poised, with her makeshift stake, to impale the battery of the ALIF-8.

The *tulpa*, which had consumed Akachi's thought-body and, due to the binding of Lazarus's blood, his real one along with it, emitted a terrible shriek beneath the searing light of the full moon. The repulsive parasite, revealed for what it was, thrashed within the prison of the lifeless exo-suit on exposure to imperfect darkness. As it clawed at itself and its surroundings and her, the General was so disoriented to find them thus that she was nearly swept by its gray hand. The freak twitch of a dying metallic arm offered protection enough for her to spring away in pursuit of an assault rifle that would now prove far more useful. By the time the thing extricated itself from the ALIF-8, the General was ready to unload a satisfying magazine into the twisting thoughtform. When that was empty, she was upon it with the pole; and by the time the pole broke in her hands, the thing was dead.

Panting, covered in the black blood of that entity that dissolved at her feet into a substance not unlike the oil of the exoskeleton, Dominia looked up to find the encampment of distant Hunters, having ascended from belowground, watched from the negligible safety of their tents. As they began to reveal themselves from their labyrinth, most in superstitious horror but some in what appeared to be genuine awe, the General threw down the remains of her makeshift spear. Amid the slick of the leftover demon floated the dentist's false teeth, his glasses, and the ampule that once was private trophy of his rule. This, the General secreted before addressing the crowd.

"Those of you who do not like what has happened here, leave. Tell your like-minded brothers in other cells to do the same. The rest of you belong to me."

Absolutely no one moved, save for what it took to translate her words. A few men laughed. Several adjusted their grips on their guns. She didn't blink.

"Bring me my traitorous whelp, René."

A murmur rose amid some of the men. When she did not move, the murmur gathered to a clamor and movement rippled through the crowd. René's shocked cry pierced the night, along with the sounds of violence. The discharge of a gun concerned her until, thirty seconds later, the thrashing martyr, too new to be truly dangerous (or even competent), was dragged through the crowd and tossed at her feet by a party of several soldiers.

He began, as usual, with, "Please," but, exhausted of hearing him beg, she snatched him upright and covered his mouth. With the blind and temporarily mute martyr under her arm, Dominia scanned the crowd again, and lifted her voice in command to the man who watched.

"Lazarus. Come out."

The crowd hushed. Again, the only sounds that rose from them were the necessary ones—the ones required for the men to part so Lazarus, having been who-knew-where, could meet Dominia with the placid calm of a person who knew precisely what was about to happen. She presented René's filthy, whining face, one hand still over his mouth and the other now resting on his forehead to drag open empty eyelids. Lazarus splashed the water so abruptly that René could only scream, as had Dominia.

Around them, Hunters murmured, and the General lowered René to the ground while he screamed about the alleged pain and burning; all the while, he clawed and kicked. Lazarus stepped away, replacing the flask on his person, to watch with a barely suppressed smile. Abruptly,

René's sobbing relented to the hilarious gasps of a small child who realized they had not, after all, hurt themselves.

"I forgive you, René," Dominia said, as gently as she had ever said anything to the professor. "For everything. Open your eyes."

To the wild astonishment of the Hunters, he did.

"I can see? I can see—I can *see!*" René sprang up, screaming the words, clutching his face, his eyes wild. From the depths of the crowd, Tenchi emerged, looking just as amazed to cry at his cousin, "René?"

"Tenchi! Oh my God, I can see you! My own eyes, my real eyes— Tenchi!" Giddy, the former professor ran for his cousin and, in a move that surprised them both, swept the man in his new martyr's arms as if his portly cousin were a tiny girl. "I've never been so happy to see you!"

"Others among you who suffer from ailments, come to us and we will cure them." Dominia looked from face to face in a crowd that dropped to its knees, and she experienced that thrill her Father felt while grocery shopping. Too bad she had to ignore the pleasure of pride in favor of the right thing. She kept waiting.

"Who among you needs to be healed," she repeated, and Lazarus translated in Arabic, Farsi, and one or two other languages she didn't recognize offhand. Now the first man, perhaps not much older than René but limping as though he were twice that, made his unsure way to the martyrs. He paused some meters away, began his sentence with "I—" and then, after reluctant consideration for the General, spoke to Lazarus in Arabic.

"This man says he has killed many of our kind, and pleasurably."

"And I have killed many of your kind, and pleasurably. You need healing."

Lazarus repeated this in Arabic, while, with hesitation, the man drew closer. "We forgive you," she told him while Lazarus blessed him. For this man, the change was less pained, but no less wonderful to behold: in seconds, his leg remembered how once it walked, and ran, and danced, as now it did so before his brothers-in-arms.

The line of men that grew proved three hours long. When all was finished, and the night found it still had room for rest, the General had her army.

XVIII

Shvu'a

Not as many men left in the night as Dominia had expected. In the aftermath, most deserters crawled off not because she was a martyr, but because she was a woman, and a lesbian. The unit was better off without them; she hoped the rest of the Hunter cells would follow suit, though she had the feeling this one, which had observed the miracles of her battle and Lazarus's many healings, might splinter off from the rest of the terrorist group, and perhaps manage to maintain ties to one or two small units. Fine by her. She wanted nothing to do with the Hunters, except for those who respected the notion of change.

Although she had been invited down into the tunnels and thus, the true encampment, Dominia refused that night, seeing them as too close to that prison that she'd shared with René. She slept in bliss, better than she had in many weeks—her whole adult life—beneath the open sky. Without fear of the rising sun! Glory. The next morning, she and Lazarus instructed the formerly crippled, selectively English-speaking pilot, a man whose nom de guerre was Farhad, to introduce them to those who remained. She thought all the while of Valentinian: particularly when one man, too young to have run off to such awful war games as indicated by his enthusiasm for Dominia's exploits, burst out in the delighted Arabic of an excited boy.

"He says you are like, ah, a 'magician,' Mahdi," explained Farhad, smiling a little, himself. "Making Tobias disappear."

After a few such interactions, it became apparent that Tobias had not been well liked in camp, but his leadership had been accepted. The dead dentist had been right on one count: they were an exceedingly superstitious group of people, men desperate for a faith to fill the empty, violent hole inside. The dentist's fundamentalist Christianity had not mattered to most of the camp, which leaned more toward the Islamic branch of Abrahamianism. That they had seen him appear out of thin air had been enough, much as simple observation of the General's bloody victory had set them straight again. This became clear when she recognized Farhad had called her "Mahdi" as a title. The word rang a bell with the Arabic- and Islam-illiterate General, though she could not remember its context.

"Is that 'General'?" she asked Lazarus as they rounded a corner in the mine-shaft-like tunnel system to the hand-carved rooms where "acquired" women slept or cried or kept their children quiet.

"No—it's an Islamic thing, or it used to be before the Hunters stole it. The Twelfth Imam, who will dispense justice and battle al-Masih ad-Dajjal during the apocalypse."

Trying not to roll her eyes, the General said, "They were calling me 'al-Masih ad-Dajjal' until last night."

Farhad, overhearing them, explained, "That was the fault of Dr. Akachi. The true al-Masih ad-Dajjal and Iblis misled him, as he misled our people. The world. If what you told us last night is true, about the ship and the hospital, then Iblis has gone to enormous lengths to ensure all societies view you as we are viewed. A terrorist."

Though she may have inherited an army of them, the title blanched her face with irritation. "I'm not a terrorist. I've never bombed a marathon because the Hierophant was there."

"If you wish different means"—the man gave a shrug—"that is up to you. We will follow. But the tools we have used on our jihad until now have been useful."

"Against your own kind," the General snapped, having seen plenty enough of the kidnapped, abused women. "Your guerrilla methods mean nothing to the Hierophant, to any martyr. It would be like humans fearing the collusion of cows. Collect the women and bring them to the surface with whatever things they've been allowed to keep. They're leaving."

Looking as though he had been slapped in the face, Farhad turned helpless eyes toward Lazarus, then back to Dominia. "Mahdi, please. These *sabaya* are fair property, granted us by Allah: men of all faiths, Abrahamian or not, keep women in this camp. Not even Akachi meant to separate us."

That was where she'd heard that title before. Her brain presented her with the fact at as inappropriate a moment as ever: there was a science-fiction novel, about a man who was Mahdi of a bunch of space people—it was one of her favorites as a kid, after she got out of dystopian fiction and into straight sci-fi stuff. Turned out a huge series about a guy—a displaced duke—who had named himself after a space mouse contained a bunch of deep, metaphysical stuff. Proof that sometimes even beneath her Father's tight censorship, foreign notions had slipped through the cracks, protected by the veil of literature. Every story she had ever read had prepared her for this journey, in a way. How funny; how frightening. How reassuring. The nature of her mission was amplified by the fiction as she gazed into the face of tragic reality.

"That's because it wasn't Akachi's duty to dispense justice." She spared a glance into one of the chambers and met the thoroughly tired eyes of the woman within it, who grew slightly more awake in the face of her confusion to see a free female staring back. "Send all the women up. If any are left behind, I will know, and there will be consequences."

Farhad, gritting his teeth, watched the martyrs turn the way they'd come, then snapped in Arabic for the listening women to do as they were bid. On the surface, Dominia waited beneath the sun. Soon, confused, displeased rabble drifted from the many entrances to the tunnels below. Beneath the ground, a loudspeaker emanated through the halls. One by one, the women emerged, thrusting their hands over their eyes and squinting in the light, huddling together in a mass of covered heads and ankle-length gowns. Pain clutched the heart of the General, particularly to see the children, but she kept her breathing level right along with her head.

"This encampment has changed its allegiance." Lazarus translated her words in curt Arabic. "The process of this change will be long and painful for the men, but for you, the change will be sudden and joyous. You are all free, now."

As a murmur arose, half excited and half frightened, one woman on the end spoke up. "To go where?"

A fair question. Jerusalem, even from Dominia's short drive to an industrial suburb nowhere near the tremendous city's center, sat in sorry tatters. Beyond all the traffic and crumbling cement sound walls, her drive with Tobias had revealed innate war-inspired poverty, with many empty and unkempt businesses tended by none but impoverished citizens. Unable to work due to injuries or lack of status, the extremely poor could not even lease and herd genetically engineered goats as those in rural regions. When the Hunters had fallen upon the city, the city model had become unsustainable, and in the face of a staggering death toll alongside crumbling infrastructure, the whole state of Israel was no longer exactly prime real estate.

"Well," began the General, "the Hunters own buildings in Jerusalem." She based this assumption on the single factory she'd visited, but this was true in less a legal sense and more a territorial sense when it came to the city. Indeed, it was just beginning to settle on her that, although other groups would murmur, technically it was not her group that was the splinter faction. Those who refused to follow would be splintering from *her*. In sweeping Akachi from his place, she had become the leader of the Hunters, inheriting their property along with their war and reputation. Not all bad, she supposed. "It is not desirable to go back to a place of painful memories, I know—for most of you, Jerusalem was not even your home to begin with. But that is a place to start, if you wish, or if you wish, I will gather the resources to send you to your homes."

Another English-speaking, now-former *sabiyya* spoke up with disdain. "Look at the big Western heroes, fixing slavery. Some liberating army! Half of these women have not even been to school. Their homes are destroyed! The ones here longest think al-Mawta have displaced the martyrs and now rule the world. They are mad, ill!" The girl's eyes filled with tears. "If I had stayed any longer, maybe I would have been.

They killed my father, my brothers—what is there for me now? What is there for any of us?"

Distant footsteps reverberated through the Earth; the General mistook them for those of her belowground men amid a mind which sought a means to soothe such pain. "Maybe I can't help you. But this is Lazarus," began Dominia, until the old man caught her gesturing hand.

"They won't know who I am, most of them. Women around the Hunters aren't allowed to study their doctrine. Not beyond the basic Abrahamian parts of it."

"Why is that?"

She felt the Lady's voice seconds before she heard it, rattling deep in the center of her own diaphragm, and the diaphragms of all those many around. *They know it takes few steps, upon learning of Lazarus, to learn of Us; and once a woman learns of Us, the world of men has lost her forever.*

Dominia, startled by the clarity of the voice, turned to see the litter, still in the distance, borne by the four older Water Bearers who had whisked away the Lady. Where the others had vanished to, or where the rest of the many women of the temple had gone, the General could not be sure. Nevertheless, it was with an admixture of relief and pleasure she saw, walking in procession before the litter with a parasol that shaded her ornately decorated dreadlocks, fair Gethsemane.

These women are Ours, the Lady declared. *We told you, Dominia, you would lead Our army. This is that army; so are the men belowground, though they do not yet know.*

Smirking, and forgetting, perhaps, that the distant face was only Miki's in theory, the General arched a brow. "I did the killing, but it's your army?"

All armies are Our armies, borrowed or stolen. We've stolen this one back. Or would you, General, reject the gift We offer in exchange? You'll command an army thrice the size of this, if only you would battle in Our name.

Here, the General was reluctant. Now divine and inter-dimensional politics were muddied into an already filthy matter that looked ever more like war. She could not believe in her heart the things known by followers of the Lady, no matter what miracle she had seen or what festival she'd attended. Perhaps this was related to her bitterness over Valentinian's abandonment. Yet, she somehow could not shake the idea that her reluctance to tout the banner of any one self-proclaimed deity was borne, in part, from knowledge of what Valentinian would want of her. He would not want to see her kowtow blindly to any one faith. But did that mean she kowtowed to him? She wasn't sure. They hadn't discussed it. Was she being a child about this, like a girl who thought if she were good enough, her parents would reclaim her from martyrdom? Was she, deep down, acting out of hope that right behavior would draw the magician back into her sphere?

"I can teach my men to battle in your name," the General allotted, "because they cannot do battle without a name to do it in, and my name isn't enough. That is why I must do battle in my own name: nobody will do it for me, since everybody's so busy fighting for you."

You do battle in your name, and the name of the magician, mused the goddess as Her litter paused at respectable distance. The parasol-holding Bearer lowered her sunglasses to wink at Dominia. The latter flushed, but did not move, and did not deny the increasingly apparent position of her neglected fealty. *Very well. This is fair. You will come to Us in time, as do all women. And all Our women will come here. You have the drives?*

Farhad, graciously, had shown these to the General and the mystic during their tour of the tunnels. Dominia assured Her of this until the goddess bobbed Miki's silent head in pleasure. *Very good. We shall summon Our scattered women to the city of Jerusalem; the time is long overdue.*

Perhaps the city's name on divinity's dream-breath was what stirred memory of the wailing souls looking for God in the Void. "I was shown a vision of Jerusalem in—Your waters, I guess. The Ergosphere. Is it true? Are all those people lost souls?"

There are many who seek Jerusalem and cannot find it, because they have been misled in life, or have misled others. Jerusalem, herself, is a pure and holy place. She is not responsible for misdirecting signposts. Those souls you see suffering are martyr and Hunter, murderers who repent in public but do not come to God in their hearts, those who are false of faith or lack the emotional faculty to experience it internally in its truest sense. They are half-formed souls swathed in robes of guilt and shame. It is better to spend an entire life unconscious than to dally with religion and swear half-true oaths.

This bothered Dominia as much or more than the thought of soulless spirits wandering without identity in the Void. What a tahgmahr religion could be! After running her hand over her forehead, the General waved toward the tent that had once belonged to Tobias. "Why don't You go ahead and take that tent until we find someplace decent in the city?"

No: We will remain with the women for now. Speak with Gethsemane.

Hesitant even as the named human closed her parasol, Dominia pressed, "There's nothing I can do for You?"

Your most important duty is to listen. Go, General. Dominia relented to the gentle tugs of the Bearer upon her arm. *You were right. There are many changes to be made. The ones within yourself are no exception.*

In the cool shelter of the tent, the General sank into the chair once inhabited by Tobias to find Lazarus had not followed but remained outside with his divine ménage. Grateful to be alone with the woman who poured wine from the bar cart set against the far side of the tent, Dominia said, "You didn't warn me about everything that was going to happen, and I get the feeling you knew some of it."

"Such a warning would have only made my work harder." So she had known. All the Bearers must have. "I think it was difficult enough to relieve you of the burden you felt toward poor Cassandra, who would, I know, not wish to see you suffer."

That was quite true. Yet in all the tumult of the past week, Dominia had not had the luxury of guilt. She had become so swept up in the wildness of events, she had not even felt guilt for her lack of guilt: the true sign of...well, some sort of progress. As the earthly body of the nymph neared, wineglass in hand, Dominia extended an arm. The woman responsively filled her lap. "I haven't given up hope that I'll see her again," said the General, determined, the faint impression of the recent dream still fresh in her mind. "But I don't think Cassandra is my priority right now."

"There is too much to be done." After pushing the cup to the General's lips and forcing her to take it in her hand, the Bearer drew from her boot a small black phone that activated at the touch of a delicate finger. "I have been asked to show you this. It was an encrypted broadcast, transmitted to the upper echelons of your Father's military personnel."

The recording that played was more subdued than those featuring Cicero and Theodore; yet, for its gentleness, the message was grave. At a plain desk before a stained-glass window of himself blocked almost entirely by the high wingback of his chair, the Hierophant sat with mournful expression. To his left elbow stood the Lamb, whose face inspired a pang of sorrow for the theoretically gentler of her two parents but who, nonetheless, was her enemy.

"Oh, children." The Hierophant heaved a piteous sigh. "It is with such pain we find ourselves thus. But, I am sorry to say extreme measures must be taken when faced with insurrection and terrorism such as that committed by my daughter, Dominia di Mephitoli. You are already aware of the bounty on her misguided life; but I do not wish for you, my men and women of the military, to think there is nothing you can do to help your country but remove the increasingly apparent head of a dangerous and, frankly, evil regime.

"This world of ours demands a certain order. Much as animals in the wild possess a predatory hierarchy, the same can be said of conscious beings. What are men and martyrs both but animals, ensouled—souls, embodied? The predators and prey together form an elaborate web whose spinner we dare not hope to know. Each thread, delicately balanced against its neighbors, comes together by nature's plan and animal's instinct. That which eats functions with that which is eaten in careful harmony. Yet, it is always in the instinct of those predators imbued with consciousness to rise above the natural order and inspire full submission in their prey—even knowing the damage this may cause the structural integrity of the web as a whole.

"This dilemma—the choice between symbiosis and conquest—is one that has haunted me for over two thousand years. When I must see my martyrs die, my children lose their lives in the sun and good people meet the horrific end of starvation, I wonder if symbiosis is the just choice. These past weeks, since the betrayal of my daughter and the bombing in Kabul, I have begun to determine it is most assuredly not.

"The time for symbiosis has ended, sorry though I am to say it. The time of the martyrs to begin seriously considering global dominance is now. To that end, I wish to give you a gift. My beloved Lamb has informed me that the time for us to reveal our plan has come. Over the next several years, military and engineering capacities will all be directed toward one particular goal: the sustainable blackening of the sun. This is no fancy, no comic book plot. This is the true inheritance of the martyrs. This is what I give to you, children. Your Father has eternally walked in the sun. Soon, all of you will join me."

The clip ended. Gethsemane, studying Dominia's tense face, slipped the phone away. "Do you understand what he's saying?"

"It's practically a declaration of war. Yes—I understand what he's saying."

There was no one, save perhaps Cicero, who knew as clearly what the Hierophant said when he spoke. This time, however, the translation was easy for anyone. As soon as he felt comfortable, the martyr army would be coming, and it would not be coming for her. It would be coming for Lazarus.

"We will have many forces, General," cautioned the Bearer, still studying the martyr's stoic face. "But we will need more than that."

"We'll need, among other things, a preemptive strike." With the edge of the glass pressing into her lower lip, Dominia marveled at how her Father could be so cordial in his hostility. For her part, she was full to the brim with only the latter; she wished, was tempted indeed, to sweep into the Ergosphere to confront him, though that would do no good. Dominia did understand, however, what drew Valentinian to spend time with the Hierophant: for she, even with Gethsemane in her lap, felt quite alone in the middle of that camp.

"You disappeared after the ceremony."

"I intended to meet you here, General."

"And the rest of the Bearers?"

"They are attending to the women who escaped the temple, and organizing the rest."

"But what of the magician? You must know where he's gone."

"Must I?" At the martyr's stern expression, the human offered a thin smile. "He is in the Void, General. The Ergosphere. I have seen him in dreams. He meets me there to educate me."

"On what?"

"On doing better service to you. I have been committed to your cause. I am afraid, however, that I am good at this juncture for little more than company."

"I get the feeling you're good for more than that." The martyr contemplated the evasive girl and slipped Cassandra's diamond from over her own head. After a moment, she hung it around the neck of the Bearer. "Can you keep her safe for me?"

"As though she were my soul."

"Thank you." With a sideways smile for the gem that glittered in the low golden light of the tent, the General felt for an instant the graze of Cassandra's fingertips down her cheek. "Would you leave me for a time?" she asked the woman, who nodded, but faltered before standing.

"I was also asked to give you this." Gethsemane withdrew from her other boot that familiar deck of playing cards, dropped in the throne room of the Lady and left far behind with her revolver. "When I dreamed of him after the temple, I found this on my person. I am not sure"—she admitted with a shifty look away—"it was entirely a dream."

"Did he say anything about my gun?"

The laughing nymph ducked from the tent. "That you'd ask about it, anyway."

Just as well. For now, she was surrounded by guns. Not having it here inspired the hope that she would have it back when she needed it. The comfort provided her by the deck of cards was more reassuring than any antique weapon, anyway.

Less comforting was that message from her Father. How strange to think, a mere six months before, the General would have been on the receiving end of that video—would have been filled with patriotic vigor. Well...not quite so much as she would have been as a youth. Still, she had not expected her life to change in the severe ways it had: certainly not at this rate. She had never expected, not once in her life, to be called a terrorist. Yet, here she was. The head of a cell of them, and the leader of an army—arguably greater in size, for all the Red Market women, than units she'd led for the Hierophant. And with intentions she respected, if under the guidance of the Lady. There was a kind of self-respect in that: perhaps that was what she was learning. She wasn't clear. She only knew that she had changed, and very much. But the most profound change of all was her instinct to genuflect before those cards.

Alone in her tent amid her growing army, Dominia di Mephitoli prayed for victory against the Hierophant. She was not sure to whom the prayer was addressed; but, if God wasn't listening, the magician certainly was, and he would help her prayers be heard. That, somehow, proved more reassuring. But somebody else also listened—somebody who thought or wished or dreamed he was God, though he coyly danced around the subject whenever asked outright. Somebody who seemed next to her in a sandalwood haze, whose specter knelt beside her. Somebody she so loathed to see here, in this place, in the midst of victory, that she kept her eyes shut and prayed: raised her voice: all but shouted her supplications for the divine against the smugly spoken words of the Hierophant's unwelcome phantasm. A being so real her own ears heard him say:

"You'll have to let me know if you get a response."

Had to get the last word, didn't he?

[ed.: The following is a copy of the Rosary of the Holy Martyr Church as it is practiced in the time of Dominia di Mephitoli. It is the English version of a prayer most popularly said in Modern Mephitolian, which appears to have its structural root in Latin while containing many words of Germanic influence. As the General has high familiarity with many works of English literature and her companions use it regularly, it seems probable English is used as a lingua franca.]

THE ROSARY OF THE
HOLY MARTYR CHURCH

Make the Sign of the Cross

In the name of the Father, and of the Lamb, and of the
Eternal Children.
Amen.

Recite the Creed

I believe in God, the Father Almighty,
Creator of heaven and earth,
And in the Holy Lamb, his Second Son, our Savior.
He was preceded by his Brother,
And borne of the Hierophant's blood.
He suffered under humanity's reign,
Was martyred, died and was buried.
He descended into hell.
On the third day, He rose again.
He was shown Acetia,
Returned to Earth,
And is seated at the right hand of the Holy Father.
He has come again to judge the living and the dead.
I believe in the Eternal Children,
The Holy Martyr Church,
The communion of saints,
The forgiveness of sins,
The resurrection of the body,
And life everlasting.
Amen.

One "Our Father"

Our Father,
Good servant of God,
Hallowed be Thy Name.
Acetia come,
Thy Will be done,
On earth as it is in heaven.
Give us this day our daily flesh,
And forgive us our weaknesses,
As we forgive those who fail us by their weakness.
And lead us not into heresy,
But shepherd us from ignorance.
Amen.

Three "Hail Lavinias" in the
Names of Faith, Hope, and Charity

Hail Lavinia,
Full of Grace,
The Lord is with thee.
Blessed art thou among women,
And blessed is the miracle you represent,
The Protein.
Holy Lavinia, Daughter of God,
Pray for us sinners now, and at the hour of our death.
Amen.

One "Glory Be"

Glory Be
To the Father,
And to the Lamb,
And to the Eternal Children.
As it was in the beginning,
Is now,
And ever shall be,
World without end.
Amen.

The Mysteries
(Repeated Five Times)

1 "Our Father"
10 "Hail Lavinias"
1 "Glory Be"
1 Elijah's Prayer

Elijah's Prayer

O my Elijah, forgive us our sins, save us from the fire of hell, lead all souls to heaven, especially those Lazarenes who are in most need of Thy mercy.

Hail Holy Hierophant
(Said After Five Mysteries)

Hail Holy Hierophant
Father of mercy, our life, our sweetness, and our hope. To thee do we cry, poor banished children of Acetia. To thee do we send up our sighs mourning and weeping in this valley of tears. Turn then, most gracious advocate, thine eyes of mercy toward us, and after this our exile show us the blessed fruit of thy blood, Elijah. O clement, O loving, O sweet Holy Father.

Pray for us, O Sacred Servant of God,
That we may be made worthy of the promises of the Lamb.
In the Name of the Father, and of the Lamb and of the Eternal Children.

Amen.

Don't Miss Book II of
The Disgraced Martyr Trilogy

THE LADY'S CHAMPION

JANUARY 9TH, 2020

M. F. Sullivan is an author and playwright currently residing in the town of Ashland, Oregon. An avid student of the occult, Sullivan fills what little time she does not spend writing with reading, attending the local Shakespeare Festival, and the company of her significant other. With the trilogy finished and behind her, she is already hard at work on yet another series. She loves cats, baking, painting doll heads, and 5-star Amazon.com reviews. Sign up for essays and book release updates on www.paintedblindpublishing.com, and consider leaving a nice note on Amazon while you're browsing the Internet. It would make her day.

www.ingramcontent.com/pod-product-compliance
Lightning Source LLC
Chambersburg PA
CBHW031646100726
47898CB00006B/1992